AT THE MOON'S INN

The Library of Alabama Classics,
reprint editions of works important
to the history, literature, and culture of
Alabama, is dedicated to the memory of
Rucker Agee
whose pioneering work in the fields
of Alabama history and historical geography
continues to be the standard of
scholarly achievement.

At the Moon's Inn

Andrew Lytle

With an Introduction by
Douglas E. Jones

The University of Alabama Press
Tuscaloosa and London

Copyright © 1941 by Andrew Lytle
Copyright renewed
Published by arrangement with the Author

Introduction Copyright © 1990 by
The University of Alabama Press
Tuscaloosa, Alabama 35487–0380

Library of Congress Cataloging-in-Publication Data

Lytle, Andrew Nelson, 1902–
  At the Moon's Inn / Andrew Lytle ; with an introduction by Douglas E.
Jones.
    p.   cm.
  ISBN 0-8173-0511-4 (alk. paper)
  1. Soto, Hernando de, ca. 1500–1542—Fiction.   2.   America—
Discovery and exploration—Spanish—Fiction.   I. Title.
PS3523.Y88A93   1990   90-35203
    813'.52—dc20   CIP

British Library Cataloguing-in-Publication Data available

Contents

Introduction

Douglas E. Jones

The publication of this edition of Andrew Lytle's *At the Moon's Inn* coincides with the four hundred and fiftieth anniversary of the historic event on which the novel is based—the march of the Spanish conquistador Hernando de Soto through what is now the southeastern United States between 1539 and 1543. The most famous of all Spanish expeditions in *La Florida*, Soto's army of some seven hundred cavalrymen, footsoldiers, and support personnel was the first major force to penetrate the interior of these unknown lands north of Cuba and east of Mexico.

Published in 1941, *At the Moon's Inn* was the first novel about Soto's disastrous experiences in the New World. Lytle's research on the novel began in the mid-1930s, about the time that President Franklin D. Roosevelt appointed a federal commission to make a thorough study of Soto's expedition and to report to Congress its recommendations for a suitable commemoration of the four hundredth anniversary of the event. The final report of the U.S. De Soto Commission was published in 1939 and is an excellent work of historical research.

Using many of the same archival materials studied by the Commission, Lytle skillfully weaves an adventure story about the history of Spanish efforts to establish a controlling presence in the New World during the first half of the sixteenth century. While focusing on Hernando de Soto's misfortunes in *La Florida*, Lytle also introduces into the plot elements from other efforts to claim the region for the Spanish Crown.

Upon the accidental discovery of America by Columbus in 1492 on his search for a western route to Asia, the Spanish quickly capitalized on the prospects of empire in this unknown land. After conquering Hispaniola, Puerto Rico, and Cuba, the Spanish as early as 1513 extended explorations from the Caribbean into the Gulf of

Mexico. Juan Ponce de León in 1513 made an unsuccessful, and fatal, attempt to plant the flag of Castille in America after sailing around the tip of present Florida and up the western coast as far as Tampa Bay. His was the first Spanish expedition in North America. After Ponce de León's failed attempt, the Spanish sent others into the Gulf of Mexico to determine the geography of the region and to secure Spain's claim to *La Florida*. As the leader of one of these voyages, Alvarez de Piñeda produced the first sketch map of the entire coastline of the Gulf in 1519, the same year that Hernan Cortés established a Spanish presence at Veracruz on the Mexican coast. By 1521 the Aztec Empire and Mexico had fallen to Cortés. The rewards of conquest were staggering—jewels, gold and silver artifacts, slaves, new lands for colonization, and converts to Christianity. For gold, glory, and God, Francisco Pizarro in 1521 sacked Peru and brought the Inca Empire to its knees. One of the brave captains of this company was Hernando de Soto, who returned to Spain a wealthy and honored man, although still in his early twenties. As his share of the booty, Soto received 180 pounds of pure gold and 360 pounds of silver. Horsemen and footsoldiers, respectively, received one-half and one-fourth of this amount.

With their treasure ships plying the waters between Peru and Spain, it was imperative for the Spanish to keep England and France out of the race for these new lands and their riches. Control of the coastal regions of the Gulf of Mexico, especially modern-day Florida and Cuba, was essential to this end.

Ponce de León was not the last conquistador to fail in establishing a permanent presence in what is now the United States. The next seeker of fame and fortune was Pánfilo de Narváez, a veteran of earlier campaigns in the Caribbean and Mexico, who was commissioned by the Spanish king in 1528 to explore and conquer *La Florida*. After a series of fierce attacks by Indians north of Tampa Bay, the several hundred survivors escaped by sea on a flotilla of small, leaky boats and rafts in an attempt to reach Veracruz. Most of the company, including its leader, were drowned in a hurricane off the Texas coast in 1529.

Each subsequent Spanish attempt to establish a foothold in the New World benefitted from the experiences of those who went before, as some survivors of each unsuccessful expedition almost invariably appeared on the rosters of later ones. Some of Pizarro's men later shipped out with Narváez—and died. A few who endured the Soto expedition were with Tristán de Luna in 1559–60 when he landed with more than one thousand soldiers and colonists at or near modern-day Pensacola Bay, Florida. This effort to lay formal claim to the new land also ended in failure. It was not until the establishment of St. Augustine in 1565 that Spain had a permanent colony in what is now the United States.

Although the Spanish had charted the entire coastline of the Gulf of Mexico, noting particularly the location of bays and rivers, they had no idea of what lay in the interior of the southern part of the North American continent. Not until the expedition of Hernando de Soto—and the concurrent one of Coronado through parts of the American Southwest—did the Spanish learn anything about the native populations, the terrain, or the existence of precious metals in this new land.

After returning to Spain from his successful expedition with Pizarro, and before that with Pedrarias Dávila in Nicaragua, Soto dreamed of mounting his own expedition to *La Florida*. The wealth he had brought from Peru did not satisfy his desire for personal fame and more treasure. Using his newly acquired influence, Soto gained for himself the Governorship of Cuba and the title of *Adelantado,* a royal commission to explore and exploit.

Soto pledged his personal wealth to the enterprise and recruited additional support from some of the gentlemen who were eager to accompany him. With the expedition financed, Soto and a large contingent departed Spain in spring 1538 for Cuba, the staging area for the operation.

After nearly a year of preparation, the army boarded a fleet of small ships (probably seven) and sailed from Havana for the west coast of what is now the state of Florida. Toward the end of May the fleet dropped anchor in a large and protective body of shallow water which the Spanish termed "Bahía de Espíritu Santo" (Tampa Bay), and the four-year drama began to unfold.

Most of what is known today about this adventure is chronicled in four primary documents, three written by participants soon after the expedition ended and one resulting from interviews with survivors forty years later. All differ widely in reliability and completeness. All accounts have been in English translations for years, but essentially they are unknown outside of scholarly circles.

The first account, unpublished until 1851, was written by Rodrigo Ranjel, Soto's private secretary, who kept a diary during the expedition. This document is incomplete and covers only the route from the first landfall at Tampa Bay to north Mississippi between 1539 and 1541. The second, published in 1841, was written in 1544 by Luys Hernando de Biedma, the Factor of King Charles V of Spain. It was the "official" report prepared immediately after the expedition, but it is woefully brief. The account of the "Gentleman of Elvas," an unidentified Portuguese nobleman with the expedition, was written in 1557 and is a timely record uninfluenced by other chronicles.

The last and longest of the known chronicles of the Soto invasion is a 1591 narrative by Garcilaso de la Vega based on the testimony of several of Soto's soldiers years after the event. The primary source for the narrative by Garcilaso, the son of a Spanish officer and Inca mother, is thought to have been Gonzalo Silvestre, one of the characters in Lytle's story and probably a minor figure in the expedition. Considered by some modern scholars to be the least reliable of the chroniclers, Garcilaso nevertheless is responsible for the popular legend of Soto as a romantic hero, the manner in which Lytle presents him here.

In the first two chapters, Lytle draws in characters and incidents of earlier attempts to gain control of lands and riches in the New World. Here he introduces Soto, a mere boy who will earn his spurs with Pedrarias Dávila in Nicaragua and his reputation as a bold cavalier with Pizarro in Peru before mounting his own quest for greatness. Later, as Soto orchestrates his own expedition to the New World, Alvar Núñez Cabeza de Vaca, the treasurer and one of only three survivors of the ill-fated Narváez expedition, warns Soto about the folly of his plans. Also brought into the story early is Gonzalo Silvestre, Garcilaso's source. Other historic characters and related events appear throughout the book, evidence that Lytle did a thorough job of research.

Events described in chapters three, four, and five occurred between Tampa Bay and what is now the state of Georgia. It is here that the Spanish first encountered oppressive heat, frightful hordes of insects, rough to impassable terrain, little local food, and hostile Indians. Transporting an enormous amount of equipment, weapons, and supplies, including an ambulatory larder of some 300 Spanish pigs, the army moved northward from the landing site along a route proposed to bring them to the Bay of Ochuse (probably Pensacola

Bay) in October of the next year for supplies and communication with the outside world.

Soto's strategy, learned from Pizarro, was to ensure the cooperation of the natives by holding the town or provincial chief hostage until guides, bearers, food, and other desired services had been provided. This Spanish tactic was known to some of the Indians Soto encountered—they remembered only too well Ponce de León and Pánfilo Narváez. Furthermore, the chief was less important in these native societies than in those of the Inca and Aztec; consequently, hostages were only of limited value to Soto.

The Indian town of Anhaica, recently discovered by archaeologists in downtown Tallahassee, Florida, was Soto's first winter campsite, in 1539–40. It is likely that the site was at or near the one occupied by the Narváez expedition in the winter of 1528–29. Harried by the Indians throughout their stay there, Soto and his army moved north and east into Georgia and the Carolinas in the spring.

The chapter "Cutifichiqui" is based on the name of the principal town of an Indian province thought by some scholars to have been in modern-day South Carolina. Here the female chief gives Soto the only "treasure" he finds in the New World—a large box of worthless freshwater pearls.

The last two chapters describe increasingly difficult travel and dramatic incidents in North Carolina, Tennessee, Alabama, Mississippi, Arkansas, Texas, and possibly Louisiana. During this part of the march the Spanish fought two major battles with the Indians; the first almost certainly took place somewhere in Alabama and the other at a town named Chicasa, possibly south of Tupelo, Mississippi.

The Mauvilla chapter focuses on the devastating battle between Soto's army and Chief Tuscaluza's warriors on October 18, 1540, at the provincial town of the same name situated probably in the Black Prairie region of west-central Alabama. No other conflict between American Indians and Europeans in the history of the United States exceeded this one in size and consequences.

The expedition was en route to Soto's planned rendezvous with his relief fleet at the Bay of Ochuse when the trap was sprung at Mauvilla. It is likely that Tuscaluza, the "Black Warrior," called in both his own people and his allies to put a stop to the Spanish deprivations in the region. Thousands of Indians took part in the battle, but they were unable to prevail against European cavalry and firearms. The battle ranged back and forth from morning until late afternoon before the Spanish could claim ultimate victory, but they paid a heavy price for it. It is here that Lytle begins to build the Soto legend of tragic hero.

After the battle at Mauvilla, in which the Spanish suffered heavy casualties and the loss of much equipment and supplies, Soto ignored the pleas of his officers—and the threat of excommunication by one of his priests—to abandon the venture and to continue south to the Gulf of Mexico and the planned rendezvous with Captain Francisco Maldonado's supply ships at Pensacola. The existence of the fleet was known only by Soto's most trusted lieutenants—a ploy to avoid mutiny by his army, which had suffered much and gained nothing.

Unwilling to return to Spain in disgrace, Soto put his now ragtag army on the trail westward toward the Mississippi River. After suffering the consequences of the Chicasa battle, Soto regrouped his battered and demoralized command and continued west to become the first European to see the great river. After wandering through Arkansas and parts of Texas during spring 1542, hoping to find precious metals in the mountainous areas, Soto and his band returned to the great river. Here Soto died on May 21st.

Now under the leadership of Luis de Moscoso, the army attempted to reach Mexico overland through Texas. Finding nothing but poor and desolate country, they returned to the Mississippi and built boats for a fiercely contested escape downriver to the Gulf of Mexico and safety at Tampico, 800 miles away. About half of the original 700 expeditionaires ultimately returned to Spain.

The expedition of Hernando de Soto was a failure. He established no settlements and found no wealth—except some inferior freshwater pearls—because there was none to find. Gold did exist in what now is Alabama and Georgia, but it was of no significance to the Indians, who lacked the metallurgical technology of their Aztec and Inca contemporaries to the south.

The Soto expedition, however, did leave an indelible mark on the native Indian cultures of the Southeast—the introduction of virulent European diseases. Some scholars estimate that mortality rates among the native population may have exceeded 80 percent within five years of Soto's arrival. Some heavily populated regions seen by Soto were unoccupied only twenty years later, when some of Tristán de Luna's men attempted to retrace parts of the earlier route in search of food.

Andrew Lytle skillfully crafts Soto's saga into *At the Moon's Inn*. Through the eyes of Nuño Tovar and others the reader senses the full range of emotions experienced by the players on this particular stage of world history. This is a story involving mid-sixteenth-century conflict between European technology and Stone Age craft.

A native Tennessean, Mr. Lytle is a 1925 graduate of Vanderbilt, where he associated with the Fugitive poets. He studied drama at Yale, then went to New York, where he acted a season on the professional stage while doing research for a biography of the Confederate general Nathan Bedford Forrest.

Lytle contributed an essay to *I'll Take My Stand* (1930), the Fugitives' important critique of the ways modern science and technology were affecting Southern life, thought, and values. As Thomas Carlson has written, "Lytle associated the decline of Southern tradition with the decline of the West, 'the gradual fall from a belief in a divine order of the universe into a belief in history.'"

Bedford Forrest and His Critter Company was published in 1931, and Lytle's first novel, *The Long Night*, appeared in 1936.

Andrew Lytle spent two years on the research for *At the Moon's Inn* and five years actually writing it; some of the materials he read were in medieval Latin. Colonel John R. Fordyce of Arkansas, Vice-Chairman of the U.S. De Soto Commission, assisted Lytle by translating some of the Spanish materials into English. The book places the reader at the center of one of the most dramatic events in America's history. Lytle draws us into the political and social life of Soto's times and makes us participants in this fateful march into the unknown reaches of *La Florida*. We share with members of the expedition their anticipation of gold and glory; the heat, cold, and hunger they suffered; the Indian attacks they repulsed; their growing anxiety about mere survival; and finally their realization that all is lost—that *La Florida* is not *El Dorado*. In the end, we learn not only about personal ambition and collective deprivation, but also the earliest recorded history of our own country. Clearly, Lytle views this violent intrusion of modern Western culture into a land peopled by hunters and growers of maize as a portentous parallel for the South that was emerging in the 1940s.

Following publication of *At the Moon's Inn*, Mr. Lytle taught history at the University of the South, at Sewanee, Tennessee. He taught creative writing at the University of Iowa and, from 1948 to 1961, the University of Florida. In 1961 he returned to the University of the South, where he served as editor of *The Sewanee Review* until his retirement in 1973.

Mr. Lytle is the author of *The Long Night* (1936), *A Name for Evil* (1947), *The Velvet Horn* (1957), *A Novel, Novella, and Four Stories* (1958), *The Hero with the Private Parts* (1966), and *A Wake for the Living, A Family Chronicle* (1975). He lives at Monteagle, Tennessee, in a cabin that has been his home for nearly fifty years.

AT THE MOON'S INN

Chickasaw

Coste

Coça

Autiamque
Nilco
Guachoya
Quigaltam

Athahatchi

Piachi

Mauvilla

Mississippi River

Bay of Ochuse

GULF   OF

The Route of Hernando De Soto
1539–1542

Adapted from a Map in the Final Report of the
United States De Soto Expedition Commission,
1939. This map shows the route used by Andrew
Lytle when he wrote *At the Moon's Inn.* Continu-
ing archaeological and historical investigations
are causing scholars to modify their views about
the precise route of the expedition, and it may
never be known with absolute certainty.

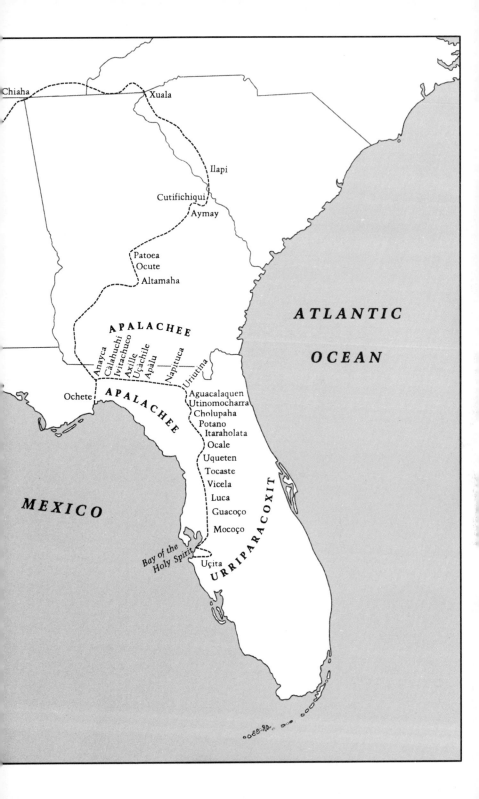

Chiaha

Xuala

Ilapi

Cutifichiqui

Aymay

Patoea
Ocute
Altamaha

APALACHEE

Anayca
Calahuchi
Ivitachuco
Axille
Uçachile
Apalu
Napituca

Uriutina

ATLANTIC

OCEAN

Ochete

APALACHEE

Aguacalaquen
Utinomocharra
Cholupaha
Potano
Itaraholata
Ocale
Uqueten
Tocaste
Vicela
Luca
Guacoço
Mocoço

MEXICO

URRIPARACOXIT

Bay of the
Holy Spirit

Uçita

1

THE FEAST

The Feast

THEY were alone in the quiet room. It was the hour of fire. Here in San Lúcar, as in all His Majesty's possessions, it is the time to rest, to reflect, to count over one's sins. It is above all else the hour to be alone. There sat Silvestre at the table. He, Tovar, stood at the window in this inn at San Lúcar, where all ships set out for the lands beyond the Ocean Sea, whither he had set out so many years ago. He could smell again, until now the intervening years were banished by that odour, the earthy mustiness of the adobe walls in all their length framing the window at the far end which, in turn, confined the sea. At first his eyes could see nothing but that window and the glittering surface of the water, the busy wharves, the galleons and caravels riding at anchor, so far below and beyond. He felt that but for this single outlet the long room would have lacked any location. After a while he discovered how, with too much looking, the sea itself might seem a picture on the wall and might thus more perfectly disconnect the room from the solid world. Or it might induce a state of mind even more perilous, for if one stared long enough, hour by hour until time lost its measure, the painted scene could take on a kind of life of its own. Upon that sea the mind might travel spheres and hemispheres not chartered in Christian geography.

"Tovar?"

At the sound of his name he turned and walked towards the table where he had left the youth. The boy was standing with his mug upraised. "To Florida," he said with wide bright eyes, turned recklessly Tovar's way, "and our part in it."

Tovar raised his own mug and drank. As he lowered it,

empty, he caught for a moment his own reflection in the mirror hanging on the wall behind the youth's head. He saw the dark, oval-shaped face, the large brown eyes lined by smudges of revelry, the high brows which gave the lids a bare look. With a shock he saw, for the first time, his features had about them a look of indecent exposure, as if they had been meant for a smaller face. The jaws might have torn a sheep apart; yet the mouth seemed almost too small for meat. To look at it now he could scarcely believe that once on the plains before Cuzco, in the full heat of battle, opened wide and yet not wide enough for the heaving lungs, an arrow had passed through it, tearing his cheeks and turning him around in his blood.

He shifted his eyes and met the eyes of the boy. They were staring with the frank appraisal of youth, but only at his scars. The glance he had got of himself, all the particular markings which set him off from other men, none of these had young Silvestre seen. To the boy, he, Tovar, was only a veteran of the Peruvian conquest.

Tovar filled their mugs from the pewter flagon. The mugs clinked. "To you, Gonzalvo Silvestre—that you may so charm de Soto he will take you with him to Florida."

Seated at the table, with their mugs before them, the two men faced each other. Silvestre leaned forward and said eagerly, "He will enlist me, don't you think? You had no trouble getting to the Indies?" His voice faltered. "Did you?"

Tovar looked for a moment at the mingling of hope and fear on the fair clear features, the wide, slightly drooping shoulders on the not too stalwart body. He hesitated a moment and then began: "You must understand that in Andalucía I was a rider until my eighteenth year on the ranges of Vista Hermosa. . . .

—At that time ran the finest herd of fighting bulls ever known on its pastures, and it fell to my lot with three others to drive them to Seville for the Fêtes of the Holy Cross. They were

[10]

noble animals, savage enough, but I who had been with them from their tenderest calfhood knew they would take their punishment kindly. Once, I remember, as I lay in the filth of my body there in Panama, ready and indeed anxious to die and be judged, my thoughts returned again and again to their beautiful strength and grace. I could feel again on the pads of my fingers their slick coats under which the muscles rolled, and I who was parched from rottenness felt that I had quenched my burning with sweet and clear-running water. I saw them charge valiantly into the plaza and paw the sand, bellowing. I saw them leave in their sandy wake, all their strength now turned to weight and their valour mocked by the wide dull horns of the oxen who dragged them away, and I thought must pride and passion come to this, be hung to the mild feet of the gelded?

We travelled by night when we drove these kings to Seville. Always you travel by night with those marked for death, for the danger is great. The foolish peasants crowd around and the young men in the towns. The last stretch is most difficult, for you must push ahead even through the day. How little I knew as we herded our brave ones together that last time and drove them from the pastures, forcing the oxen to the front with our lances, for these the bulls knew and would follow—how little I knew that for myself, as well as for my charges, had begun the first slow steps in the long dance of death. So it seemed as I lay there in Panama waiting for the priest.

On the outskirts of Seville we put up at an inn. Although it was fête time, a corral had been saved, for did not we bring the sacrifice to valour? I ordered old José to guard them. Later we would all take our turns at watching, but it was important that the most skilful rider should soften the strangeness of the town for our savages. They had never before left their home, and there was much to offend them. It was two hours until the rising of the sun before all had been properly disposed. I then passed through the stables to the sleeping quarters. There were no beds, but I was told I might arrange myself in the

[11]

kitchen. I wrapped my cloak about me and lay down in a corner near the hearth, with the great jars of oil at my back. I never sleep in towns with my back exposed. I was not alone. The floor seemed covered with hunks of slaughtered meat. I closed my eyes, but I couldn't sleep. The stink of the night sweats on unwashed flesh curdled in my throat. I lay there, saying, Nuño, you had better go out and sleep at the moon's inn. Here you will choke. But I was weary, and my legs lacked a nose.

Women near the hearth were busy making monks' sighs and broiling lupins to be pedalled about Seville on the morrow. The light from the fire twisted their shadows as they walked, and the gross cook hung over the steaming pot, her jowls swinging like a mastiff's and her eyes as dark as drying blood. The women moved always in shadow, like souls in purgatory. But there was one. When she came into the range of the hearth, I did think the yellow light a man. Its long fingers clutched at her reins and made the cloth at her breasts into damask. I must have dozed with my eyes upon her, for I was awakened by a voice calling "María!" It was the man near me calling out in his sleep. He sighed. It was not a sigh for a man to make. I heard a low laugh and looked up. There was the young woman rubbing her foot on the sleeper's mouth and he in his dream covering it with kisses. She was almost astraddle me. My eyes were good, I was young, and I had seen no woman for months. I grabbed her ankle and fixed it to the floor. "María?" I whispered.

It was that word which sent me to the Indies. There in Panama I cursed it; but here, now, seated with you, I bless it. If I sinned those months in Seville, I made confession. María was loose in the hilt and had a deal of honey in her hips. And was I to ask what she was about? I let the riders go back to the range without me. I told them I'd follow. I can see now the gloomy looks of old José as he rode out of the inn's yard, the tip of his lance bright in the sun, as rusty as old bacon upon his trout-coloured mare. He rode away and never once looked behind. That was his way of dismissing me. He knew better than I, for never again did I set eyes on Vista Hermosa.

I was more innocent than lads my age. The prairies are nature's retreats, for we riders lived the most of the year as remote from the world as monks. We went for days and weeks at a time lacking any society, and what we had was of men of our own calling, silent and contemplative men given at moments to passionate action. We did not contemplate Our Lord's wounds. Our beads were the genealogies of herds, but these we said as faithfully as any priest. I have seen things strange and mysterious in the new lands; and once on my first voyage out, months from land, sick to death of my narrow quarters, weary of my companions and myself and feeling a growing terror of the sea, I lay upon the deck and watched the stars for comfort. In the Indies they do not sparkle as in Andalucía but shine with a steady beam. It is this which tells you you have left behind you Christendom. Suddenly—I thought I was dreaming—a marvellous sweetness blew through the air. Almost at once the watch called, "Land!" I leapt to my feet, but nowhere could I see it. I had expected wonders, I'd heard sailors tell of monsters who would crush both ship and crew before the slime of the deep could slip from their jaws—but this, a land with a fragrance, to be smelt far out to sea, no man had told me of. I stood bewitched, and yet, lad, it did not match the awe I felt when once in Andalucía, on a range it was not my habit to ride, I saw a bull, black and fierce, grazing a little apart from his kind. The herd, as though sensing his nobility, did not intrude upon his solitude. The master herdsman was by me. "Do you see that animal?" he asked. My eyes answered him. "He is of the line of Geryon the great Hercules came here to tame." We reined in our horses, and I sat quite still as his voice, secret as at confessional, told over the animal's descent.

I tell you all this to show you how little I knew of the world. Naturally I thought the woman could love no other. A man, when he is young, will always think he alone is a woman's delight. One day she said, "Nuño, take me to Mass."

"Not today," I replied.

"Why?" With a woman it is always why.

[13]

"I have an ounce of gold," I said, "and I must first find some place to hide it."

"I know a place," she said and tossed her pretty head.

"I'd as soon put it in the king's highway," I said, laughing in good humour. She slapped me on the buttock and we fought and frolicked about the inn's yard.

"See. Put it in your mouth and come." She panted so prettily from the scuffle that I agreed to go.

As we knelt, three sailors came in asking alms to have Masses said to the Virgen del Carmen. Out of my eye I saw them make their way towards us. Each held the corner of a handkerchief which had a few coins in it. How could I know they were not sailors? I could tell now in a glance, but then I was my ignorant self and in love. There was I with my teeth clamped firmly over my treasure and María by my side. It makes me smile to think how I guarded a mere ounce of gold, I who have seen the Inca's ransom. Ah, well. The sailors knelt beside us. I never saw the damned pray so devoutly. All went well—all went well for me, I mean—until after the *Ite Missa Est*. Then one of them let go his hold of the handkerchief, and the coins rolled over the stones.

The most evil-looking one stood up with the arrogance of a guard at the Tower of Gold. "Señores, let no one move," he commanded. "All this coin belongs to the Santísima Virgen."

"Look for the ounce," the second one cried; "the ounce of gold."

Everywhere around us eyes went scurrying like cockroaches. Then one, the evil-looking one, said angrily, "The ounce of gold for the Masses to María Santísima. Who has taken it?"

An accomplice in the crowd pointed to me. "This villain here," he said. "He put it in his mouth."

Simple fool that I was I clapped my hand to my mouth. A sailor snatched away the gold and wrapped it, oh, with such wrath and contempt, in the handkerchief. I was crowded back against a pillar and abuse heaped upon my head. In the confusion the robbers naturally slipped away. María fought and scratched. She told the innocents they had connived with

[14]

thieves. She told them much else, and they were glad to set me free. How beautiful I thought her indignation made her. Back at the inn this indignation vanished. Nor was that all which the day took.

At night, as was my custom, I slipped up the stairs to her room. I knocked once very softly, but only once, for I heard a low voice saying, "Thine eyes are brigands." I didn't believe my ears and called sharply with my mouth against the wood. There was whispering, short and furtive; the creak of a floor board, then silence, the voluble silence of people listening. Fury seized me as I smelled the straw dust from her bed. I knew what had made it rise. I beat upon the door, but it was locked. Then I realized I was in my shirt and unarmed. The saints were kind, for I had wit enough to retire.

I slept no more that night. Early on the morrow I descended to the kitchen. There she was looking as innocent as a calf. I walked up and took her by the arm. "Who is he?" I demanded. "Where is he?" For answer she reached down and bit my hand. It was no love bite, and I slapped her against the chimney. The eyes that I had seen melt in their sockets for love of me turned the colour of hot iron quenched in water. I didn't move. I couldn't see, sick as I was with anger and shame, the tears washing the ill fortune of the night from my face. María edged away from the chimney, glancing like a muley cow. The instant she was out of reach she threw her insolent hips about. My eyes followed them, and I must have looked stupid and clownish, but it was only that I was wondering how ever I had thought there was honey in those hips. Then she threw her head back on its swelling neck.

"Our rider," she said to those gathered near, "has been listening to dreamers again."

Between us stood the big pot out from the fire. It steamed lazily as the cook threw in the ingredients for the puchero—two handfuls of garlic, a side of bacon, twelve pigs' feet, a peck of onions. I counted the ingredients as if the puchero were some strange dish and I studied how to make it. "Yes," she said, "our fine rider rides the plains and pricks the bulls with his lance, so he thinks he may ride and prick where he please. But in Seville"—she paused to make my punishment more unendurable; the cook's red fat hands hovered at the mouth of the pot—"in Seville there are better ones than his."

I could feel the faces at the door and windows strain with laughter. She made no effort to contain her own. Its harsh cruelty drove away my shame. The bystanders could barely wait for my reply; they well knew there was none that I could make. The silence hummed. As if to relieve it, the cook reached up and flung a leg of mutton in the pot. The liquor splashed, and she slapped at her cheek. At that moment I turned all into fury.

"Señores," I said, facing the kitchen, "you have been kind to a simple country fellow. The meat you served me was seasoned to my taste, perhaps a little old and tough, but only a Turk would examine the teeth of a guest. No, it is I who have let it grow chill. But it shall not be said of Nuño de Tovar that he ill requited Seville's hospitality," and with that I seized María and lifted her in my arms. She lost her breath from rage, bucked and tried to bite, but I closed her mouth with my hand. "And so, Señores, I give it back to you as hot and better seasoned." I swung her over the bubbling puchero and dropped her, butt-end, into the pot.

My triumph was perfect. I did not leave that day, for I was not done. I knew she would try to have her revenge, and her revenge would make mine complete. All morning I waited, with each hour growing more sick of the place and longing for the open plains. I had the grace to stay away from the inn, yet I could be easily found. But as the hours turned and I was left unchallenged, I began to look for a trap. After siesta I joined several men for a game. We withdrew to the shadow of a wall. The cards ran well for me, and I forgot for the time my difficulty. Then just as I had picked up a hand—I had seen, I remember, the mounted knave of cups, the king of coins, and several small clubs and swords—suddenly a bundle was flung

[16]

into the midst of our game. It might have fallen from the sky, except that the paper wrapping was greasy and smelled of fried fish. We looked up. There stood a baratero, older than I, wrapped by a ragged coat and strutting with the air of the king's chamberlain. He was one of those adept at the use of the knife worn by the little people, the navaja. As you may know, the baratero lives by blackmailing gamblers. Since he demands very little, gamblers had rather pay than fight. No one had seen him arrive; no one seemed disturbed. My companions thought he had come for his percentage. But I knew better. With the point of the navaja he undid the paper very delicately. A pack of cards lay inside, and face up on the deck was the Ace of Swords. Looking only at me, the baratero said, "Here no one dare play but with my cards."

If there had ever been any doubt in my mind, it was now dispelled. In his voice I heard the voice of the penitent sailor. And the voice I heard that night? I assumed it was the same. Suddenly I smelt the sharp staleness of straw dust in my nostrils. Slowly I took his measure, from the dirty turban to his pale insolent face.

"You will give me half the stakes," he said.

My companions protested. I silenced them.

"Comrade," I replied, "we have cards."

Our eyes ran together, and I felt mine had been dashed by the sea's wash. "Make haste, boy," he said impatiently; "hand me my profits." He reached out his hand and I drove my long knife into his cards.

"Here," I said, "the profits are paid only at the point of the navaja."

My companions rose to their feet and stepped back with the ceremonious gravity the occasion required. Perhaps they had arranged the scene. Of that I cannot be sure. If so, they acted in my service.

The baratero drew his cloak about him. "Let us make a journey," he said.

The navaja has its rules, its honoured strokes, as well as the weapons the great people use, and these I had learned on the plains. The baratero was ignorant of this. He had seen me ride in with my lance in the air. He did not mean for me to leave in so proud a fashion. María did not mean it. We reached a place of privacy, and the baratero laid aside his cloak—I give his rags this dignity—he laid it aside with the gesture of soon picking it up again. I knew that I would have no easy time of it. There were the scars of many fights on his face, and on his right cheek one in the shape of a sail. Some great fighter had left that, for it is the classic cut. Skill and nerve and speed are all required to make it.

He raised his navaja. "Should this viper bite you, pharmacy can bring no remedy."

"I hold the knife of extreme unction," I replied and kissed my hilt.

With that we fell to.

It was a pretty fight. He had the ease of a man who fights often. I was more aggrieved. Of that, perhaps, I cannot judge. We both were quick, we both did hate and long for the other's death. In one special way I had the advantage. I had taken him by surprise, for he thought to find me easy sport and had not studied where to cut. From the beginning I knew what I would do.

I ignored the face and throat. They were the easier and obvious places. I played instead about the waistband. But I was cunning. I only took a thread now and then, feinting always about the face and throat. The band was well frayed before he understood my attack. He was furious, but I think in his fury there was fear, for the moment the band had slackened enough to fall about his hips, I might bide my time. My companions sighed with admiration.

It ended suddenly. I made a beautiful slash, just enough to let it slip upon his hips. I forced him to advance and retreat. It began to unwind in earnest. A voice said gravely, "Go for a priest." These words put the baratero into a frenzy. Snatching at his turban, he threw it at my face. I caught his blade beneath

[18]

my throat. He ducked to fling sand in my eyes. I saw the moment was upon us, abandoned my guard and, stooping, swung behind him. I cut through his back bone at the middle part.

María, I knew, would not rest until she had seen me swing. I could see her following the sound of the little bell through the streets of Seville and a voice asking alms "to say Masses for the soul of an unfortunate who is about to be hanged." At best I would be lodged in the house of little wheat. So I fled to Seville to lose myself in its narrow ways. Wandering near the river and wondering what to do, I heard a fifer and drummer beating near the Tower of Gold. I asked the reason. Men were being enlisted for the lands beyond the sea. I did what any one must have done in my circumstances. I enlisted⌣

Tovar paused, lifted his mug and drained it.

"Then you had to flee, it was not of your choice?" Silvestre asked wonderingly.

"I followed my fate," Tovar replied.

There was a moment of silence between them, when Tovar continued:

⌣This adventure passed through my head, as I lay dying in Panama. The fever consumed from memory all but this, so that I was again that lad fleeing his follies. Again I stood upon the deck of the pinnace as it dropped down the Guadalquivir, passed the plains where the bulls charged the river, burying their legs in the reeds, bellowing and shaking their heads at the ship; passed a drove of horses, their tails raised in flight; and, moving with the tide, drew near the bars of San Lúcar. The prow of the ship coasted slowly towards the dangerous sands . . . a voice said, "The man's not dead."

Sharp, violent jabs of anger at last opened my eyes, for I lay swooning in that sweet weakness which despises the world.

[19]

Dimly I saw the figure of a priest and beside him another, bending over me. The other one said, "Father, I've seen men get over this," and, leaning over, he picked me up in his arms; he picked me out of my filth and corruption and carried me to his lodgings. With his own hands he nursed me back to health. My sight was weak and blurred, but for a moment, as he leaned over, I saw the bristly beard on the long, flat chin, and the eyes. Compassionate they were, but it was not compassion that I saw. They lay far back in his head, so brown they shone black. The skin of the sockets looked white, as though they had been drained of blood. Sharp and lustrous, never eyes to be taken by surprise, and yet I had the feeling they rather looked in than out and looked not to see but to devour. Perhaps it was my own fevered vision, but they seemed to be sinking into his flesh, towards that dark interior where lay the only sustenance able to glut their hunger⏤

Tovar paused and looked narrowly at the boy. "That man," he said, "was Hernando de Soto."

He continued for a few moments to search the boy's face, but he saw no understanding, only a blend of youthful melancholy and excitement. "De Soto was then," he said casually, "a captain in Pedrarias' service. We met just before he entered upon the Peruvian conquest. I followed him there, I followed him back to Spain, I stood by while he married the Lady Ysabella de Bobadilla, the daughter of his old master, Pedrarias, and I will follow him to Florida. . . . But come, lad, we must be off to Seville. He gives a feast to the great who have helped him to the conquest of Florida. We have a hard ride if we would reach there in time. There could be no better moment to present you."

Tovar rose and picked up his cape and gloves. The boy quickly reached his feet after him. "One last toast," Silvestre said. His face was flushed as he turned a dizzy stare upon the older man. "I give you de Soto, the Lord of Florida."

[20]

Ceremoniously the two men drank and then hurried from the room.

2

Doña Ysabel de Bobadilla knelt in the oratory where she alone might come. She let her dry hot eyes rest upon the cool whitewash of the walls, draw towards the altar. Here was sanctuary. Here Our Lord did hang in alabaster, his precious wounds intricately worked in garnet. She sank into that miraculous privacy where the heart is free to seek for comfort out of the blood's confusion. She would not delude herself. There was no easy comfort, no comfort without knowledge, but she could find relief in the search for it. Deliberately she began to put together the critical segments of the past which, if they could not resolve, might illuminate the nature of her dilemma. . . .

Inevitably the tangle of memory unwound at Rostro the time de Soto first came to live and serve as page in her father's house. How he happened to be there she had forgotten. It mattered little or too much. She was a child, not so much of a child that she failed to notice the dark boy with the long chin standing near her father's chair at meat. He stood apart, strong in pride even then. One of the pages pointed him out and made fun of his looks. It was his earnest glance, she supposed, his suspicious and haughty reserve, and the roughness of his clothes which made him ridiculous in their eyes. He seemed to be playing the part of a great hidalgo. But even so early he was shamed by his poverty and the sense of dependence it gave him. She knew this now, but who could have thought a lad of such tender years had such vanity? A lack of property was not a thing to make one of noble quarterings sensitive. Not in Spain.

She ran to him and said, "My name is Ysabel. What's yours?" He smiled and she smiled. She thought she had a friend to play with and humour her. Her sisters scorned her childish games. The older pages had their heads turning upon

[21]

courtesy, how to manage a horse and how to drive their lances at the target in the court of arms. But the smile vanished. He had heard the snickers as she ran up.

"My name," he replied, "is Hernando Méndez de Soto y Gutiérrez Cardeñosa."

Her father, Don Pedro, the Bishop of Burgos, and the others about the board smiled to see such pride and reserve in a stripling. She saw only the slim bones showing through his jerkin. "I'll call you Hernán," she said. At this the pages could not contain themselves. Don Pedro frowned away their mirth, but he could not frown away Hernán's feeling of shame.

His father and mother were dead. His mother had some remote connection with her house. That, she supposed, was how he came to be at Rostro. He already knew how to ride and the sergeant who taught the pages liked his grave courtesy and showed him favours. The horses of most mettle were given him to try, because of his voice and hand. He always spoke softly, but the tones did not caress. Those who speak so, she had noticed, animals obey. His young companions were soon ready to be friends, but he never forgave them that first reception. He was amiable and easy in his manners, but when any offered the way to intimacy he withdrew into that reserve all had come to know.

It fell to the lot of Carlos, a cadet of a rich house, to be his companion in sword play. One day she came upon Carlos in the kitchen patio, downcast and aggrieved. She was twelve and in a few months would be turned over entirely to a duenna; but she still had the freedom of a child and a child's simplicity. It seemed to her that day that nobody should be sad, for Hernán had brought her from the hunt a wild boar's bladder. He blew it up, put pebbles in it, and gave it to her for sport.

"Look, Carlos, what Hernán gave me," she said, innocently thinking her pleasure would make him gay.

"Anybody can cut out a bladder after the beast is dead," he replied. "If he'd brought you tusks, that would be something to boast about."

[22]

She was unused to surly answers. She said angrily, "You've never killed a boar. You have no courtesy and all great soldiers have courtesy."

Her rebuke had added to his misery and she told him she was sorry, when to relieve himself of the thing on his mind, he recounted how he had found on the hunt wild honey in a rock, had led Hernán secretly to the place as a special act of friendship. Hernán seemed eager at first to share the find; but suddenly, without explanation, he withdrew into himself, saying he cared little for honey. This rebuff was too plain to ignore. As Carlos said, anybody likes honey found wild and made from the flow.

After this there came a great shifting in the household. What caused it she no longer remembered. Perhaps it was some difficulty in the reign of the mad Juana. The Flemish courtiers had turned away from the court the old favourites of Ferdinand and Ysabella. Among these were the Bobadillas. Whatever it was, it put her happily in the care of her mother's cousin, the Marquesa de Moya, and she went to live in her town of Segovia.

This moving about made the break between childhood and womanhood abrupt enough. She was taught those things a woman of her station should know, but mostly she remembered the time the Marquesa's maids spent curling their hair, how they smoked it with sulphur and wet it with *aqua fortis* to make it shine and afterwards spread it in the sun of the dog days. And the elixiviums they made to wash it in, and the sweet herbs they beat out for scent. But later there were suitors, and her days were full and gay at the Marquesa's small court. Breathless she opened her eyes and breathless she closed them at night. Memory of her childhood rarely crossed her thoughts. How often since had she thought, especially out of the weariness of years in waiting and disappointment, that but for that first intoxication with the world, that whirl of the senses wherein youth casts the skin of innocence, nunneries and monkeries would be the common dwellings in the land. But to a maid of sixteen the world seems as long and mild as an Andalusian winter. All its good things lie about for the taking. One needs only to wait and choose. Then suddenly it happens there is. one thing you want, one out of many. In your guilelessness you wonder at your modesty. You reach for it; it eludes you, dancing just out of reach. You dance after it gaily, for it seems only another sporting with innocent pleasure. It still eludes but you go freely on, never stopping to question; then suddenly you hear the strains and see the narrow way where each alone must go the long dance of death.

One day the Marquesa called her into her wardrobe and told her that her father had been appointed governor of the first great armament to be sent out to Golden Castile. The Marquesa would accompany her to Rostro and they must be on their way by San Sebastián's day. She was not told her mother would bear her father company and secretly thought the Marquesa had fine matches to discuss with her parents.

At last the day came to leave. The heavy carriage rolled into the outer yard behind four large blue mules and the ten asses stood patiently under their load of chests and boxes. Four of the Rostro servants sat their horses, with bucklers around their necks and rusty steel caps on their heads. Swords lay between their legs and the saddles. Crossbows were slung to their backs, but it was plain from the way they moved their shoulders they would use them ill if any need arose. She ran down the steps to greet them and they smiled foolishly. And then a voice from behind:

"Have you forgotten me, Ysabelita?"

She turned and there he was, standing by his horse.

"Hernán!" she cried and ran to embrace him.

The duenna took her by the arm. "You are no longer a child."

At that moment the Marquesa came down the stairs. "Come, girl," she said dryly, "be as effusive as you like at our journey's end, when we know better this young man's worth. The roads are full of brigands, Sir Captain. I hope you know your trade."

Hernán made her a low and gallant bow. "I know, Your Grace, whom I have in charge."

With that he handed the Marquesa into the carriage; then he took her hand. It may have been that she was off balance, but he pressed it as he helped her in. She supposed now that then it was done. Perhaps it was the shock of seeing him in his first manhood, so comely and straight standing by his horse, a little man but every part put neatly together. In the carriage she tried to recall what he looked like. He wore a breastplate and round steel cap so burnished the light slid sharply about his chest and head. She remembered the dark, restless eyes. And that was all. But then he rode up beside the carriage and she saw the clean legs encased in tight-fitting leather hose, the plain sword, and the careless way he handled his lance.

Halfway on the journey they reached the mountains. It had been rough enough before, but here the carriage seemed to leave the road entirely. After a wearisome morning they settled down to the rhythm of the jolts and tried to doze. She must have fallen asleep. She looked up and the carriage had stopped. Her first thoughts were that the horses were blowing, but it was far too still for that. The Marquesa's eyes, blue though they were, had turned as hard as two black beads. "Don't be alarmed, child," she said, and drew out of her hair a small knife. In her lap, her hands folding over it, it lay like a crucifix.

In her corner the duenna was snoring. In the curious silence the gross noise frightened her a little. She glanced out of the carriage window. The guard had drawn his sword and fitted the round buckler to his arm. He sat forward and looked before him as though he had trouble in seeing. She heard the hard clicks of a horse charging. There was no other sound for a moment; then savage cries leaped through the gorge. But she heard only the horse galloping.

"Jesumaría!" The guard spat the word. "He's opened his windpipe."

She felt a lump in her throat. The guard looked behind

him abstractedly, kicked the horse. The animal moved as if the earth were slipping beneath its feet.

"In God's name, fellow," the Marquesa said, "throw it down and draw your weapon." The other guard, she saw, was fumbling with his crossbow. Before the man could obey, something slapped the carriage and its whole frame quivered. The Marquesa drew in her chin. Above her head an arrow had split the coach's quilted lining. A thread of cotton floated into the air and settled slowly at her feet. "Draw back as far against the cushions as you can," the Marquesa said.

The shouts drew nearer. The asses stampeded and the four blue mules moved restlessly in their harness. The guards from behind rode up, she took the sounds of horses to be the guards, and from everywhere about rose the noise of battle, yells and grunts, the thud of the laying on and metal striking metal. The duenna opened her eyes and looked wildly about. The eyes fastened upon the carriage door. A head wrapped in a filthy turban had thrust itself through the window.

"Rape! Rape!" screamed the duenna.

"Restrain yourself," the Marquesa said sharply. "The brigand hears you."

The brigand looked carefully at the women. He was reckoning, she could see, their ransom. Very calmly the Marquesa spoke. "Sirrah," she said, "take your head out of my carriage. Your nostrils stink."

He flinched, then moved further in until his breath blew into their faces. "Your worshipful ladyship will stink ere long," he said.

Very daintily the Marquesa raised her handkerchief to her nose, but not so far as the eyes. They met the brigand's stare. It was quickly done. The turbaned head jerked back through the window, the nostrils slit and flapping loosely about the bone. The Marquesa wiped the knife with a small lace handkerchief and threw it after him.

"Praise God," the duenna said, "how neat Your Grace did slit it, and both sides too. That comes from consorting with

[26]

queens and kings. I vow he'll remember you every time he raises his hand to blow his nose and cannot find his nostrils." Then she laid her finger beside her nose and, leaning forward, said mysteriously, "It was the face of my dreams."

"Listen," commanded the Marquesa.

The noise of the fighting was moving up the gorge. It moved quickly, for even as she listened the sounds ceased altogether. There was silence and then a horse came up at a springing trot, bent before the carriage its curving neck, splashed all over with flecks and clotted blood. Hernán swung from its back.

"Are you unharmed?" he asked.

He looked only at her. His voice was still harsh from exertion, and its tone made the question sound perfunctory. The sense of power and control his body gave out seemed out of place with the soft and beardless chin that, as he looked at her, with the lance in his hands, his steel cap beaten in against his ear, gave him no battle-scarred look but a jauntiness, and his bottomless eyes ... it was this, this softness and this hardness which made her want to comfort him. After ever so long she heard the Marquesa, "We *all* are unharmed."

She thought she saw him blush, but she looked quickly away. Briefly he said, "The inn should be two furlongs distant. There we shall lie tonight."

Bowing courteously, he mounted and gave the orders to go forward. No sooner had they settled down to the jolts of the road when the duenna smacked her lips and said, "If Your Grace did but know the fright I got when I opened my eyes upon his leering ugly face. I have a habit, long I've had it, of dreaming."

"Indeed?" the Marquesa asked.

"Indeed, my lady. All I do is close my eyes for goblins and sorcerers to leap about my head. My brains are beat as fine as the sage the Barbary slaves flail before the gates of Triana. Holy Mary knows how I suffer at this sport, more than a hundred scratching monks who lay the rod on. But such a dream

[27]

this jolting road did put me in today. My backsides: if Your Grace could but see them . . ."

"No doubt," the Marquesa said.

"A giant Moor with a nose and eyes and a mouth used me so. A sorcerer too he was. 'Some Christian dog has killed my horse,' he growled; then looked at me."

"No."

"But yes, Your Grace. I dropped upon my knees, in my dream, mind you, and wrung my hands . . . so. 'Oh, Sir Moor,' I cried, 'use me any way you will, but spare a poor Christian maid.' But he waved his wand, white like those the major-domos carry. I would have said more . . ."

"No doubt," the Marquesa agreed.

"But when I opened my mouth such a whinnying and neighing did I hear. 'A horse! Thank God, a horse!' I cried. But then a fly, a green bottled fly, lighted on my neck. As I made to slap it, I felt a twisting of my rear, and a swishing of hair across my sides. Oh, Your Grace, I wept and wept to think a gentlewoman had a tail. And then the turbaned Moor leaped upon my back and rode and rode. We raced until I thought that nowhere does it say that horses are in Paradise. At this I grew so sad to think of all the sins I might have done, I slowed my pace. The evil Moor dug me in the flank and every time I slowed my pace he dug my sides, and I would kick and fart."

The guard leaned over. "There is the inn, Your Worship, just above us."

The Marquesa nodded. "You have just saved a gentle-woman from a sorcerer."

"A what, your ladyship?"

"'Tis only a dream, Diego," the duenna added and smiled.

The guard rode off and in less than an hour they drew up before the inn. . . .

Everything seemed to work according to some bold design. Don Pedro was grateful to Hernán for his prowess, as much for the Marquesa's sake as for his daughter's. So it came about that Hernán had, as the Marquesa's favourite, great liberties. Often

[28]

Ysabel and he were alone together in the Marquesa's chamber. At night they would sit in her reception chamber or in the great hall with the rest of the household and tell stories. At times there would be dancing. She could see now upon the hearth the vine branches crackling about a green log partly up the chimney, with the bugs and ants running in and out, trapped on the bark. There was such ignoble desperation in their scurrying that, as she watched, she scarcely listened to Don Pedro telling what His Majesty's captains did in the islands and firm land of the Ocean Sea. But mostly she would seek Hernán in his corner and he would look back, but never when Don Pedro spoke of fishing gold out of a lake with nets, of how the Indians held it no more than bright pebbles, or of the times they chased the savages with Irish hounds for sport, and once how a certain captain hanged thirteen by the feet in the name of Our Lord and His twelve Apostles.

The Marquesa lifted her head at this. "I'm an old woman," she said, "and I have seen much that is evil in my time. But I like not that kind of sport. Nor would Queen Ysabel have liked it." Her voice rose a trifle. "I doubt me if my mistress would have pledged her jewels for that Columbus if she had known that Christians would mock Holy Mary's Son in such a way." She crossed herself and fell silent.

As the pause lengthened, Ysabel had turned to the Marquesa. "They truly loved, did they not, Don Ferdinand and the Queen?"

"Ah, child," the Marquesa answered, "they are both dead now."

"But tell us, Your Grace," Hernán asked eagerly.

The Marquesa raised her heavy eyes and let them rest for a moment upon him. Hernán grew confused and stumbled with his words. "I mean," he said, "it would please us all. We would be honoured. . . ." The Marquesa's eyelids creased with something that might have been a smile.

"Do tell us, Your Worship," the duenna added, "for there is nothing so royal as the love of kings and queens."

[29]

All gathered that night in the hall waited for her to speak, for they knew that the old queen had held the Marquesa the closest of all her court.

"Spain is now united," she began, "and all Christian, but when Their Majesties met to plight their troth it was far otherwise. Queen Ysabel was then heiress to the throne of Castile, but she had powerful enemies. She was not even safe in Valladolid where she held her small court. As a stroke of policy her friends, led by the Archbishop of Toledo, betrothed her to the Infante of Aragon. How well I remember waiting for that first meeting with Don Ferdinand. She and I were alone in the long room of the palace. She held a missal in her hands. The Ave Maria had struck, and she crossed herself. I saw how white was her face. She was only eighteen, I but a little older, and I felt a great longing to comfort her, for it was pitiful in one so young to play so bold a game. And I knew that policy or no policy the Infante must please her. I said, 'I know it's a great risk, Infanta, but the Archbishop is answerable for his safety. Every precaution has been taken in passing the frontier. He travels by night disguised as a servant, tends the mules and waits on his companions at table.'

" 'He can't be far away by now,' she whispers, listening to the bells.

"But the hours carry us deeper into the night and still we are alone. Long ago we have ceased to speak. Then midnight strikes at San Pablo and, while it is striking, the tapestry withdraws. Under a sudden glare of torches and smoke the Archbishop appears. Behind him, almost concealed in his travelling cloak, follows the youthful Infante. There is a pause. Don Gutiérrez de Cardeñas steps forward impatiently and points at Don Ferdinand. 'Look at him. This is he!' The Archbishop puts aside the too zealous courtier. 'Your Highness,' he says in formal tones, 'I bring you your affianced lord. May God and Santiago ratify your choice.'

"They look at each other. Slowly her face colours and I know that all is well. She takes his hand and lifts him from his knees and they withdraw to the far end of the room and sit within the shadows of the royal canopy. But even there, my children, though it was plain they pleased each other, policy balanced against soft eyes. Castile was the greater kingdom and the princess did not mean to deliver it over to Aragon. But when they returned to us, it was settled. 'I am ready, my lord,' she says to the Archbishop—how fair she looked surrounded by the smoking torches—'to wed the Prince. Give us your blessing.' "

The Marquesa paused, the fire popped on the hearth there in Rostro and she saw Hernán's eyes glued upon her. She dropped hers, fearing her father might notice, for Hernán's stare was bold.

"What a romaunce," the duenna cried. "Queens do have it all," she said, sighing.

"Romaunce," the Marquesa repeated, and her voice was hard and brusk. "The princes were too poor to pay the expenses of their wedding and the journey into Aragon."

"But God smiled upon this match, Cousin," Don Pedro said. "Did not Their Majesties drive out the Moors and add Granada to the Spanish Crown? And did they not make Spanish policy great in Europe and give to Castile vast and rich possessions overseas, where even now I go to serve their grandson?"

"*You* tell *me* how much greatness was in her life?" the Marquesa answered a little sharply. "I could fill an evening with her greatness. But it is not of that I think tonight." Again she paused and then said quietly, "I am thinking of the end she made. It was in the Castillo de la Mota that she had come to die. God smiled upon the match, you say? And all the greatness it brought to Castile? I doubt me if the Indies were much comfort to her then. She was only fifty-four. She who had made the world so full lay upon her couch, alone except for me and waiting as before. But this vigil she kept with bitter thoughts, for in her retreat she had seen the enemy's face."

The Marquesa's eyes, drawn to the fire, grew distant. The silence of her listeners surrounded her.

[31]

"In the vaulted hall the gilded pendants hang above her head. Screens of tapestry give her privacy. Not far from the bed stands the altar and the Sacrament. The lighted tapers fall cruelly on her face and on that skin which has lost its clearness. Her eyes, once so unalterably blue and kind, are squeezed in their sockets. Only her majesty remains and that disciplined calm which rarely left her. Everywhere she may look is the symbol of the two names, Ferdinand and Ysabel . . . in the escutcheons on the walls, stamped upon her missal, on the table which holds the crucifix; on the great chairs, and cut into the silver dish bearing strong essences to revive her. These were more than dynastic markings, say you?

"She opens her eyes and stares vaguely at the light glancing diagonally through the casements. 'Marquesa,' she calls to me, 'What news of the King? Where is Peter Martyr?'

" 'Here, Your Highness,' answers the secretary, standing in the shadows by her head. 'A great victory has been gained by Gonzalvo on the Garigliana. The French are driven out of Naples.'

" 'Ah, is it so? But the King? Where is he?'

"There is silence.

" 'His Highness was last heard of at Gerona,' answers Martyr, 'with the army.'

" 'War, always war,' she sighs. And then she takes my hand. 'Beatrix, I see by your face that something is amiss. The King's absence, what does it mean?'

"I replied, my voice was strained, 'His Majesty is safe with the army at Perpignan.'

" 'The Princess Juana?'

" 'She has left the castle. She refuses to return unless she can leave at once and join the Archduke in Flanders.'

" 'Who attends her?'

" 'None. She escaped alone. But her people have been sent after her.'

" 'Now Heaven protect us. Martyr, call here the Archbishop.'

"I knelt and put my arms about her. 'My dearest mistress, these fancies of the Infanta will pass. She loves the Archduke madly.'

" 'It is not returned. He cares only for the succession.'

"The arras is lifted and her confessor, the Archbishop of Granada, presents himself. She rises with difficulty to kiss the episcopal ring; then falls back among the pillows.

" 'I pray you, my Lord Archbishop'—her voice is low and fluttered—'by the love you bear me and the King, to bring to this castle the Infanta Juana. Tell her from me that it is her health that prevents her from joining her husband. As soon as she is recovered from her lying in, she shall start, in case the Archduke refuses to join her in Spain.'

"The Archbishop waits until the Queen has recovered her breath somewhat. 'What I can do, Your Highness, I will do.'

" 'Go—go at once,' she commands.

"I lift the dish of essences to her nose. It revives her somewhat. Her voice is more composed as she says, 'Now, we are alone, as once before we were alone. Believe me, daughter, I have no false hopes. The end is near. If only ...'

" 'Shall I send an express to His Majesty?'

" 'No,' she answers wearily. 'Let me not trouble him. He knows I am ill. Perhaps ... but no matter.'

"We waited there for the King as in Valladolid, but he delayed. The enemy crossed the frontier before him. He, too, travelled secretly and by dark. There was no blaze of torches to announce his arrival, no one to cry: Look at him. This is he. There was no need. As I held her hand, I felt it tighten in mine. I saw her eyes look narrowly upon the arras through which all must come to reach her presence. I turned quickly, but the room was empty save for us. The arras hung unmoved to the floor. And then when I would speak some word of comfort, I saw that I was alone."

A silence came over the hall after the Marquesa was done, and Ysabel was crying. It seemed to her a pitiful thing for so great a queen to die in such a way, or die at all. She sought

Hernán and their eyes met. His said: I would never leave you so. The fire had died, leaving them in shadow.

As the company rose to part for the night, he came and stood beside her. "Oh, never, never . . ." she whispered but could not finish.

She thought he had lost his voice, but at last he said, "I'll wait for you here, by the hearth." There was such a sweetness in his tones she could feel her stomach grow tight to its very well.

The duenna took her off to bed, babbling all the way to their chamber, "That poor queen, there's no pity in any man, king or varlet. His Christian wife dying and him off to the wars. They call it off to the wars. Off on three legs I call it. Even then, even while she was taking the last Sacrament, I've no doubt he was smelling around that eighteen-year-old Germaine de Foix. Well, God knows all. What's the matter with you, child? You're as white . . ."

"Am I white?"

"As white as milk. It's your little heart grieving. Come, the Queen is done with hurting and you are in your days of grace. There's plenty of time for weeping and for rue."

The duenna talked on; she scarcely listened but made haste to get between the covers. She thought the duenna would never be done with her clothes. First she took her cap off and the skewers out of her hair. Then over her head she pulled her dress and petticoat. As she undid the band which held the hoops, rust showed upon the linen. From where Ysabel lay watching, she thought how it must always be moist under the fleshy folds about the duenna's waist. Next, she arranged her hair. The way the night cap went on displeased her. She took it off and did it over. She ate six oranges, one after the other, and threw sweet herbs on the fire. She scattered holy water about her bed. At last she said her prayers and, groaning, rose from her knees. Still she did not go to her bed. The girl despaired. Hernán would never wait, she knew. Or worse, he might come to seek her out.

The old woman walked idly about the room, opened a chest

and went through the clothes. Ysabel could hear her yawn, and in a little move heavily to arrange bottles of elixirs on a table near the bed, take sips from three. Finally she blew the light, squatted on the jordan, and crawled into bed. She twisted about for a while and then grew still. She belched twice and afterwards it was everywhere quiet in the room. Very softly the duenna began to puff, then settled into loud and regular snoring.

At last she was free. She waited a little to make sure; then slipped to the floor and stood in the shivering air.

She had forgotten how long the corridor was and how dark. Through the bare glow from the hearth she saw him standing in the shadow of a tapestry. He had seen her first and whispered her name so as not to frighten her. She ran into his arms and they closed about her. If he had not held her against his leather shirt she must have fallen; and yet in their innocence they did not clasp like lovers. They held tightly together as frightened children do. She became aware of his warm breath travelling over her face. Once he called her name with his lips at her ear. He drew her behind the tapestry and threw his heavy cloak about them. As he drew its folds, everywhere that his lean fingers touched made her feel that much his. And they roved nervously along her throat, cold and moist. He lifted her face, and she looked up to take his kiss.

They sat together without words. They sat until it was very dark and the hearth a misty red. In his arms it was warm and dark. She could no more see his face, but their breaths met and crossed and his blew sweet about her face. "Tomorrow," he said, "I'll ask Don Pedro for your hand."

"Not tomorrow," she said, holding tight his hands. "Wait until he leaves. Then we'll find a way."

Hernán must have understood her fear but he replied a little coldly, "My four quarterings are noble. It is only fortune that I lack."

"Yes, I know, but wait a little."

The coat had fallen from their shoulders. Their hands were clasped so tight she could feel the bones rub together. "No," he said. "I want to hold you always mine." He was shaking her.

"You hurt," she said. Her mouth was dry and she began to tremble, for it was suddenly cold.

He pulled the cloak about her and brought her to her feet. "I want to hold you honourably," he said.

She must have understood it all, for her plea was desperate, sitting beside him in the black chill when the humours of the night are most hurtful. Naturally then she did not know what now she knew, but in the very fulness of innocent love she had glimpsed the crooked way, how beset it was. In those minutes there she might have turned him aside, but she had only her feeling to urge and it was not enough. A woman will go straight to her desire. It is the man who is devious in his house of pride.

She slept no more that night. Hollow-eyed and pale, her throat tight and dry, she presented herself before her father and mother after early morning Mass. The three of them were alone in the chapel, her father in his chair, her mother beside him. "Are you ill?" Her mother asked.

"No, Mother," she replied. "Father, Hernán has a suit to ask of you." Now that she had said it she felt more calm and assured.

"He's a worthy lad," Don Pedro answered in perplexity. "But why does he not come himself? I've always dealt generously with him."

An instant she hesitated and then spoke it out in a breath. "He is going to ask for my hand."

At first Don Pedro seemed not to understand; then his hands struck the arms of the chair. She saw the knuckles grow white. She could not bear to look at his face; it frightened her. But she knew she must say it out or do the damage she had tried to prevent.

"I love him," she said. The words seemed to go no further than her lips. She tried to concentrate and make them carry. "I will have no other for wedded lord. I will. . . ." Her throat closed in fright.

Don Pedro strained but could not rise from his seat. She felt

[36]

her mother forcing her towards the door. "For God's sake, man," her mother said to the steward, "unlock the door and let us out."

Outside they stood an instant. From behind, muffled by the door, she heard the crash of the chair. They hurried away. She had scarcely reached her chamber when, below in the courtyard, there came the clatter of hoofs. She rushed to the window in time to see Don Pedro righting himself in the saddle. The horse leaped and he galloped through the open gates.

It was late when he returned. Hernán had been waiting in the yard. He ran forward and took the bridle and helped her father to dismount. The boy asked for an audience and it was granted at once. She had meant so well. She had thought if her father could see her desperation, it might soften his violence. She had no hope of his blessing. But all her fears were vague. She was as yet innocent of the cruel manner of his punishment. Don Pedro's ride seemed to have put him in fine humour. He made Hernán sit at table with him in his wardrobe, and with his most courteous and gentle manner told the boy it was not his blood—with that no house could be displeased; it was his lack of fortune, not entirely; it was rather his lack of spurs, of a bearded chin, and of a name for valour in his own right. He had a proposal: if only Hernán would follow him over the seas, the field was broad enough for fortune and for name; if he would prove himself a worthy and valiant man, then he, Pedrarias, could think of no reason to deny him. But naturally Hernán must understand that he should see no more of his daughter, just once to say farewell in the presence of the duenna; then he must be off to Seville and there take ship.

Hernán was taken so unawares that he agreed to every condition. At least so had she understood it then, but now she knew that Don Pedro had little to do to persuade him. He came to her grateful and enthusiastic. She had little heart to tell him her misgivings. Young as she was, she knew that few, through fair means or foul, ever returned from across the enchanted waters. She did what only a woman can do: she promised to

[37]

wait. Half in love and half in despair she gave that promise. He vowed to return a conqueror rich in spoils before he would claim her. Both promises were kept. How well were they kept. She waited. He returned. Seventeen years of waiting for her. Seventeen years—of what for him? Sitting there before her embroidery frame in the convent, she felt the shadow of a presence, felt the needle tremble in her fingers, and looked up. There he stood with the insubstantial promise of the world upon his lips. He had not forgotten. In the moment of his triumph he had crossed the seas to lay the new world's treasure at her feet. He had made the promise to a girl of sixteen. The woman who rose to take his hand was thirty-three.

3

She had withdrawn from the dining patio with her maids. De Soto had closed the door behind her, shutting her out from the banquet board where he remained with his friends of Peru and those he would persuade to follow him to Florida. It was a heavy door, all studded over, with a Moorish arch at the top. She was left standing before its barrier, unable to leave or rid her sight of it. In her own house, in their house, she stood like a stranger, with deliberate scrutiny counting the studs, those iron warts which marred the rich wood's flame. She would say: If only I can count the iron spikes studding the boards, I might yet be able to move away. Solemnly she counted, like a child doing ciphers, but the vision blurred, the bolts melted and spread, or they danced, stabbing at the thick and impervious barrier, and above the roaring in her ears she heard, far away: Iron and the tree; iron, and the tree where all passion is impaled. Her ears grew calm and at her back skirts rustled anxiously. There was whispering, and then:

"My lady is faint?"

"Go," she managed to say and, when her women refused to stir, she turned. "Go now, to your rooms. At once. Good night and God keep you."

Their wide skirts swept the floor of the entrance hall, their shoes tapped the tile as they retreated. She watched the last skirt serpentine against the turning wall, saw it disappear, and knew at last that she had put away the unreality which is the world. At last she was alone with her decision. How many months had she fled into the dishonourable refuge of the day's measures.

Around her she felt those familiar noises with which the night settles down to its vigil. She could feel the darkness sifting through the cracks, curling under the doors, licking the white façade of the Moorish house until it hung, a gray shadow, over the street. At that instant she felt—she freed her thoughts, it mattered not to what perilous region they might carry her—behind the stillness she felt a presence, almost physical, casting night for its shadow, watching behind it, waiting. . . . She crossed herself and murmured a paternoster. And then she heard it. Through the still house, out of the stiller night, it struck. It fell upon the topmost marble stair, moved with sure progression into the court, crossed it to the front gate. From there it turned, as strangely she knew it must, towards the corridor where she was. It was a common sound, no more than the majordomo bolting the night out. Alonso Ayala, with so much treasure stored within, always made the last rounds himself. Why did she listen with such expectancy? Why did she feel released into the full stream of her part? Mechanically her hands fell to her skirt, straightened it, afterwards to the lace in her hair.

The doors opened, two footmen stepped in and stood inside with snuffers like pikes in their hands. The page's torch flared in the entrance. Alonso appeared as though blown by its smoke and glare. Without pausing, he swung down the corridor, stepping with too much force, as if he expected the flags to roll beneath his feet. He looked like a sailor in disguise rather than the highest functionary in a Spanish house, but a fabulous sailor. The feather in his cap was long and pointed. It curled and popped as he moved. A chain of linked silver rolled upon the

[39]

chest of his soft brown tunic and his sword leaped about the crease below the buttocks. He might have been any age, she thought, for his face was as dark and scarred as a patched boot, and no eye could tell whether the wrinkles had been put there by time or weather.

He saw her at once and advanced as if he had expected to find her there. He was not alone. Besides the page, another man followed behind. This figure seized her eyes at once. He was dressed in black, with a great coat hanging from his shoulders. He moved with such ease and grace his clothes did seem to hang in air, hiding without touching his body, and beneath his broad-brimmed hat there lurked his face. She thought of a pilgrim being ushered before a shrine. On one side the coat fell straight to the floor, on the other it bulged, making him look, as he drew nearer, like a woman whose child has slipped out of place. She watched him approach. He is a gentleman, she thought. He came closer and she said, He is an unfrocked priest; he stood beside her and, seeing the eyes only, she almost cried, He is possessed!

His voice slipped between his lips, "It was kind of you, Doña Ysabel, to wait up for so late a guest."

He took off his hat. Thus suddenly exposed by the torch, she saw the face. Face, did she say? Only the lips and eyes were alive. The skin had dried upon the bone. It was peeling, leaving splotches of amber upon a smooth and deeply parched surface. She stared at the pied mask, at the eyes which had seen too much and asked, Is this the phantom I summoned in my folly?

"It is my honour"—Alonso Ayala raised his voice—"it is my honour ..."

She started. "Yes," she said.

"It is my honour to announce Alvar Núñez Cabeza de Vaca."

With hat in hand, the brown hair falling to his shoulders, the gentleman inclined his head. "My face interests you, my lady?" There was neither shame nor irony in his voice. "In Florida, my lady, a Spaniard is more improvident than the serpent. He casts his skin twice a year."

[40]

She could only murmur, "I didn't know the distinguished survivor of the de Narváez expedition was expected."

"I was not expected," he replied; waited a moment for her silent inquiry. "In the Indies it is the unexpected which one does well to expect."

"If you will follow me, Señor," interrupted the major-domo.

"I've come to wish Don Hernando Godspeed and to leave with him a small gift from the land he goes to pacify."

He lifted his coat. His arm clasped a chest, a very small one, iron-ribbed and leather-bound. It was a stout box, battered, and the salt of many seas glistened in its broken facings. She could but wonder through what strange and outland places it had gone, strapped upon brown backs or washed in the bilge of how many holds or hurled against the cabin walls as the heavy seas took ship and crew where God willed. But she wondered most that the little box should seem of a colour of his skin and a part of his flesh. Alonso Ayala's hand was upon it stroking its rounded top, and his fingers sought the rough leather, the dull and rusty bands, with a tenderness which made her seek his eyes against her will.

Ayala's voice dropped to a furious whisper, "Gold?"

De Vaca smiled curiously. "What you get in Florida for your pains."

"Don Hernando"—Alonso spoke roughly—"is with his friends in the small patio."

"My husband"—she stayed him with the question—"my husband had hoped you might return to Florida in his armament?"

De Vaca bowed with mock formality. "If the daughter of Pedrarias will forgive the stale jest, Florida has already enough of my skin."

Bowing, he turned away. Ayala's impatience had already carried him to the door which opened as de Vaca reached it and, with continuous movement, closed behind them both. In that moment, brief though it was, she saw a hateful illumination on Hernán's face and in the eyes of his companions. They were

[41]

clustered around the table in the dining patio. The cloth had been removed. The blue night shone through the palms and orange trees. Around the flowered borders the grass was fresh, dark, and soft. Over the southern rim of the arches which held up the cloistered walks she could just make out the bright cluster of the Goat stars and on the long table the bright warmth of the tapers, now melting down the silver holders; but neither in the Heavens nor in the earth did this light find its source. It set the guests' eyes ablaze, and yet it chilled. It glowed upon their faces; yet they were white and stricken. Their senses reeled with surfeit, but not with wine. Suddenly she understood! Into that cheerless revelry Núñez Cabeza de Vaca had thrust his unwelcome presence, into all that burning fell the cinder from the ash heap.

The smoke from the page's torch blew across her face. "Careful, boy," she said.

He turned upon her the small sooty face, the round staring eyes. "It is Saint Lazarus come from the dead."

"Speak no disrespect of the gentleman."

"Oh, no, my lady."

"For ten years he wandered lost and God knows in what privation through many and remote lands." She paused, divided by her thoughts.

"Is it there my master would go?"

"Hush, boy," she said. "Now you may light me to my chamber."

At her door she bade the page good night. She smiled at the boy, but her smile was not for him. She knew now what she must do. Hastily she dismissed him, in the midst of his bow, and, turning, hurried into her chamber.

4

The guests were reseating themselves with that easing of flesh and loosening of garments which the withdrawal of the ladies always leaves about the board. Tovar was slower than the rest in sitting down. Perhaps it was that his chair was opposite the entrance into the dining patio, but he saw Doña Ysabel pause, after de Soto had handed her into the corridor. He thought he saw her stiffen as the door swung to. He could not see the expression on her face, but he had a passing feeling that something was amiss. He gave it no thought. De Soto was hurrying back to his guests. He came like a man who may now settle down to serious business. Silvestre's voice rose from Tovar's side, "There's a captain for you."

The black wine was streaming over the guests' shoulders like frayed cords. It struck the mugs with a spattering hiss. In the midst of this pleasant noise de Soto reached his seat. He stood for a moment as though he was taking the measure of his guests. A gold chain hung from his neck, upon the dark rich clothes. The short black hair bristled at his head, belying the softness of his luxurious attire. Easily he dropped into his seat.

Tovar raised his mug. "I give you our host," he said, "Don Hernando de Soto, and the pacification of Florida."

The guests stood up to drink this toast. There was nothing dramatic in their action. They seemed to be performing the usual amenity. But there was a difference: the wine was drunk with an added seriousness, for all there waited in the knowledge they had not been bid to this house for the pleasure of their society alone.

As the guests sat down, scraping the tile with the benches, Tovar saw with surprise that the Marshal of Seville kept his feet, his arm thrust high over the table and down the heavy gold cup the wine spilled, staining his hand.

"I arise, knights and squires——" the old lord said, while his eyes swept those settling under their food and drink. So deliberate was his manner that even the vaguest sight sharpened at his glance. Then he raised his eyes to the open sky. All watched him standing in his black satin coat, the large sleeves slashed and showing the Holland's cloth of the shirt beneath. The newly replenished tapers brightened his hair, thin and white and too scattered to cover the places galled by battle gear.

Carefully, so that no unseemly haste might mar his dignity, he shifted his gaze to the cup. "I arise, Captains," he repeated, "now that healths go round."

Hands flew to their vessels as if they were swords. Moscoso de Alvarada beat the table, shouting, "Wine!" Don Hernando beckoned to the butler. From the orange trees and the cloisters of the patio servants ran, some stumbled, with their skins and flagons. The black Spanish drink poured to the cup's edge, it poured to overflowing and spattered the smooth oak boards. Then the attention became so perfect that the guests seemed to be hearing only the water falling in the fountain.

The Marshal straightened his already stiffly held back, and he would have looked a man barely turned from his prime but for the cords loose at his neck.

"I was at the fall of Granada," he said and brought the cup in ceremonious gesture to his chest. No man wondered that his words fell too heavily from his lips, for the jaws in the long and scarred face had a crushing look. He paused. Several made impatient by the wine already in their blood were holding their arms outstretched. He did not look their way but waited until, one by one, their arms fell and the cups rested quietly upon the table.

"I was at the fall of Granada," he repeated. "Six hundred hostages had been assembled in the Christian camp, when Gutiérrez de Cardeñas took possession of the Alhambra and the other fortresses and fixed the Cross upon the highest tower. Three times the Cross was raised and lowered, and every time the infidel Moors wept and groaned and cried aloud. Their lamentations had been a pitiful thing to hear if the soldier can feel pity in the moment of triumph. Then from the tower the herald called: *SANTIAGO, SANTIAGO, SANTIAGO; CASTILLA, CASTILLA, CASTILLA; GRANADA, GRA-NADA, GRANADA, For the most high and powerful lords, Don Fernando and Doña Ysabel, King and Queen of Spain, who have this day won this city of Granada and all its lands through the might of their arms, with the help of God and the glorious*

[44]

Virgin His Mother and the Blessed Saint James, and with the aid of our Most Holy Father, Innocent VIII, and the help and loyalty of the peers, prelates, knights, hidalgos, and corporations of their kingdoms. Then the herald ceased, and the tower and the Cross quivered to the blast of cannon and mortars. The trumpets blew and the narrow-tubed clarions and all manner of martial music, to show our joy."

The old lord said no more for a while. He waited in the image of his youth, loath to pass on, but even the varlets could see he was not done. The restless men about him had grown quiet. Although it had been forty-five years since that Cross had been raised over the last infidel kingdom in Spain, several wept as if it were only that day and all breathed harder, feeling the triumph to be their own.

Suddenly the Marshal's voice rang out, "That day the Crescent fell in Spain forever!"

"Santiago!" As one breath it sounded in the night.

The cups and goblets and mugs were drained, the guests sat down, but the old lord still kept his feet. With lowered voice he went on:

"I was a young squire then. Now I am old and think of many things a young man knows nothing of. That youth Hernandarias"—he glanced towards his grandson across the table—"nothing will please him but that he must follow Don Hernando to this island of Florida. I tell him that lances may be broke for the Holy Cross in Africa, where the infidels still plot and dream of field and tower we drove them from. And I tell you all, Christendom is nowise safe, not while Soliman gathers his Janizaries and Arab horse in Constantinople and the French Judas casts his eyes upon Milan."

He stopped for breath, or to measure his passion that it might not grow discourteous, and then looked again upon Hernandarias. He spoke sadly, "It may be young men no longer care to break lances for Her Ladyship's honour."

"Ah, but think, my lord," said the young friar, Juan de Gallegos, "how large a camp have Christians now to wander in." He leaned forward, the grey cowl fell jauntily on his shoulders, and his eyes seemed blown to a glow by his voice, and his face, wonderfully pocked, looked like a square brown cinder. "And consider how God from the time He first created the world hath reserved unto this day the knowledge of the great, the rich, and the plentiful Ocean Sea. I, the meanest of His servants, cannot think but that He has chosen to honour us from out all Christendom, as the instruments of His will.

"The equinoctial line hitherto unknown and thought un-inhabited by the writers of antiquity He has discovered to us filled with people—fair, fruitful, with a thousand islands rich in gold and beautiful pearls. The South Sea, Peru and Mexico. From these domains riches which do shame the East begin to pour into proud and thirsty Spain. Think you not His will is clear?"

Lobillo whispered to his neighbour, "There's a priest who speaks like a man."

"I know," said the Marshal with scorn, "what is brought from those islands and continents which block the route to Cathay. And I ask you, priest, are we merchants and Jews? Shall we let perish our immortal souls for a policy like unto that of the Venetian state which pays tribute to Soliman that courtesans may have spices in their meats, that prelates may swell their tongues with saffron?"

No man answered the Marshal. All eyes were upon the table. Don Hernando leaned slightly forward, listening with perfect courtesy.

"Do you think, sirs," the Marshal said in a fresh spurt of breath, "that I say these things because I am old and have forgot what it is to fight? You will much mistake me then. I have been to the wars and served under the great Captain while most of you were still wrapped in your napkins. I know what it is. It is a joyous thing, is war. You love your comrade so in war. When the quarrel is just and your blood is fighting well, tears rise to your eye. On seeing your friend expose his body so valiantly for Our Lord, a great sweet feeling of loyalty and pity swells your heart. Then you prepare to go and die or live with him, and for love not to abandon him. Out of that there comes such delight that he who has not known it is not fit to say what it is. Do you think that a man who fights so fears death? He is so elated that truly he does not know where he is."

"My lord, your pardon, but a Christian may love and fight in the new lands."

Tovar's voice left no impression of rudeness, for the Marshal had paused and there seemed no more to be said. Yet because of the half-revery induced by the old man's speech, Tovar saw the guests shift in their seats and look abruptly towards him.

Some one whispered, "He is de Soto's friend."

The Marshal also looked in his direction but he did not see him. Tovar could tell by his voice. It was puzzled and remote. When he began speaking again, it was a man thinking aloud.

"Granada fell in 1492. Later that year your Columbus made such a hole in Christendom I fear me it can never be plugged. I had seen the adventurer about Their Majesties' pavilions earlier in the siege. I had thought him an alchemist. I knew he was no soldier. And, for truth, he did turn out a kind of alchemy." The Marshal hesitated. "Yes, a kind of alchemy, for too much gold pours into this frugal land. Remember this, young captains. On that blessed day when Doña Ysabel rode in triumph into Granada, she held in her hands the sceptre of Castile. It was a slight thing of silver gilt. Yet it had brought low the Infidels who had usurped our kingdoms for seven hundred years."

He thrust the cup before him. The lights made it glow. With all eyes upon it, he thundered, "Señores, I give you poverty, that poverty of the Cross which is Spain!"

With one great swallow the Marshal drank down his toast. The guests, half-rising, half-sitting, looked foolishly at their empty mugs. The Marshal took his seat with an air of triumph. He did not know that he had drunk alone.

The night's ceiling hung low about the patio, so that the guests seemed to wait neither in darkness nor in light, but in a

[47]

sort of purgatory of the air, and they stared across the table as if each saw his image in the face opposite. Momently the heavy scent of the blossoming orange blew through the fumes of wine. The odours mingling above the table acted like a drug which sharpens the wits but sets them adrift. So it seemed to Tovar. It may have been that he had drunk too deep. Suddenly Lobillo, the youngest to come out of Peru with de Soto, stood up so abruptly his seat fell over. Spreading his arms like a man swimming, he said, "I smell the dark sweating," then, swaying slightly, sat slowly down upon the floor.

"My lord," de Soto said quickly, diverting the attention from Lobillo, whose friends were assisting him to his seat. "My lord, you have such words that my attendants forget their service." He nodded, and the waiting cups sang and spattered. Gracefully he lifted his mug and inclined his head towards his guests, "Come, gentlemen, let us soften our words."

In the pause which followed he looked squarely upon the Marshal. "Your Worship," he said, "I would read you and my other guests a thing I have here." He was very grave, very courteous, but his voice told his guests he had accepted the old hidalgo's challenge, that unforeseen intrusion which had disturbed the perfect sympathy he required for the success of the occasion.

As he spoke, he rose from his chair, taking a parchment from out its pearl-beaded tube. For a moment he looked across the board, as if he were balancing the future before his eyes. He lowered them and began to read:

"I give you, the said Captain Hernando de Soto, power and authority for us and in our name, and in that of the Royal Crown of Castile, to conquer, pacify, and populate the lands that there are from the Province of the River of Palms to Florida, the government of which was bestowed on Pánfilo de Narváez"— his tongue curled at the name—*"and further the Province of the said New Land, the government whereof was in like manner conferred on the said Licentiate Ayllón."*

The guests who had never left Spain listened like men

caught at their ease by a sudden emergency; but the conquerors of Darien and Peru, Moscoso de Alvarada, Lobillo and the rest—their eyes were veiled like merchants, yet merchants not born to the trade.

De Soto raised the sheet. *"Also we will confer on you the title of our Adelantado over the said two hundred leagues which you shall select and make known for your government in the said lands and Provinces you so discover and colonize, and will likewise bestow on you the office of High Constable over those territories in perpetuity."*

He lowered the parchment.

"Sirs, I have just read you the King's words. His greatness does not fear the Moors nor Soliman's Janizaries. His care is for all his realm and the extension of our holy faith. It is my pleasure to serve him wherever he may send me. Where I go, goes the King's authority. Where I set up my government, there will be lands and servants for those who follow me." Quietly he rolled up the parchment and thrust it back into its pearl-beaded tube.

He had made his titles clear. There could be no doubt, no reproach against such authority. Captain General, Governor, Adelantado, High Constable in perpetuity—High Constable of the world's end. There in Seville he sat in promised greatness, dividing spoils and vassals in a land he had never seen, might never reach, as calmly as if he were laying down clauses in a contract for the transference of so many geiras of olive trees or rents from the silks of Granada. The world's end—could man in his frailty go there? Or, might he return home again? Was it this which had made him pause with so much scorn at de Narváez' name, that luckless gentleman whose temerity had carried him to the outer provinces of the earth's corner to perish—to Florida to perish? Whose courage and luck did not match his arrogance? Tovar looked at those who had been to Peru. Certainly they had no doubts. At that instant he understood how set apart were these men, himself included, who had pursued the falling sun.

But it was not for their benefit de Soto had invited his company to dine. That morning, clattering out of the court yard, had gone the heralds with fifers and drummers, the Moorish drums riding high in the saddles, to beat up recruits for his armament. Over the highways of Estremadura, Leon, Andalucía, the two Castiles the horses would go. Nor would they stop until they had trod the floors of wastelands, falling without sound upon the bottoms of wildernesses, where the after-gloom of creation still lingered, secret and inviolate.

He must be sure of enough men and captains of skill and power in Spain. That was why so many rare dishes, rarer wine, had been served up this night. Was his display of confidence enough to make these hidalgos sell their property and follow him? Were they enthusiastic enough to bring family pressure upon the Crown to receive those Royal posts of Factor, Comptroller, and King's Treasurer, posts always fat in a rich land? The word must travel that Florida was as rich as Peru, and intrigue at Court was one sure way of releasing this word. The Adelantado had silenced the Marshal, but that was not enough. He was waiting to see the effect of his words. The pause was too long. Juan Gaytán broke it.

"Tell me, Don Hernando, do crockadiles eat men?"

Gaytán was the nephew of Cardinal Cigüenza and had come here tonight to make up his mind whether or not he wanted the office of Treasurer. Tovar did not like the question. It seemed to him irrelevant. But de Soto answered as if it were the most natural of all questions to be asked.

"They do," he said. "And men eat crockadiles. The suet of a cow crockadile is as sweet as the gums of Araby."

There was another pause, a short one—then:

"What weapon," de Biedma asked, "will be most effective in Florida?" There was a precise and metallic ring to his voice.

"No weapon."

"No weapon?"

"No, Señor, but an animal."

De Biedma's eyes, which never blinked, now blinked and the moisture which was always in them glittered.

"The horse," de Soto continued, "is feared by these Indians as a god."

"Is it true," Gaytán asked, "that once in Peru you shod your horses with silver?" His voice carried the faintest note of incredulity.

"Señor," Tovar said sharply, "in Peru silver is trash."

"I would have shod them with gold"—de Soto's eyes for the first time that evening grew informal—"for I saw from afar the golden halls of Cuzco."

"*Cuzco!*"

The word fell into their midst like an arrow. The men of Peru drew together and leaned forward on the table, and the air in the patio grew so still the flames of the tapers now bent, now lifted, to the rhythm of their breath.

"God showed us great courtesy that time," he added quietly. "To a handful of Christians he delivered a kingdom."

"God's miracle!" Juan de Añasco flung out the words like an oath.

De Soto paused, continued evenly, "I was one of three sent to Cuzco to hasten the delivery of the Inca's ransom. You know the amount: a room filled with gold; twice filled with silver. Those who had gone before me were too brutal, too unseemly, let us say, too eager. The treasure was slow arriving in Caxamalca." He leaned forward, placed his hands before him on the table. "In Peru there is a bird called the comine bird. Its breast is no larger than my thumb nail. Upon this breast grow the turnsole feathers, slender and delicate, the colour of very fine gold, although some have the hue of a goldish green. A mantle of these feathers covered the trough where the Sun god slept. The trough itself was of plated gold. Upon this mantle, covering this trough, lay the god, a disc of solid gold made in the image of the sun. Around him slept two hundred of his wives, daughters of the greatest lineage in the land who had sworn to live apart from men for his pleasure. The room held enough treasure to equip the Emperor's army sent down into Italy."

The Governor sat back in his chair. He seemed charmed by

[51]

the spell he had cast. In the silence the guests reached for their mugs. They drank in great gulps and then Juan de Añasco rose to his feet. He swayed and righted himself by the board.

"Sir Governor, Adelantado," he said, and his blunt tongue had been softened, "we have dined at your board as only the Emperor, the greatest appetite in Christendom, knows how to dine. But not even he in his lone splendor has had such a roasted yearling stuffed with pig, nor such breasts of capons brought before us simmering in rose water and sugar, nor such fowl and geese until Castro's arm grew heavy with carving. And for such good meat, the cakes you served us, browned in pans of bubbling oil which we dipped in honey to soothe our smarting tongues. And the cool pomegranate and purple figs to lighten the blood you have spiced, and the tent-red wine to make it rich again. All this have you served us, but only now do we begin to feast."

The guests shifted and resettled themselves in their seats. De Soto smiled and waved de Añasco to his stool.

"My Worships, you overpraise my poor food. The least among you may serve such dishes for your daily meals—in Florida."

The brown faces of the guests turned white; their mouths worked but could not utter the name which in that moment had become their talisman. "There remains—" de Soto seized the moment before it could spend—"one last hid secret of nature. You think Peru is rich, and rich it is. But Florida. . . . Think of a land where the air is forever soft, the rivers wholesome from coursing through earth that is never free of gold; think of a climate where a man is rarely driven to close chambers with the cold, nor ever burns his shins before the fire which will make him old before his time by resolving the natural heat of his body. Think of all this and you will be in Florida, the lords of that land."

Tovar felt a jar. The jar of a door swinging shut. There was no noise, but with that sense which governs in the instant of tension he understood it was the door into the corridor. The walls of the patio had been breached. The breach was closed. The air smashed by the door and its jamb eddied, spent itself. Under the open sky the patio was as close as a cell. This same sky which hung so low over Christendom, did it lie as quietly over the Ocean Sea and over that Wilderness which was its other limit?

The guests swayed slightly. De Soto bent slightly forward. "We know by experience," he said, and his voice found its equilibrium in their ringing ears, "that the vein of gold is a living tree which spreads from the root through the soft pores of the earth and ceases not until it discovers itself to the open air, where it shows forth certain beautiful colours instead of flowers, round stones instead of fruit, and thin plates instead of leaves. These are scattered by rivers and springs and violent floods, for it is held that such grains are not engendered where they are gathered. The root of this tree, philosophers say, goes down to the centre of the earth and there takes nourishment for its increase, for the deeper men dig the larger they find its branches. Some are as small as a thread, others as large as fingers. In Hispaniola miners have chanced upon entire caves borne up with golden pillars. This has spread the belief that the abundance of gold begins there. But, gentlemen, I am of another opinion. I believe this golden tree sprouts in the gardens of the North Pole. This pole, not the Southern, is the golden pole." He paused just longer than an intake of breath, and then:

"Florida lies to the north of Peru, to the north of Golden Castile, to the north of Mexico, BUT to the south of these gardens."

He was done. The guests seemed not to know that his voice had stopped. It was, rather, that they had ceased to listen. Bent forward and stilled, with only their chests rising stealthily, they stared, as if the sound of his words had taken on a precious but very fragile mortality which any movement, even the lash of an eye, must destroy. De Soto leaned back in his seat. His armament would not lack for men.

And then out of the vacuum:

[53]

"Do I smell the air of Florida?"

The voice which spoke might have been of the air, so thin it was. And pervasive. The guests stirred, as out of some magic wax. They looked at one another in unbelief. Instinctively Tovar knew where to turn. Under the arch of the patio, near the door into the corridor, stood the majordomo and behind him what might have been his shadow.

"Don Alvar Núñez Cabeza de Vaca," the majordomo announced and drew back, but not out of hearing.

De Soto frowned and rose to greet the visitor. "Cousin," de Gallegos called out lustily and lunged to his feet. Micer Espindola threw open his arms. "I must embrace my cousin," he said, and slid under the table, crying as he sank, "Some villain has greased my seat."

De Gallegos paused behind his chair, looking foolishly towards the entrance. He saw no one. He saw no one, for de Vaca was advancing unseen by all but de Soto's eye. De Soto, the Indian fighter, watched him in the silence he made, a gliding darkness in full travelling cloak, until suddenly, before the guests could set their faces for the greeting, he appeared out of the night. The flickering tapers lit up his splotched and peeling face.

Romo leapt up. "The plague," he cried and stumbled over his chair. Benches and chairs clattered to the floor.

"Hold, hold, Señores," de Soto called sharply. "This is my guest."

De Vaca advanced into the full light, curiously smiling. The servitors ran among the chairs, setting them to rights. With a few empty jests those who had risen in terror, glancing furtively, resumed their seats. In the embarrassed silence de Soto turned: "You come among Christians, Don Alvar, like an Indian."

"Forgive me, Your Worships, but you see a Christian who has lived a naked Indian. For ten years I was cast away in Florida, but in all that time my skin remembered it was Christian and never ceased to shed its heathen layers." He smiled and brushed his hand across his face. "No, Señores, it

[54]

is not the plague, but Florida knows how to leave as deep a mark."

De Soto beckoned for a chair. "You bring honour to this house, Señor." He paused, added dryly, "But you come late to the feast."

"Not too late to pray God's blessing on your venture, I hope."

De Soto inclined his head, but only long enough for courtesy. "You have not changed your mind?" he said. "You will not accept my terms and come with us?"

"Your terms, my lord, were too generous for my services, too frugal for my knowledge. Perhaps the time will come in that land when you may regret the ship you refused me."

"Perhaps, Señor, but not such regrets as your lamented Governor, de Narváez, must have had when the shallow barks in which he fled that land opened and spilled you into the sea."

"It is true, Don Hernando, that of all the armaments which have gone to the Indies none has found itself in straits like ours, or come to an end alike forlorn and fatal." De Vaca's voice was low, but his lips drew back from his teeth for the bitterness of his tongue. "The love for action and the service of our Prince," he said, "are common to all men of spirit, but there be great inequalities of fortune, the result not of conduct but only accident, nor caused by the fault of anyone but coming in the providence of God and solely by His will. Hence to one arises deeds more signal than he thought to do, to another the opposite in every way occurs, so that he can show no higher proof of purpose than his effort, and even this may be so concealed that it cannot of itself appear."

"There is but one fortune I trust, Señor . . . this!" De Soto struck the table with his dagger. The steel quivered in the wood, the hilt blurred with the motion, and then grew quiet. Stilled and bright, the Cross of Santiago stood upright in the spilled wine. The breath rasped in the throats of Estremadurans, the slashed and pinked bloods of Castile, the men from Peru and Darien. With their eyes upon the Cross's image, they made its sign.

[55]

With elaborate care de Soto loosed the blade and returned it to its sheath. Hoarse and trembling, voices whispered, "Santiago!" And the young priest was standing.

"Speak you of gold?" he asked. "Speak you of the sword? Then you speak of avarice and pride." He paused until the scattered attention was focussed by his voice. "Avarice and pride be the two worms in the forked tongue of Satan. One sucks at the heart until it is cracked as an old wineskin, but the other festers the meat of your soul. And spews it out a hull, and spits it out a shred. And the fires of torment and damnation flare in Hell. They flare afresh, these fires that never die, for though the hull be empty and the shred dry, they drip with the grease of sin.

"The people of Florida perish for lack of the Word. What will you bring them? Salvation?" He reached forth his arms, slowly let them fall. "No salvation. You will bring them the sword. And what will you have of them? A crown in Heaven? No crown. You will take of them their riches and the labor of their hands. Will you be lost? Perhaps you will be lost. But there is hope. I bring you hope, for the Word is more cunning than sin. For to that dark and ignorant land you will carry the Holy Cross, and that Cross will bring it civility and the true faith. To those who are perishing for lack of the Word, the Word that is iron, the Word that is tree, and the Word that is the bloody thorn—cleaved by iron, bled at the thorn, died on the tree but did not die—that Word shall set them and you free."

The priest made the sign over the board and quietly took his seat.

Tovar looked around and the tears were rolling into the beards of the guests—to think that sinners might bear the Cross, that their mouths were no longer defiled for the Word they would speak, that their wilful hearts knew, if but for this moment, the infinite mystery of God's mercy.

De Soto broke the silence. "Fuentes," he called to the dining steward, "bring me three soups for my guests." And turning to those about him: "We will eat them in honour of the Blessed Trinity."

These Lords of Florida, for such did most of them now consider themselves, were pleased to find their governor anxious to praise the dynasty of Heaven. Tovar was pleased to notice their rising respect for his master, and did not at first notice that de Vaca, for the moment forgotten, had risen. He was standing near a small chest he had set upon the table. He was putting a key into its lock. One by one the guests leaned forward to see what it would bring forth. Lightheartedly Baltazar de Gallegos addressed his kinsman. "What, Cousin, have you there? Some treasure from Florida?"

De Vaca's long and speckled fingers rested on the lid of the chest. His eyes lingered on some memory, and then he spoke. "Only four men of all that numerous armament of the Governor de Narváez escaped from Florida with their lives. I was one of those four. Another a negro slave. And Dorantes, my companion. After we had found ourselves in a safe haven, Dorantes and I agreed to ask the government of that land and swore an oath not to speak of what we had found. I crossed the ocean. He remained behind. But I was too late. The grant had already been made. Because of my oath I may not divulge what you would know, but this much I may tell. It will be a parting gift from one who knows better than you what you are undertaking. The gift lies in this chest. If you are wise, you will value it above all treasure. I have seen the time I would have given all the pearls that do pasture in the meadows of the sea, the gold of Peru, and the pride of power for it."

There was some uneasiness at his words, but mainly the greedy curiosity as before the discovery of a new thing never before known to the world. De Vaca lifted the top of the chest and, reaching his hand into its body, threw an ear of maize onto the table. He reached down again and brought up a buskin and some laces of curious leather. The silence was profound. Disbelief and anger flashed about the board.

Presently Gallegos said, "You jest, Cousin."

And Tovar insolently, "What brings you here, Señor?" He snatched one of the lacets, and it lay coiled and streaming through his fingers.

"I bring you the secret of Florida, my Captain," de Vaca answered gently. Tovar looked for some mockery on the pied face, but it was unchanged.

"This . . . this lacet, and this maize." Tovar picked the ear up and tossed it down with such force that the grains broke and scattered.

De Soto—out of his eyes Tovar saw him—from his waist upwards stiffened with contempt and fury.

Then still gently from de Vaca's lips: "A lacet, you say? True, it is a lacet, but it is also all that is left of the skin of His Majesty's factor." Biedma, who was a candidate for this post, paled. "And this"—de Vaca reached for the buskin—" once covered the back of a captain of foot."

Tovar turned his eyes slowly down the amber and cured length of the skin; then tossed it after the maize. The guests started and pressed the backs of their seats.

De Vaca proceeded calmly, "The rest of the conquerors, all save their buttocks, were eaten by their companions"—he hesitated, reached over and picked up the ear of maize—"for lack of this."

Gently he put down the maize, closed the chest, locked it, and covered it by his cloak. "And now, Señores, I must leave you," he said. "I am on my way to Valladolid to ask of His Majesty another government. My people are in the street below. We are already late, if we would out-march the Andalusian sun." Bowing once to the table and once to his host—de Soto did not return the courtesy nor rise from his seat— de Vaca turned away and disappeared beneath the arch at the patio's entrance. There was a slight sough as the door closed. Tovar heard a gasp. It was the youth Hernandarias vomiting.

The soups to the Blessed Trinity were tasted by the steward and by him sent to the board. They sat in ceremonial order, and out of the silver dishes a fragrant vapour rose and spread over de Vaca's gifts. Zeilam's cinnamon, Beledi ginger from Calicut, cloves from the Islands of Molucca hung like incense and spiced the air. But the air soon staled, and the soup turned sour in its immaculate dish. The guests had paid their respects and departed.

5

Doña Ysabel looked at her reflection in the mirror. She had just fixed the brilliants in her hair. Slowly she turned her head. It was lovely, lovely. The small stones—how cleverly she had hidden them—did not flash but made the hair move in liquid flow. They had been a happy thought, the brilliants, especially since the hair was down, flowing over the soft stuff of the Peruvian gown. It made her seem all flesh, a fairer flesh than ever grew on the bone. Quickly she ran her hand over the small vials of crystal, paused before one of the ebony no larger than her thumb, a perfume brought from Damascus at twice its weight in gold. Her trembling fingers took the stopper, sent it skimming over the hair, lightly behind the ear. She closed her eyes, almost swooning with delight. Grasped her throat. Her breath, her breath—she was as giddy as a girl.

She fled to the window, threw back the half-parted damask curtains and breathed deeply the cool spiced air. The hollow knots in her breasts softened, dissolved, and the breasts began to rise and fall in slow deep pulsation. How strong were myrrh and the secret oils which dissolved its resin! Through her chamber window blew all the airs of the rounded world, but they did not blow away the heavy scent rising before her face, curling and waving like scented vapour. She leaned forward, listening like one taken by surprise. There was only silence; then up the narrow street, mounting to the iron bars:

"Hail Mary, Most Pure, one o'clock and the night fails."

The sereno! Was it so late? He would come any moment now, for the banquet must surely be over. She rushed back to

[59]

the dressing table in sweet panic. How her cheeks were flushed! She felt them with the back of her hand. They were as red as clay. She dug the coney's foot in chalk and patted until the dust rose about her head and face, falling slowly to the table. She threw down the foot, noticed the table's gay disarray; then with a critical eye she looked again into the mirror.

Her gaze was bright and daring. The tapers softened the skin, washed out the wrinkles about the eyes and the two faint lines at the mouth, but the little bulge at the chin—no matter how she lifted or turned her head—that remained. And then her courage failed her. It was no use. She would never be able to bend him to her desire. She felt a sudden pity for herself until, deliberately, she began to remember all the secret things between them. In the glass her eyes ran together, blurred.

It was the voice in the wardrobe which brought her to herself. Hernán's voice, bidding good night. She turned in time to see him come into the room. He came forward a few paces and stopped. As she rose, she felt her heart sink to its pit. It held her fast, as if it had been a physical weight; but she would not be taught despair.

Aslant the window a luminous shaft stained the bed, spilled over onto the floor. Through this she walked towards her husband, stopped upon its edge for him to see her and come. But he did not move. Slightly stooped, his eyes fastened to the floor, he remained in close thought. She noticed that he had forgotten to close the door. After a while she heard herself say— her voice sounded cool and distant:

"The feast is ended?"

It was not what she had meant to say at all.

Slowly de Soto raised his head. "Ysabel?"

"Yes."

"You are not asleep?"

"I have waited for you."

He came over and took her hand in his. He patted it idly and let it fall. "Thou art the best of wives," he said and turned away. Slowly he took off his coat and let it fall upon the seat.

An arm of the slashed and full-bodied sleeve dragged the floor. She felt the need of desperate, startling words. She wanted to say: Look at me, your wife!

She said, "All did not go well?"

"Until the end. Cabeza de Vaca came with malice to chill the spirits of the Florida men."

"Yes, I know." Her voice was flat. She felt inside her a red spot of anger swelling. What perversity put words in her mouth so far from her purpose? He lifted his head.

"You knew, you say?"

"We met in the corridor."

"Going?"

"No, coming."

"You wandered through the house at so late an hour?"

"I did, my lord."

"Attended?"

"Unattended."

For a moment she felt the sudden strength of hope, but in the pause she coolly examined his gaze. It said: This my wife, who keeps my house with such fine management. A woman capable of all affairs. Ah, had he thought: This my love, to love. What did she wandering through dark corridors where the whispers lie in wait?

He looked away. "That was an Indian trick he played me, with his maize and string of Christian hide."

"What trick? What hide?" She felt herself grow strange with fear, and the words were on her lips to ask him not to answer when he said,

"Out of hunger de Vaca's companions ate one another when they were cast away in Florida. He brought to my table a shoe lacet made from the hide of one. He meant to terrify my guests, to thwart us, keep us from riches he himself might not have."

The words struck like a blow, and she stepped back. At last it had come—suddenly, as a phantom solidifying the air. Out of the first instant of horror she felt growing, stronger each breath, a sense of relief, for at last the Enemy had made himself

[61]

tangible. All evening had she not sought to confront him? Had she not, in the secret places of her mind, heard the rattle in the brush? The warning? Watched the slow unwinding coils and the long glide? Felt the scratch of the scales? And out of the cool slime sucked in the malevolent air of Florida, that outlandish island or continent so abandoned of God, the very principality of the world, where renunciation must forever fail? There could be no more abandoned acceptance of the world than for brother to eat his brother! Eat of the ever-dying flesh and go down quick into hell! And then in the instant flash of vision she saw those ghosts of men, forlorn in their desperation. She saw the bone, the sterile bone, in its labour crack its shell, the thin and cannibal flesh be rent; and in the blinding truth of revelation, as if she had been transported, she watched the starving Christians fall upon one another, their long teeth tear the dusty flesh and be broken on the bone. And they gnawed and tore at one another until one alone remained, lying upon his back, his lipless jaws moving in supplication. And, aloof but present, she felt such pity that she stooped and leaned over to hear the low whistle of his words. And out of his mouth there came such a stench as of corrupting myrrh so that she almost swooned, and the words, "Oh Christ, one drop of your blood"— and a low petulant wail like a sick child's—"one drop and I am saved." She looked hard at the face, and she saw that it looked as Hernán must look when he had died. She came to herself crying, "Stay away! Stay away!" And then more calmly. "Hernán, give over this Florida. It is an evil place."

He sat perfectly still, like a man stunned. Slowly he rose and took his wife's shoulders and pushed her into the column of light. She could see in his stare surprise, then disbelief. She spoke hurriedly,

"Let us take the goods you have won and live among the worshipful of our station. I've waited so long. Let us have some pleasure in ourselves."

He reached forward and ran his hands gently through her hair. Instinctively he did what a man does when the woman he loves shows signs of unaccountable hysteria, and she felt pity for him. She closed her eyes and put her long white arms about his neck, drew close until she felt the familiar slope of the hard shoulders. He must think a delicious weakness seized her, but the game of love she had meant them to play, she had meant to mean so much, was now another game. "Hold me fast, love, or I shall swoon and fall away." She thought bitterly, I am a harlot simulating passion.

"No man in Christendom is so blessed as I," he said, and there was triumph in his grasp and voice.

In spite of her sorrow she smiled tenderly at his innocent simplicity, innocent in spite of the evil things he had done or would cause to happen in his name, for already his caress by its familiarity had kindled the familiar desire, and he had forgotten its purpose. She said, thinking how easily she would turn him, "You do love me above all others?" He grasped her almost roughly and she freely pushed her advantage. "You must say you do."

"I do."

"You will stay here with me, won't you?" Her voice urged secretly.

In the pause she realized that she had gone too fast. His arms loosened their hold. She heard his reasonable tones, "My love, what would I do in Spain?"

She knew that she must consider well what next she said, but her fright made her look at him, and looking hurried her speech. "You may buy farms and great herds of sheep in La Mesta," she said.

"Am I a man to play shepherd or serve as lackey at Court?"

"Oh, you don't understand." Her voice was becoming desperate, but he did not hear.

"No, we will found a great house, a princely house, in the wilderness," he said flatly.

She stiffened. Already he had dropped his hands and his voice no longer caressed. In bitterness and futility she turned away and walked down the column of light. She felt its chill,

[63]

for the moon was on the downslope, and the iron bars against which she leaned were cold. "Did you think," she said finally, "it would be like this—never together, with great waters, a thing greater than they, between us?"

He answered hastily, and the haste in his voice told her that he feared she might return to the strange and unaccountable mood. "You won't stay long in Cuba. Somewhere on the coast of Florida I'll build a town. I'll fetch you there at the first safe moment." She could see him, although her back was turned, leaning forward. "You will be mistress of a kingdom," he whispered.

"But did you think it would be like this?"

"I'll leave you as Governor of Cuba in my place. You will be safe in Cuba, and Cuba will be safe with you. The daughter of Pedrarias and a Bobadilla will be respected there—and obeyed. And I say it to you, my Ysabel: I never saw a woman more fit to rule. And the expedition will not fail as the others have. You will sustain me with supplies. We will buy grazing farms for cattle, and at the proper season slaughter the wild hogs. Corral remounts for the cavalry. A successful Adelantado must foresee every contingency. He must . . ."

"But did you?"

"Did I what?"

"Think it would be like this?"

"Like this? Like this when?"

"Oh, long ago."

He considered. She turned and faced him directly. She saw him frowning. "I promised to return to you," he said diffidently. "Didn't I?"

"Yes, you returned."

"With treasure."

"With treasure, as you promised."

She saw him look as if to say a gentleman can do no more.

"But I keep thinking of that lad and the way he held me and promised."

"What lad?" he asked coldly.

She did not answer him.

He said stiffly, "I would not have held you to your promise."

"Behind the tapestry at Rostro he waited, and I ran into his arms." She turned again to the window. Possibly he would not, but she could not bear to see him fail her. "It was not his words. It was his arms which had promised all delight."

"Oh . . ."

She turned fiercely, "What have we done with our youth? Those seventeen years? Where have we lost them?"

"Some of them"—he spoke evenly—"were spent in Peru. Riches do not come easy."

"You do not understand me at all."

"Yes, I think I understand," he replied with weary vehemence.

"Don't speak to me like that."

"Like what?"

"Like that."

"Ranjel sleeps in my wardrobe, you know."

"Why didn't you close the door?"

She was in deep distress to watch the evening, this crucial time, perversely waste itself in quarrel.

"Come," he said more gently. "Let's not have words." And he came towards her in an open, affectionate way.

Something in his manner—it was too noble perhaps—made her say against her will, "You murdered my youth. Now must you widow me?"

He laid firm hands upon her. She flattened her arms against her sides. "Don't touch me."

"All right. I won't."

"You stink of wine. You and . . . and your men of Peru. All of you sodden with wine. Pretty conquerors you will make."

"Be silent, woman. Any one of them is fit to rule half the world."

The smear of light passed his face. The hollows it made below the eyes, at the mouth, at the base of his nose, turned all his face to bone. The silence tightened. She could hear him breathe.

[65]

He was looking at the bed hung with its green and gold damask, at the white tapestries draped upon the walls, at the brass lamps burning by the bed, such as are kept in Moorish harems. He raised his hand and waved it with sharp pointing motions. "This is what the men of Peru give their wives," he said and pointed again, as if he felt the inadequacy of his words. He dropped his arm uncertainly and walked once up and down the room, slowly and in troubled thought. He stopped near her with the intense arrested motion of one who in ambush hears the enemy's step.

"Do you know," he asked, "what it is for a captain to lose himself and his men, of his own free will to lose them in the uncharted tracts of a new found land, ignorant of the quality of its air, of its food, even whether there be any for Christians to eat? And everywhere a mystery which his presence there compels him to make plain. Do you?"

He waited for her to show some sign she had grasped the essential meaning of his words, but she could not answer him. He continued: "That captain is like a navigator whose card has been swept clean of all direction, and he somewhere upon the great and the plentiful Ocean Sea, utterly without bearing, under a sky where the stars, even, differ from those in our circle of the heavens." He lowered his voice and leaned forward. "And suppose it happens that he never finds himself in that land, and his men are brought to such straits that they eat one another like Caribs." His voice took on a strange, enraptured tone. "What prince in all the known world commands such desperate measures, such unfailing obedience?"

Again he waited for a sign from her, but she walked away in a daze. As she passed him, he stepped forward and grasped her shoulders. "You do understand?" he asked and shook her slightly.

His lithe dark body made her feel how complete was her defeat, and yet she knew he was innocent of any triumph. She raised her shoulders, and his hands fell away. Later, standing by the bed, with the lamp's speckled light upon her, she tore the brilliants from her hair. Slowly and clumsily she took them and let them fall. They slapped the back of the table, swung in the lamp's way, sparkling dully. The covers of the bed had been turned back, neatly, ritual-wise, and the blossoming orange had been scattered there. She reached over, lifted the sheet, and crept beneath. The covers fell, billowing for a moment; then settled upon her crouching form. All brittle did she feel where the linen spread, too sharp at the feet, falling away towards the breast and lightly clinging there.

She was conscious of nothing, and then she heard his silent speedy movements as he stripped him of his clothes: the sinking of the bed as he rolled the trunk hose down the brown and wiry legs, the pat of the jerkin striking the seat, the white flash of the Holland's shirt, and the noise of the mattress as he got in, all naked, beside her. He reached under the cover. "Love?" he asked gently. And when she made no response. "What a fool I was to talk away the night." He leaned over her. "What's the matter with you? You're like tallow in a mould."

She began to cry, without sound, but each tear as it fell shook all her being.

"Now, now," he said. "What's the matter?"

"And I had thought," she replied, "we would make such gallant lovers."

"And haven't we?" And to break her silence. "And won't we?"

"All that's over now."

"It's just beginning," he asserted with exaggerated emphasis.

"It's no use," she repeated.

Weeping had unbound the stiff cords of her despair, and she lay beside him, relaxed as in sleep. He had disarranged the covers, and she saw the thin gown clasping her body or hiding it, and it seemed a pitiful thing. And then like a thing out of the night she heard his voice, harsh through stops of breath, and the deep bare chest hovering above her, the long shadow descending:

"No, Hernán, no!"

[67]

"Yes."

She put up her hands. "Not now," she said and lost her breath. "Oh, not now."

Her arms folded in. Her head whirled as thick and stifling pressed down upon her a sweet and unbearable odour. It was that of corrupting flesh! Cannibal! She opened her mouth, but no sound came; and then she felt herself grow heavy and inert.

In the chamber it was still. In the long narrow street there was the hush of the dead, and the dead grey light made the walls distantly visible. Out of the greyness, sourceless yet clear, rose the sereno's voice:

Hail Mary, Most Pure, two o'clock and a morning fair.

2

THE OCEAN SEA

The Ocean Sea

Tovar stood upon the beach in Havana and watched the fleet preparing to set out for Florida. The trumpets blew, the drums beat, and from the sea a stiff breeze took the standard and spread the royal arms of Spain upon the air of this far post of Christendom. The long lines of Indians and soldiers paused, with the supplies they were carrying to the ships, and watched the standard go by. Diego in all formality bore it upright against the wind on its way to the flagship, where it would lie folded inside its chest against the day when, thrust into the sands of Florida, it would claim that land in the name of His Sacred Caesarian Majesty, Charles, the fifth of that name.

For the first time in weeks Tovar felt the old quickening of his pulse and a return of his desire for outland places. The armament at last was almost come to its goal, with Florida only a few days away, ten at most, after thirteen hundred wearisome leagues of water, a year of recruiting in Cuba and gathering horses and supplies. The sound of the trumpets died away, burst afresh upon the air.

So had they sounded, dulled momently by the rounds of artillery, that Sunday morning, Saint Lazarus' day, when the fleet set out from Spain. De Soto kneeled in the sands at San Lúcar, folding his hands within the hands of the President of the Council of the Indies. The President's voice rose above the lap of the waves: "You, Hernando de Soto, do swear and take oath of homage as a cavalier and hidalgo, one, two, and three times; one, two, and three times; one, two, and three times, in accordance with the custom of Spain, to hold the lands, towns,

[71]

and fortifications which may be settled in the land of Florida, its confines and its ports, for the Royal Majesty of the King, Don Carlos, our Lord, and for his service; and as such you will defend them both in peace and in war as a good and loyal vassal of his, keeping in all things the service of His Majesty. And you will obey and comply with whatever you may be ordered by His Majesty, under penalty of being declared treacherous and of falling into evil state and of incurring the other penalties established by law, which are incurred by gentlemen and persons who break the oath and covenant of homage made to their king and natural lord."

The Governor had answered that in all things he would keep his loyal service. Then the standard with its insignia and sign of the Holy Cross was blessed and put into his hands, and afterwards he held a muster of his troops, to which the Portuguese came with splendid arms and the Castilians very elegantly, in silk over silk and many plaits and sashes. As this finery did not please him, the Governor ordered another muster, with instructions for each man to appear in his armour. The Portuguese came as before, and these he placed near his standard. The armor of the Castilians was poor and rusty and their lances for the most part worthless, but those he liked the Governor enrolled.

There was never such a prosperous armament to go out of Spain. Six hundred men in seven ships. The company of Portuguese under André de Vasconcelos, and from Salamanca, Jaen, Valencia, Albuquerque and other parts of Spain many persons of noble family. The Marqués of Astorga, after talking with the Emperor, sent his brother Don Antonio and two other kinsmen, Francisco and Garcia de Osorio. Don Antonio disposed of an income of two thousand ducats in the Church and Francisco of a town of vassals in the district of Campos. Luis de Moscoso, the Camp Master, took his two brothers. From Badajoz, Pedro Calderón and the three brothers, Arias Tinoco, Alonso Romo, and Diego Tinoco, kinsmen of the Governor's. Baltazar de Gallegos sold houses, vineyards, a rent of wheat, and nineteen geiras of olive trees near Seville. He was made Chief Constable over the fleet and army and took along his wife, as did Don Carlos, who had married the Governor's niece. With other known and rich countries it was usual to lack for men, but such were the hopes of Florida that many who had sold their property were left behind.

Then he, Tovar, had been Lieutenant-General of the army and captain of the *Magdalena,* the second ship of the fleet. He stood upon her high decks, the last of the ships to pass in review down the roadstead of the harbor. When she hove in sight of the flagship and he saw the great cross loosed in the stern sheets, what hope and promise, what pride did he feel! So close did the *Magdalena* come to the Governor's ship he could make out the features of those on board. Upon the forecastle Doña Ysabel had gathered her maids against the gilded railing. In a blue velvet gown with wide sleeves, slashed and palely glowing from the rows of watery hyacinths sewed into the cloth, with a gorget of emeralds about her neck, she looked more like the lady of a conqueror returning from a conquest than one at the setting out. The *Magdalena* moved on. He passed slowly by her ladyship, by the halberdiers of the Governor's guard, with their arms grounded upon the deck, by the gentlemen grouped outside their quarters, some already green from the pitch of the waves; and then hovering above the decks and water rose up the poop of the *San Cristóbal.* Slightly withdrawn to starboard, the Dominican Hernando de Mesa, going out to Cuba as its first bishop, stood among his clerks. In the air before him he was making the sign of the cross, his lips murmuring into the wind and the wind blowing his robes tight about his legs.

But the breeze broke invisibly about one figure, that of the Adelantado, alone and to the rear where the poop curved the highest. On one side of him, towards the ships he reviewed, the standard of stiff satin damask popped and fluttered. On his other side lay the sea. Stiff and silent in his ceremonial harness, de Soto stood where he could be seen by the entire fleet. His

[73]

cuirass, rising to a sharp ridge at the centre of his body, sliced the meridian sun. Bright and slick shone the armpit guards, the rere braces, and the great braguette covering his stomach. At the neck a thin linen collar turned neatly over the hauberk. Here his head seemed to rest, all head and no body, precariously balanced upon the frail white cloth. The plumed casque drew down upon his eyes like a hood.

That day the *Magdalena* had been appointed to keep the rear. She passed the hazard of the bar and waited. Then one by one the navios, the galleons and the caravels gave their canvas to the indifferent breeze and glided into rougher water. The boat ahead when it had reached a certain distance, as though it were linked to the one behind, seemed to jerk it into line, for all at once the sails of the after boat fluttered from the masts and stood out in the lane of travel. And so it went until all with arrogant ease and heavy pace held forth upon the top of the sea. On signal they scattered over the placid surface and wandered for a while without design; but gradually the ships turned themselves, coming at last to rest, half-mooned upon the horizon, the fleeter caravels outriding the ends. They lay quite motionless with every stretch of canvas, from mainsails to the white drivers, straining to free themselves of the hidden masts. And then, as he watched, before his very eyes the boats began to shrivel, until they seemed no more than toys on a pond. One moment they were in sight; the next they were gone; and then, as far as the horizon it was as vacant as on that second morning when the waters divided from the waters.

Twice he had crossed the Ocean Sea. Many ships had he seen slip over the horizon. But never before had he felt that sense of utter vacancy as on that day the fleet set sail from Spain. Now he could see it all, now that he had time to remember it, since another commanded the *Magdalena* and served in his stead as second in command; now that he lacked all responsibility for the armament and for Florida, there was time for memory.

If the fleet had touched at the Grand Canary instead of at

Gomera, he would not be idling now or turning back his thoughts, bitterly. He, not Porcallo, would have charge over victualling the ships and loading them with supplies and horses. But to Gomera de Soto went, to take on wood and water and replenish his stock of bread and wine, for the Count de Gomera was cousin to Doña Ysabel on her mother's side. He met de Soto at the wharf, clad all over in white, cloak, jerkin, hose, shoes and cap, for all the world like a gypsy king, and at the parting gave a natural daughter of his as waiting maid to Doña Ysabel. From the first Doña Leonora had charmed de Soto and his lady; indeed she had charmed them all, for she had fateful eyes. Pale green they were, at times almost grey, and beneath them the skin was of a light transparency. One never looked into them, but at them, for any gaze glanced off. They seemed all surface, without depth; and yet they only seemed so.

But there were other things to do than think of the colour of a lady's eyes. Indeed as day passed into night, and night into day under the monotonous skies, one did not think at all, but endured—the close quarters, the evil smells, the tasteless food, and the growing boredom as wide and deep as the sea which made it. But at the end of May the fleet came into the waters off the coast of Cuba, near the town of Santiago where the government sat. On Whit Sunday it made its way into the harbour.

It would have gone differently, he liked to think it would have gone differently, had the Governor landed at Grand Canary and not at the port of the island under the sway of her ladyship's cousin. Even if the Count had not sought for his daughter a good marriage in the Indies, even then, he, Tovar, would not now be standing on this beach, ruined in fortune and disgraced; or if Porcallo had kept to his estates at Trinidad. . . . A pair of green eyes, an old man with a fat belly, these had been his undoing; if not his undoing at least the occasion for it.

There are certain persons who are like leaven to dough. As soon as they appear, events follow in their train. They may or may not have the force of a Porcallo. They may be as innocent

[75]

as nuns, in no way profiting, indeed ignorant of what they bring about. Purely instrumental, they are like the hollow places of whirling winds that so damage lives and property in the Antilles. But in this instance it can be said that Porcallo profited, at least he came to have his way; but this, his having his way, perhaps was mere accident.

When Porcallo first came to Santiago, Tovar watched him narrowly, knowing how anxious de Soto was to receive him, for Porcallo was the first man in Cuba, owning more riches than four ports put together, with a stable of fifty mares, wide holdings in land and mines and repartimientos of Indians. It was said that his presence in the island alone kept the Indians from revolt. He came galloping one forenoon into Santiago with grooms and outriders and six spare horses for himself, all of them stallions. Father Francisco of the Rock was standing by Tovar's side. The priest said, "What's got on the devil's back is spent on his belly." Tovar had turned, wondering to whom the priest referred.

Down the grassy street Porcallo came, holloing to friends, shifting his lance from breast to breast in salute to others, until with much confusion and spirit he drew up before the Governor's house. He threw his lance, twisting and singing through the air, to an Indian servant. A groom ran forward to help him dismount. He swore in the heathen tongue, kicked at the groom, and leapt to the ground in a heap. The thin legs gave beneath the great trunk without spilling him quite. He tottered, adjusted his balance, and slowly rose. He stood upon his feet without any quickening of breath. It was not vanity, then, that string of stallions, but simple need. Porcallo had pushed them hard, coming a long way from his estates at Trinidad, in the very centre of the island. To do this guest especial honour de Soto came out in the yard to meet him. The two lords paused to take each other's measures, and then with grace and ease Porcallo advanced lightly towards the Governor. Lustily he threw his arms about him, lifting him off his feet as if he had been no more than a piece of cork.

[76]

"So," Porcallo said in a pleasant growl, "this is my little cock of Peru."

De Soto recovered his dignity, stepped back and looked carefully at his guest. "At last you have come," he said.

Porcallo did not hear. He was beckoning with outstretched hand. Behind him a servant snatched a mastiff whelp from the wallet at his saddle bow. In one motion Porcallo grasped it and offered it to de Soto. "To take with you to Florida," he said. "Its dam has the finest nose and the best jaws in all the Indies. She knows the scent of every Indian in Trinidad. I've seen her fall on runaways and spare the baptized by the smell of holy water." He laughed a long growing laugh which made all who stood about his own; then putting his arm about the Governor, he led de Soto into de Soto's house.

As Tovar followed them in, he thought the priest's words irrelevant. It was not until later that he began to remember them. Very shortly after his arrival Porcallo began to leave the impression that he was the army's patron. He had managed it with great cunning. He made handsome gifts with a free hand, sold ten geldings to good but needy men, to be paid for out of the first smeltings made in Florida. If de Soto noticed or feared his growing popularity, he gave no sign. Always he was courteous to Porcallo, frank about his needs, equally frank about his intention to make the island supply them. While for all his pretended frankness Porcallo became evasive about what he could or would do to push the preparations forward.

One day the two of them were inspecting a storehouse of arms. De Soto handed Porcallo a crossbow. "See what fine weapons we have," he said. "Strong stays and fittings, and yet the whole will not weigh more than two pounds. That will make a difference on a long march. And we have workmen to look after them, for as Your Worship knows not a day passes but they get out of order from dampness."

Porcallo handled the weapon, glanced expertly at the fittings. "What would I not give to be twenty again," he said.

They passed on to the arquebuses. "Here are some fine hand guns of light metal. I especially chose them, for those made of

[77]

iron are quickly eaten away with rust." De Soto threw a gun to Porcallo. "What would you say it weighed?"

Porcallo balanced the weapon, squeezed his pig-like eyes. "Thirty pounds," he said.

"Between twenty-five and thirty pounds, all of them," the Governor replied.

They had withdrawn to a corner of the room and were looking back over the array of pikes and guns. Suddenly Porcallo turned. "Don Hernando, no better armament has come out of Spain. It is plain: you will pacify this Florida." And then very casually, "How would you like to take me with you?"

De Soto said as casually, "For a man of your wealth and station to risk a long campaign . . ."

"I'm not too old to gamble," he said vehemently.

De Soto raised his hands against the absurdity of such a possibility, said thoughtfully, "A gentleman of your distinction could take no less than second place, but that I have given to Tovar. We would feel it great honour to have you along. What would satisfy you?" He asked suddenly.

Porcallo paused. "As Your Excellency has said, I could not well take less than second place." He waved this aside as a man accustomed to be liberal. "On the smelting we could agree. But I will be plain. What I need most is Indians. They die to spite me. I was delayed in paying your Excellency my respects—how it humiliated me." He placed his hand over his heart. "But just as I was setting out a steward of mine got word that all my Indians had agreed to hang themselves. It's a vicious people. But this steward is a shrewd fellow. He discovered the appointed time and place and met them with a rope in his hand." Two hard white spots came into Porcallo's eyes, and he smiled as the blind do in their private knowledge. He resumed: "He told them to go hang themselves. He would hang too, and if they thought they had been put to hard labour in this world, they would learn their mistake in the next." Porcallo for a moment almost closed his eyes. "A cunning fellow, no? But I confess the whole affair was unpleasant." Porcallo looked

[78]

directly at the Governor. "I will be satisfied with the largest repartimiento of Indians. And perhaps when a ship returns to Cuba for supplies, I may replenish my stock of servants." He waved his hand lightly.

"It would be worth many sacrifices to have the support of your arm and counsel," de Soto said. His voice was cool, polite, and noncommittal.

Porcallo blurted out, "Fifty horses will I furnish and bread and work to feed you for three months. More, if the harvests are good."

This was what de Soto had been waiting to hear. He said, "I think, Señor, we can come to an agreement."

As they left the building, Porcallo added quite casually, "Naturally, Excellency, come what may, you may command my services."

So Porcallo had the last word. In the form of an amenity he had made a threat, disguised but plainly a threat. Certainly the Governor could command his services, but could he command their performance? Porcallo knew that he alone had enough goods to fill out the stores and the animals to mount the body of cavalry de Soto thought necessary for the conquest. It was a delicate matter, but Tovar wondered why a man secure in so many riches, a man beyond his prime, would risk so much for a few boatloads of slaves. And then he remembered how Porcallo had been Velásquez' first choice for the conquest of Mexico.

A week after Porcallo left for his estates, the port of Santiago was thrown into turmoil. The drums beat in the plaza, couriers galloped to and from the farms, where many of the soldiers were quartered, and at the harbour wood and water, all the supplies so far collected, were being loaded into the holds of the ships. Word had come that Havana had been sacked and burnt by French pirates.

It was decided in council to send the fleet there with all the foot, and also Doña Ysabel and her household. De Soto charged his lady to repair the damage and see that Francisco Aceituno begin his work on the stone fort at the harbour's mouth. For two days and nights neither Ranjel, Tovar, or the Governor slept. At the end of the second night all the necessary orders had been issued. Five days later the fleet weighed anchor, under the care of Don Carlos.

It was one of those gratuitous strokes of ill fortune which sent Don Carlos instead of Tovar in command of the fleet. If only Tovar had gone, as he might have expected to go, being second in command, the damage could have been prevented, at least postponed until after they were all in Florida, and once in Florida, with communications cut, he might have hoped for grace. So it seemed to him then, and so it seemed to him now. He did go to the Governor and ask to be put over the fleet, but the Governor denied his request, saying he would be needed to command the cavalry and judge the worth of the men. There was nothing more Tovar could do. He disguised his chagrin as well as he could and threw himself with zeal into his duties.

The Governor marched straight for Havana, taking a small body of the cavalry with him. Tovar was left in the interior of the island, to scatter the troops among the various towns and thus distribute the burden of their keep. He had expected to remain at some intermediate post, where he could be in touch with all the troops, see to their training, and hear complaints. But one day, less than a month after the Governor's departure, he received a summons to appear with all haste in Havana.

By impressing horses he arrived within the week, but he did not go straight to the Governor's chamber. He felt that he could not face him until he had relieved his anxiety. He asked first for Doña Ysabel. Without delay he was shown into her closet. He stood for a moment, not moving, to accustom himself to the abrupt change of light. It was a very narrow but long room and the ceiling was high and on the outside wall ran a platform and small openings for purposes of defense. It seemed to him a strange place for a lady's closet, until he remembered how the army must have overcrowded all the dwellings. The only light came through the loopholes in the outer wall; and, as he waited, he watched it pass below the ceiling timbers in narrow beams, as brightly opaque as columns of quartz, leaving him to stand below in a kind of perpetual cockshut time. And then, out of the half-light, he heard a sigh, so low it seemed the heavy air had shifted within his hearing, and coming hard upon it, the words, "God may consent, but not forever." He waited an instant and turned. It was not as he thought. He was not alone.

Doña Ysabel sat at the far end of the room, without attendants, in a gown of black velvet, looking straight before her. He saw at once she had not heard him come in, and the usher had not announced him, thinking, no doubt, she was in some other part of the building. For a moment Tovar stared at her ladyship. With the shadowy lace drooping about her hair, her curving nose as frail as bone, her lustrous eyes staring out of space, she seemed the Queen of Darkness. It was unseemly of him to watch her unawares. As softly as he could he walked towards her and dropped upon his knees. He heard a short intake of breath, nothing more; saw the coiling velvet move and knew that she had risen. She said his name. As he kissed that cool, that firm white hand, he felt it tremble. Then she bade him rise.

It was a few moments before he could speak. He asked after her health, and then he trusted himself to ask after the health of Doña Leonora. He thought he saw her lips slightly curl. She said,

"Have you seen the Governor?"

"No, Señora, I came first to you to pay my respects."

"It was kind of you," she said coldly. "But I will excuse you. Don Hernando has an urgent matter to discuss with you."

He bowed once and then walked out of the room.

De Soto did not come down from the high seat to greet him. In the short passage from the wicket to the Governor's presence Tovar saw the eyes, which had never shown for him anything but affection and confidence, blur with the remote stare of authority. Tovar bowed, carefully fixed his gaze no higher than the point of the Governor's beard. In this fashion he waited. And then the words,

"Doña Leonora de Bobadilla, my ward, is with child."

Tovar raised his head. He could not speak.

"It is true, then," de Soto stated coldly.

He said, "I did not know."

"Is it true?"

"I called upon Doña Ysabel." He could say no more.

"You will answer me, Señor."

Carefully Tovar released his breath.

"Is it you?" De Soto was leaning forward, waiting for him to answer, as if the sound of his voice with a magic of syllables would undo the fact, the bitter and stubborn fact. Tovar felt a spasm twist the lines of his mouth, draw them tight, pass; but he could not speak.

"It *is* you then," de Soto said and flung himself from his seat. For one moment Tovar felt the scalding eyes and then they went away. From behind came the fall of steps, the steps slowed, and at last a voice, strange but no longer impersonal. "You knew the pledge I gave to the Count de Gomera."

Slowly de Soto returned to his seat. The two men faced each other across the long silence. "Why did you do it?" When Tovar gave no answer, the question was repeated, almost in supplication, "Why did you do it?"

In the pause de Soto's face recovered its strangeness, the mouth moved but the words seemed to come from the other end of the long room.

"You will deliver to Ranjel the warrant of your rank." And then: "The audience is ended."

"I must find a priest," Tovar said aloud and then remembered the salute of the two halberdiers before the government house. The burden of that sign of authority, his automatic acceptance of it, became all at once unbearable. He turned about. It seemed no more than a minute since he had left, and here he found himself beyond the houses of the town. Suppose the guards had been relieved. . . . He hurried his pace. With relief he saw them leaning on their weapons. "You must know," he said and paused vaguely as the two halberds a second time rang against the steel plates, "you must know I am no longer due this courtesy." The guards did not return to rest but looked sharply at each other from under their beavers. "I am Nuño de Tovar, a plain gentleman who keeps a horse and bears arms."

"But naturally, Your Worship," the smaller guard said quickly.

"I am looking for a priest."

"Father Dionisio de Paris has just passed going to the chapel."

"Thank you. Thank you very much," Tovar said and wandered into the street. That voice and that question: Why? Why? Why did you do it? Why? He must find an answer. He must confess and be absolved, but first he must find an answer. The force of the necessity made him stop and look about him. He saw that he had gone in the direction away from the church. Then he knew how his senses had been struck and his wits confused by the sudden judgment of his sudden act. He waited where he was to collect about his despair the frayed toil of will. This despair, unfleshed as a shade, alone gave him being. He must grow more solid, or he was lost. Only then could he draw close in the secret box— "Father, I . . ."

That afternoon of the bull feast. That began it. But how could he have known? What made him lift his eyes at precisely that moment? What made him lift them at all? The last bull had been difficult, cunning and without spirit. Only four other lancers had taken the field. He recalled their names, faces, what they wore, the quality of their mounts, as if the exact succession of detail must disclose the truth. He had drawn the animal away from Enríquez whose horse had shown herself a trifle too heavy. . . . His own little sorrel had charged, feinted, retreated with admirable skill, and the bull had been left spent in the centre of the plaza, opposite the Governor's stand, where

[83]

Doña Ysabel and her maids sat under the green bower. Perhaps it was the murmurs of admiration which made him raise his eyes as he backed the sorrel away, refusing to kill, out of pride leaving that to others. Perhaps . . .

She was leaning forward, her mouth parted. Her naked eyes opened to his, and in that instant pause he took their innocence. She recoiled, and he felt he had had her wholly in a public place, but a place where the throng, its common sight carefully averted, moved by unseeing. He looked again, but her gaze now fell midway between them. Seconds later he noticed the play had gone wrong. Enríquez had come too carelessly forward, misjudging the temper of the bull, and the bull had charged him on his off-side. Enríquez was falling. . . . His leg slid comically over the saddle; his lance toyed with the swelling neck; the nearest gentleman had levelled to charge. . . . Raised upon the lunging head, the upright hoofs pawing the air for balance, the mare seemed light as straw. Her nostrils told her courage, but her eyes he could not forget. Shocked into a roundness, they withheld for a moment in their shallow film of fury the coming blindness. Out of her belly, where the intimate horn had sunk, a thin pink stream stood erect, playing like a fountain.

Now that he remembered, it was clear that but for this mishap, from which he could never be free . . . Untroubled weeks would pass, and then Leonora's stare, safe there under the green bower, and the swelling power of the bull's neck, somehow never parted, would startle him in the deep night. Or riding alone through the noon woods he would remember it, grow sudden in his seat, straight and trembling and his charger trembling. Nor could he be eased by the spur, the strain of leather, the flying turf, or the curving jerk of the saddle. Yes, it was clear but for that feast of bulls . . . Why did he not take warning?

And then came that evening he and Silvestre returned to their quarters, sharp from gaming and nowise ready for sleep. In all those weeks he had never been freer from thoughts of her. The business de Soto sent him on in distant parts of the island had sweated out the idle humours of feast and holy days. He had returned feeling as one feels the first days of a campaign, purged of the grossness of camp, marching through a country rich in grain, the enemy still to the front but close enough to stiffen the march, the scouts appearing, disappearing like wraiths. To look to your horse, to your harness and weapons, and at the end of each day watch how the sweat has deepened at the grip the colour of your lance. This brings a kind of peace, an innocence, where all is simple and straight, where each small act becomes in itself complete and fulfilling.

They stepped under the low lintel and stopped. He touched Silvestre. A grey streak hung for an instant before his face . . . Silvestre's sword. He could hear him breathing deeply. They waited for the shadows to lose their false substance. In that moment he felt a pleasant surge of power. His body was quicker than his wits. The darkness moved; he heard it rustle. "Put away your blade, lad," he said aloud. "It's the wrong weapon."

"It's what?" Silvestre whispered.

"Make a light."

Silvestre raised the ship's lamp over his head and they looked down at their bed rushes. "Well, well," his friend said, "our reputation has gone before us."

Two Indian girls were lying among the rushes. They looked at the light and then gravely at the two men.

Silvestre said mysteriously, "See how brown they are. In daylight they are cinnamon coloured."

"Never mind their colour. Are they baptized? I always take care to have them baptized."

Silvestre hung the lamp from its chain. It swung the shadows about the room. "What a wonderfully hospitable world," he said gaily.

"Indian women are bad spinsters," Tovar replied. His voice tried to be humourous.

"At least mine's a Christian," Silvestre called out louder than he need. "She has a cross through her nose."

Tovar did not answer him. With surprise he noticed he had

[85]

been talking like a priest. What he should have been feeling he did not feel at all. He saw only how young she was and pitied her. But in her stare he found something too strange and formidable for pity. She showed neither fear of him nor interest in his person. He had thought their host was being agreeable; but suddenly, as he looked at the girl, he understood that she had come to his bed of her own free will, as casually as she might pause by the clan pot and squat there to feed. And she would leave his bed when it was done, and to the soft pat of her disappearing feet there would come no pause, no looking back. To sin with her would be like sinning with himself. Silvestre did not hear him leave the room.

He stepped into the patio and said, I can no longer flee. I must find again, tonight, the old peace. He looked across to the Governor's lodgings where Leonora was sleeping, and in that moment he understood that the night was not of one darkness but of many. How could two beguiling eyes cause him such uncommon longing? How could they take away his nature? He had never asked more than to beguile, be beguiled, and then pass on. Fortune's son has no time to wait for the banns to be read out in church. His feather whose frailest barb he had kept inviolate with a straight thrust and a ready guard no woman had ever tampered with before. "My son," his first captain had said, pointing to his cap, "that feather is the mark of your trade and the seat of your honour. Look well to them both. They are of a like frailty." He did not fear for his honour so long as it stood on the point of a lance. But to leave it in hostage, to be plucked like a goose, with him off wandering over the wide world, dishonoured and not know it. That was not for him, not for Nuño de Tovar. Nor did he think it just to bind himself in holy sacrament with a woman and leave her to languish or to sin. So had he thought; so had he meant always to carry himself, free from all things save fortune's toss.

Fortune's toss . . . He was far more gravely involved than that. Already he had sinned with her in thought. In thought he had betrayed his friend's confidence. And if not lightly done,

[86]

but passionately surging within his heart, had not the consequences of the imagined act seemed light? Had he not said over and over, I think dishonour, I think dishonour—only for the words to dissolve into sound, and sound into the senseless inflexions of an unknown tongue. He stood in the centre of the patio, his hands clasped to his side. He closed his eyes, screwed them tight. He was surely bewitched . . . the White Paternoster—fire, flood, evil spirits, dogs and wolves. Evil spirits. Rapidly under his breath—

White Paternoster, Saint Peter's soster,
What hast ye in the one hand, white book leaves?
What hast ye in the other hand, Heaven gate keys?
Open Heaven gates and strike Hell gates,
And let every chrysome child creep to its own mother!
White Paternoster, Amen!

He opened his eyes carefully. He felt the earth stand solid under his feet and he a solid man upon it. But his flesh lay wearily upon him, languidly weary as of a body freed of pain. Out of this body his mind rose light and clear. He could go to his bed now and sleep. His flesh grew porous and a warmth sank tingling to the bone. The girl seemed wonderfully desirable and strange the terror he had felt that he, a Christian, might never draw love from her Indian heart. Silvestre would be asleep . . . he was never bothered by thought, but then he . . . With a light step he hurried towards his quarters.

He had gone but a little way when he stopped, transfixed. Coming towards him was a figure barely lighter than the surrounding darkness. Its lines were dim, the features blurred, but one glance and he began to shake. He must have a tertian fever. No. No evasion would serve him now, for in his heart he suffered another chill and kind of burning. Despite that night makes shadows of all who walk its province, his senses said, It is Leonora. In its progress the figure faded and grew darkly solid, moving swiftly and with purpose. What would

[87]

she, if it were she, be doing to show purpose at the hour when animals leave their holes to prowl, she so gentle and demure in her ways? Had his eyes tricked him? The carriage of the body, the lift of the head, the indefinable signs of recognition—these he still saw, but with such distortion that what seemed most familiar was become most strange. And then he fastened upon that quarter where the body takes its balance. There was no form to be seen. Only motion which the darkness bred, flowing, bold and free, the hips of a woman who has knowledge and is unseen.

At last now the decision was out of his hands and the long race for honour lost; but waiting there in the deeper shade, where she must come, he husbanded his breath like one who has not lost but has still to make the race. She entered a space lit by the quarter-moon, so close to him that with a single bound he could have stopped her in his arms. But he let her go by, stirred by what he saw, unable to stir. That same power which drove him into the night and her from her bed surely did not work whimsically. Yet in her blinded stare, exposed for an instant by the vague moon, he understood that she wandered in all ignorance of him. He opened his lips to call her name; then closed them and followed her.

Beyond the storerooms on the west side of the patio lay an open space and a little away the forest. The distance he knew to a rod, for he had measured it. He had even spoken to de Soto, for his eye told him the town was open to attack from that side. But as he looked now, the clearing had narrowed to a thin lip, slanting from the sky down the black and solid mass of growth. In this space, just beyond the buildings, she had paused. He could see her leaning forward, scanning the forest wall as if to find an opening. And then she began to move towards it, walking a little faster. His own stride grew longer, but his boots made no sound in the coarse grass. There was no sound in all the world, only the heavy stroke of his blood dividing the silence. Did she know he was behind? Did she sense his desire? Did she fear it and flee it?

[88]

She reached the outer curtain of trees and, never hesitating, disappeared into the black waste. The darkness had holes, and in her flight he saw her dismembered, an arm thrown forward, a head extended on its curving neck, peering, once a shoulder, and once he thought he saw her heart ... He began to run, and as he ran he clutched his sword. What but a lover's meeting could draw her so fearlessly into this savage place?

He dodged the outlying trees and brush. Before he could come to a walk, the outer night had vanished and the deep ways closed about him. Just ahead, on a cattle path, he saw her. There was no light but he saw her, a moving wedge and the path a long mark drawing behind her. As he went along, he could feel the roots snatch at his clothes, the coiling tendrils brush his legs. Overhead, out of sight, beyond the swinging ceiling of vines and lesser growth, where the great trunks reach, the forest's lid stretched even with the dark. He thought, We alone, two Christians, are alone in this place, wandering by ways known only to the things that crawl, and that fly, and that creep. O Christ, the wild dogs ... Terror stopped him where he was. He could not see them, but her they must be watching out of eyes which hunger made to burn, drawn on by her scent, dragging the stiff hair of their undersides, now quick, now low for the spring. Mother of God ... The second time that night he opened his lips to call her name, and the second time failed. She had stopped and was turning out of the path.

He saw her grow still, raise her hands, and part the thicket. And then she was gone. He plunged down the path, straining like a man who hurries through water. He forsook all caution, and at the place where he had seen her last, he took the labyrinth in his hands.

Roughly he dug his way in, tearing clothes and flesh. Once he tripped and fell. Afterwards he grew more cunning, softly calling her name, pausing in the stillness which returned him no answer. He said, I must find my bearings, but what bearings were there to take in a place where she who was its pole had vanished to make a jest of him? And then he found himself

[89]

walking more freely through an open set of trees, guided by their black trunks through the lightless way until suddenly the trees fell away and left him standing in an open room. He turned as a man who is trapped; then more carefully examined where he was. Rotting trunks lay piled about the edges of the clearing, but in the centre of the place there was little obstruction. Cautiously he raised his head. Above, at the end of a long funnel, he saw a patch of light.

He lowered his head. She was standing before him.

"Leonora?"

She did not start or cry out but brought her hand against her breast. "You," she said at last, and after they had stood together for awhile, "Why did you run away?"

"What are you doing here? Whom do you meet?" He spoke not as he had thought to do, in anger and accusation. His words lacked body, blurring an anger which had already spent itself.

She began to laugh, at first softly, then by growing runs, each louder than the one before, rising in brief gasps but never shrilly rising. "Stop that and answer me," he said harshly. But she did not stop. Not until the monkeys, like troops of obscene birds, began to scream and chatter did he understand. He took her in his hands and shook her, and after a while she grew more quiet and trembled less.

In his arms her breathing grew more regular. He found a hammock made of vines and took her there. They sat on its edge, listening, erect, he with his arm in support about her. With a few low chirps, softer than a bird's, the last monkey went back to sleep. So profound was the silence he would never be able to breach it by speech. Leonora shifted slightly; then said, "It was too much."

"Too much?"

"To find you jealous of yourself. To find you at all."

His arm dropped beneath hers.

She said simply, "I come here where I am free to think of you."

"This is no place . . ."

"When I saw how you ran away, I used to lie awake and pretend you lay at my side. But it was only Mexía." She sighed. "I grew jealous to think she was so close to you . . ."

"Close to me?"

"Being close to me." And after a pause, "I could no longer think of you but of what kept us apart. Of how kind was Doña Ysabel, but how strict. Of the Adelantado whose man you were. At times I did fear to fall asleep, for I knew I must dream. . . . One of the maids might wake and hear me call your name."

"Would that be so great a sin?"

She lowered her head. "One night I saw a bar was missing in the window. At first I went no farther than the yard, but that lacked privacy, too . . . the watch. And there, so close to your lodgings, I would argue why we didn't meet. But here . . ." Her voice died away and she lifted an arm, vaguely gesturing.

"To think . . ." he said.

The vines slipped and pressed them together and back upon the hammock. His eyes travelled the long funnel overhead, through the luminous mist drifting upwards. Far away the lid stretched over the top like a piece of silk held up to the light. Suddenly he said, "We might be together at the middle of the world."

He felt her flesh give about his hardness and against his ear the hot and moist lips. No words but the violence of her breath—"We are quite alone now." He did not move or make a sound, and then secretly she said, "Not even the celebrated Court of Angels can see us here."

The blind spasm released its grip and into his clearing vision, suspended between sky and earth, appeared the leg drawn in pain, the arms outstretched upon the bar, as in rest, the side droop of the head and upon the sweaty brow its circle of thorns. Tovar leaned forward; the parched lips were murmuring. He listened and faintly in his ears, *"Eloi, Eloi, lama sabachthani . . ."* Still parted, the lips grew still.

[91]

"You are in trouble, my son?"

The figure blurred and swam dizzily and, when his eyes cleared, it hung small and lifeless above the altar. The whitewashed walls of the log church enclosed it like a tomb.

"You are in some trouble?" The voice repeated.

He turned. "Father, I . . ." He was looking into two eyes set wearily in the lean face.

"Perhaps I can help," the priest said and averted his head. "Will you come with me?" Turning, he began to walk away. His sandals moved noiselessly over the dirt floor. His soutane gently slapped at his heels.

Involuntarily Tovar followed, but his eyes drew towards the crucifix . . . his steps followed his gaze. He stopped abruptly; the priest moved on. In front of him, out of the rough Sanctuary, four green leaves sprouted from a ghostly stem. "See! See!" Tovar cried. His voice was hoarse and cracked. Two women looked up from their beads, startled and afraid. The priest stiffened, turned slowly about, and down Tovar's outstretched arm swiftly sent his glance. "What is it, man?" He asked sharply.

"The sap, Father! In God's house." He was not understood. Deliberately, pausing with each laboured word, he repeated, "The wilderness grows here, too."

"Calm yourself, my son." The priest spoke softly, as to a child who is hurt, and then started towards him. But Tovar had turned and was walking rapidly out of the church into the bright glare of the meridian sun, rising in waves from the open square.

2

"Know ye who shall see this testamentary letter that I, the Adelantado Don Hernando de Soto, being of sound body and free mind, such as my Redeemer Jesus Christ has been pleased to bestow on me, believing firmly in what believes and holds the Holy Mother Church, in the most Holy Trinity, Father, Son, and Holy Ghost, three persons and one only true God, promising as a faithful Christian to live and die in His Holy Catholic faith, mindful of the blood that Jesus Christ shed for me as the price of my redemption and endeavoring to repay and satisfy so great benefit, knowing that death is a natural thing and that the more I shall be prepared for it the better will He be pleased, I declare that I commend my soul to God, who created it of nothing and redeemed it with His Most Holy passion, that He place it among the number of the elect in His glory . . ." De Soto paused, and then said briefly, in contemptuous dismissal, "and I order the body to the earth of which it was made."

It was the sudden change in his voice which made Silvestre look up. He was under the pressure of last-minute instructions to the governors of the ports. At last the Governor was about to make the entrada. Ever since Tovar's disgrace Vasco Porcallo had tremendously speeded the preparations. He gave plentifully of his own stores which, added to those already gathered, gave supplies more abundant than could have been got together in Spain for an armada: three thousand loads of cassava bread, twenty-five hundred shoulders of bacon, twenty-five hundred hanegas of maize, besides beasts on hoof for the settlement and for the butcher to be in readiness for Florida on the return of the vessels. Juan de Añasco who had sailed along the coast of Florida, scouting for a landing, gave the final impetus. The army had given him over for lost when he and his men reached port after having been cast away on an island, where for a month they had lived on pelicans and crabs. They went all the way from the seashore to the church on their knees, fulfilling a vow made in their desolation. The reports they brought made all think there never was such a land as Florida, and two Indians taken in that land by signs spoke of gold. The men could not wait for the day of departure! . . . In all this haste the making of a will seemed only one other thing to do. And then de Soto's voice, sudden, exultant, discarding the body, consigning it to thirst, hunger, all pains, so that the final weary anguish, when it comes, may seem one more rehearsal of the daily immolation. The hour was upon them!

The Governor's three scribes, one after the other, looked up. He continued:

[93]

"First, I command, should God take me from this present life on the sea, that my corpse be so disposed that it may be taken to the land wheresoever our Lord shall be pleased it shall come to port, and should a church be there or should one there be built, that it be deposited therein until such time as there are arrangements for taking it to Spain, to the city of Xerez, near Badajoz, where it be consigned to the sepulchre where lies my mother, in the Church of San Miguel." He paused. The scratch of the quills filled the air with petulant haste. . . . "And in that church I order that of my goods a site and place be bought where a chapel be built that shall have for its invocation Our Lady of the Conception, in which edifice and work I desire there be expended two thousand ducats, one thousand five hundred in the structures and enclosure, and five hundred in an altar piece, representing the same Invocation of Our Lady of the Conception; and I order that vestments be made, with a chasuble, two dalmatics, an antipendium and a cope, with three albs, and a chalice with its cover, both of silver, and two other chasubles for daily use, for which I direct there be paid of my goods other three hundred ducats. And I order that the mentioned vestments be of silk, of the colour which to the patron and my executors, and to those of the said chapel, shall appear well. And I order that of my goods be bought a perpetual rent of twelve thousand marevedis, in good possession, which shall be given to a chaplain who shall say five Masses each week for my soul, the souls of my parents, and that of Doña Ysabel de Bobadilla, my wife. And he shall be appointed by the patron of the chapel, with the understanding that should there be a clergyman of my line who desires to be chaplain, it be given to him in preference to any other, and that he be the nearest of kin, should there be two or more."

De Soto walked towards the scribes and looked over their shoulders. Silvestre saw how straight he was, even as he leaned forward, and how the shoulders of his servants drew about their parchment, as if they had something which they must hide. Silently and with the ease of a body which leaps before its will he had turned and was looking towards Silvestre. His dark eyes were tender and his voice. He looked away. "Also, I order that if the body of my father or of my mother be in Badajoz, or in any part whatsoever, not in that chapel, they be taken out and brought thence and be entombed there where my body shall be, or should be placed, which is in the midst of the chapel, in such manner that the foot of the sepulchre adjoin the footstone of the altar. And thereon I order to be placed a tomb covered over by a fine black broadcloth, in the middle of which be put a red cross of the Commandery of the Order of the Knights of Santiago, that shall be for use on week days, and another pall of black velvet with the same cross in the midst, with four escutcheons of brocade, bearing my arms, which escutcheons I wish and order to be likewise placed on the chapel, altar-piece, and railing, and vestments, in such manner as to the patron and executors shall appear most becoming."

He paused, reflected for a moment. . . . "Also to the end that this chapel and chaplaincy be kept in repair and appointment, the chapel and the income alike, I order that Doña Ysabel de Bobadilla, my wife, be the patroness; and, after her, should God give me children, I desire the patron to be my eldest legitimate son, or my eldest legitimate daughter, should I have no male child, that they, or either of them, who shall be the patron, may buy the site for and make the said chapel and do all the foregoing appertaining to it, and buy the said twelve thousand maredevis and appoint the chaplain. And should God not grant me legitimate sons or daughters, I order that after the life time of my wife, the patron be Juan Méndez de Soto, my brother, and after his life, his eldest son; and if he be without a male child, I order that the successor to that patronage be the eldest son of Catalina de Soto, my sister; and should she have no male child, let the successor thereto be the eldest son of María de Soto, my sister; and if it happen of the designated patrons there should be no issue male, I order the patronage to succeed to the next nearest of kin, being always male.

"Also, in order that the chapel and vestment and rent for the chaplaincy may always be available and that in each year, on All Saints' Day, a Mass be sung and another on All Souls' day, with its vigil and offerings of bread and wine, there shall be a perpetual rent of five thousand marevedis, on good possessions, to be bought with my goods. And I order that they be used in no other way than for what is expressed.

"Also, I order that on the day my body is interred, it be followed by the curas and the clergy of the parishes, with their crosses, and by the orders there may be in the city aforesaid, and that there be paid them what is customary. And I require that each cura, with the clergy of his church, sing a Mass on that day, and they be paid what is usual. And I order that on the same day thirty Masses be said for me and that there be paid therefor what is customary.

"Also, I order that there be said twenty Masses of requiem in the said chapel, for the soul of the Captain Compañon, and that what is usual be paid for them.

"Also, that there be said twenty Masses of Our Lady of the Conception.

"Also, I order that ten Masses of the Holy Ghost be said in the chapel.

"Also, ten Masses of All Saints.

"Also, I order that ten Masses be said, five of them of the passion, and five of the wounds . . ."

The door opened and Alonso Martin, chief pilot of the fleet, strode hastily in the room.

The Governor looked up. Silvestre looked up. The Governor's eyes met the pilot's. For a long moment there was no sound but the scratch of the quills, and then the Governor's voice, sudden and quiet.

"Yes, Señor?"

"Excellency," the pilot said, "a stiff wind has just risen, blowing out to sea."

One by one the quills grew still, the hands which held them suspended in air. Silvestre held his breath in his teeth.

"Give orders," the Governor said at last, "to embark the men."

There was a slight, a very slight tremor in his voice.

3

THE WILDERNESS

The Wilderness

TOVAR leaned over and adjusted the horse's breastplate. He ran his hand between the plate and the shoulder and felt the pad. In the dark he had drawn the straps too tight. It seemed all right now. Carefully he went over the animal's other furniture, pulled the saddle, slipped his finger under the girth. He could not afford any galled places . . . not today or any other day in Florida. He had only one change of mounts, and for what lay ahead that was none too many. He smiled and felt his stiff whiskers draw, put his hand on the horse's neck and patted it. "I don't want anything to take your mind off your business, old girl," he said and took the reins and tied them to his lance. The lance stood out of the sand, slim as a reed, as strong as gut. It was a beautiful object. If a man had never seen one before, it would make his hands itch to use it.

He looked about the camp. It was still dark, but there was just enough light to make the fires lie closer to the ground. They glowed in flickering lines upon the high land which sloped down to the beach. Not twenty minutes ago some six hundred men had lain about them, wrapped in blankets, as still as bundles of merchandise laid out for auction. But now they were deserted. Nothing gave a camp so abandoned a look as deserted fires. The infantry had gone to hear Mass at the other end of the beach and the cavalry was being set in order for the march. His eyes travelled down the squadrons. Moscoso had divided them into four of fifty each, one in the wayward, two in the battle, and one for the rear. He could hear him arguing pleasantly with an hidalgo who had his own opinion as to which squadron he and his retainers preferred to join.

These private gentlemen fought well enough, but he, Tovar, liked the discipline of mercenaries, especially in a new land where they had no opportunity for mutiny. The voices travelled clearly and sharply over the moist air. There was no sense of distance in the early morning. Everywhere he felt a closeness, even in the murmuring of the infantry hurrying from Mass. They had made short shrift of it.

The air off the bay blew chill and he walked down to the nearest fire. As his feet crunched in the sand, he said aloud, "This is Florida," hoping to feel some unique emotion, but he felt only the delayed tension that any march in the presence of enemies would arouse. He thought it strange and began to reckon how long the armament had been on the way. From Havana to the sighting of the Bay of the Holy Spirit had taken eight days. How short a time that seemed in comparison with the voyage from Spain and the stay in Cuba. Today was the thirty-first of May, 1539. Considering that the fleet had left San Lúcar on the morning of Saint Lazarus in April of thirty-eight and that yesterday was the festival of the Holy Spirit, it had taken altogether about thirteen months. Thirteen months merely to sight the land to be pacified . . . when first he saw the coast of Florida, he had been leaning over the poop's rail straining at the horizon. He was thinking, he remembered, that it took the eyes of a mariner to keep the horizon always sharp. His eyes grew hazy with too much looking, especially if there was nothing to see, and there had been nothing that day but the same blue troughs of water, the choppy crests, and the sky drawn down like a tent. Nothing until that thread of a line appeared between sky and water. He had scarcely noticed it— so many times the light at sea had deceived him. He was turning away when the lookout shouted, "Land away!" He ran up the ropes, grasped tight lest the swing of the ship should cast him into the sea. What he saw was a dirty smear on the sky. Later, at one certain moment, one startling instant, the land stood out of the gulf like a great green meadow. But that quickly passed, leaving no memory to sharpen the monotony of a closer view. Closer, but not close enough. He could see Florida, but he was too distant to feel it. Now that he was landed, warming himself by a fire made on its soil, he still could not feel it.

The trumpet blew. The lancers kneeled in the sand by their horses. Tovar went forward, took his lance and dropped on his knees to be blessed. The trumpet blew again, and he swung into the saddle. By the time he reached the front of the column every man had his seat and was waiting. Moscoso had shown him a delicate attention by assigning him as a guard over the guides. This kept him out of the ranks and allowed him the privilege of riding with the officers of the Royal Hacienda and those gentlemen who had attached themselves to the Governor's household. Since he had been ruined, he liked it best this way. It gave him the freedom of movement he needed for what he planned to do. Moscoso would be all right as long as the conquest prospered, but his desires were narrow. And Moscoso liked his ease too well. As for Porcallo—he was an old man. He had done his part in furnishing the horses. Of these nineteen had died at sea, a heavy casualty in a very valuable article of war. It had made Tovar ill to see the swollen carcasses roll and leap in the gulf. They might have been disporting themselves but for that unmistakable stiffness and the unresisting flow before the waves . . . the dive below the surface, the four legs rising like an overturned table, dripping water out of the hoofs and water rolling off the swollen barrel.

His disgust had made him turn away, but he could not turn away from the image of Leonora, his wife, standing there on the beach in Havana after they had parted, swollen in her middle, with dry eyes, red as a hawk's, drawn back in her head, as though they were being pulled by the weight of the child she was carrying. His child. Well, it was her child now. If only she had not stood there in that wooden fashion, with the tic at the corner of her mouth . . .

Two horsemen rode between Tovar and the bay. He looked up. It was de Soto and Gómez Arias. De Soto raised his arm and pointed up the bay. "The town lies two leagues that way?"

"Yes, Excellency," Gómez replied. "Near the beach and abandoned when General Porcallo seized it."

"And there is a tidal river between this point and the town which we will have to skirt?"

"Yes, Excellency."

"How far up do we have to go before we cross?" Moscoso asked, riding up.

"Some leagues, from its appearance."

"We must push off, then," the Governor said sharply. "Is the infantry in formation?"

"They are in line ahead. As the cavalry passes, they will fall in behind."

"And the rear?"

"One squadron of horse for the rear."

"Good," the Governor said and rode to the head of the column. Rising in his stirrups, he looked down the rows of lances, quickly towards the swamp forest to the front and right. Then he gave the word to move forward.

The Indians lifted slow feet, walking one behind the other. Behind them their guards, the Governor's household, and then the cavalry. As the horse came up to the infantry, the first light broke out of the sky and turned the beach a dirty brown. Footmen who were late ran across the line of march to their squads, but the companies stood at rest like a broken wall, dim, the colour of the ground, and as he passed, Tovar could see the moisture on the beards of the men in the front ranks. It gave them an unwashed look, but their eyes, he noticed, were bright and eager. As de Soto passed, voices raised ragged and disconnected shouts. He bowed once, and his plumes dipped low over his eyes. Moscoso galloped up and slowed to a walk by the Governor's side. They spoke together in low tones for a hundred yards, when abruptly the Camp Master pulled his horse's head around and galloped to the rear. Veterans called gaily to him and he lifted an arm in reply; then quiet settled over the column. Half a league down the beach the Indians skirted a small stream and turned into the forest. They disappeared into the deep gloom, one, then another, and another, silently as into a suck.

Alvaro Nieto, the other guard, approached the narrow opening. Suddenly the sun came up and splattered his armour. For an instant the light splinters exploded at the edge of the thick green foliage, and then his back plate grew dull as lead. The vines and shrubs jumped about his shoulders. They snapped like rotten strings. He rode on unnoticing. His form grew dim. Behind, as though from a long distance, came the commands to the column to shift from double to single file. There was no other sound but the push of hoofs into the spongy sod, the light slap of twigs against armour, the flowing creak of saddles. Tovar turned in his seat. Behind him rode the Governor, half solid, half shadow. The horsemen followed like shades.

They came to a tidal water. The vapour rolled over its surface in sheets. The guides entered, sank down to their thighs, their legless trunks gliding smoothly upon the body of the mist. The horses stepped high, pulling and setting their hoofs down soundlessly, while hidden beneath its cover the earth boiled and sloshed. The air clung to Tovar's reins like a poultice. His shirt of mail pulled at his shoulders. In front of him the Indians, steadily rising, floated out of the mist and stepped into an open stand of water oaks. The great arms of the trees touched and crossed and from their branches the moss undulated slowly, dead weed in a grey sea. Somewhere the morning birds began to sing.

Without warning the oaks gave out. Upon the edge of a swamp of water lilies the column halted for the guides to consult. Tovar looked up at the open sky. With surprise he saw how far the morning had advanced. The mist had burned entirely away except for slow-rising wisps about the seams of the flat green leaves. He rode in to test the depth and his mare sank up to her knees in grey mud. The guides grunted and pointed towards the south, inland and away from the town. This way they led the column, walking along the edge of the swamp

[103]

until the lilies ran into wide mud flats. Beyond glimmered the tidal river Gómez Arias had reported. The army received it as a reassuring sign, for this river, too wide to be crossed near the Bay of the Holy Spirit, they must follow until it narrowed. But there was no sign of a path.

The ways grew deeper, the footing less solid. The horses began to blow and frequent halts were made to rest them and close up the column. De Soto ordered the guides to find more solid ground, and when they seemed not to understand, he threatened to throw them to the dogs. At this they turned inland, but the ways did not greatly improve. The army must have gone three or four leagues, certainly the day had far advanced and the direction of the march was still away from the town, when he stopped the column again. He rode up to the Indians and pointed to the left. The chief guide shook his head and swept his arm three times towards the south. De Soto shook his finger across a marsh and said sharply, "Ucita there." The Indian pressed both hands down towards the ground and then folded his arms. His body was greased and his face streaked with red and black gashes. Suddenly Tovar remembered the man had not been so greased or painted the night before. Where did he find that grease and that paint?

He looked more closely at the Indian. He would not have known him for the captive Añasco had brought to Havana on his return from Florida. And yet he was familiar in another way. . . . It came to him. He looked like the Indian who had jumped from the palmettos. The same marks, even to the blue circle about the mouth. Two days ago with the first horses to be beached, he had gone with Porcallo to beat up the country. They were going through a pine forest undergrown with palmettos. They had ridden for half a league, seven Christians, all indifferently mounted, as the horses had suffered from the voyage.

Tovar had just remarked to Porcallo how blown the animals seemed when the old man cried out, "Look sharp!" and levelled his lance against a palmetto thicket. Yelps like a dog running

[104]

in pain came out of the thicket, but Tovar could see nothing. Yet his companions were charging. His own animal plunged and whinnied. He scarcely could hold her in. Still he saw nothing. And then Osorio's horse skidded to its knees, tried to rise, fell slowly over. Osorio was picking himself up . . . Añasco swaying to right and left around the trees . . . and then, in front of Porcallo the cinnamon-coloured giant sprang from the ground. His arrow struck Porcallo's plate, veered off. Deftly the Indian took another out of his hair. Long and black, it was trussed up on top of his head and the topknot filled with arrows. Porcallo was upon him. Arrow drawn back to ear, lance and arrow almost touching . . . the grunt and tumbling back-leap as Porcallo passed over him. A floundering among the palmettos and Porcallo turning in twice his length, but the large bay walked stiffly. The animal stopped and, swaying slightly, dropped to the ground. Porcallo leapt off its back and stood for a moment bewildered. And then he raised his head. "What are you holding back for?" he bellowed. Tovar released his grip and sped into the thicket. The palmettos slapped his legs; he felt a blow and a hum: an arrow quivering in his saddle bow. Vague forms flashed behind trees and then . . . and then Añasco's lance butt sticking through the angle of his arm, out of the hunched over back, jabbing at the ground. He drew up. "Where are the rest of them?" Añasco did not raise his head or answer him. He let his eyes follow the lance to the Indian squirming on his back, the blood glistening, sweat glistening, and the arrow in the large brown fist jabbing at the horse's flanks. "I've killed him. Why doesn't he die?" Añasco said hoarsely. The horse behaved magnificently, jumping from the arrow without freeing the lance. Grease and sweat and paint smeared the red body. It had lost its duller colour. Could it be that as the Indian weakened, his skin came alive from a struggle of its own? The free red hand reached for the lance, tightened about it, but it slipped on the staff, left a stain. Did the savage think he could lift the weight of Añasco's body? Again the hand reached for the lance and this time its grip froze to the wood. Slowly—he could not believe what he saw—the Indian pulled himself upwards, the lance sliding further into his body, the wound spreading and welling with blood. For a moment the Indian held himself spitted in mid air. Suddenly gathering all his strength he drew back the hand with the arrow . . . the up-raised arrow wavered, slipped through the fingers and the body slipped down the lance and struck the ground with a thump. The two Christians did not speak for a while. They stared as if they expected to be surprised by some impossible feat. "He's dead now," Tovar finally said.

The same paint, the same trussed hair but without the arrows. As Tovar looked at the guides, standing so insolently apart, the uneasiness he had felt all morning came to a head. That was war paint they had on. They were bewildering the column, leading it into swamps to lose it—or worse. Not since that first and only encounter had the Spaniards seen another savage face. Certainly the Indians had not fled from fear as the captains seemed to think and certainly there were many in this country. Their smokes had risen all along the coast the moment the fleet had been sighted in the gulf. He looked at the swamp and the thick marshy forest. No horse could run here. His face began to smart. He raised his arm and wiped away the sweat and biting flies. The guides ought to be thrown to the dogs.

"These Indians either do not understand or they are misleading us." Tovar recovered his attention. De Soto was talking with Moscoso. "But the day is too far advanced and the army is too tired to go any further. We'll make camp on that dry ground on the other side of the swamp. I should say roughly we have come four leagues."

"At least that," Moscoso replied.

"Tomorrow follow the guides another league. If they don't lead you to the river, send out scouts and find a crossing. It can't be impassable this high up. If necessary take axes and cut your way through this jungle, but there ought to be a path. I am going out with a scouting party before dawn. If I find a ford, I'll sound a trumpet and you can overtake me. At any rate you have your orders."

The camp was still asleep when the scouting party moved off. Tovar quietly joined it. The Governor neither ordered him back nor made him welcome. In the dark his presence was ignored. De Soto had picked his men well. They were all veterans of the Indies and they rode some of the best horses in the army. Otherwise the party must have lost itself in the swamps and the dark. The Governor rode ahead and let his horse pick his ground, but guided him with that instinctive sense of direction which his many years in the wilderness had given him. Twice they had to stop and cut their way through a tangle of vines and shrubs. With the first light they heard the morning trumpet at the camp. The Governor ordered silence and readjusted his direction. They had wandered some three crossbow shots too far south. At sunrise they found the river. Its banks had considerably narrowed. A brisk wind made the mists boil like steam. Large white flowers, as big as small funnels, hung from the trees in the midst of oblong and cordated leaves. A kind of wild squash climbing the branches fell over the water. In the top of a dead cypress a large bird stood alone, the colour of horn, about three feet high. It looked grave and melancholy, its neck drawn in upon the shoulders and the beak resting like a scythe on its breast. Quickly the horses plunged into the water and crossed to the other bank.

The going was hard until they came to a greyish-looking plain broken with islands of trees. The Governor had stopped and looked at the sun. He opened his mouth to speak, when Añasco said, "Look!"

Two deer stood frozen in the tall grass not a bow-flight away. They turned and fled and the Christians gave chase. One, a buck, turned off into a stand of pine. Tovar followed the flash of its tail. Shouts rose on every hand, he was gaining and so did not notice that the pine was playing out. He lost the buck, his horse began to flounder, and he spurred him.

The last thing he saw was the shaking bush where the deer

[107]

had passed, and then he came to, lying on the ground. It took him several moments to realize what had happened. Indeed, he did not know. He listened for sounds of the chase. It was perfectly still. He tried to rise, but a pounding in his head made him lie back down. It was then he discovered that he had run out of the pine and lay on the floor of another marsh. The green roof came down almost to the ground, the branches of the trees, some of them so low a standing man could touch them, mingled with and were caught and bound by the tendrils of vine. The stems were as large as his arm, twisted and looped in a motionless, timeless strain, their deep grip about the vitals of the earth and doom in their coils. He dismissed this fancy: the light was failing. He must have lain unconscious most of the day. Carefully he picked himself up. He began to sneeze. Each sneeze struck his head like a hammer blow. He felt his butt—it was cold and damp. He had lain in one of the shallow pools which pocked the marsh like running sores. The water looked like bile and bred a noise. Then it came to him that he had fallen in a place where it was always twilight. Something stirred in the thicket to his front. He drew his sword and stalked the noise. Softly he parted the bushes, looked over a palmetto. He heard himself laugh. It was his horse caught by her reins, almost hidden by swarms of mosquitoes and flies. They rose and fell as she stamped and shivered. He became aware of his own discomfort and slapped his face and rubbed it, and the little black flies rolled off like sweat. Fanning with his hands, he untangled the horse and led her back out of the opening they must have come through when he was struck to the ground. He saw his lance, snapped in two. He picked up the butt-end and threw it away. It was no longer of any use. He cupped his hands and holloed. No answer came back. He waited and holloed again.

Not until later, after he had turned the horse in the direction of where he thought the bay might be, not until then did he reflect upon what a fool he had been. If Indians were anywhere near, they had heard his voice. It was not a heavy voice, but it carried well. This thought pushed him on. He must have wandered for an hour before the mare found a path. He did not discover it at first, only that the going was easier. Often he had come across open stretches which went well for a while, but this time it became clear that the horse was following a beaten way, for the leaves underfoot were packed, not hard but enough to seem flat, and they gave ever so slightly towards the centre. He was certain, when the path went up a rise which fell away on either side into another of the many swamps he had waded through or passed around that day. The horse picked up and his own spirits began to rise, as the ridge spread out and the ground became firmer on all sides. And then without reason the horse began to balk. The day was far along. He gave her the spur. She leaped to one side and his head flew back and cracked his neck against the steel hauberk. Lights streamed from his eyes and through the lights he saw a deer, but a deer poised in the air, its head raised among the branches of a tree, still as the leaves. . . .

He crossed himself and patted the horse. Surely this land was magical. The deer they had jumped in that evil plain were no deer but phantoms which had scattered to draw the Christians to their ruin. He had had some such feeling of impending disaster when he followed the Governor, but his thoughts had been of ambush, not apparitions. And then through his fears came the shrill and insistent noise of birds quarrelling. He listened. They at least were no phantoms. The path was the path. He could feel the horse between his legs. Slowly he raised his eyes. Nor did he lower them. A large buck was hanging from two limbs, with the skin of its legs blowing gently before a breeze. He looked more closely. The eyes had been pecked out of its head and the skin of its barrel split and sewed together again. Under the neck the stitches had broken, and pumpkins and squash, beans, gourds and strings of maize pushed through the opening. About these the birds he had heard were fluttering and quarrelling.

He felt like shouting, for that buck had been hung and

stuffed by human hands. In his relief he dismissed all thoughts of danger and relaxed the grip on the bridle. The horse took the bit in its teeth and ran. He urged her on, dodging and bowing before the festoons of vine and low-hanging limbs. Suddenly the forest fell away. He was galloping in sand. Salt air blew in his face. The houses were almost upon him before he could pull up. Men, Christians, were moving in and about them. He saw the brigantines at anchor in the bay, the standard of Castile unfurled on top of a mound, behind it a great open-mouthed house, and a voice, "God save you, Señor." He felt a stinging in his eyes. He had arrived, safely arrived, at the Port of the Holy Spirit.

2

Tovar stepped back and surveyed the piece of artillery. The men watched his eyes to see if he was pleased. They stood by the side of the piece stripped to their waists, their bodies glistening from toil. It had been hard work dragging the piece to the mound, but now it was set, with its long barrel pointing towards the forest. "That will serve, I think," he said. "It won't do much damage, but it will make a lot of noise." The men turned away with reluctance and began to pick up their jerkins. They did not put them on at once but held them in their hands, look-ing at the cannon as if they were loath to leave it. A few stood about in that lost way common to workmen who have finished a difficult task. Tovar let the cool air blow over his body. It felt good, for this was a hot country and he was tired. His gaze rested on the sails of the ships still anchored a good distance down the bay. The small boats were going between them, un-loading. He would be glad when all the supplies were stored away on land in the two long houses which had been left to receive them. That would mean that the last hazard from the sea was behind.

The army was busy putting its base into a state of defense. Porcallo was felling the trees a crossbow shot about the town so that the horses might run. Captain Vasconcelos was handling the logs, piling those to be burned and dragging the most perfect to the wall that was building. Two squadrons of horse had been put to this work. The noise and shouts had settled into a regular rhythm, but earlier in the day the camp had been in great confusion. Porcallo stood behind the squads, shouting to them, keeping them moving, galloping out of the smoke and blaze of the brush fires and the falling timber. At times, leaping through the brush, he seemed on fire himself. The old man was doing well. He never allowed the cutting to grow slack. When the ring of axes slowed up, he brought in a fresh detail and shifted the weary to piling brush. Gradually he took over the direction of any task which came into the range of his quick nervous voice. If horses stalled, he would ride up, "Do you want those animals to lose confidence in you? Double the team." His voice was the one constant point from which everything moved. Only the crash of trees could muffle it. Once ten fell together and he shouted a long lusty shout. The fall mashed every voice but his, and in the wake of the wreckage it rose, "Strip and quarter them." Tovar felt envious.

The Governor had spent most of the day on the mound, seated in front of his lodge where he could oversee the work and be reached for orders. At times he would rise and pace the mound, slowly and bent over in thought. Or he would stop and look towards the forest into which all of his guides but one had gone. He would stare for minutes at a time, oblivious of all around him, as if by staring he could make the forest open up its mystery; then abruptly look away and resume his pacing. Perhaps he was more worried than he had pretended when the loss of the guides was reported. One he had sent away with promises of friendship to the near-by tribes. The guide did not return. The others disappeared while their guards were sleeping. This loss could mean serious, even fatal delay. De Soto could not go on with the conquest until he had made contact with the natives, and for this he must have interpreters. The alternative was to march in ignorance, and such a course might easily lead to the kind of wandering which had proved so fatal to de Narváez. This even the pages understood. The army was worried. Squads stood about their shelters and discussed the situation. The negligent guards kept out of their way.

When the Governor came before his lodge and saw the entire army debating the news, he called to them to draw closer to the mound. "These Florida Indians are not coming to throw themselves at our feet," he said. "They will either stay out of our way or try to do us harm. I hope to win them to peace, but whatever they do we must match and overmatch their cunning. I hear we have lost our guides. Very well. We must take others. And when I say we, I do not mean the army. Each single man in this armament must think of how he can seize, outdo, outfeel the heathen." He paused. His eyes lost all expression. Behind his long beak of a nose and the hungry face, they looked like two round pools of oil into which water had splashed. "Our scouts," he continued, "have discovered several paths. We don't know where they go, but a path goes somewhere, and a path is used. We must find who uses it." His eyes fell on Baltazar de Gallegos. "Señor Constable," he said, "I want you to take our remaining guide, forty horse and eighty foot, and go towards the northeast and see what you can find. And you, Captain Lobillo"—the tall, youthful captain stepped forward—"take fifty men and go to the east. Cavalry will be useless to you. The ground is too swampy. Limit yourself to bowmen and gunmen with the proper amount of sword-and-bucklers. Each detachment is strong enough to avoid surprise. I have one other word. Bring back as many Indians as you can, as many chief men—above all the caciques." Then he faced the army. "As for the rest of us, we have enough to do to put this port into a good state of defense."

It was not his custom to take the army into his confidence, but by his act he had restored its calm and put heart into the day's work. Now, in the late afternoon, the work was far along. Two more days, Tovar surmised, would see the curtain up, the gates hung, and the runway cleared of trees and brush. He ran his eye along the cannon for a final inspection, then walked towards de Soto to report. "The artillery is in place, my lord, with ladle, rammer, scourer, and a hundred rounds of powder and ball. Would you like to look it over?"

De Soto raised his hand for silence. His eyes were fastened upon the forest beyond the clearing, his head lifted and slightly turned. "Did you hear it?" he asked.

"Hear what, Excellency?"

"Guns."

Tovar strained his ears, but he heard only the familiar sounds which the pioneers had raised all day. He noticed that the tempo was slower. It had reached that hour when men and their work come to an equilibrium of balanced resistance. Hands are laid on but do not grip. The axe falls of its own weight. The horse pauses at the command and even the voices of the drivers rise perfunctorily, as if all sound were withdrawing against the coming night.

"Lobillo is in trouble. Ribera!" The Governor called his page.

The boy ran out of the lodge. "Yes, my lord?"

"Buckle me up." His voice rose sharply. "Fuentes!"

The steward came running. "Excellency?"

"My horse and sound to arms."

The trumpeter flattened his lips against his teeth, licked them, pressed the trumpet to his mouth. His eyes bulged and the long blast struck the forest and rebounded. The raised axe hung on air, heads caught, Porcallo whirled his mount, sat forward. The trumpet quavered, broke off. For an instant silence hung over the town, and then Porcallo's voice shattered it. Men leaped over logs, ran out of their huts with weapons in hand, stumbled and fell. Drivers snatched at their animals' gear. Horses, with heads up, sniffed the air, curvetted, and with riders on their backs galloped towards the rallying ground. But de Soto looked beyond the turmoil he had caused. The page fumbled with the buckles of his armour. A groan ran up with his mount. He swung easily into the saddle, took his lance from Viota, his other page, and then slid down the mound, leaning back as the horse lunged to keep its balance.

[113]

When Tovar reached the square, the soldiers had been reduced to some order. The squadrons of horse were forming in
the town streets, the bands of foot in the clearing. The arquebusiers and bowmen had spread out in an arc and were moving
into the forest. They had scarcely disappeared when Lobillo's
men began drifting towards the Port. That morning they had
marched away in one compact body, laughing and jesting, strid-
ing confidently into the undergrowth. The squads who came
into the clearing with that quick-dragging step of men too
weary to falter were not the same men. They hurried by their
companions drawn up to receive them without any sign of recognition, their ears turned slightly to the left in strained attention.

Guarded by sword-and-bucklers four Indian women came
in, walking in single file. Moss skirts drawn about their middles
lapped at their thighs, but from the waist upwards they bore
their bodies as stiff as uncured leather. There were three or four
wounded. The more hardy walked alone, but there was one
who passed supported by two companions. He slumped forward and favoured his left side as he walked. An arrow stuck
out of his back. It had pierced his shirt of mail. He spoke and
his companions eased him down by a stump. They were bending over him as Tovar came up. He could hear the hard
laboured breath, and the man's lips were drawn back to the
gums. Red saliva bubbled at the corner of his mouth. "What's
happened?" Tovar asked. The man rolled his eyes and let them
rest on Tovar's, and then he looked away. Tovar repeated the
question.

"Indians."

"How many?"

"Indians."

As the officers gathered that night in the Governor's quarters, they came with heavy faces. Lobillo did not try to disguise
the truth. He had made his formal report: fifty Christians
driven in by nine Indians. It seemed unbelievable, yet believe

it they must, for no officer would boast of such dishonour. The Governor had summoned him for details. The other officers, captains of foot and horse, the Camp Master, the King's officials, and Porcallo had been invited for discussion. The Governor was standing by the fire waving each man to his seat. He honed his eyes upon their faces, and as each captain entered and bowed, they grew a little sharper.

Lobillo was the last to enter. He did not speak for a while but sat in the firelight, his large boyish hands falling between his legs. He had washed his face and combed his hair, but a smudge of fatigue darkened his eyes. His beardless face shone in the firelight, and he looked younger than his seventeen years. The glances of his fellow officers plainly indicated they thought him too young for his post. He sensed their thoughts and kept his gaze on the floor beyond his feet. All the attendants had been sent out, and the shadows pressed the captains closer to the fire. It burned in the centre of the lodge, and as it burned an odour of musk and stale grease rose with the flames. Overhead the smoke swirled and rolled. Tovar had not been summoned, but he quietly took his seat by the large earthen jar of water near the entrance.

At last Lobillo looked up. With constraint he said, "One of my men is dying. He has asked for a priest."

The silence continued after his words, and then Porcallo spoke. "Didn't you get your hands on even one of them?"

"Only the women. When we surrounded the huts, they all jumped into the water and swam to the other bank."

"You crossed after them." Porcallo was insistent.

"The river was deep. I tried to find a ford." Lobillo paused. "They swam with their bows held over their heads. Two of my men were wounded. We thought we would have to leave them in the water, the arrows came so thick and so true."

Porcallo had been leaning slightly forward, listening with slack mouth, incredulously. He shook his head and sat back on his bench.

"What disposition did you make of the troops on the retreat?" de Soto asked. His voice was mild.

[115]

Lobillo turned away from the fire and faced the Governor. He gesticulated with his left hand as he spoke with a heavy but even flow of words. "I threw the bowmen on our flanks with orders to keep under cover. To each I gave a sword-and-buckler for support. The rest I put in the wayward with the women and the wounded. I kept to the rear and directed the arquebusiers. The path was narrow, for much of the way a marsh on each side. As soon as a gunman fired his piece, I sent him forward to reload."

"That's what I would have done," de Soto said.

Lobillo looked gratefully at his commander.

"That way you kept up a continuous fire," Moscoso said.

"We shot when we could see anything to shoot at. They were running about. It was hard to aim. I must be plain. An Indian can shoot three arrows to every bolt that leaves a cross-bow. The arquebus is all right in open woods, but it's too clumsy for the kind of wilderness I've been through." Lobillo turned towards Porcallo for the first time. "My men did well, General." He spoke calmly and with the confidence of one who has knowledge even if he is not believed. "The sword-and-bucklers charged when they could. But what could they do, running in glue and held down by their harness? The savages go naked. They ran away and, as soon as our backs had turned, were upon us again."

He reached behind him and brought forth his buckler. "Look at this." The room had been quiet. Now it grew still. Driven up to their shafts in the buckler, from the split bull's hide to the feathered tips seven arrows made angles of the air. Gingerly Moscoso touched an arrow with his thin and bony fingers. He pulled and the shaft came out with a jerk. "It's a good thing I'm not pulling this out of you, Lobillo," he said.

"Indeed it is," the Governor added and turned the shaft slowly in his hand. "You would still be carrying the head in your body."

"You mean we would be burying him," Porcallo said, and his voice rang boisterously through the lodge.

The Governor carried the buckler closer to the fire and very gently began working loose another arrow. "Yes, Señores," he said looking up with admiration, "these are very skilful warriors. Every head to an arrow is so tied that it comes off in the body." He returned the buckler to Lobillo and went back to his bench. "The devil is cunning," he continued softly, "but I understand his policy. For twenty years I have fought all kinds of Indians, those who eat snails and dig roots with their hands and those who keep such state as no Christian prince could afford. All of them serve the devil, some poorly but always with patience and cunning. There is a secret to the conquest of the Indies. Cortez was the first to understand it." He paused and let his gaze fall upon his officers. They sat a little forward. "All power lies in the person of the Indian ruler. Seize him and his subjects will obey us."

He rose and walked to the fire. His face fell into shadow, but the light from the fire outlined his body in a faint red glow. "Did you ever think why it is the Indies have been so long unknown to Christians? I have thought about it in the long watches and the idle times that come to every soldier. It is because Satan has made of these worlds his private domain. He has made contracts with the caciques. The articles are as plain as the links in Biedma's mail." Biedma started, drew back. "To the caciques the wills and bodies of their subjects. To Satan the souls of all."

De Soto waited to judge the effect of his words. There was a long silence, and then Porcallo lifted his shoulders. "Souls?" he asked. "My grandfather the Sun. My grandmother the Moon. My cousin the eagle. Can you have a soul and claim kin to a bird?"

The Governor regarded his general gravely. "Señor," he said, "His Majesty's conscience is sorely troubled over this matter. What troubles him concerns his vassals."

"His Majesty's conscience . . ." Porcallo shifted impatiently on the bench.

"Yes?" De Soto waited.

"His Majesty's exchequer rather. I'm not his priest to speak of his conscience. I was thinking, my Lord Governor, that what troubles His Majesty are his gold fleets, whether they will reach San Lúcar in time to keep him solvent."

De Soto stiffened. "The solvency of His Majesty's government," he replied coldly, "is no doubt of the first importance to His Majesty's Council. But our concern, my General, is the conquest of Florida. I will add: our concern is tactics and strategy."

Porcallo looked strangely at the Governor and bowed his head, half formally, half humourously.

"Perhaps in Florida the Indians are different," Juan Gaytán, the Royal Treasurer, said. He looked directly at the Governor as he spoke.

De Soto returned his look. "You would understand me better, if you could have seen Atahualpa in prison," he said. "Confined to one small room he still ruled Peru. I have seen his greatest vassals, governors of provinces, generals of armies, wait at the entrance of his cell for an audience, sometimes for days, and when audience was granted take off their sandals and enter with small burdens on their backs as a sign of their humility. If Atahualpa deigned to raise his eyes in recognition, they fell to the floor in gratitude."

"And yet Pizarro executed him," Gaytán said slyly.

"In my absence. And besides, that was his one great blunder." De Soto raised his hand in the smoking air. "And Satan has blundered. By the power he has given to the caciques we will undo him. We shall bring the Word to these lost souls, the Word made image, Holy Mary unfolding in pity and travail the passion of Her Son. The Word shall be our triumph, our lash, our chain, and Satan enchained on his rock, for no longer may he elude the long gaze of Christendom."

"Take care, Excellency."

The officers started. De Soto dropped his hand. Father Francisco of the Rock was moving swiftly into the circle of the fire, speaking as he came. "Satan will be enchained in God's time. Take care, Señor Governor, you do not commit the sin of pride."

De Soto crossed himself. "There is only one enemy, Father."

"Pride is above all sins the most subtle. Take care." Abruptly the priest turned to Lobillo. "My son, I have confessed your man. He is calling for you, but you must make haste."

Lobillo looked wearily to the Governor for permission to withdraw, and at the same instant de Soto grew tense. "Did you hear it?" he asked. The captains had reached their feet and without formality were hurrying towards the entrance of the lodge.

Tovar had heard the cries, or what sounded like cries, and had reached the edge of the mound before the others. Lobillo was the last to arrive. As he came up, Porcallo turned on him. "Be quiet!" he muttered. Fury covered Porcallo's face but even as he turned away—it was perhaps some trick of light; the night was bright and cloudless—it changed to cunning and he grew stiff as a dog on a point. And so the captains stood, waiting, listening for a return of the sound. Moscoso was the first to break the tension. His shoulders relaxed and he began to breathe freely. "We must have heard some animal. There be strange beasts in these parts."

"I heard it," Porcallo whispered vehemently, and as if he had been crossed, "I know what I heard."

"It was men shouting," de Soto said.

The milky light washed the beach, divided the huts, lay flat upon the town yard and, streaming through the clearing, vanished at the forest wall. The moon had made each hut into a target. Where were the sentries? Had they heard or had the fluid dark plugged their ears, stopped their mouths? And then suddenly the silence rushed into the pit it had made. Giddy, with ears roaring, Tovar drew back from the edge of the mound. His glance fell on the horses. Tied to their stakes, they stood quietly chewing before their log mangers. As he looked, they arched their necks. Their ears grew sharp. A stallion whinnied . . . then shouts, clear and hard by. A sentry fired his piece. Beyond the town a voice called to arms. It was drowned in a fresh volley of shouts.

Tovar fixed his eyes upon the forest. The shadows seemed deeper where he looked, less shadows than mouldy stains that would never dry. He saw them waver, split their dark centre. A horseman sprang out, galloping. Other riders leaped up as out of a well.

"Gallegos."

"He's not due back for two more days," Porcallo growled.

De Soto took one glance and began speaking. "Throw the crossbowmen and the arquebusiers around the town. Mass the horses on the beach, the pikes on the beach, my halberds in the square. The sword-and-bucklers in support of the bowmen." He singled out with his eye the officers who were to execute these orders and then, turning, ran towards the steps of the mound. At its foot was a horse kept always saddled.

The officers scattered.

Tovar made slow work of pushing his way through the crowd. He hesitated to enter at all, thinking it best, if Gallegos was being driven in, to turn about and ride down the beach and put himself on the flank of the enemy. Before he could act, he was caught between the halberdiers and a sudden back shift of footmen and horse, all mixed together and crying for their commands. A hand grasped his reins and he saw two startled eyes behind the upthrust beard. "What's happened, Captain?" Tovar shook his head. The hand freed the reins. And then from the front a trumpet sounded the levet of victory. The camp paused and grew at once more orderly. Lighted by torches, de Soto was riding into the square. Gallegos was at his side, his large frank countenance smiling, his hands waving to show there was no cause for alarm.

The Governor stopped before his halberds and stood up in the saddle. The murmuring died away. "Gentlemen and soldiers," he said and his voice was full and clear, "we have at last a guide and a tongue." Shouts interrupted him and he waited for silence. "The Constable has found a Christian, one of de Narváez' men, held captive by the Indians."

Tovar heard a great intake of breath, then hundreds of voices crying as one voice, "A sign! A sign!"

De Soto motioned to the Constable. Not until he raised his gloved hand did the army grow quiet. Then he began to speak in his thin nervous voice. "The Christian is still behind. I rode ahead to bring the news. I can't tell you very much, for when he talked, he used four Indian to every Spanish word. But this much we did learn. His name is Ortiz, Juan Ortiz. He is from Seville. He is of noble birth. He was taken by the cacique of this very town of Ucita. The Indian's daughter saved him from burning and later helped him flee to a friendly tribe. There he was well received and promised by his master to go freely to his own people should they come again to Florida. That promise his master kept. He was on his way to us when we ran into his escort. That's all I know but here is the man who took him."

Alvaro Nieto rode a little forward into the light of the pine-knot flares. Their wavering flames fell across his face until it seemed like a face under water. The silence was perfect. Tovar could hear the sputtering of the flares. Nieto did not raise his voice. "We had just come back to the path when we saw the Indians. Nine or ten of them, all painted, with feathers in their heads and bows in their hands. Large bows too, as big as my wrist." He clamped his wrist with his fingers and held it up to view. "We thought they had come to spy on us and rode them down. They fled to a near-by wood, but several seemed uncertain what to do. One of these I almost ran down, but he parried my lance with his bow. I turned to charge and as I balanced myself, I could see the Indian trying to think. You never saw a man try so hard to think. I was almost upon him, two lances away, when it came to him." Nieto paused and then said slowly, "I saw the sign of the Cross in his eyes. He holloed, Holy Mary! and Xivilla! Xivilla!" Nieto relaxed in the saddle. "I pulled up and sat there looking at him, feathers, paint, fish bladders and all, the bladders blown up at his ears and shining like ransom pearls, and I said, "God save you, I would never have taken you for a Christian." Then I reached down to fling him up behind me"—Nieto's voice grew slow and mysterious—"and when I gripped him, he was as slippery as an eel."

This image, in the silence it created, hung before the eyes of the army. It seemed to the soldiers a hard thing that a Christian had been brought to such a pass and they breathed a deep sigh, half pity, half relief. The sigh had scarcely died away when for the second time that night shouts rose out of the forest and horsemen galloped out of the black pit into the moon's blind haze. This time the army did not run for its arms. Heads were lifted, eager and stilled, and eyes fixed on the shadowy forms riding down upon the camp, eyes veiled as in the presence of destiny, for hidden among them rode one who had been lost that all might know the way.

3

Father Francisco of the Rock tied the cords of the amice, dropped the flowing alb over his head and quickly, with deft and accustomed fingers, fastened the girdle about his middle. His server handed him the stole. The cords of the girdle were brought up, looped, the maniple slipped on his arm, and then with care he put on the rich and stiffly embroidered chasuble. Abstractedly he looked through the door of the hut. The altar stone was in place upon the cypress log, the crucifix stood up, slim and pure, before the great dirt wall of the mound. Upon the corporal the Sacred Vessels waited. The flames of the two candles, he noticed, twisted and curled before the morning breeze. He should have ordered some kind of screen. He turned to his server to bid him find something, changed his mind. The army had already gathered, the entire army. They had never shown themselves so eager for worship before. He would speak to them on the vice of curiosity. He continued to look abstractedly at his server. That Cacho was a worthless lad, slothful and he feared already marked with every sin. Assisting at Mass in spurs. Perhaps, though, there was nothing vain in this. It was only the way the boy wore them. "Cacho, take off those spurs." The acolyte looked as if he would disobey; then leaned over and reluctantly unbuckled the straps. The spurs dropped to the ground with a clink.

He must perform well this morning. The Governor had asked Mass to be said especially for this Ortiz. For twelve years the Christian had gone without hearing God's Word. Twelve years ... the man had forgotten how long it had been. He had had to ask the time he was cast away. It was fearful to contemplate, this loss of the knowledge of time. Day following dark day, time hurrying him to death and judgment, when time would be no more, and he so deep in savage sloth as not to know or care. One had only to look to see that he had been wholly lost. There in the presidio rubbing the Governor's shoulders for greeting like any heathen until even the Governor had mistaken him for an Indian. "No, no, Ortiz, greet your lord in a civil way," the Constable had said and laughed.

It was not a thing to laugh about. There was too great levity in certain quarters of this armament. Ah, Holy Mary, ever Virgin, is it not enough that Your Son has died once so bitterly for man? Is the spirit so weak, so ready to fall into forgetfulness, that each morning He must be sacrificed afresh? Must He each day cross the brook of Kedron and climb the Mount of Olives, climb anew to his agony, to the kiss of betrayal? Must He stand by the Roman Pilate's couch as he laves his hands and hear, Crucify Him! Crucify Him! from the lips of those who when He went down into the city sang hosannas and cast palm branches at the feet of his ass? Ah! Jerusalem! Jerusalem! Thou that stonest the prophets! How often would I have gathered ye under my wings as a hen doth her chicks, and ye would not! Ye would not!

"Look, Father," Cacho said. "Juan Ortiz dressed in the black velvet the Governor gave him. ... How strangely he walks."

Father Francisco raised his eyes.

Beside de Soto's brisk step Ortiz swung wide his legs and

set each foot down in place after the other. He twisted his neck as though the collar choked him. He scratched himself. It was a cool morning, but sweat gathered in beads on his forehead.

"—besides he gave him his second best coat of mail, a breast-plate of silver gilt and . . ."

"Peace, boy," the priest said sharply.

Ortiz paused uncertainly. The Governor was sinking to his knees and crossing himself. For an instant Ortiz watched his superior; then quickly followed him to the ground. Father Francisco sighed. *At least he has not forgotten to do reverence before the altar. . . .*

"Did you speak, Father?"

Perhaps after all the Church is wise to make daily the Sacrifice of Our Lord, the Sacrifice which consecrates, the Consecration which is the Sacrifice—Christ Himself offering Himself.

"It is time, Father. The Governor looks this way."

The priest nodded his head and followed the acolyte out of the hut.

In nomine Patris, et Filii, et Spiritus Sancti.

He had come to the foot of the altar.

An object came between Ortiz and the crucifix. He ran his hand over his eyes, removed it: the priest was bowing and striking his breast—*through my fault, through my fault, through my most grievous fault.* Standing at a distance, contrite, the concealing heart punished, bruised, and humbled; the human race fallen and driven from Paradise: four thousand years of misery, sickness, and death, four thousand years of repentance for sin and hope in the promised Redeemer.

Again that promise was about to be fulfilled. If only he could quiet his body. Spasms had seized it the moment he sank to his knees, all trembling, before the Presence on the altar. Out of the forest at his back the light which flows before the sun fell upon the silver cross and, as he watched, it ran with blood. For him it ran. He beat his breast in a frenzy of remorse and fear and hope, and then he grew very quiet, his head thrown slightly back as though transfixed suddenly by a blinding light. In that instant he felt the darkness of his purgatory slip from his eyes . . .

He was pulling towards the shore, he and González, dipping their oars in the limpid water, pulling towards the letter held up on the stick by the Indians. Surely there was no treachery. The companions they had left on the brigantine were over-cautious. Obviously it was a letter left by de Narváez telling where he had gone, and to find him they had been sent out from Cuba. It was their service to look into so plain a clue. And then some impulsion had made him look back. The brigantine was riding at anchor and it seemed that all on board were dead. The tiny men hung, motionless, over the gunwales; the sails drooped; at the water line the small craft leaned on the sea. In that moment he knew that he and González were lost. He turned to González to speak of his forewarning, but González was bending over the oar. And what could he say to him? The Indians ran down into the water and pulled them ashore. Others came whooping from the forest. González drew his sword. Once he heard him cry out, only once so quickly was it done . . . on the sand the flat and naked trunk quivering and spurting blood, the dark sponge of sand, an arm, a leg, the hair, the very privates of his companion swinging in the air. Cries and whoo-whoo-whoops. He shut his eyes and then he felt a stinging at his shoulders. He was being pulled along a path through the forest.

The priest ascended to the altar, bent over it.
Oramus te, Domine . . .

A short distance from the gulf, but deep in the forest, the Indians halted and built a fire. All but two scouts who went off to stand watch gathered around in silence as the war leader stretched González' scalp on a hoop, tied it with gut, and carefully, so as not to burn the hair, dried it over the coals. This done, the savage took a red paint from his pouch and painted

[125]

the scalp and the hoop. His server brought a branch of the green-leaved pine, and to this the hair was tied. Then calling the scouts, the leader set out again on the path. As he, Ortiz, followed in file, his eyes would not turn away from the arms and legs of González scattered in the hands of his captors. "He was here. He is gone—gone." He repeated the word as if by repetition he might surprise the meaning, but the words were like the sounds of a foreign tongue. He began again. "An hour ago he was alive and pulling at the oar." He tried to see him, but just as González' form was about to appear an arm or the hoop of hair swung before his eyes. Then the leader whooped and answering whoops came back through the trees. He turned cold: they had reached the Indian town.

The trees gave out at an open ground on one side of the town. As they came in view, the Indians spread out in single file, each a few yards behind the other, whooping and insulting the prisoner. They entered the yard singing the death song, raising at intervals the shrill whoo-whoo-whoop. Women and children, young warriors and old men came out to meet them. In the centre of the yard stood a pole. To this his captors tied him and then carried the hair and González' members into the town. His turn would come soon, he thought, and as he began to envy the fate of his friend, the crowd gave way. An Indian of great dignity was coming towards him, at his side an old man with an owl-skin headdress and claws through his ears. Seven tattooed warriors followed close behind. Ortiz looked narrowly at the Indian but something made him avoid his face. He was crowned with eagle feathers. From his shoulders fell a skin held up by an attendant. About his ankles loops of shells tinkled as he walked. Upon his arms he wore bracelets of shell. Upon his breast hung a copper plate. And then, as he drew nearer, Ortiz saw the face. Below the feathered head, below the malevolent eyes, two holes gaped for nostrils. Through a lipless mouth teeth parted in a perpetual snarl.

Slowly the Indian approached. Like doom he bore down on the Christian. On he came to within a foot of the pole. Ortiz pressed his back to the wood but the Indian had stopped. He tried to look away but the cold red eyes sank into his and held them fast. Strands of flesh about the death-like holes trembled as the breath sucked in and out. A long time the two men confronted each other; then slowly large tears gathered under the flaming lids and rolled down the tattooed face. Suddenly the cacique threw back his head and gave a wail of despair. The cries were taken up and rose through the crowded yard. At the height of the wailing the cacique fell upon Ortiz with his hands. The long nails scratched at his eyes, tore the flesh from his face. As suddenly the cacique turned and walked away.

From where he was tied, Ortiz could see the war leader's house. In front of it, on either side of the doorway, two rows of women faced each other, singing in their soft shrill voices a solemn, moving air. They would sing for a minute and then keep perfectly silent for a long interval, when they began again. And as they sang, they gave their legs a small muscular motion without lifting their feet or bending a joint. All night they kept this up. Every two or three hours the war leader came out and danced about his war pole facing the door. Three times he went around it, against the sun, whooping and singing.

Towards dawn Ortiz fell asleep. He had scarcely closed his eyes when he was aroused. His guards were stripping him of his clothes. Half-dazed, he leaped up and kicked out about him. They struck him with a club and he came to his senses. Overhead he heard a hissing and popping noise. He looked up. A burning brand had been tied to the pole. Moccasins were being put on his feet, bear skin with the black fur turned out. At one corner of the yard women were piling brush and sticks under a low scaffold. Black on his feet; fire over his head. He had received his sentence. Black is the sign for death.

Around the corner of the yard the Indians gathered. Between him and the scaffold women were forming in two lines. He saw them go to the leader of the party who had taken him and give into his hands an herb. Suddenly he saw he was naked. He began to shiver and shame overwhelmed him. The cacique

[127]

passed with his family and nobles and sat himself on a bench covered by brush. At a signal from the cacique the guards unbound Ortiz' hands. The women began to jeer and shake their sticks. At the head of a line an old woman, her thin grey hair falling over her face, danced, her long, dry paps flapping at her sides. Feebly she raised a stone hoe and shook it. A girl turned about, lifted the moss over her rear and thrust it towards him. His guards pushed him forward. He held back. They jabbed him with the ends of their clubs. Not until then did he understand what they meant him to do. He took in his breath and began to run down the lane. The sticks and hoes fell upon his back and shoulders. He dodged and struck out at faces which came too close. Behind he heard the clatter of sticks beating together. Half way through he stumbled. As he was going down, a blow across the eyes blinded him and he lay for a full half minute and took his punishment. A fat leg came down by his ear. He grabbed and bit it, jumped up and butted his way clear, caught two women off balance and rammed their heads together. Gales of laughter greeted this stratagem.

When he came to, he was tied to a wooden frame. The frame was raised in the air and two old men were putting clay on his hair. He looked at his feet and his hands. They began to throb. "I am a Saint Andrew's cross," he said. And then four men lifted him and carried him across the yard to the scaffold. He began to notice the sounds, the death whoops and shaking of rattles, but most of all he noticed the high, shrill yelps of the women. He got a whiff of smoke, a crackling persistently travelling, like a lone man running through brush. So would the last man run on the day when the graves open and give up their dead. . . . A yellow flame leapt up at his side. It was thin and without heat. Under him he felt a round spot of heat. He squirmed out of its way. The cords cut into his flesh. A hot awl bored at his ribs, melting and spreading. He raised up. It still bored. Another struck his backbone. He began to scream. His screams were drowned by the laughter of the Indians. . . .

The priest returned to the centre of the altar.

Kyrie, eleison.

    Lord, have mercy upon us.

Christe, eleison.

    Christ, have mercy upon us.

Mercy, mercy, mercy. He was lying on the floor of a cabin, his dry lips moving in supplication. Soft hands were spreading a cool paste over his blisters. He closed his eyes not to see for fear it would cease, in fear that it was not true but an illusion of pain. The hands continued to soothe, and where they passed the sharp throbbing grew duller and he could feel the heat of the fever. He tried to remember what it was to suffer from fire but his senses were dull and blank. Pain cannot be heard or seen or touched or smelt. It lacks a taste. It has no memory. Under the cool hands his mind wandered, grew drowsy.

When he awoke splinters of light fell through the cane walls. He had slept into doom and out again or was this another station in his progress? He sat up, but the motion twisted his wounds so that, leaning on his arms, he made a low moan. It was then he saw the girl. She was standing by him and words came out of her mouth, and she pointed to the couch. The skins were damp and his own odour was mixed with the stronger smell of cat. Watching the girl, he let himself carefully down on his side. She did not come nearer or move away. Her hair hung loose over her shoulders and the moss skirt hung loose about her thighs and as they looked at each other he understood it was she who had saved him from the frame. And then an old woman passed between them and gave him a cool, slimy drink out of a conch shell.

He did not count the days, but quickly, so it seemed, quickly, his body mended, although there must have been a time when the flesh under his blisters had mortified. By bending and straining his neck he could see the track of worms. How close, he thought, the worms had come to the full measure of their feast but for his luck, the unaccountable, the against-all-odds luck. Or was it luck? What had she seen in him, scratched and bleeding beyond any comeliness? Had it been pity or had it . . . The old woman, her mother, the first wife of the lipless, earless, gaping cacique, had said, moons later—when he had come to be held in some esteem—had said that it seemed to them—to them—a pity for one so young, without war honours, a boy with smooth and unpricked skin, to be burned like a fighter who has brought in much hair. And when the girl had begged his life of her father, the cacique saw only the child he loved. He forgot the dishonour the Christians had done him, forgot his mother thrown to the dogs. Her he could forget now that the hair of González had released her spirit from haunting the eaves of the lodge. Little did he, Ortiz, think that comfort would ever come from seeing the hair of his friend waving at the end of a pole. This scalp had saved his life, for once the dead are at peace the living do not recall them to mind lest memory renew their sorrow. But Ucita, though he could forget his mother, found always fresh cause to remember his shame and his grief. Dipping a shell into the great jar of water, he would see the two holes where his nose should be, the fangy teeth, the clipped ears such as adulterers have. And he would hurl the shell into the jug, raise the whoop of grief.

Ortiz would hear and flee to the woods and there he would stay until the girl, coming upon him like silence, would tell him it had passed. He might return to the town, not to the lodge but to the hut of the wind clan whom the skunk, Ucita's clan, called nephew. Then quietly one day he would sit down with the uncles of his master, dip into the same pot with him and them, first throwing a choice piece of fat into the fire to make it merry. But as the days passed and he grew strong and well, the cacique's anger returned. The Indian would not look at him or in any way recognize his presence, but once by chance Ortiz turned and saw him watching, and he knew that some evil was preparing in the cacique's mind.

But those days he was too weary for thinking or fear. The women set him to menial tasks but mostly he brought in the wood. They gave him a stone axe and thongs to tie the sticks and all day he must pass through thick woods to be torn by thorns and brush and worn away lifting and carrying. How simple one good Biscayan axe would have made his task! The sun brought sores to his shoulders and chest; the wind parched them; the heavy loads tore them afresh, made them bleed. And then he would lie down by the wood, too weak from weariness and bleeding to drag it or lift it. In those moments his comfort was the Lord Jesus who had suffered and bled for him.

One morning a man of the potato clan ran out of his house with a lighted brand and waved it over his head, lamenting and crying out; then he dipped the brand into water and watched it sink down. The cacique's wife came out of the lodge and stood by Ortiz and all the people came out and watched the Indian. "What happens, old woman?" Ortiz asked. She replied, "The spirit of his son has left its body." When he returned that night, green boughs of mourning hung all about. For four days the child's kin, at morning and evening, whooped and cried around the house where it had dwelt so that its spirit would not linger to haunt them. The morning of the fifth day the cacique spoke to Ortiz, "You will watch the bones of the dead," he said.

Stepping in their tracks, he followed the two old beloved men. At first he had been pleased at his change of occupation but now that he was on his way to watch the dead his thoughts turned sober. Instinctively he felt that his position was more precarious than at any other time since he had been condemned to burn on the frame. He had begun to understand the beloved speech but more than that, he had learned somewhat the things the Indians held taboo, especially of the dangers to the sacred fire in polluted people. He had watched the women at their time of the moon slip into the woods to stay until their uncleanness had passed, and in that time he knew how careful they were never to let the wind blow by them to others or wash in water that would flow by the town. He had seen war parties withdraw into the lodge of their leader and fast for three days, with a Knower watching the youngest to make sure they drank the white drink and kept away from their women, so that no pollution could damage the ark of war and bring disaster upon the war party. It was indeed serious to watch the dead, or he would not be so carefully escorted. Four times they had made him wash in the stream and chew green tobacco until he had retched and vomited. And the girl had slipped him a sabbia to keep him from harm. It was wrapped tight in white deer skin and tied to his flap. Very carefully she had taught him the song to sing and what to do to make him see well at night. She had tried to steal a true male sabbia, for that had many powers. It could charm a deer within range of the arrow and what could charm a deer would charm a woman. She had said this openly and frankly, coming close so that the moss about her middle teased his thighs and he reached out to take her but she shook her head. They could not have love with him as he was, a boy set down among women. So the cacique had planned, although it was known to all when she saved him from the frame that she had seen he was good and without blemishes. Perhaps soon now, if he guarded well the bones. But there were many perils—the wolves that would come stealing the breath of the bodies they loved and the ghosts of the dead who were like wolves of the air. And then she gave him some hilis hatki to chew. This would drive away the ghosts, but he must watch the old beloved men as they approached and do as they did. And then she slipped away, for he would be called to purify himself and she must not be seen. . . .

The priest finished the Collect. He placed both hands upon the Missal and faced the east. *O Orient, splendour of light eternal, thou Sun of Justice, come and enlighten those who are sitting in darkness and in the shadow of death*—Ortiz watched his lips, moving swiftly and soundlessly, as he read the Epistle. He could not hear but through the priest's lips passed all the prophets, soundlessly to the ear but crying in the heart, out of the wilderness smelling of goats, in the streets where the stench

[132]

of the market rose with the words. . . . And that one man sent from God who is not the Light but is sent to bear witness of the Light, the Light born not of blood, nor of the will, nor of the will of the flesh. . . .

The old beloved men were no longer moving. He stopped at their heels. He was not abrupt and yet his motions beside theirs seemed violent and clumsy. Their very stillness was motion, the motion of sap hidden under the bark, their walking a kind of flowing, an unobtrusive extension, an integral part, of the wilderness which enclosed them and him. Not a leaf shook as they passed, but where he went vines and thorns leaped to bind him. An overwhelming feeling of strangeness oppressed him. He would never discover the mystery of this absolute oneness between the Indians and their world. And yet to live he must do more than understand it.

They were taking hilis hatki out of their pouches. Quickly he put some into his mouth and began to chew it. He tasted the earth which still clung to the herb and his spit ran bitter, and into his nose crept an odour, sweet and faintly nauseous, a thin cool odour which stuck like glue. He chewed and watched. The old men spat out of one corner of the mouth, then out of the other. Turning slowly and with slow dignity they spat four times each way; and as they moved, the stuffed horned owls on their heads turned and bowed, turned and bowed, and their red eyes watched him as he followed the ritual, step by step. Then his mouth grew dry and silently he dropped the root at his feet. The old men had faced about and were viewing him gravely.

The oldest put two darts into his hand and pointed to the green thickets to the right; then, stepping around him, the Indians departed. Not more than a hundred paces away he saw through the trees what looked like great eagle nests, but eagles do not build in the low forked limbs. "They build in the tops of the highest and the deadest trees," he said aloud. All at once he felt an acute nostalgia for his wood-gathering, the buffets of the old women and all the contempt which had been heaped upon him since he had cried out at the frame. He looked at the darts. They were good ones, flint-pointed and balanced well. He gripped them tight and began walking towards the burial ground, and then drifting through the air he smelled the same cool sweet odour, invisible, resistant, clinging yet penetrating, surrounding him yet passing, and suddenly thick with nausea. He reached up to brush it from his face. It had saturated his hands. He leaned over and wiped them on the ground. It rose in waves from the ground. Holding his breath, he pulled moss out of the trees and stuffed it in his nose. The moss was corrupt. He tore it out, drew in his breath. His stomach heaved but he held it down and ran into the centre of the burial ground. There surrounded by the rough log coffins caught haphazardly in trees or resting on frames, he slowly freed his lungs, tried the air. One short gasp and the full force of afterdeath, streaming in viscid flow from the adipose substance of the dead, tightened like a vise about his middle and threw him to the ground.

With lips clenched he thought the borders of purgatory must be like this, and hunted for those bones which were driest, for he knew that when the bones were utterly clean Ucita's people gathered them into the house with the owl on its roof, the owl with the red bead eyes. He found a tree and sat down by it, burying his face in his arms, and waited for the retching to cease. He must have dozed, for when he looked up it was dark. A slight wind was at his back and the air had blown almost clean. Across the yard he could see the glow of the expiring fire which had burned at the foot of the child's coffin. Not trusting the wind, he held his breath and brought away on a piece of bark enough live coals to make a fire of his own. This was a serious business, his fire, for in this coastal country when the sun went under, the air grew chill and damp. He had awakened shivering. He fed the coals with moss and twigs and blew them into a blaze. He broke off dead limbs, picked up what down wood he could find and soon had the flames leaping. He warmed himself on all sides. Once through the yellow swerving light he thought he saw the coffins shift and swell. He smiled at this, so much better did he feel now that he was warmed and cheered. He was even beginning to have some liking for what he had to do. He was alone, in a disagreeable place, but he was alone and that was something he had not known for months. Sleeping in the round lodge with Indians of all ages and sexes where the air was never free of smoke nor the room of smells, he had not realized how much he had missed the privacy of Christendom. Even in the woods gathering sticks he had felt eyes spying from behind every bush, and in the town the Indians went freely about and strangers would walk into a dwelling as if they were come to their own house with an "I am come." And the only reply, "Good, you are come." They would leave as suddenly. "I go now." "What, you go?"

But when the fire fell into its coals and the night settled thick and close about, to guard the dead did not seem so good a thing. He reached into his pouch and took out the sabbia and rubbed it vertically over his eyes; then horizontally. This would help him, she had said, to see the wolves and other scavengers who were now his enemies. Yet it was not the wolves but the lids of his eyes which troubled him. They grew rough and dry and his head rolled heavy as a stone. It was a long straining to keep awake. At first he had been able to follow the sharp soft snap of a twig, hear the soft pads, he thought he could hear them, as the animal trotted away. Perhaps it was a fox or a mink, or even a rat. And once he had seen shining the still eyes of a cat. Many of the grandfathers of Ucita's people are out tonight, he said softly to himself, but I shall waste no darts on them or else I shall have to pay forfeit to their kin. But the time came when he no longer heard. The time came when there was no time, only the heavy slow effort of the will to stiffen his neck and shake out the heavy fog which settled over his eyes, which blew thick and slow through his eyes, into his head, weighting it, pulling it down, down, and a down ... down ...

Dominus vobiscum
Et cum spiritu tuo
Oremus ...

He sat up, his eyes all awake and his heart beating: it was broad light. Voices wailed, low and then high. He leapt to his feet and in a glance took in the coffins. They were all intact. Where the child lay, two women sat before it wailing. Their white mulberry bark mantles they had drawn over their heads. He could not see who they were. Obviously the child's mother and grandmother or two old aunts. He wondered if they had seen him lying asleep by the dead fire. If they had, they would surely report it. Perhaps their grief had saved him. His luck rather. Suddenly he remembered that malevolent look on Ucita's face and knew why he had set him to watching the dead. The cacique had foreseen the trap of the long vigil, that almost irresistible drowsiness that comes to all who watch without relief, that comes just before dawn.

Carefully he walked towards the women. They did not hear him approach. Overnight, he repeated it, overnight he had come to walk like an Indian. He moved into the sound of their voices. "Why did you leave us, Little One? Did your bow not please you, the one your uncle gave you to make war on the rats and flies?" The woman paused as though listening for an answer and the older one's wails fell into a low, an almost voiceless moan. The woman continued, "Did your playboys displease you? Perhaps you feared the gartooth's scratch? It was but to make you manly. The Dog-cacique told you he would not kill you. Had you not enough to eat? Long did I let you suck—Why did you leave us?"

Very quietly he slipped away and when he came near the town, he washed in the stream four times and then went to the sofki pot to eat, without fear of polluting the holy fire. Afterwards he lay down on a skin. He lay under a great water oak, and the hanging moss stirred the grey air over his face. He had thought to sleep all day and prepare himself for the night's vigil, but sleep he could not. To stretch at his ease without any to bother him was so great a freedom that he lay in a kind of stimulated doze, awake and yet with all the ease of sleep. The old women no longer abused him and the old men, the young warriors, saluted him respectfully and called him Ispani. He knew he was still a slave but at last he had a name. Idly he thought that to be free among Christians is to have a place, but to be free among Indians you must have a name and a name must be won. You must bring in hair or do some great feat on the hunt or pass the examinations set by the Knowers and learn to read the secrets of nature. None of these proofs did he have to his credit and yet they had given him a name. The fighter receives his after he shows the scalp. What had he, Ortiz, shown? Nothing, for to move among dangers is not enough with Indians. And then it came to him: they had given him a name because they considered him as one lost, and bravely lost.

Accept, O Holy Father, Almighty and Eternal God, this unspotted Host which I, Thine unworthy servant, offer unto Thee.

Back in the burial ground towards the close of day, his hours of rest, unrest, gone, for who is cunning enough to forfend the many ghosts that wander the caverns of the wilderness or upside down walk the roads most used by men, wandering in search of their substantial kin, crying blood for blood that they may travel west; or when their own kin fail them, take blood, any blood, to speed them on their way to the land of the Breath-Holder. This was what the Indians were thinking when they called him Ispani. Nor did they forget that he must watch in darkness when wolves see and man is blind.

—grant that by the Mystery of this water and wine . . .

He heaped wood onto his fire. This night he would not fall asleep, nor any other night. Ucita should not pay off his score with him. It would be hard at first but in time he would learn to turn night into day. He would escape. The chance would come. There was the cacique of the Mocoços. He had asked for him. The two tribes were at peace but they would not always be

[137]

at peace. Some fine day a boy would covet to sit with the men or he would ask a girl to lie with him and she would jeer and say she was unworthy to lie with one who has brought in so much hair. And the boy would hide where the Mocoço people went to fish and get his hair. And the path would run red. Then he would get his chance. Until then he must wait and keep his watch.

We offer unto Thee, O Lord, the chalice of salvation ...

Waiting would not be too bad. A man could be put to hard measures and still find life bearable. It would be more than bearable if he could persuade the girl to lie with him. She had made it plain that she had saved him for this very purpose. The cacique had thwarted them by setting him down among the women, but that was over. Nothing now stood in the way but his occupation. Just how that interfered he was uncertain. She probably feared to follow him into so many known and un-known dangers. Perhaps it was taboo in a burial place. He must find out. Certainly the odour of corruption did not make for love. But there were other ways, there must be other ways. The days were long and the woods deep, but how the nights would pass if she would spend them with him, if not actually here, then close by, near enough for him to be at hand if any-thing should go amiss. There was a fine retreat near the spring, where the moss made of the ground a bed, deep and soft and cool ...

He rose from before the fire lighter than a deer. Out of the darkness she came walking towards him. Everywhere it was dark but she walked in an even light. And then he was beside her, close enough to touch but he did not touch her. He called her name yet no sound came from his lips. He reached to draw her to him but without moving she evaded him, smiling and shaking her head. Not now, she seemed to say. When we have passed the dangers on our way, but not now. She took his hand and they began to walk up the air. Strange, he thought, that one can walk the air, and yet it is no different from a path. He could have fled had he known. She was smiling and holding his hand. She was smiling when they reached a broad way strewn with stones shining of milky light. Why, this is the spirits' road, he said and she replied, Yes, of course. Then I must be. . . You are, she replied.

How easy it is to die in Heathendom, he thought. No purgatory, no hell, no sins to account for. Only to travel without tiring, without hunger or thirst, across the sky to the land of the Breath Holder. What is it like in that land, he thought. Lacking breath, he had only to think to speak and she, thinking, replied, It is a warm pleasant country where maize grows all the year and springs never dry up. In that land the nuts drop of their own accord near the crackling stone, the bear jars overflow with grease, and on the fire pots of sofki and venison forever simmer, for in any moon the hunter may hunt knowing he shall never lack for game.

It's a good land, he said. Let us make haste.

—There are no red towns but all are white and the people dance and play ball and feast without interruption, and that place which the fighter has loved most on earth he shall find again and raise his lodge.

—Let us be off.

I have loved, O Lord, the beauty of Thy house and the place where Thy glory dwelleth.

She had scarcely ceased to speak when the broad way they were travelling ran into a body of water. As far as he could see there was nothing but water, and his heart fell within him. Not one piragua lay on its bank.

This is the first danger, she said. If a woman has sold herself to a man and then sleeps with another, even though her ears are not cropped or her nose cut off, the water will not part for her. And if a man has spilled his own blood, he must swim, if he can swim it.

I have killed no man, he replied, and looked hard at the girl. She returned his look.

Like others, she said, I have had my pleasure at the time of the busk dances, but to no man have I sold my freedom, to no man until now.

Without pausing she walked down upon the water and he followed her. Before his eyes the water parted to right and left and the path of milky stones rolled through it. The winds blew down and stood up like mounds of dirt, and they passed through without hurt.

But I have walked in my innocence; redeem me and have mercy.

The path rose through curving hills, the ways grew rough and full of stones, and the stones made caves. In these caves and along the ledges before them he saw where tribes of snakes had raised their towns. And on the path they danced and rolled the chunghe stone. Some shook their rattles, the big bull snakes beat the drum and around the fire, coiling and uncoiling, the Highland Moccasins danced the death dance. Slowly and cautiously they raised their heads and struck the air, and out of the rocks there came a noise as of a thousand pots hissing and singing.

Let us find some other way, he said to the girl. We cannot pass here.

There is no other way, she replied and pulled baksha branches, wrapping them close about his body. These will stop their fangs, she added and took his hand and led him through the stamping ground, and as they passed the fangs struck the baksha like hail.

The priest turned to the people:
Orate, fratres . . .

They climbed to the top of a mountain, a mountain so high

that, standing on its very top, they could see the underside of the sky. Below lay a plain and beyond another mountain. There our journey ends, she said, where the sky ends. Between those two peaks we leave the path, passing out under the sky to the land we seek, but first we must overcome two other dangers.

What are they? he asked.

Without replying she led the way down into the plain. As they approached, he could hear from afar the whoops of death and the noise of men fighting. At the foot the path curved about a rock so high the sun never reached its base and, as he went around it, he could smell, rising from the slimy floor, the odour of the dead.

Let us hurry on, he said and, stooping beneath an escarpement, came out of the mountain onto the plain. She was beside him. He heard her say: Take this pipe and blow the smoke, first to the north, then to the east, and to the south, lastly towards the west where we go.

But he did not hear, watching the battle as it moved from side to side across the valley's floor. From above the valley had seemed a wide plain, but now he saw it for what it was, a basin with neither inlet nor egress except by way of the mountain they had come down and the one yet to climb. Eagerly he looked towards the last barrier, but it lay hidden in mist. And as he looked, the battle spread out before him. At the same instant he saw it in part and as a whole: each Indian who behind a tree pulled his bow, each separately and all together as they crept through the grass; each insult and whoop of defiance; each axe that fell and split a skull; each knife that took its hair—and those farthest away seemed of a size with those who fought near by. In between the two parties lay the path they must travel and over it the arrows so sped that they made a flickering darkness, and so fast the air whistled one shrill never-ceasing moan. And out of this clearly he heard a bell ringing three times and a voice saying *Sanctus, Sanctus, Sanctus.*

Who are these who fight and never die? he asked.

—They are those who walk the path without pipe or tobacco.

[141]

Outcasts. Hunters and fighters who have died without proper burial.

—And must they fight forever thus?

She nodded her head. —Once struck by an arrow you may never leave this plain. But take this pipe and smoke it as I have directed and we shall pass invisibly by.

Very carefully he blew the smoke to the north, to the east, the south, the west and, as the smoke rose and disappeared, the sound of fighting died away, the warriors vanished, and the path ran unblocked over the stilled grass to the forest which circled the mountain at the other end of the basin.

We may now walk without fear, she said.

Be mindful, O Lord, of thy servant, Ortiz ...

—Be mindful of your step, Ispani, as you climb. All our dangers are past but one and that one you alone must overcome.

—What is it?

—You will see.

He did not press her further, for suddenly he began to shiver. This chill is strange, he thought, and then he saw that frost lay heavy on the ground. The forest stood out in a clear cold light, bare of leaves. Brown shrivelled clusters hung in scattered patches to the oaks. The bark was tight and grey and dead. The sun fell to the ground in broad slick strips. Tree shadows lay athwart the strips flat and black and sharply lined. Where am I, he wondered, that a glance may bring winter where all was green and pleasant?

Hurry on, she said.

Walking faster, he came out of the forest to the foot of the mountain. Ice covered the path. A frozen river winding among the blue-white slopes fell motionless into a gorge. Out of the gorge a wind blew, driving the snow, piling it in heaps, and bringing to the upper air an endless blizzard.

—So this is the danger each faces alone, with no mantle to cover us, no sticks for a fire.

—Not yet. Climb.

—Climb to our death.

The dead cannot die; climb, she said and, speeding before him, disappeared into a flurry of snow.

Wait, he called and leapt after her.

Almost losing but never quite losing her, he followed running up the frozen path. The snow blinded his eyes, his feet drew tight with pain. They burned, they throbbed, they lost all feeling. He ran clumsily like a man in heavy shoes. He ran until he came to a place swept by winds. The ground turned soft. Not ten paces away he saw the girl. Bent slightly forward, she pulled along the path. Her hair and the most of her skirt stood out behind her, streaming through the air. As he watched, she jerked forward and stopped and the hair settled about her shoulders. She motioned to him and he came up beside her. The wind fell away, the air grew mild and all about them the sides of the mountain turned yellow green, buds swelled on the trees and underfoot strange herbs were in flower.

How is this? he asked.

Big winter, little winter and the wind moon . . . all have we passed. Now we are come to the planting moon. Look before you, she said.

He looked and saw that the mountain was no longer steep but sloped gently upwards into summer. From tender shoots to the full-grown stalks fields of maize followed the slopes. In the distance thunder storms passed, twisting and shaking the fields. In the very distance there was the brown look of drought.

There are still other moons, she said. The mulberry, the blackberry, the big ripening moon, and after them the black water and the whip-poor-will. There are many moons but only the four sacred seasons. Of all things they are the last.

Then all now is simple, he said.

—You carry your darts?

He held them up.

—Then let us be on our way.

Into winter, out of it; into, out of, spring; through summer, summer's heat, summer the ripening time, out of it and into autumn. And at last they came to a place where no seasons were. Time they had left where the path began. Now they stood in No-place, the last station. All the way they had walked, through every danger but the last, out of time, out of the seasons, out of space. They saw the sun's bed, where he slept with the moon. They saw night and day.

There, she cried.

—Where?

—There.

Two stones no taller than a man enclosed a passage. On either side the sky came down. Straining his eyes, he saw at the passage end a point of light, clear and bright and of such a blue that it struck pain at the back of his head.

Now, she said.

—Now?

—Throw well your darts, or we are lost.

As she spoke, down the passage a great wind rushed. Strike this with a dart? he shouted, but the words blew back into his mouth . . . he was being sucked towards the entrance, the point of light went out, he stumbled and fell to his knees; then darkness bolted from the mouth of the cave. It passed over him and pinned his back to the ground. It screamed as it passed and overhead he heard a noise as of the mainsails of a ship popping in a storm.

Up, before it dives, she cried.

Then he saw the eagle curving on the air, its wings outspread and its talons drawn up against the smooth white breast. From the tip of each tail feather hung the hair of a hundred scalps. The bird soared like a thing of down, curved into a spiral, and for one long instant held itself poised in space; then it reached down its open beak, folded its wings and, like a ball, dropped from the sky.

He sighted along the dart, flung it. With a side sweep the bird caught the shaft in its beak and broke it.

[144]

Too soon, the girl cried.

He waited until he saw the two small nostrils in the beak. He raised his arm and let the last dart fly. It went straight and upward. The eagle screamed and caught itself in its flight.

Now run for the cave, she shouted.

—Where is it?

—Here! Here!

A dull heavy thud struck and the dark fell between them. Where? he shouted. Where? returned his voice, high and strained, and then he felt himself standing alone in a vast silence, then in a tight, close, too familiar place. His body was taut, his arm raised, and his hand clasping the darts. At his feet spread a soft red glow. Even before he looked, he knew that he had leapt up out of a dream before the ashes of his fire and in that instant he received the full impact of the world. And then out of the woods beyond the burial ground he heard a thing being dragged through the brush, haltingly, unresisting. . . .

He did not wait to think but ran where the corpse of the child rested on its frame. The frame was empty. The over-turned coffin lay on the ground. He turned it over with his foot—it was empty. His body was cold and running with sweat. He held his breath and listened. No sound. Perhaps he had never heard it. Perhaps he had heard it in his dreaming and, like his voice, it had persisted into consciousness. There was no time to lose. Quickly, instinctively, he entered the woods. Creeping, listening, alert and calm, he moved swiftly through the undergrowth, and yet carefully he broke apart the brush and set his foot down as though he stalked the unquiet ghost of the dead. The night air was cool and heavy. He had gone a short distance when, cooler, heavier, throat-stopping, the odour familiar above all others drifted across his path. The trail was now plain. He followed it.

The priest spread his hands over the oblation.

His foot came to sand and scattering palmettos. His nose

gave him warning and then his ears. Somewhere to the front he heard a crunching and suddenly a low growl. He stiffened. Near the ground, within casting distance, the darkness shifted. It shifted in silence. As he waited, his eyes explored the distance, measuring, isolating. . . . The darkness moved again, the crunching began again. Slowly he raised his arm: the dart swished, the blood rushed to his ears. He heard no muffled growl, no slipping away, but his hand was salty. He threw again. The second dart went wide of its aim, and he realized the spot of darkness which had been his target had vanished into the general darkness the moment the first dart left his hand. Suddenly he was shaking, all his nerve gone; yet he forced himself, unarmed as he was, to stumble about the palmettos hunting what he feared to find and yet must find. Suppose he had not struck the beast? Suppose it was lying in wait, wounded and cornered? Had it done away with the corpse of the child? Had the corpse, even, been stolen while he slept and he now pursued some other beast?

Chilled and disheartened, empty of courage, he returned to the burial yard. He threw twigs and sticks on the fire, and it popped and blazed. He looked at the flames, leaping with cheer and warmth. They brought him no comfort. And then before the heat the scars on his back began to twinge and draw. With a start he drew away. Slowly, as a man turns upon his doom, he turned to the fire. His gaze was still fixed upon it long after the flames had fallen away when, hours later, the dawn came and time returned quietly to the forest. So was he standing when he heard the Indians file into the burial yard.

Take and eat ye of this, for this is My Body.
The bell rang three times and the priest, kneeling, adored the Sacred Host and, rising, elevated it before the altar.

He waited for the discovery, waited, waited . . . a woman cried out in a high shrill wail. . . .

[146]

*Take and drink ye all of this, for this is the Chalice of My
Blood of the new and eternal Testament. . . .*

The bell rang, the priest knelt and, rising, elevated the
Chalice.

In a moment they would see him standing apart . . .

Striking his breast and raising his voice, the priest:
To us sinners also . . .

They seized him and led him, bound, before Ucita. They did
not tie him when they brought him to the slave post. His two
guards, Big-Handsome-Child and Two-Fell-Together, motioned to him to sit down and they sat on either side of him. He
took this to mean that at least he would not be condemned until
the scouts who had been sent on the trail of the missing body returned. Ucita would want to deliver him up to the frame. Such
had been his plan in giving him the bone yard watch. But the
Indians would hold a council on him and even Ucita would
not go against its expressed judgment. At least it was not customary, but then he was not sure whether a custom had been
established in a case such as his. Big-Handsome-Child and Two-
Fell-Together belonged to the White Deer hasomi. This was
encouraging. If his death had been predetermined, they would
have put guards of the Fish hasomi over him, since the mother
of the child belonged to the Fish people.

Holding the Sacred Host, three times the priest made the
sign of the Cross over the Chalice—three hours of agony—and
twice away from it—the flesh and spirit are parted. The Host
and the Chalice are slightly raised:
It is ended.

The Indians were gathering before the long council house.
They entered according to rank. First Ucita with Him-Who-

Leads-the-Cacique-by-the-Hand on one side and Mococo-Killer, the war leader, on the other. After them the beloved old men. Their flesh was like rotting wood, and the bracelets of fish teeth and pearls hung loose on their arms, but they held themselves erect and walked slowly up to the open piazza where gradually they faded into the cool shadows of the house. Then came the inihama, the second men. They passed through the town yard, haughtily, indifferently; then more quickly the ibitano and after them, the toponole. He saw them all out of the corner of his eye, for decorum ordered that he must show no interest in anything that bore upon his dangerous position.

Father . . . Thy will be done.
Over the Chalice hovered the body of Christ. The priest broke it and, holding the fragment in his hand, three times made the sign; then the fragment fell: the blood and the flesh were joined.
May this mixture and consecration of the body and blood of our Lord Jesus Christ be to us that receive it eternal life.

He must show no fear, either now or at the time of judging. Nor too much insolence. Insolence on the part of a prisoner is expectation of death. His guards would be watching to report his slightest movement. Even though they sat with averted heads, he was not fooled. He must show the same supposed indifference.

Lamb of God who taketh away the sins of the world, have mercy on us.

Outcries announced the return of the scouts. They filed across the yard towards the long house. What did they carry? If only he could look. He could feel the tension of his guards and hear the low sounds of the Indians who were not allowed in council. And then he listened to the slow beat of his heart.

[148]

*I will take the bread of Heaven and call upon the name of
the Lord.*

He was standing. The guards pressed his arms against their
bodies. He walked between them. The bear grease on their
bodies was hot and slick. On the piazza two beloved old women
were brewing caseena. One fanned the fire with turkey feathers.
The other stirred the drink with a gourd until the dark liquid
frothed, and out of the handle he heard the talk of the brew.
He passed with his guards into the house. *Lord, I am not
worthy.* . . . Ucita's skull-like face confronted him from the royal
bed, impassive under its perpetual grin. Arranged according
to their castes the Indians sat in council. He felt their eyes upon
him as he moved between the beds, but his own he kept at
Ucita's feet. And then when they had reached a certain distance, Big-Handsome-Child and Two-Fell-Together raised their
hands twice to their faces, saying, Hah, he, hah, hah, hah!
From all the beds came the response, Hah, Hah! And then his
guards went to the warriors' bed, and he was left alone. He did
not move, or move his eyes. The silence grew.

To his lips the priest raised the Bread of Angels, laid it upon
his tongue. And drank of the precious Blood. It was no longer
the priest who lived. Jesus Christ lived in him.

Ucita pointed to the floor. Slowly he dropped his eyes.
There at his feet lay a wolf and out of its breast, running along
the grey sandy floor, was the handle of the dart. He took in his
breath and held it.
At last Ucita spoke. "The little child is found and not far
away the thief is found—dead." From all the beds came grunts
of approval. He almost dared to hope. Behind him he heard
a low humming, and a Waiter, bowing and singing in a low
tone, went by him to Ucita, holding before him the conch shell
of cassena. Ucita took it and drank and the Waiter sang, and
when his breath was out, Ucita lowered the shell and handed it

[149]

to the first councillor. The Waiter sang as before. As it passed from mouth to mouth, Ucita broke into a sweat and with great composure leaned over to vomit, spewing the liquid onto the floor at his feet. When all the first and second men had drunk, the Waiter came to him.

His hand shook as he reached for the shell. He drank deep of the bitter stuff.

May Thy Body, O Lord, which I have received, and Thy Blood which I have drunk, cleave to my bowels; and grant that no stain of sin may remain in me ...

He began to sweat, a nausea seized him. He leaned over and the warm bitter liquid spewed out of his mouth.

Ite missa est.

There was the murmur of a great throng moving and a voice said, "You may rise now. It is over." And then he felt a jerk at his arm. He turned his head, his eyes focussed. De Soto was smiling and his hand was on his sleeve. "You live again as a Christian, Señor. Among Christians."

4

THE MARCH

The March

A<small>ND</small> you have seen no gold?"

Ortiz shook his head. "No gold."

The captains and men leaned forward, waiting for him to contradict himself. De Soto did not move, but he saw the blank look of disappointment on their faces. With an easy and confident voice he said, "How far have you gone into the interior?"

Ortiz struggled for words. "Two days."

"About eight leagues?"

"Leagues?" Ortiz reached for the meaning. "Leagues? Ah, yes, about ten leagues."

De Soto smiled, said heartily: "Why, that's no distance. No distance at all. Great treasure is never upon the rim of a land." His voice grew direct again. "Have you heard of a better land?"

"Urriparacoxit. Great prince. Caciques on the coast all pay tribute. Plenty maize and beans."

De Soto seized on this. "How far?"

Ortiz turned and pointed to the northeast. "Twenty, thirty leagues, maybe."

De Soto slapped the arms of his chair. "That's what I've waited to hear. Gentlemen, Ortiz brings us luck. I only want to be certain of supplies. I have no doubts of gold. Florida is so wide that in some part of it we are bound to discover a rich country." He stood up. "Señor Ortiz, choose from among the Indians one who speaks the language of this Parra . . ."

"Urriparacoxit."

"Thank you. Tell him to go to this Urriparacoxit and say

[153]

that I, the child of the Sun, want peace and friendship and permission to pass through his territory. Be sure to find out what
he knows of the country beyond. Also send another to your
former Indian master and say that I am on my way to visit
him."

Under strong escort the Governor pushed hard and came
within sight of Mocoço's town the afternoon of the day he left
the Port. The lancers drew up in battle array, upon a flat open
space opposite an arbour recently made of fresh-cut bushes.
Ortiz advised the officers to dismount; and he slipped down
from his horse, stiff from his ride, and drew near the Governor,
dressed in a linen shirt and velvet cap, the only clothes he was
as yet able to wear.

The pages had scarcely led away the horses when a loud dis-
cordant music came from the town, and shortly after ten
Indians, armed with darts and bows, walked through the trees
which screened the dwellings. Hard behind were ten others
blowing away on rude cane flutes, without harmony or regu-
larity. And then a tall Indian, in middle years, with his body
marked by figured pricks, advanced with an easy carriage.

"Mocoço," Ortiz said to the Governor.

Mocoço's crown of feathers, eagle tails rising out of swan's
down, raised him above his attendants. To his right limped his
soothsayer, to his left walked his first warrior. Close by were
his wives and sons, not one missing, and after them hundreds
of his people. He entered the arbour all alone and sat in a
squatting fashion on green pine boughs. Looking all about him,
he let his eyes fall upon the Christians, as if he had just discovered their presence.

Porcallo drew near the Governor's ear. "We'll never have
another chance as good as this."

"Yes?"

"Hundreds of them and all in our snare."

De Soto frowned and shook his head.

Two old men were crossing the open space in the direction of

[154]

the officers. They stopped before the Governor and spoke to Ortiz in full low tones, asking the strange caciques to join their master in his arbour.

"I'll stay behind," Porcallo whispered, "and when he engages you in his long harangue, I'll give the order to seize them."

"I forbid it," de Soto said.

"But it's slapping fortune on the arse."

"This Indian meets us in good faith," de Soto said rapidly out of the corner of his mouth. They were almost come to the arbour. Mocoço was rising.

The cacique stepped forward and took de Soto by the wrists, then by the elbow, and then rubbed his shoulder nearest the heart. Without haste, in the same fashion, he greeted Ortiz and after him each officer in turn. He listened attentively while Ortiz explained the rank of each and then he sat cross-legged on the ground, motioning to the Christians to join him. A pipe was brought and he drew the smoke through its long stem, blowing it towards the four points of the compass. At last he blew a cloud upon de Soto, and then he handed him the stem. The pipe passed from mouth to mouth and during this time no one spoke.

After a long pause Mocoço said, "Most high and powerful lord, though less able, I believe, to serve you than the least of these under your control but with the wish to do more than even the greatest can do, I appear before you in the full confidence of receiving your favour, as much so as though I deserved it and not in requital of the trifling service I rendered in setting Ortiz free, a thing I did, not only for the sake of my promise but because I hold that great men should be generous. As you exceed all in your command over fine warriors, so in your nature are you equal to the enjoyment of your desires. The favour I hope, great lord, is that you will hold me to be your own."

"A very civil greeting," the Governor said.

"It loses much by my halting speech," Ortiz replied.

"Say to him that for freeing you, although he has done no more than keep his word, yet am I very grateful and henceforth shall hold him as a friend and brother, and in all and through all favour him."

The cacique listened carefully as this was translated. He did not reply at once but kept silent to give his guest time to recollect, in case he had anything more to say. Then he spoke again, saying that he was unworthy to be called brother by so great a man. Nevertheless he took comfort from it since four caciques of the coast, Orrigua, Neguarete, Capaloey, and Ucita, had threatened him for his release of Ortiz. De Soto hastened to assure him he had no cause for alarm. The Christians would help him against all his enemies, especially enemies made out of friendship for them. Mococo became more direct. His spies, he said, reported war parties gathering in a town of Ucita's, not far from the Port. De Soto was glad to hear of this. If Mococo cared to return with him to the port he would see how well he, de Soto, was able to destroy those who opposed him.

Mococo showed pleasure at this and ordered a fire to be lighted on his left and a large jar of water to be set at his right. Then he stood up, rolling his eyes and shaking his head furiously, while from his throat deep guttural sounds came forth. Suddenly he gave a horrid yell and all his people yelled after him, striking their hips and rattling their weapons. Taking a wooden platter, he next dipped water from the jug and turned with it towards the sun and spoke a long while, his voice rising and falling in a monotony of violence. Until the sun began to drop below the trees, his voice filled the open space in the woods, and all the while his people kept silent. After one last talk to the sun, now fast sinking, he turned upon the Christians and sprinkled water on their heads. "As I have done with this water," he said, "so may you do with the blood of your enemies." Then picking up the jar, he hurled it on the fire. The steam flared and covered him. Through it he called in loud fierce tones, "So may you put out their fire and take their hair!" Then he turned, crying, "Hah, Ucita! Hah, Ucita! Hah, Ucita!" His people answered, "Hah, Ucita!"

Very calmly he resumed his seat.

2

Ortiz took a gourd and dipped water out of the large jug before the Governor's quarters. He drank all of it and hung the gourd to its peg. The ground all about the jug, he noticed, was damp from the waste of drinking. It had not been so when the Indians lived in their town. Weeks had passed since the treachery of the envoy to Urriparacoxit. Mocoço had come and gone, leaving without being able to witness the power of Spanish horse. Porcallo had found the town of Ucita deserted. He threw his guide to the dogs and returned to the Port, disgruntled a second time at the loss of slaves. Ortiz did not like him. He was neither Christian nor heathen. He was Porcallo and, since his foray, a discontented Porcallo. This discontent, very plain to Ortiz, had given a rallying point to the disaffected. Men were saying the army would never leave the Port. Others complained that Florida was a barren land and no fit place to settle.

But this de Soto whom Ortiz had come so accidentally to serve was a good captain. He was both bold and prudent. Ortiz liked the way he had treated his Indian friend, nor did he think de Soto's courtesy entirely a matter of policy. De Soto was grateful. Out of this gratitude he had entertained Mocoço well and sent him away with gifts, as well he might, for the garrison to be left at the Port, when the army advanced, would now have a friendly tribe in time of trouble. Yet the more Ortiz thought of it the more he felt a kind of shame. De Soto had bought this friendship at a small price, a cap and a shirt and a dagger. He felt shame, too, for his part in the pact, shame that Mocoço, wise in council, devoted in war, could be so easily bought. Perhaps this was unjust, for naturally Mocoço had no sense of the value of his gifts. Perhaps he, Ortiz, was

[157]

merely feeling out of sorts. . . . No, he must be plain with himself. He was ashamed because he had informed on the woman who had persuaded the envoy to Urriparacoxit to desert. But she had brought it on herself. She had boasted.

"This will have a good effect," de Soto said from his chair. "I hope it will have a good effect." His eyes ran restlessly over the square where the army had gathered to witness the execution. "On both the Christians and the savages."

Ortiz followed the Governor's gaze. The Indians, those captured and those lent by Mocoço for bearers, gathered near the spot where Ucita's bone house had stood. It had had a bird with gilded eyes on its roof but most of all Ortiz remembered the odour which came from its dark insides. He had rarely passed the door, but he could never forget how it had smelled. Not so much the smell of death as of darkness, as of a place where darkness bred. Nothing now was familiar any more, not even the lodge where he had dwelled with Ucita. The palisades, the soldiers' messes, and the cleared space around the town had changed the appearance of the world. It would have taken the Indians years, with fires at the trunks of the trees, to have cleared away such a space. De Soto had done it in a week. That was a dangerous, hostile act, an act of magic. He smiled to himself. There he went thinking like an Indian again.

Baltazar de Gallegos, coming up the steps of the mound, crossed to the Governor and saluted.

"Take this chair," de Soto said.

"A fine spot from which to witness the play," Gallegos said. "I'll bet you five pesos of gold the dog Brutus will be left with the carcass."

"I'll take the Irish bitch," de Soto said negligently. "But I called you here for another purpose. I'm going to send you to this Urriparacoxit. Ortiz here will go with you. You can pick up a guide from Mocoço."

Gallegos did not answer. The drums beat in the square, the trumpets blew, and the woman was brought in between her guards. Gallegos let his eyes rest for a moment on the squat solid-walking figure and then he turned to the dogs. They leapt and pulled at their leashes, barking and whining. "They must have been fleshed on her," he said.

"They were, and I have kept them from their food." De Soto looked briefly at the dogs. "That Brutus is a valuable animal. I mean to allow his master a town of vassals, a small town." His voice grew direct. "You had better take about eighty horse and a hundred foot. I don't want anything to miscarry." He looked squarely at the Constable. "You understand nothing must miscarry."

Gallegos slowly bowed his head. "The men haven't enough to do."

"It's not that. I could take them in tomorrow. They would follow me."

"Close quarters breeds fear and other bad humours."

De Soto leaned forward. "But they must demand to be led."

Up to this moment the woman had kept silent. Now she turned and insulted her captors and the insults were those that men least like to hear. Her words, Ortiz knew, the Christians did not understand, but her gestures left little in doubt. Neither de Soto nor Gallegos seemed to hear her.

Gallegos said, "I don't quite know what you mean."

De Soto raised his head as though he had just heard the woman's shouts. Suddenly she ceased. In the silence, not her silence but the silence she had made in the crowd, de Soto said carefully, "I mean that you must draw from this Urriparacoxit what the army wants to hear."

"It wants to hear one thing."

"Exactly."

"But suppose Urriparacoxit lacks the knowledge of gold?"

De Soto let his attention rest on the guards: they were untying the woman's hands. He said, "He must not lack this knowledge."

From his collar a dark colour, deeper than the brown of his skin, travelled up Gallegos' face. His voice was even and cool, but it trembled slightly. "You are asking me to lie."

De Soto kept his gaze on the square. The guards were drawing back from the woman. She shouted after them. The barking mingled with her voice, and then there was only the sound of growls and yelps. The woman had grown perfectly still.

"I do not ask you to lie."

The keepers freed their charges and the dogs bounded across the sandy square. The woman half turned her body and the animals were about her. She stood quietly and dropped her hands between her thighs. The dogs growled at her feet but came no closer. Brutus' master prodded him from behind. The woman moved; the hound jumped. She dropped her head, threw her arms forward and walked backwards, digging her heels into the sand. Then all the dogs leapt and she went down before them. Ortiz waited for her to scream, but there was no sound but the growl of dogs worrying their game. Out of the whirling noise two mastiffs leapt high, their fangs cutting at each other's throats.

"No, I don't ask you to lie. But there is a skill in questioning Indians. I have found them to be a very astute people. If they learn your desire, you will find them anxious to assist and direct you, so long as it is beyond their own territory."

"I see."

"And unless we enter the country, we shall certainly find no gold."

"There's none here."

"A captain must take risks." De Soto paused. "What the Indians say to you you will report in a letter I can read to the army. But you will send another letter for me alone. In this second letter you will report on prospects of food and what you actually find. No rumour."

Gallegos did not reply.

"I do not believe this dishonourable, but if your conscience objects ..."

"The main thing is to get the army under way," Gallegos said.

"That's right, and quickly under way."

[160]

"I'll go."

"Good. Luck seems to follow you."

The broken swell of men arguing rose from the square. The two captains looked below, watched for a moment a dog trotting away with an arm in its mouth and then their gaze turned to the centre of the square.

De Soto counted five golden coins into Gallegos' hand.

"That Brutus is a remarkable animal," he said.

3

The boar came peacefully into the circle of men and torches. Juan Ruiz, the carpenter, led him by a rope tied to the ring in his snout.

"You are sure he is the right one?" Tovar asked, examining the animal.

"Do you doubt it, Señor? Regard him."

"If he is not the right one, we'll be chasing pigs all over Florida."

"He is the grandfather. In the army there is not such a gallant. For the favour of the red sow he has killed already one lover, ripped another." The carpenter waved his free hand towards the hind quarters. "Where in all Florida is there such pride?" The boar lowered its head, grunting contentedly and sniffing at the ground.

"All right," Tovar said, nodding to his men. "A man to each leg. Got your needle, Coles?"

Coles, a small man with sharp eyes in a flat face, held up a threaded needle.

Tovar gave the signal and four men seized the boar's legs and threw him on his back. The animal screamed and kicked against the weight of his captors. Ruiz stood squarely on his feet and, with the rope jerking in his hands, held the plunging head, drew it back. With a serious expression he watched the tusks. Tovar jumped across the animal's middle and rammed a stick in its mouth. The screaming grew more frantic. Froth gathered on the tusks. Tovar nodded to Coles. The tailor kneeled by the head, the torchbearers drew near and Coles grasped the boar's upper eyelid delicately between two fingers and jerked the needle through it. He waited a moment, the needle in air, his eyes upon the shaking tusks. From the sties lying against the palisade set up a great din, extravagant in fear and sympathy. Tovar leaned his weight forward. "Hurry up," he said. The tailor moved his fingers deftly, sewing the lids together. Tovar could feel the animal, now fastened to the earth by six men, quivering and his own arms trembled from the strain. Coles finished with one eye, moved to the other. He knotted the thread, clipped it and rose to his feet. "It is finished," he said.

"Let me out of the way first," Tovar ordered and jumped clear. "Altogether now."

The boar leapt to his feet, stood for a moment with his head upraised and then ran blindly about in circles. After a while he grew quieter, tearing the ground with his tusks.

"To think," Coles said, "that this needle which has sewn brocades and silks...." He shook his head. "Surely a man who seeks to improve his fortune descends to strange practices."

"Stake him to that tree," Tovar ordered. "You had better watch him, Ruiz, until it comes the swine squadron's turn to fall in."

"Swine squadron. That is very humourous, Señor."

From within the walls of the Port the trumpet sounded in one long blast, then quick short notes. The men stiffened a moment, then scattered in the darkness. "Assembly," Ruiz said.

Tovar watched the men disappear through the great log gates, into the flickering glow thrown out by the fires. The army would be under way before light, but he had plenty of time. His squadron would be the last in line, twenty lancers all told. To assign so many sergeants and hidalgos to drive pigs through Florida had the appearance of a grim jest, but he was content. The time might come, he had seen the life of expeditions hang upon ignoble things, when these very sows and their pigs would save the army. Only he had wished ... he had had one moment of hope when Vasco Porcallo threw up his command and returned to Cuba. Now that he reflected, it had been a foolish hope. But since Cuba and all that had happened there was far behind, farther than the seventy leagues of water which separated the two lands, it was not unreasonable to think that de Soto might forgive and, for the good of the conquest, restore him to his command. He should have been the one, not de Soto, to ride off at first cockcrow with the advance and the engineer, Maese Francisco. That was the function of the lieutenant-general, to go ahead and build bridges and scout before the main divisions of an army. It was certainly not the commander's place.

He paused at the gates to let a squadron of lancers walk through. Sleep was still on them, their voices were thick with the rheum which settles in the night, but the words sounded distinct and heavy with meaning. It is strange, but just at dawn words seem always full of truth. It is not until later that they become literal and driven by purpose. The damp air had a strong odour of horses and leather. The smell was good. For the moment the men riding slowly to their post in the wayward seemed invincible. The dim light fused corselet and helm and leggings into one solid piece, solid men of iron. But so had they looked when Porcallo led them to Añasco's support that day he tried to land on the island where the Indians had gathered too close to the Port for comfort. When Porcallo had arrived, the Indians had vanished and his pursuit had come to nothing. The few women he brought in made his lancers look ridiculous, and he was ridiculous enough himself, covered with mud, an eye swollen and running from the dirt he had got from his fall. He, Tovar, had warned Porcallo not to pass through the swamp, impossible for man or beast, but the old man would plunge ahead and his horse had fallen, pinning him under. By the grace of God he got out with his life and on the way back to the Port he was amusing enough, mumbling to himself, "God damn these caciques that live in slime. Origua ... Urriparacoxit ... Coxi, Cuxi, Cuckold, Urri, Ari, Riga ... to

[163]

the devil with a country where the names are so infamous. From such beginnings there can be no good middles or ends."

Porcallo, now on his way to Cuba. He came in July 8 and the next day had sailed away on the *Magdalena*. What passed between him and the Governor would never be known, although the men parted with public composure. It was said in the army they did not speak kindly to each other. Certainly but for Gallegos' letter this disaffection in one so high in authority must have done damage to the army's morale. But after the public reading all discontent vanished and the men became of one in their desire to enter the country. Perhaps Porcallo's failure told him he was too old for the conquest. Perhaps, but avarice ignores age and no man in the Indies had so fine a nose for profit. No, it was plain Porcallo was not impressed by Gallegos' letter.

Now that Tovar thought of it, it promised no particular thing. It spoke of several towns where the army might winter, with a great plenty of maize, fowls, turkeys kept in pens, herds of tame deer. It also spoke, somewhat vaguely, of trades among the people and so much gold and silver that the warriors wore casques of these metals when they went to war. May it please God for this to be true, but he must see to believe.

The squadron of lancers cleared the gate and Tovar passed inside. Within the walls the whole town was bright from the morning fires. The companies had already formed in the main street and he could see the officers with their torches inspecting the ranks. The hum of low, rapid speech filled the air. The formations at the square were still in a state of confusion, but it was the confusion just before order. At the head of the column Diego Tinoco, the Alferez of the army, sat his horse. The standard of Castile had been unfurled and the folds of the cloth fell motionless about the staff, hiding Tinoco's hand. On both sides sat his guards. From the dark shadows of their faces their noses burned from the reflection of the fires.

He stopped by Tinoco.

"We'll soon be off," he said.

[164]

"Yes, the stars are fading."

"It will be a good day's march."

"Eight leagues, I believe." Tinoco replied formally, and after a pause, "a good stint for those who walk."

"Will the drums beat?"

"We leave quietly."

Tovar raised his hand. "God be with you."

"God be with you, Señor."

Tovar saw his own squadron and the page with his horses. They had withdrawn as far as possible from the sties. Hurrying towards them, he passed the Governor's guard. "Your men are over there, Tovar," Espindola called out.

"Gracias." It was a good sign, he thought, for all to want to talk on this morning, a sign of common understanding and purpose, which makes for a good march or a good battle. "Your company looks well," he replied, pausing.

Espindola glanced quickly over the ranks and saw the uniform line of halberds, grounded and leaning slightly forward. Each man was fitted out from boots to casque and the Governor's arms were embroidered on their tabards. Espindola said with emotion,

"It will be a hot day."

"The air is dry and warm for this time of morning."

"I slept on the beach last night."

"Did you hear whether the Governor expects to reach the river of Mocoço in time to build his bridge today?"

"So he hopes."

A group of shadowy horsemen rode towards them. "The Camp Master," Espindola said. They fell silent until Moscoso and his household drew up beside them.

"Well, gentlemen, we are about to be off," Moscoso said. He sat his mount easily and his voice was casual. "By the way, Tovar, the women, the priests, and the land stowaways will fall in just before you. I've put a squad of bowmen to their front. In case of trouble you are to take charge. But I look for nothing."

"God be with you all," Tovar said and walked towards his men. He made a quick inspection and mounted the dappled grey. The grey was not so good in a charge nor so intelligent as his mare, but for a march he would carry well. Besides the gelding had a fast running walk which he could keep up all day. It was for that very quality he had paid the extra six pesos of gold. Tovar put his hand forward to smooth the mane. At precisely that moment a stillness spread over the column. He saw Moscoso pause to speak to Tinoco and then go through the gates.

It had come. Tinoco was leaning forward, peering through the dim, fading darkness. Suddenly he sat back in his saddle, gave a low order. The standard moved forward. Running along the column from front to rear there came a long strung-out creaking and rattle of armour. The column was tightening up. Espindola struck the ground with his lance: "Halberds in column of twos"—the lance spun upwards—"March!" With weapons dressed the halberdiers followed at a fathom's length from the tail of their captain's horse. The light from the fires ran down the curve of their polished blades, caught the points, splashed the back of their casques. They marched out of the gates, grew indistinct, disappeared.

There came blows and curses, soft but vehement. The lead mule, packed high with the Governor's chests, would not move. It took the blows and then began to kick methodically. Two varlets ran to hold the chests in place while the confusion grew. Steadily, without intake of breath, the head driver began to curse. Gradually the mule's ears grew to a point. The driver's voice reached a crescendo of scorn and profanity: "—thou son of an ass, thou son of the grandson of an ass, thou impotent, slick-tailed, long-eared, bastardly, left-handed, long-braying cousin of the wide and loose c——ted jennet who bore our Lord into Jerusalem . . ."

The mule moved off, the pack mules followed in line, setting their small feet solidly and soundlessly down. Four squads of lancers closed up the rear and then a platoon of crossbowmen. They passed with an easy stride, their weapons slung to their backs, and as they walked the iron bolts clanked dully against their thighs.

He scarcely saw the Indian porters. Their bodies melting into the lightless haze, they might have passed unseen but for the fardels of supplies on their backs. When the sword-and-bucklers followed in their broken line, Tovar felt the shock of a long gap in the column and he saw how small were the men, their armour illy-matched, their swords hung according to fancy. But each buckler lay in place against their shoulder-blades. Towards their rear came the few Indians taken at the Port. From their necks hung the chains which bound them together. The chains fell in loops, marking their distance, but they neither swung nor made a sound. Very little to show for the first six weeks in Florida. Very little . . .

"Did you speak?"

"No."

He did not turn to answer Silvestre. The Portuguese lancers were passing. Leaning forward in their saddles, they rode with a haste and yet they went no faster than the column moved. The red glow of the fires flickered on their armour, but as the last of the company reached the gates they took on a grey and unsolid look. Only the slim stout lances seemed real. On all sides now the huts appeared out of the murky air. He saw the mangers, the corrals, the cheerless faces of Calderón's men who had been ordered to remain at the Port. "It's almost day," he said to Silvestre. "Tell Ruiz to untie the boar."

He waited for the priests, the two Spanish women, the servants and sailors who had jumped their ships, all the unfit of the army, to move out of the way and then ordered gaps in the sties let down. The hogs, grunting and squealing, trotted through the lane made by his men. In the clearing beyond the gates Ruiz was drawing the rope from the ring in the boar's snout. The animal turned to locate the other swine and, as they surrounded him, Silvestre prodded him with his lance, driving him gently along the path of the army. The sows and shoats followed without urging, lancers on their flanks and rear. Tovar felt a swell of pride: the plan was going to work. To the front, beyond the clearing, the rear squad of bowmen had reached the forest. As he watched, the last man was drawn into the dark tangle of trees.

He pulled out of line and let his men file by. He turned and looked once towards the Port of the Holy Spirit. The first light of dawn was falling across the spiked top of the palisades. Beneath in the cold shadows, crowding through the gates, the garrison watched him in silence. He wondered when, if ever, they would meet again. They, too, must be wondering. Silently he raised his hand in salute; then, spurring his horse, he felt the warm decaying air close about him.

4

It was well after dark when the army reached the river of Mocoço. Word passed down the column to make camp. Orders were to spread out along the river, but the footmen had already dropped where they halted. It had been a hot day, the army had crossed two rivers, and still it had made its eight leagues. Eight leagues is only a moderate day's march for horse, but it is more than infantry, even well-seasoned infantry can do. Yet the foot had done it. But once stopped they could not go the hundred paces to the river. The Indian porters lay in a circle about their baggage. The arquebusiers had stacked their pieces. The bowmen and sword-and-bucklers lay across the path as though they had been felled in ambush. As Tovar passed, he heard a few snoring. The rest lay like the dead.

At the river he found the Portuguese watering their horses. He let his own drink, counting the noisy sups lest he drink too much, then walked him towards Moscoso's quarters. "You are the man I am looking for," Moscoso said. "I want you to set the watch in the rear. All mounted. The foot is too blown."

"So I noticed. Where are we?"

"Scouts report the Governor a league to the east. He went

upstream to build his bridge. What have you done with the pigs?"

"I made a pen out of brush."

"Good. Santiago is the countersign."

"Does the Governor know our position?"

"His scouts gave me his position and returned."

He noticed what fine humour Moscoso was in, said, "You've made a good march."

"Gold, comrade. It makes light feet."

On his way to the rear he too felt elated at the good start the army had made. But the test would come at Ocale. That was the looked-for land. There lay the treasure. If not there, then somewhere. It was remarkable what the march did for a man. The doubts and fears which took hold in Cuba he no longer felt, and yet nothing had happened to change his forebodings. But gold or the lack of it lay in the future. There were more immediate problems to think about. Tomorrow the army would pass out of friendly territory.

He set the watch and poured maize into his casque for the horse. He measured it carefully. In each bag there was enough to last man and beast a week. He broke his bread in half and, while the horse ate, chewed the dry flat pone slowly. And then he cut a small piece of cheese. He licked the crumbs out of his hand and walked a short distance into the woods. At a grassy place he staked his horse; then he threw his saddle under a tree and lay down against it. His hand touched his lance, the sack of maize, his casque, sword, shoeing kit, his plates. The plates were still warm. The morrow, he judged, would bring as sultry a day, for the night air had barely begun to cool. There was no sound but the slight rustle of horses moving about the shrubs and the hum of diving mosquitoes. He pulled on his gloves and wrapped his scarf about his face. Then he turned on his side. In the distance he heard an owl calling. . . .

"Get up." He opened his eyes. It was light. Silvestre was prodding him with a lance. "The army is under way. I thought you were lost."

[169]

He jumped up. Through the trees he saw his men saddling their mounts. Quickly he put on his plates, but before he could reach his command the army had begun to move. Just as Bautista's wife came up beside the woman Don Carlos had brought to attend him, the pull of the march reached the camp followers. He had certainly overslept. The swine trotted out of their brush pen, spreading wedge fashion behind the boar and rooting in the ground. It had not taken them long to learn. They would run ahead of the lancers, forage, when the horses overtook them run again.

Going at a slow pace, the army did not reach the Governor until the sun was two hours high.

The river was narrow and de Soto was throwing two bridges across it. In the centre of the stream Master Francisco had sunk piles put together like ladders. Across the top rung he was laying trees lashed together with vines. The Governor met his officers at the bank of the stream. His pages were by him. One held his helmet, the other his buckler. His brown, close-cropped hair lay in tight kinks over his head. His beard curled from the dampness. His eyes were steady and grave.

"Your march was well timed, Señores," he said.

"Do you build two bridges out of courtesy, Excellency?" Moscoso asked amiably.

"One is for the horses. The banks are too steep for them to swim." His voice was sure, almost gay.

The officers stepped out of the way of a tree being dragged to the bank.

"We will be able to cross in thirty minutes. Impress on your men that once over the river we enter unknown territory. If we are attacked, let every man run for cover. A tree, a bush, whatever comes to hand. This does not apply to the lancers. If there are signs of Indians, no talking. Speed and silence." He let his eyes fall speculatively on the tall youthful form of Lobillo. "You will divide the baggage. We drop the porters here. Añasco, you the food. And now, Señores, are there any questions?"

"How far to Urriparacoxit?" Biedma asked.

"We have come a third of the way," de Soto said and waited a moment; then, "God speed you."

"And you, Excellency."

Once out of Mocoço's province the trail grew wider. The army contracted its column and moved steadily through an awful forest of live oaks, into one of palms and magnolia, out of this into pine. The trees stood wide apart and every way was an avenue. The trunks rose eighty, ninety feet into the air and their topmost branches drew together in a solid cover. The bright noonday sun shimmered among the tops, throwing shafts of dusty light across the gaps in the upper limbs. Tovar lowered his eyes. On the floor of the forest it was afternoon. The small men and horses wound slowly through the shaggy trunks. Their feet slid as in sand. The infantry walked stiff-legged, digging their heels into the slick mulch for purchase. The air was still, heavy with resin and bark dry to crumbling. The head of the column halted. The men were dismounting. Word came back, from mouth to mouth, "A five minute rest." Tovar and Silvestre sat their horses for a moment.

"What does it smell like in here?" Silvestre asked.

"Resin."

"Again."

Tovar sniffed the air carefully. "Dry hot pine."

Silvestre looked down one of the long avenues. "To me it smells as though some prince had made through here his marriage progress."

"You are sick for home," Tovar said; and then quickly, "It does have an odour of flares."

Father Juan de Gallegos came up and asked if they had water to spare for the woman, Ana Mendez.

"She is Carlos Enríquez' charge, Father," Silvestre said but he gave the priest his flask. Tovar was taking the bit from the mare's mouth.

5

The pines grew thinner. Oaks and hickory began to appear.

The going got rougher and from under the broken slopes of hillocks small streams ran into the low, fenny ground, trickling among deep banks of fern. Scattered about on thick-set hummocks cone-shaped plants expanded with hundreds of crimson flowers. The pace increased at the front and the companies followed unevenly, picking firm ground to walk on. The horses constantly dropped their heads to snatch mouthfuls of the tall and succulent grass. As the forest grew more open and light, Tovar saw that the army had lost its formation. Suddenly through a grove of cabbage palms the sun flashed from the surface of a lake. It disappeared, appeared. Automatically the pace of man and beast picked up. In thirty minutes the army came out into a small burnt-over savanna skirting the western edge of the water. It was by now late afternoon. The order came to make camp.

As he led his horse to drink, Tovar met the Governor and several of his captains squatting on the ground near the lake. Before them lay rotten chunks and brands and old ash heaps. "None of these is fresh," de Soto said, "but we must keep good watch tonight."

The horses were turned into the savanna to graze. Tovar took off his armour and came to where his page was pounding out maize in a wooden mortar. Near by Silvestre was stooping over a wide clay dish the Indians use, sifting meal through his shirt of mail. Over the way those too hungry to wait parched maize at their fires. Tovar let his eyes run over the camp. Smokes from scores of fires rose in straight blue columns through the hazy air. A slight wind blew off the lake. The smokes bent slowly before it, swirled upward and broke. Everywhere voices called cheerfully, and foot and lancers wandered through the piled armour and saddles, visiting their friends. In a hummock of trees young Carlos Enríquez lay with his head against his saddle, his body stretched upon the ground, watching the woman Ana. She was kneeling by their fire, with one hand before her face, drawing coals out with a stick. She did not take her eyes from her work, but Tovar

[172]

could tell by her movements that she knew the boy's gaze was on her. He wondered if Enríquez had fouled his father's nest. The army's single piece of artillery stood alone and, for the moment, abandoned on the outskirts of the camp.

It was no longer Tovar's business, but the piece was too exposed. He cast his eyes about for Moscoso to tell him. He was just about to ask Juan Coles if he had seen Moscoso when a rabbit jumped from a clump of grass and bounded through the camp. Coles jerked back his head. "Hare," he shouted. The camp was in turmoil. Men shouted, raced, threw their helmets and sticks across its flight. Midway of the camp the rabbit circled. The soldiers were closing in. Three men dived and the rabbit disappeared. He followed its path by the turning heads. A great shout: it was running clear, springing across the open savanna towards the horses.

In that instant Tovar saw what was to happen and there was nothing he could do to stop it. There went the rabbit and there the horses stood, heads up and ready to bolt. A mare leapt up and ran into the animals behind her. And then they began to run, those on the outer edges trotting sedately with tails to wind, necks thrown out. They ran faster, and then the herd seemed to explode from its centre. The Governor's stallion was out in front. He turned in a wide curve towards the forest, the others behind him. The pounding hoofs rose into the steady momentum of a charge. Legs bent, manes showered, tails streamed, a driving wedge of one hundred and twenty backs struck the walls of trees and broke. In a few minutes not a horse was in sight.

Stunned, the motionless army leaned forward, its eyes frozen upon the spot where the animals had vanished. And then without cries or shouts the men began to run. Desperately, empty-handed, without pausing for weapon or halter, they ran. Officers called, but they did not hear. They swept on steadily into the forest, and a second stampede swept in the wake of the first. The more cool-headed had snatched up their bridles. A few, after the first running had spent itself, returned for others. In

[173]

the first rush of panic Tovar grabbed Silvestre and his page by their arms. "Pick up all the halters and bridles you can find. Slip them over your lances and follow me."

At the entrance to the grove he paused and looked behind. Some score of men were still drifting out of camp. He seized a sergeant. "Go back and keep those men there," he said. "Arm a watch and throw it about the camp. Do you understand?" He shook the man.

"Yes, Captain, I understand," the sergeant said.

Once in the woods he found the speed of the men had slowed. He passed fifteen of the Governor's guard returning under the command of a sergeant. Not a man of them held a weapon, and he noticed they looked clumsy without their arms.

"Have you seen the Governor?" The sergeant pointed vaguely to the front. "He's up there."

"How do you know?"

"He sent me back with these men."

He located de Soto by his voice. He was walking along in his shirt of mail and boots, his sword at his side, his lance in his right hand, ordering the men to spread out. The companies were so confused it was impossible to get them together, but he sent Lobillo to the west to take charge, Moscoso to the east, the other officers in between. Once they came up to the horses, he ordered, they were to swing the two wings together and draw a circle about them. Vasconcelos he sent back with a detail for halters, calling the men by name who were to return. He saw Tovar and motioned him to the far left.

At a running walk Tovar and his companions moved out on an arc. They had gone half a league before they happened on the first animals, five grazing in a small group to themselves. It was late. The shadows had crept up the trees and were overspreading the limbs. Soon it would be dark. The horses heard them and trotted off a short distance. Tovar waited until Silvestre and his page had made a wide circuit and got to their front; then he walked slowly forward, keep-

[174]

ing the trees between him for a mask. But the horses heard him and trotted off again, and then they saw the two men to their front and halted. They threw up their heads but they were too tired for a hard gallop. This gave Tovar his chance. Running from behind a tree, he leaped upon the back of the nearest. After the first spurt the animal no longer tried to run. Tovar slipped the bridle over its head and rode up to the others. They offered no resistance. By dark he and Silvestre and the page were mounted—and armed.

Shortly after midnight a hundred horses had been rounded up and brought into camp. There were still some twenty at large, but the emergency was over. Fortune had smiled upon the expedition that night but all understood how close the conquest might have come to a shameful ending. The Governor personally set the watches and ordered the men to sleep with their arms at their sides; then with a picked body he returned to round up the last of the animals.

Not until Lauds was the army together again and under way. From the start the foot showed their lack of rest. By Terse the insects swarmed over the heads of the column and the men began to straggle. Halts became more frequent than on the previous day, and longer. At fall-out the men dropped full length to the ground and lay there without speaking. Each time the march resumed they fell in more slowly. But the Governor did not make camp until he had reached his objective, a lake named St. Johns. It was then two hours after dark. The distance covered a little less than three leagues.

The next morning the sun came up red on an endless plain. Islands and promontories of oaks and bays projected into its rim from the lake side, and low-growing shrubs, stunted by fires, grew out of the sandy earth, stretching as far as the eye could reach. To the north and west the horizon drew down bright and shimmering. The mist burned quickly off the lake. Only the deep high forests on the eastern border promised relief, and here the shadows made a narrow shade. Once under way this promise of shelter, meagre as it was, vanished.

The column moved off across the plain. De Soto rode from front to rear, saying, "Keep closed up. We've a long hot walk ahead. No straggling." His voice repeated itself monotonously and then he turned about and galloped to his place near the front.

The army moved through the plain like a polished wedge. It had been under way less than two hours when Tovar noticed the men looking over their shoulders at the sun. For the first time since they had left the river of Mococo the companies kept their proper distance. They went at a steady pace, the foot with long easy strides keeping well up to the horse. In the distance whirlwinds of dust twisted into the air, travelled at a gathering momentum, then died away. Shafts of light flashed from casque and plates, heads bent before the water flasks, but the water was hot and left the stomach swollen and in a few minutes the throat was as dry as before. The dust rose in clouds and settled heavily on the air above the column. And then the army came to a place where the shrubs grew wide and thick. It slowed its pace, winding its way through the thinnest parts. Only the weapons of the foot could be seen, here and there the casques of the tallest men. In places the horses disappeared. The shoulders and heads of the lancers advanced like men upon palanquins. At a wild stretch of glittering sand and pebbles the shrubs gave out. The men drew to the limits of their shelter and looked silently, anxiously before them. To the north and west the heat flowed from the ground in waves, drawing a watery curtain before the horizon. Far to the east the forest had shrunk to a murky shadow. Overhead the sun stood at a quarter to meridian. The order came to fall out for a thirty-minute rest.

Slowly the men scattered through the scrubby bushes, seeking what shade they could find. The lancers undid the cinches and the heavy saddles fell to the ground. A few of the horses plucked at the tough, wiry grass, but the most of them stood quietly panting, their withers and backs dark and slick with sweat. Tovar took his comb and curried the gelding. Lather lay at its mouth and under its tail. Its body was steaming. He tied the reins to a cactus and walked over to where the men had gathered about a skin of reserve water. He could feel the sweat, hot, trickling lines running from under his arm pits, down his back, between his breasts, tickling his navel. The water-bearers said over and over, "Careful now. Don't waste it." Tovar waited his turn. Those whose flasks had narrow tops were turned away lest the water be spilled. Tovar got half a measure. He took a swallow, washed it about his mouth and slowly let it trickle down his throat. It had a brackish taste. His thirst grew stronger. He took another sip and held it under his tongue and then walked back and poured half of what remained down the gelding.

As he lay down to rest, the order came to fall in. Surely the time had not passed. He looked up and tears rushed under his lids. His eyes shut tight but for an instant they had swum helplessly in the white molten pool of the sun. He picked up his gear and reaching through the dark nimbus blindly saddled the gelding. He could hear the captains calling to their men and de Soto's voice in different parts of the brush, now close, now at a distance. It sounded cool and fresh, yet it was hard and he knew the freshness was of the will. Gradually his vision cleared upon the companies forming. The men hung back upon the edge of the shade and the officers were going along pushing them into the open. Slowly they found their places and stood hunched up and shivering. The Portuguese took up the march at a walk and drew the Governor's guard in their wake. In ragged formations the companies fell in behind, with stragglers half-running, half-walking, to overtake their detachments. Añasco and Biedma rode among the bushes driving out the last of these. Finally the column gathered itself together and crept through the full blast of the midday sun. De Soto and his retinue rode on the flank, behind him at the middle distance came Moscoso and, just off the rearward, Añasco.

By one o'clock the army took a five-minute halt. With the corners of his eyes drawing from the glare, Tovar scanned the plain. In no direction could he find its limits. Even the forest to the east had disappeared. The most hard-pressed of the foot gave their weapons to the cavalry and sat for the few minutes in the shade of the animals. When the march resumed, many had to be lifted to their feet. At the next halt the order went out to remain standing. Tovar's thirst could wait no longer. He drained his flask. A few drops fell to his breastplate, hissing softly. The fever on his cheeks and head burned inwards. He began to feel light-headed and lifted his casque.

"I'm being stewed in this kettle of armour," he said.

"It's hot," Silvestre replied.

"It is."

A man stepped out of line. Añasco rode up to him. "Get back," he ordered hoarsely.

"I want to make water."

"Hold your water. You'll need it."

"But I want . . ."

"Get back in line."

"Here, grab my stirrups," Tovar said. "Give me your cross-bow."

De Soto was standing in his saddle, alert, with his hand over his eyes, looking before him into the waste of sand and heat.

More and more the foot dropped back and caught at the lancers' stirrups. By now the army had lost its formation. With effort Tovar lifted his eyes. He thought he could see a smudge along the horizon. And then from among those walking before the mules a man lunged into the open and stood swaying upon his feet. Slowly he dropped upon his knees and hands. Moscoso and Añasco rode up and dismounted. As they were lifting him, he slumped forward in their arms. Father Francisco hurried to his aid and bent over him. It was a few moments before the Governor noticed the commotion and gave the signal to halt. Hoarsely the officers called out, "Keep to your feet. No sitting. Keep to your feet."

"Who is it?"

"Why don't they put him on a horse?"

"Prado."

[178]

"Prado? The Governor's steward?"

"What are they doing?"

"Died of thirst."

"Prado dead?"

"Died of thirst."

It did not take long to make the shallow grave. The army moved slowly by the slight mound of sand and then gradually, ever so gradually, increased the tempo of its march. Tovar opened his lips to speak and saw Silvestre a length ahead. He spurred his horse. The gelding walked a little faster and after a long while he reached his companion's side. "If the army stops again, there will be more to follow Prado," he said.

Listlessly Silvestre looked around and stared. His face was streaked with sweat and dust, his half-closed eyes drawn and hollow.

Somewhere up front a voice called, "Shade." The word travelled from mouth to mouth like a sigh, and the army stiffened with a fresh strain of will. Through the sweltering air a long green tongue reached far into the plain. Towards this the straggling column pulled its steps. The heat lessened as the sun moved westward, but the green stripped oasis grew no larger. And then as grass grows after a rain, it began to rise from the parched earth and behind it, across the entire length of the horizon, the long shadow turned into bushes, the bushes into miniature trees, and the trees into hope.

An hour later the wayward rode into the lip of a high and open forest, broke rank and ran towards the deep pools of bubbling springs. Tovar was among the last to enter. Coming suddenly off the plain, out of its glare, he felt at once shut up in darkness and at the spring he found off to itself he looked down into water that was black, yet clear. He jerked off his casque and sank his head into its icy depths.

6

He awoke with the drawing of hunger in the roof of his mouth. The night before he had eaten his last bit of cheese, rather he held it in his mouth and let it melt. There was no bread. The supplies brought from the Port had by now given out. Word spread that the Governor said they were near the borders of Urriparacoxit and that they might expect Gallegos to have food for all. With this in mind the army marched all day with good will and reached before nightfall the village of Guaçoco, set in a plain near the woods. It was deserted, its cribs were empty, but to one side there stood small fields of maize. At the sight of the tasselling grain the men gave a shout and then scattered to gather it. Later, sitting about their fires, they roasted the half-ripe ears in their shucks and ate them, a small enough ration, with the cheer that men show at a feast, for it was the first growing maize they had seen in Florida. The horses were turned in upon the stalks. In half an hour the field had disappeared.

The following day, early, the army reached Luca and here Gallegos met the Governor. The rest of his men came in Monday, July 21. They brought with them Ortiz and the seventeen Indian hostages, but very little food. They had found a few cribs in the capital town, but this disappeared the first two weeks of their occupation and since that time they had lived on the new half-ripe crop. A small amount of the old grain Gallegos held in reserve and this the Governor had put into a common lot, cooked into bread, and divided among all the men. A pone the size of the hand to a man. No one was told that there was no other in prospect. Some ate theirs at once. Very carefully Tovar cut his piece into four parts.

A day and a half from Luca lay a great swamp running for many leagues, how many Gallegos did not know, but somewhere on its other side were the towns of Acuera and Ocale. Scouting parties had explored it for short distances, but they returned with no clear knowledge of trails. Confronted by this information, the Governor decided to make one final effort to communicate with the Indian lord. He released an old man of authority and sent him to Urriparacoxit with the message that he, Hernando de Soto, who commanded the long-armed men and the four-footed animals, children of the wind, wanted peace and friendship and a way through his territory. All day Tuesday the army waited for a reply, and all that day the Governor turned his eyes to the east, but no runner broke through the brush with the message he longed to hear. Towards nightfall the captains gathered at his fire to learn his pleasure. They had been sitting in silence, with their backs to the trees, when suddenly the Governor leaned forward. The captains followed his gaze and then all resumed their former state of lassitude— the Governor had seen Ortiz returning from a foraging trip. He came out of the forest followed by six men of the guard, carrying sacks on their backs.

"It's no use, Excellency," Gallegos said. "For a month I've tried to get in touch with the Indian."

De Soto did not speak at once. He was watching Ortiz walking slowly towards the camp. Then he said, "What kind of a swamp is it?"

"A swamp."

"What kind of trees?"

"Indian cypress."

"And you couldn't find its limits?"

"My scouts went a day in each direction."

"If I could send strong parties after this Indian, I'd let him feel what it is to thwart me. I believe I could find him."

"But suppose you don't?" Moscoso asked.

De Soto got to his feet and began to pace.

"Most of the army has gone today without eating," Lobillo said out of the clear. "The more improvident longer."

"There'll be no food growing in the swamp," de Soto replied.

"Narváez didn't find any towns in this region," Juan Gaytán said.

"Narváez passed nearer the coast," de Soto answered quickly. "Rich land is bound to be in the interior. There will be plenty of food when we reach it."

"The swamp."

[181]

"I know the hazard," de Soto said with irony. "That's why I want to find this Urriparacoxit."

Ortiz came into the circle of captains. Without raising their heads the guards walked by to their messes. "I've brought some roots," he said.

"What are they?" Añasco asked gruffly.

"The Indians eat them."

Tinoco and Moscoso walked over and looked at the muddy pile in Ortiz' mantle. Tinoco moved them with the toe of his boot. "What do you do to them?"

Ortiz made no response.

"Guard," de Soto called. "Bring the Gallegos Indians here."

The cook was looking doubtfully at the roots. "Wash them, pound them, and boil them," Ortiz said.

Linked together, with chains about their necks, the Urriparacoxit walked silently into the circle of the captains and stood between their guards.

"Question them again about the trails through the swamp," de Soto said.

It was dark when Ortiz turned away from the captives to put their words into Spanish. "They don't know much," he said.

Angrily de Soto strode across the firelight and, pointing to the dogs, said, "If you lie to me, I'll throw you to them." He turned to Ortiz. "Tell them that."

Ortiz talked several minutes with the Indians. Their faces had withdrawn into the darkness, but the fire fell upon their bodies and they glowed with deep rich hues.

"They say it's bad country. They are afraid to go there. Full of witches."

"Witches," Biedma said contemptuously. "What does an Indian know of witches?"

"They say the Ocale people shout and birds fall from the air."

"Partridges?" Lobillo interposed eagerly.

The captains moved restlessly. "Partridges feed on the ground," Maldonado said in a heavy clear voice.

"They fly, too." Lobillo's voice was hopeful.

"Don't talk about birds and feeding," Juan Gaytán said irritably. "My ears are shooting with pain."

De Soto looked at the Indians for a long time and then he walked to where the cook was pounding the last of the roots in his wooden mortar. The cook increased the speed of his work. The Governor watched until he was done and then he walked back to his captains. "If I get no word from Urriparacoxit by morning, we try the swamp," he said.

The army was late in getting under way, for de Soto waited until the sun was high, hoping to the last to receive a messenger who would tell of a certain way to Ocale, or at least arriving bring the promise of enough food to stave off their hunger. But the forest remained still and close as on the past two days and so the order, at last, was given to move forward. With much straggling the column came to a small place called Vicela, paused to pull the blites growing in the gardens and cook them in water with a little salt, and this the men ate without any other thing. Those in the rearward seized upon a few straggling stalks of maize and chewed the pulpy joints like cattle. Afterwards they went beyond to sleep and, as they lay down, one man from each mess kept watch over his fire, throwing damp wood upon it to make smoke against the mosquitoes blowing in swarms from the pools of scum. All through the night from some part of the camp a man would wake up, cursing and slapping his face. Once Tovar found himself sitting, half awake, rubbing his hands. He saw de Soto in the glow of his fire, in his harness, looking across and beyond the sleeping men. Feeling suddenly a sharp swell of nostalgia, Tovar rose with the thought to join him, but as he watched he saw the other's gaze, secret, withdrawn before the darkness. Silently he lay back down and drew his mantle about him.

Just at dawn the army approached tall marsh grass, half a league wide, for the men had been aroused about Matins, not with the trumpet which had been usual up to this time but by the captains going among them and shaking them awake. And so, after marching through darkness, with the first faint smear of light appearing just as they came out into the grass, they saw before them where the swamp should have been a green, far-reaching plain. De Soto halted the army, thinking the guides had misled him and that the north was the east, for the light lay brighter over the plain. The dogs were brought and as he stood by while Ortiz interpreted him to the Indians and the Indians to him, the sun rose and revealed the true east and slowly, sharpened by the morning rays, the black waste land which had lain between the grass and the plain turned into a thick and gloomy mist and, growing, looming into view, up from the watery earth, tall trunks of cypress appeared out of the deep and broken corridors they made. Suddenly, before the eyes of all, the plain vanished. The men fell silent, staring at the flat and cumbrous tops of the cypress swamp.

De Soto turned his horse sharply about and the animal reared. "Forward," he called. His voice sounded thin and tight. In spite of his command, it was several minutes before the order was obeyed.

Once under way the army moved over the grass, beating it down, over firm ground at a good stride, and with each step the cypress appeared bigger and higher and the recesses between the trunks gloomier. Men in the wayward began to slip, and then Tovar felt the earth grow soft and spongy. Only the tufty roots gave it body. All at once, near the border of the swamp, the ground began to shake and tremble. A voice cried, "Quicksand." As at command the wayward and battle floundered in an effort to run. Captains shouted and the men returned to order, setting down their feet as lightly, as carefully, as their harness allowed, the companies advancing in a line of columns, sinking up to their ankles, the horses up to their fetlocks, pulling and bobbing along after the guides. To their flank, as the sun advanced, the great trees cast upon the underlying mud and grass a shade as wide and dark as a cloud, and the right column marched in shadow and the other four in light. From aloft

[184]

the long moss fell in streamers, fanning the upper air, and fluttering in the green umbrella tops, ninety feet high, flocks of paraqueets shelled the cypress balls. In the top of a dead tree, among the bare arms, Tovar saw the trash of an eagle's nest. At a bank of shells the trail, winding narrowly through the mud, turned into the swamp. In single file and walking gingerly the wayward turned and followed it.

As soon as the advance wound itself out of sight, word came back to send forward a company of crossbowmen. The army halted while these men unslung their bows and went to the front. As they stepped upon the shelly ridge, Tovar noticed they looked ahead like men with films over their eyes. An hour passed and it came his turn. Going ahead of the hogs, he rode into the swamp and before him he could see where the outside light ended. On every side the trunks of the cypress flanged out like the wings of a giant bat, as high as his saddle and deep enough for several men to hide in the hollows between. Mud, cracked and dried to a dead look, coated them, but where they went into the ground the mud was dark and slick. On top of the flanges the trees took a second beginning, mounting straight and branchless to their tops. He could hear men and horses slipping and men cursing under their breath. His mare, with her head down, stepped delicately along, missing the cypress knees which lay about like great dark bubbles. He did not raise his eyes; it was a place where a horse might break a leg.

He heard the water splashing before he saw it. First it began to slip among the roots, then it lapped over them, and then it came to the top of the knees. Small waves set in motion by the army lopped and lupped against the trunks. Gradually as his horse went in deeper, he heard the hogs splashing and plunging behind. He drew in his reins and dismounted. "Tie up the pigs and lash them to your saddles," he said. "One on each side for balance." His voice reverberated through the high corridors, big and solemn, and he felt that it was out of control.

It took half an hour to get the hogs tied and then he and his men set out to walk, leading the nervous horses by their bridles. All the way he was in water up to his shins. In less than an hour he came to a break in the swamp, where the cypress gave out at a body of water two shots wide. There was none of the rest of the army in sight. Only a lone horseman waiting at the bank.

"It's stirred up now," he said to Tovar, "but the trail goes under the water here. If you will follow me, I think I can take you across. Everywhere else it's over your head."

Tovar nodded and led his horse in after the guide. The water came up to his boots, ran over them; then he was walking in it up to his waist. It was warm and sluggish and he felt unclean. In midstream he had to walk on his toes. He heard the sows screaming and kicking but he couldn't look back and anyway they wouldn't drown. If only they didn't frighten the horses. After a hundred paces, he estimated the distance as best he could, the water began to recede and in less than five minutes he came out on the other bank. While he waited for the squadron, he sat on the ground and lifted his legs and shook the water out of his boots, and then as the men came out he put four each to a pack of hogs and they were quickly freed. After their recent fright the animals hung from the saddles in abject terror. He felt a sudden swell of disgust and anger that his talents must be wasted in such a way, and bitterness that he should be thrown down from his high place to herding swine.

Through the woods there came the sound of hoof beats. He looked over his shoulder at a body of lancers galloping towards him. The lead horse was the Governor's Aceituno. Its legs and belly were covered with mud and the Governor's harness was splashed and dimmed. He looked like a man at the end of a hard campaign. He pulled up and ten lancers pulled up behind him. "You'll find the army at Tocaste," de Soto said. He did not speak directly to Tovar. "It's a town about half a league from here, on a large lake. A savanna in front of it."

There was a pause. Since he had not been addressed, Tovar received the information in silence, and his men kept silent waiting for him to speak. As though he were answering a question, de Soto said, "We can't get through. The country is a network of swamps. I'm going back the way we came and try to find a crossing lower down."

He spurred his horse and plunged into the stream. One at a time his men followed. Ranjel was the last to leave.

"And you think there's no way to get through?" Tovar said to him.

"The trails are under water. The lake overflows on all sides. In some places a stiff current."

"Any food?" Silvestre asked.

"Gardens." He waved his hand, "Here's luck," and rode after his companions.

The ten horsemen were now spread out from bank to bank. De Soto was drawing out on the farther side. Without looking back he rode into the cypress and quickly lost himself. Tovar did not move until all the lancers had disappeared.

"Think," said Hernandarias, "the men at the Port are wallowing in two years' supply of food."

7

At Tocaste Tovar began to feel the draw of hunger again. As long as he was on the march he was fairly free of it, but the moment he rode across the edge of the savanna to the town and saw the men moving about the place with the air of settled boredom which a veteran body throws off as it breathes, at that moment his hunger struck him like a pain. . . . He was sure he smelled fish, fish frying in oil. He paused by a group of men building a shelter and asked them could it be possible that he smelled fish? Yes, it was possible. He might smell fish but he would never eat it. Those particularly bastardly sons of whores in the wayward had already eaten it. Fifty pounds taken from weirs found in the lake and fried in two jars of bear oil left by the Indians. Well, then, was there anything to eat? About ten hanegas of maize and one or two of beans, but these Moscoso had set aside for the morrow.

[187]

Perhaps he might find something in the fields if he rooted like his charges.

He found two immature ears trodden into the ground and ate them raw, cob and all, and at once he began to feel cramps in his stomach. Pains scattered in sharp rough points and he raised his leg to ease himself. Down by the lake men were at work and he went there to see what they were about. They were lashing limbs together into fishing rafts. As he watched, he began to feel dull in the head and more tired than he should be after so short a march. In three days he had had as many mouthfuls of food and the lack of it was beginning to tell. He must not let himself get weak. Until the army got out of the swamp, the wayward would always get what there was to eat. He turned and walked to his mess and ordered his page to saddle their horses. While the boy was gone, he inquired for Silvestre and found him in a group throwing dice. He asked him if he wanted to forage. Silvestre shook his head. He was putting up his fine dagger with the embossed handle against a cup of beans.

He and the boy had been riding for several hours, the afternoon was far along and they had found no weirs. In every direction they had been stopped by marshes or overflown arms of the swamp, and now they had stumbled on another arm of the lake, covered over near the bank by floating lawns of water plants. "Go tie the horses," Tovar said. "We'll find trout here." The boy looked depressed; so he told him to make a fire, then he cut from his mantle and sleeves bright-coloured cloth and tied the strips to his hook. He saw a place where a storm had torn a hole in the plants and as he went towards it to try his luck he slipped on the bank. All about his head was the odour of spices, his mouth began to draw and shoot with saliva, and then he saw the aromatic herb he had pulled in his fall. He took a deep breath and threw it quickly away.

At the lagoon's edge he made a cast and pulled his line close in to the thick, flat leaves. Instantly he saw the flash. He jerked, the pole bent, and he was walking out into the lagoon up to his

[188]

arms in water. Several times he thought the pole must break, but after a good hard fight he landed the fish. The page ran out to take it and was finned for his haste. "It must weigh two pounds," the boy shouted. They made their way to the bank and as he pulled through the water and weeds, Tovar struck a sunken log. He felt along it with his foot. It seemed hollow. Suddenly he reached under the water with his hand. "Here, lad," he said.

"The fish."

"Put it on the bank and come here."

The boy rejoined him, wrapping his hand as he came, and soon the two of them were reaching into the log and throwing stones to each side of them. After a little while they got hold of one end and lifted. Slowly, spilling water, the charred butt of a dug-out rose to the surface. They shook and pulled, but it would come no further. And then Tovar sent for a spike from his shoeing kit and drove it firmly into the square bow, hooked a rope about it and hitched the horses to the other end. In a few minutes the long narrow cypress boat, with four paddles in its bottom, lay upon the slippery bank.

Tovar waited until the fish was cleaned and spitted and broiling over the coals; then he stepped into the boat and pushed off from the bank. He would see what lay beyond the lagoon. Perhaps, by some stroke of good fortune, he might find where the trail picked up again. They were only half a league or so from camp and he had another hour of light. Perhaps, even, the boy might catch another fish or two while he was gone. If it didn't rain and drive him back. The sky seemed clear but storms in this country rose suddenly and with a lot of wind. He had been hearing thunder, if a strange kind of thunder, towards the northeast.

He paddled out of the lagoon into the main body of water, crossed one arm of it to a place where it emptied into the swamp. There, following the current, he passed through the narrow reed-grown mouth, into, out of, another lagoon, and came to a lake shut in by swamps and cypress and much smaller than the one he had put behind him. Upon its banks and on the small sombre islands the shrubs opened in brilliant flower, others already drawing to against the approaching dark, and high in the trees wild squash hung out of reach. Laughing coots with wings half-spread scudded over the coves, hiding in the tufts of grass. A young brood of painted teal followed a hen, skimming along the water, unconscious of any danger. Suddenly in their midst, there was a flash and foaming, a moment of fluttering and one of the teals was snapped away by a trout. The hen cried a warning and she and her brood turned for the bank. Tovar looked around for the danger. It was not the trout, and he grew still in his boat. In front now, not over a hundred yards away, a creature of prodigious strength and speed, with a plaited tail, a body as large as a horse and armoured, rushed forth from among the flags and reeds.

Its first burst of speed died away and, slowing, it came to a stop near the centre of the lake. There it drew in wind and water with a rattling sonorous sound and, swollen almost to bursting, spun in the churning foam, brandishing its tail and spewing water out through its mouth and nostrils. The vapour rose like steam; then it snapped its jaws and roared until the whole earth seemed to shake and tremble. Immediately from the opposite shore a rival splashed into the lake. Each moved swiftly towards the other, the lake boiling in their wakes. They met, their jaws clapped together and, folded in horrid wreaths, they sank out of sight. Tovar told himself it was time to leave, but his eyes had fastened upon the thick and coloured water, where they rose to the surface, their jaws popping like saplings snapped in a storm. Again they went down. Later the victor rose exulting to the scene of his triumph and the shores and the forest resounded to his dreadful roar. Cold sweat broke out on Tovar's forehead. Along the banks, where he had taken them for logs and brush, hundreds such creatures answered the champion's trumpeting. Suddenly Tovar understood the source of the thunder he had been hearing all afternoon.

He lost no more time. He turned his boat about. His battle

axe was behind him. He shifted it between his feet and paddled hard. He could hear the splashes as they dropped into the water to pursue him. Halfway to the mouth of the lagoon a large one dived under the boat. He took his axe and laid about him. Two others attacked more closely, at the same instant, rushing up with their heads and parts of their bodies upraised, roaring and belching buckets of water. Their jaws struck close to his ears. For a moment he felt stunned and swung the axe at random. It thumped against the brown-black armour and slowly the creatures withdrew, but everywhere in the water he could see long rows of white sharp teeth and above, lying far back along the upper jaw, two hard black glittering spots like stones in a setting. His only hope was to make for the bank. He paddled hard, they followed slowly, and when he next looked up, he saw the mouth of the lagoon.

Across it, in a solid line, the creatures waited. He crossed himself, said a prayer to his patron saint. He had drawn his boat close in to the bank. As it skimmed along, unexpectedly the creatures drew sluggishly out of his way, all but one that followed as far as the lake. There he felt free once again, but, still not trusting the open water, he kept close in to the bank. It was dark when he saw the glow of the fire and the boy standing down by the water.

"I thought you were lost," he said.

"I went further than I thought. Any fish left?"

"I ate all of the first one."

"The first one?"

"I've two ready for you. And four more I caught." He tried to disguise pride in his prowess.

"Good," Tovar said. "We'll eat tomorrow."

Flickering through the trees, the lights from the fires guided them towards the camp. They rode along in silence, with the pleasant feeling of lassitude which comes from eating after long hunger. Without urging, the horses moved faster and, drifting across the darkness, the low hum of many voices carried unevenly through the trees. "The army sounds in better spirits," Tovar said.

"It's great fun, isn't it, Don Nuño, conquering a new land?"

"Your spirits seem better, too. How's your hand?"

"Oh, it's fine."

For several moments there was only the sound of hoofs pressing the soft earth, and then the boy blurted out, "I knew you would find us something."

Tovar did not reply at once and when he spoke he said casually, "You know, you don't have to wait on me any more. I . . . I am not in a position to advance you."

"But I like waiting on you. Everybody says what a fine lance you are and what a pity . . ."

"Soon now," Tovar interrupted, "you'll be a lance yourself. Your exercises are improving. The first good ash I find, I'll turn it for you."

"Oh, will you?" He paused. "But I have no horse." His voice had lost all its joy.

"You ride one now."

"But she's yours."

"You can use her as long as I don't need her."

He could see the boy out of his eye, sitting eagerly forward. "I shall be a lancer."

"How old are you, Benito?"

"Fourteen, Señor. Well, almost fourteen."

"You will be the youngest lancer in the army."

"The youngest lancer . . ."

"And one of the best."

"Do you think so, Señor?"

"You've got a good wrist."

They had almost reached the plain. The watch challenged them. Tovar called out his name and rode forward. "They are making a lot of noise at camp," he said.

"Good news."

"Gold?"

"Almost. The Governor sent his secretary back for fourteen horses and the supply mules. He's found the roads broad and the way to Ocale open."

"That is good news."

"To celebrate the Camp Master has ordered a feast of the grain and beans seized this morning. That's what you hear. We leave before light tomorrow."

"Any Indians?"

"Ranjel says he was shot at on the way."

"How many?"

"He made light of it, but his horse was blown badly. Moscoso had to lend him one of his."

"And fourteen lancers for the Governor."

"That gives him twenty-four."

"Who went?"

"Only the toughest horses. Your friend Silvestre."

"Of course. He drew one of the best."

"What I wouldn't give for that pitch-colored chestnut," the sergeant said. "With the white left foot and the beautiful blaze on his forehead."

"We meet in Ocale."

"In Ocale."

But the morrow brought other things. The army set out and the men thought they had the spoil already in their hands, but their hopes were quickly dashed. Following the trail left by the Governor, not three hours out of Tocaste, they heard the Indians and before they could be located two men fell badly wounded and the horse which Don Carlos rode died under him. Moscoso threw the lancers out on every side and behind them the arquebusiers and crossbowmen at the run. He acted quickly and it was well he did. Otherwise the two couriers from the Governor might not have got through. With their horses let all the way out, they dashed by the wayward and it opened for them. The news they brought was disheartening. The Governor had found himself stopped by another arm of the same swamp. He was

[193]

trying to find an opening, but if he failed in this, he would have to turn about and look for trails towards the east. In the meanwhile Moscoso was to await further orders at Tocaste.

The army moved back in good order, with a screen of bowmen thrown around its flanks and squads of lancers in support. The Indians skirmished all the way to the cypress swamp, but at the crossing where all looked for dangerous work not a one was in sight and those who had been following at the heels of the Christians fell mysteriously away. Nor did the army run into any other trouble on the last half-league from the swamp to the town. But just where the trees opened out onto the savanna, the wayward drew itself up short and halted. Every eye was turned upon Tocaste. It was in flames.

8

Silvestre got down from his chestnut and looked out over the river. So this was the crossing, a way out of the swamp at last. Who would have thought help could come from the Indians they found fishing in the lake? It seemed too simple and easy. For a scarlet cap they had brought the Governor here. It was not a trick. Blown down by some storm, the two trees lay across the stream where the current was swift and deep. As the Indians described it, so it was. The dying sun twisted and turned with the river, twirled around the eddies, flowing into a narrow draw of the leafy cavern beyond. As he watched, the day burned out on the water. He turned away to take the bit out of the chestnut's mouth. Perhaps tonight the Governor would let them unsaddle their mounts. For two days and nights now the animals had travelled and stood by without taking off their furniture. And he would sleep, too, even if he hadn't eaten. Tomorrow they would cross. And then Ocale! There must be maize and beans, pumpkins ... treasure. Perhaps they would find a city with walls covered in gold as the Governor had found in Peru. At least there were golden casques. And if casques then ...

"Silvestre?"

"What?"

"The Governor wants you."

De Soto was sitting on an overblown tree. His two lean-bellied Irish hounds were at his feet, panting, their tongues hanging limp and moist out of the sides of their mouths. De Soto did not hear Silvestre approach. He was watching the face of the Indian Ortiz was questioning. Silvestre put himself where he would be noticed and listened to the soft tones of the strange tongue, as strange in Ortiz' mouth as in the Indian's. And yet the words must make sense: the emphasis and the gestures showed they had meaning, but it was like everything else in this wilderness: you could see it and hear it, but you couldn't understand it. Ortiz spoke the language but where was the man to make the mysterious, intangible thing it was intelligible to a Christian?

"As best as I can judge," Ortiz was saying, "there is an Ocale town called Uqueten about three or four leagues from here, on the other side of this river. The crops are good and ready for harvest, but when I speak of a yellow metal, he pleads ignorance."

"Food is what we most want now," the Governor said. "Put him in chains in case he is lying." And then the Governor saw Silvestre. "Ah, there you are."

"Yes, my lord."

"One of the best horses fell to your lot."

Silvestre bowed slightly.

"That means harder work for you."

"What falls to me I try to do."

De Soto let his eye run quickly over Silvestre's weapons, the joints of his armour, and at last came to rest in a full and steady gaze upon his face. "Our conquest and perhaps even our lives require that you return to Tocaste. Is your horse lame?"

"No, my lord."

"Do you think you can find your way?"

"I think so."

"I mean at night. You'll have a better chance to get through at night. The Indians won't attack the army, but they might try to harm two men."

"Two, my lord?"

"I'm going to let you choose a companion."

"When do we start?"

"If you hurry, you can pass out of these woods before dark." De Soto's voice made it sound easy, as if fatigue was a thing man could set aside at will, as if the roads were broad and open all the way and familiar as the King's highway, as if there were no twistings and turnings, hard enough to remember by day.... "And you will tell Luis de Moscoso what you have seen and order him to march here at once with the army. And after you have told him this, you will have him assign thirty lancers to guard you on the way back. I'll wait for you here until tomorrow night."

On the way to his horse Silvestre ran into Cacho. He was lying stretched out on his back at the foot of a tree. Near by the pack mules had been staked. Perhaps it was his utter look of comfort which made Silvestre pause. He looked at the esquire for a moment. "Get up," he said.

"Get up, hell!"

"We're going to Tocaste."

"Poor lad, hunger has gone to his wits."

"The Governor ordered me to take somebody with me. I take you."

Cacho sat up. He said angrily. "By your life, take somebody else. I'm tired and can't go."

"If you want to come, come. If you want to stay, stay. You won't lessen the danger or make it any easier."

Angrily Silvestre strode off and slipped the bridle into his horse's mouth, mounted and, without looking back, rode through the overhanging trees and struck the trail. After he had been five minutes on the way, Cacho cantered up behind him. "Why didn't you choose Vásquez? He likes to offer himself."

"I chose you because I love you," he said dryly.

"Well, I don't love you for it."

"And you can protect me."

"Do you suppose we'll run into Indians?" Cacho's voice was sober.

"It's their country."

Cacho did not reply to this and the two boys rode on in silence, at an easy canter, until they came out of the two leagues of thick and miry woods which bordered the swamps. It was well dark by this time, but the moon was rising. They had been travelling due west. Now they turned south, along the treeless plain out of which for the past two days de Soto had made his numerous sallies into the forest, only to be stopped each time by lakes and swamps. For once, Silvestre thought, if he felt fresher he would take pleasure in going straight across instead of always coming back to the invisible maze where one could wander forever. Whatever the Governor felt, and that no man knew, not once had he shown discouragement. Silvestre marvelled now that he thought of his lord. Each time they were thrown back on the plain, de Soto would take them a little further along, his eyes tearing at the forest, looking for the narrow break that would tell of a passage. Once or twice he had found a trail, but mostly the openings played out and the squadron had to cut its way with the axes. And the men riding always in silence or grunting as they struck at the vines which fell tangling their way. All day at intervals the Governor's voice would rise sharply, "Here's a trail." They would try it, turn back; there would be hours of silence and then again the voice, "There it is." And each time it came with a shock. Under this Governor's drive there was no rest for man or beast and the lancers followed out of pride until, from nowhere, in a place that seemed hopelessly bogged with marsh and water, the Indian boat drifted out of the reeds.

The slow canter was making him drowsy. He shook his head and fixed his eyes on a spot ahead, a blot of darkness, higher and sharper in line than the surrounding flat-topped growth. Slowly he approached, at a walk, at a canter, his eyes

[197]

blurring the spot into a pool, shaking his head to renew the focus, with Cacho behind and never speaking—perhaps he was asleep in the saddle—and the bush always the same distance away until at a certain moment it would grow to its right proportions, show its branches through the hazy light, stand exposed suddenly in all its parts—and suddenly, for seconds, he was fixed in time and place and the elusive plain drew to a point; then it was gone and he was looking before him for another marker. Five leagues, he judged, of this before the trail grew bad. If only they did not lose themselves in the swamp ahead they might come out at the crossing by dawn.

His legs and seat began to ache and he shifted to one side of the saddle, drawing his free leg up across the pommel. If only he could talk to Cacho, it would be easier to keep awake. No Indians would be abroad this time of night but he was afraid to take the chance. They made good targets as it was, for the moon, although it had a wide ring about it, was still bright enough to throw them into relief. The sound of the horses was lighter. Cacho's Zorruño was keeping up in perfect rhythm, or were his senses duller or . . . he turned. He was alone on the empty plain.

Carefully he forced his eyes upon every part of it. Cacho was nowhere in sight. More closely he searched again. He thought he saw a movement, a shake of a bush a hundred paces away. He put his lance in the socket of the rest and rode back, making a wide circle to come up from behind. He came closer . . . he pulled up and cursed long and hard. With one foot thrown out before him, Cacho leaned over in his saddle asleep. Zorruño was quietly grazing. Zorruño raised its head and nickered softly as he rode up. He took Cacho by the shoulders and shook him, slapped him awake. "You ride beside me from now on," he said.

"I couldn't help it."

"You've got to help it."

Silvestre's anger refreshed him and for the next quarter-league they rode at a canter but gradually the horses slowed to a walk and refused to respond to the spur. Perhaps he had been driving them too hard. He had better keep them at a walk the rest of the night and let them blow more often, for if on the morrow he and Cacho ran into trouble, their lives, the success of the conquest, would depend upon what Zorruño and Zapata could do. But if they could only go at a canter, he could keep off the drowsiness. The slow easy rock of the saddle made it harder. Already Cacho was nodding again. "Wake up, Cacho," he called under his breath.

Cacho shook his head. "Listen, Silvestre . . ."

"No."

"But just a thirty-minute rest."

"No."

"Ten minutes, then."

"Count the horse's steps. That will help."

Silvestre took his own advice. One, two, three, four . . . one hundred and one, two, three. It didn't help. His eyes had closed to slits. He must throw back his head. That would help keep them open and ease the draw in his neck. He shifted his leg again. Slow steps, steady steps of the hoofs, never breaking the rhythm, scarcely moving, the bushes rising, fading, rising, the even flow of the saddle, its low strain, the strained light of the moon in a white murk. That meant rain, and rain would keep them awake, but what would it do to the stream at the crossing and the slippery footing when the trail got bad? What was that distant rasping draw? He listened. It sounded like the hollow croaking of frogs. Frogs in the trees. He was hearing the deep forest and as he looked at its black front, he realized how nearly shut his eyes had been and how, in the struggle to hold on to his consciousness, time and space lay drowned, for the last league or two, in his will. He spoke to his horse. It walked a little faster and Zorruño, throwing his neck heavily forward, kept pace.

From out the forest the shadows swirled down upon his head, from the dark earth they turned upwards and at a point before his eyes narrowed to a twisting gyre. Drawn to its moving centre, pulled above and below, his head floated in parts, empty and swooning, and then lighter than air it hung suspended to nothing within the airless void, within the concave walls whirling within a whirl, drawing the outer dark into its private darkness, increasing until the furthest reaches of the night revolved on him as axis and all was motion and motion ended motion in a deep and pervading peace. The earth fell away, the heavens withdrew, and his eyes opened upon nothing and saw it was black and exquisitely restful. And then the darkness wavered, found depth, his eyes began to draw and focus. His heart twinged and rushed its beats—he was sitting his horse and the horse stood quietly at rest a few feet from the forest.

Near by he heard Cacho's voice. "Have you found the blaze?"

Dazed, Silvestre turned his head. Cacho, not ten paces away, was riding towards him. "I said did you find the blaze?" he repeated. "It's not back here."

"The blaze. Not yet." Hastily he said, "I think it's lower down."

He spurred Zapata and the animal stepped along the skirts of the forest and Silvestre looked for the tree where de Soto had made a wide mark with his axe. "It's a little out from the others, I remember," he called back and went towards a great oak standing apart on the plain.

It was the tree. A few paces to the west of it the trail began. In single file, Cacho riding behind, they entered upon the last three leagues of their journey. "How in God's name will we keep it?" Cacho asked. "I can't see a thing."

Zapata had dropped his head to the ground like a setter and he had to pull hard to make him raise it. They went along in silence until the horses began to snort and Zapata again pulled at the bridle. "What fools we are," Silvestre said in a loud whisper. "Give your horse his head. They know the path better than we."

He tried to remember the landmarks. The great cane

thicket. This they would be able to identify even at night. There was only one way through it, the way they had cut with their axes. Or the tree struck by lightning. But in between these marks it was easy to go astray. There was nothing for them to do but depend upon the intelligence of the animals. The Governor must have had this in mind when he picked Zapata. At the time Silvestre thought it was his own endurance the Governor had in mind, but he had been careful to choose not the right man but the right horse. He supposed he ought to take offense, but he felt only a great humility.

Not that endurance did not count for as much as intelligence. The Romero Zapata strain was known for its endurance. Its breed could go farther on less food and water than any other breed in Spain, except those animals bred by the Carthusian monks. They were as good, as loyal and gentle . . .

Zapata raised its head and snorted. Zorruño gave a low reply. "Do you hear anything, Cacho?"

"No," he replied gruffly but rode up beside him.

They kept silent for several minutes, turning their heads to the left, the direction from which had come whatever it was that disturbed the horses. There was no unusual sound. Only the tree frogs and a rain crow in the distance. Yet there had been something, for when they moved off, the horses went nervously. How long it was he had no way of knowing—he was kept busy dodging the low-hanging branches of the water oaks, couching his lance for caution and because it might snap against a tree—but at one certain spot he rode into the drum beat, the rapid, hollow rhythmic thudding and soon after a shrill half-muffled whoo-whoo-whoop of the death dance. He knew it at once. Ortiz had said there was no mistaking it.

The path curved towards the sound of the dance. As the drum and the yells grew louder, the horses trembled and increased their pace. There was no danger now of falling asleep in the saddle. At the dead tree he saw the firelight. The undergrowth was too thick to see the dancers, but they were within an arquebus shot and just as he and Cacho rode by, sparks leapt high and fell in showers through the thick black screen of trees and smoke. Dogs were barking. "They've got our scent, Cacho. We must run for it." He sank his spur into Zapata and the horse cantered briskly and Zorruño came up abreast and together they went past the encampment, rapidly through the open forest. Fortune was with them. They did not slow up until they reached the cane thicket.

"The savages mean trouble, Cacho," he said. "There's no telling how many more there are in these woods. Suppose we had slept."

Cacho mumbled under his breath, while they travelled slowly along the high wall of cane, trying to find the way through. It took longer than he had expected—the cane seemed to run for leagues and every moment it grew darker. In their flight they must have lost the way. Beyond the cane the crossing of the swamp was not more than a league or a league and a half away. He didn't remember exactly. It was hard to tell. The distance was always confused by the difficulties of the way. It might be farther. He began to think of what would happen if daylight caught them wandering. He could no longer concentrate. His wits began to scatter in panic ... and then Zapata snorted loudly. Zorruño trotted up beside him. Just before them there was a long corridor of lighter darkness. It gave. They had stumbled on the path.

He knew when he had passed through the cane by the change in the air, for there was no change in the light. Darkness had by this time overspread all things. He made no effort to see but let the horses take them forward, if forward it was. They crept along without spirit—he had only enough left to keep them moving. Zapata would stop and let out his breath, turn his head as if to say, "Let us rest, Señor." Each time it was harder to urge him forward. The air itself seemed drugged and he began to think that nothing in the world could be so luxurious as one long stretch upon the ground. He must not give in. No matter how little distance was covered it brought them that much closer to Tocaste. He thought of the gold waiting to be

[202]

looted. Gold, gold, he repeated the word. He could not remember what it was. He thought of a leg of beef. His appetite was gone.

"I can go no further." It was Cacho. His voice had a quality of desperation not to be denied. Silvestre wondered how he could speak so forcefully. "Either let me sleep" Cacho growled, "or kill me with a thrust. I am dying of sleep."

Silvestre lacked the will to protest. "All right," he said after a while. "Get down if you want the Indians to kill us."

He half saw, half heard Cacho fall to the ground and through the dark reached for Zorruño's bridle and found it. Cacho's lance fell across the saddle. He took it. Perhaps Cacho was right. A man can endure only so much. No danger could equal the present pain. But he must not fall asleep. He must set his mind and count slowly to a thousand and then he would arouse Cacho. With his lips he counted, by tens, five on the intake, five as his breath sped. It went slower and slower until each number drew out like a string of glue. He could hear the numbers dropping quietly among the leaves. They dropped faster and he counted faster to keep up with the drive of his will. A drop of water splashed on his hands, several drops. The leaves began to shake and rustle. Far away he heard thunder roll over the ground. He raised his head and took the rain full in his face.

After its first gusty violence it slackened off into a steady downpouring, streaming down his casque, running under his plates, drawing lines down his legs, warm loosening lines; and its monotonous drone made of itself a watery silence, enclosing him, secret, protective, shutting out all danger until slowly the aches of his body sped away, untying his shoulders, dropping his head upon his arms, crossed and upheld by the lances—only here the hands, frozen to the wood, resisted—and his will, joint by joint, dropped away from his skull. In dream-like lucidity, Peace, and again Peace said itself behind the still wet lips, the word as common as breath, no longer a word but a body to be heard, to be felt, to be understood. He had only to reach out to touch it. Suddenly like one who looks up from the mouth of a cave, he felt free from care and sorrow and his body fell away into rest.

When he awoke it was clear daylight. He opened his eyes but his senses delayed. The rain was over, the air soaking in spices at once heavy and light and in it the birds sang. In one long moment of wonder he looked out on this fresh new world. And then his senses leapt awake. He was wet and cold and Cacho lay in a heap on the ground. "Wake up," he called in a low command. "Wake up." Cacho did not hear. He took the butt-end of his lance and gave him several good strokes in the ribs. Cacho looked about him in angry surprise. Subdued and vibrant the full bass tones of a conch shell blew out of the swamp. Cacho got up quickly.

They rode about to find the trail, both now thoroughly awake. After some minutes they stumbled on several piles of droppings, took their direction and set out at a canter. At the border of the swamp the horses, as if they understood the necessity, barely lessened their speed. They leapt over the cypress knees, swung around the great roots, carrying their riders further into the grey-brown gloom. The conch shells came louder and closer, answering one another across the swamp. They followed like a pack of hounds. Suddenly Zapata shied and the arrow swished past his head. It struck a tree, hummed, grew into silence. Whooping barks jumped from the ground, but Silvestre saw no Indians. And then two heads, streaked in red and black, appeared above a cypress root. He saw the long steady draw of the bows, distinctly heard the twanging, the round hot cracking blow struck over his heart. He coughed. It was only a bruise, the flint head had broken on his plate. He couched his lance but the Indians stepped out of the way and disappeared. "Keep the trees to your back," he shouted to Cacho."

"Let's run them down."

"No."

If only now they could make it to the crossing, the water

would be a shield. Always shifting, he and Cacho kept the large flanged roots as cover. The arrows passed by on their flanks or lodged overhead in the trunks, sucking the air in their flight. Where the bottoms ran with water, the pace slackened. Twice Zapata slipped, but Silvestre brought him up in time. No other Indians drew close until he and Cacho reached the stream where they must pass over to the firmer ground, but here they closed in. There was no time to hunt the ford. As he plunged into the water, the canoes darted from among the reeds, long dugouts holding ten or twelve warriors each. Out of the corner of his eye he saw them, standing upright in the boats, paddling with a low rhythmic dipping and the fighters standing to loose their arrows. The woods and the water drummed with their yells of triumph.

"They think they've got us," Cacho whispered.

"There's no need to whisper," he shouted.

The arrows splashed and hummed in the water. One leapt across the surface to his front like a snake. Hissing, it struck; the feathers turned up and then it fell and floated gently, undulating with the wavelets. He heard another hit Cacho's plate.

"Lie down across Zorruño." Between Zapata's ears he saw them creeping through the brush, stealthily into the reeds on the other bank. There was no turning back. Lie close to the water and boldly thrust when the time came.

Zapata was rising up from the water; the reeds moved, he ducked. It struck Zapata's head guard, flew twisting over his shoulder. The horse stumbled with a splash. He called him fiercely, desperately, jerked the bridle. Lumbering, the animal at last got its feet. Thank God Zapata was only stunned. He heard Cacho shout, saw him thrust into the reeds and then he drew up beside him. "Don't stop, don't stop. Ride before the devil."

They fled through the broken woods, faster, faster, until shouts, Christian shouts—"Santiago and at them!"—hoarse, abandoned, mingled with the whoo-whoo-whoops, and the lancers appeared after their cries, sweeping the woods before them. Out in front rode Tovar, ten fathoms ahead of his companions. Who else had such a seat? Who else could make such a charge, handling his lance like a switch, whipping it around the trees, threading the air? He swept by and for an instant Silvestre saw the set, reflective eyes. Long seconds later the others passed.

Silvestre turned and followed at a walk. By their cries he could tell that the Indians were fleeing and halfway to the stream he met the cavalry returning. He could hear Cacho's voice telling how the arrows lay upon the water as thick as rushes on the streets of Seville at Easter. He pulled up and waited.

Tovar saw him and trotted up. "You almost got into a little trouble," he said.

The two men looked at each other and smiled.

"Take me to Moscoso," Silvestre said. "The Governor has found the crossing."

9

Moscoso set Tovar over the thirty. Two hours after dark they rode into the Governor's camp. It was deserted. At first Silvestre thought he had mistaken the place, but under the bright moon he could see the log bridge dark and plain in the water and the current drawing beneath and around it.

The Governor had said he would wait for him here. "I will wait," he had said and yet he was missing, gone, vanished. The thirty had drawn behind Silvestre to the river bank. He could feel their thoughts. They were thinking that he in his great fatigue had led them astray, but the bridge was there and where all was strange it stood forth like an old and familiar landmark. It was the Governor who had lost them in this wilderness. Had the Indians led him to this place to surround and take him? Now that he thought, they had appeared too easily, almost as if they had been waiting. Behind him the men were talking. Their voices were low and bespoke alarm, but with him there was no fear. He felt only a great and lifting exaltation. He had driven and subdued his flesh until it was as light as rotten wood. He knew now what had seemed so strange and fearful—that look of joy upon the faces of sainted men, coming from their fasts eaten with vermin and filth, who moved in the world and saw it not. He understood that Holy triumph in the wilderness, the forty days. How vain the world, and how false Satan's promise of pomp and riches! What mattered it if the Governor was lost or dead? What mattered it if the army perished? They were not lost but saved. He would disclose his revelation. It would bring the comfort the thirty now wanted and lacked. As he turned from the river bank, he heard Tovar;

"It's not the Governor's habit to tarry. He's gone ahead and tomorrow we'll find his trail. But I'll set a strong watch. The first watch of ten to remain mounted. The second watch of ten to sleep with their horses saddled and bridled, the third ten with bridles off to let the horses graze. Watches to change every two hours."

"There's no need for this," Silvestre said. His voice was high and clear. "I'll watch alone."

Tovar looked through the dark at his friend. After a pause he said quietly, "You will sleep."

"I have no need of sleep, or food, or drink. I have triumphed ..."

"You will sleep," Tovar repeated firmly, "and at once."

Silvestre heard the rapture of his words. "But listen. There's no need ever to sleep, or to eat, or ..."

Tovar walked over and took him by the arm. He said harshly, "You will stop talking and lie down." And then gently, "It is my command."

"You command it?" Silvestre's words wandered off into the night.

"I command it."

"Where?"

"Here by this tree."

"If you command it." Again his words wandered but he did not move. And then he felt the pressure on his arms and then the earth beneath. And then he felt nothing.

[207]

When Silvestre woke up, the thirty were preparing to move out of the swamp. The sounds of movement, the voices, told him. He lay upon his back unable to find the centre of his strength. The muscles in his body were as loose as strings. He must get up, he knew he must get up, but he could not find the will to stir. After a long while, he felt the old squeeze of hunger and slowly sat up. Some three hundred paces from the bank the bridge stood out of the mist. Tovar and ten of the men had stripped them of all their clothes, save for their daggers which they had strapped about their middles, and were lashing their own and the horses' gear to the saddles. Tovar swung his saddle to his head and stepped into the water. Walking carefully on account of the brush and hidden snares, the others followed one behind the other, the mist boiling around their naked waists, their shoulders, finally their necks; and then one by one they disappeared.

Silvestre got to his feet and anxiously watched the bridge. He tried to remember where the water ran deep, but his wits were still dull and heavy. At last, a few paces this side of the bridge he saw the saddle rise and float upon the mist, Tovar's head rise and float and then his naked, glistening body. He stepped up the slippery tree and walked along it, balancing the saddle with one hand, holding to the balustrade with the other. Midway he paused and looked towards the far bank and then went on. Where the bridge ended, he slipped down into the water and again the mist swallowed him. Gradually the rest of the detail climbed up and their graceless bodies clambered unsurely along, all dignity and confidence gone. Were these the same men, the riders of skill and courage, his companions of yesterday? Was a Christian one thing in clothes and another without? And why did he, Silvestre, feel shame as though he watched a procession of gelded men? He felt no disgust at sight of an Indian, no strangeness before their exposure after the first strangeness of seeing them. Suddenly he realized he had watched Tovar as he might watch an Indian.

He grew restless waiting for some signal from the other

bank. The detail had had plenty of time to cross. Had the current washed them down? Ambush? He would have heard
cries, unless the Indians had seized them one by one as they
stepped out of the misty water. He looked at his companions.
They were silent and looked gravely before them. The wait
was growing interminable. He was about to speak and suggest
that they do something, what he didn't know, when Tovar's
strong clear voice came from the other side—all was clear; send
over the next detail.

Quickly the second watch took off their clothes and entered
the stream, each man with two lances slung over his back. They
seemed to Silvestre to pass over in less time, shouting back to try
one horse. By now the mist had burned away and showed the
dangerous pull of the current. After a short discussion among
those who were left, the fattest and strongest of the horses was
driven in. All went well as far as the bridge. There she struck
the current and instead of swimming with it began to fight. A
weaker, less spirited animal would have let herself be washed to
shore lower down, but Amarilla's roan saw her master and tried
to reach him. For a while she held her own, until she lost her
head, turned and began swimming or trying to swim upstream.
At first she made headway but soon lost ground. There was
nothing to do, only if the men on the other side would stop
shouting she might recover her head. Hard work and little to
eat gave her no chance. Silvestre waited and his companions
waited until the current took the gallant mare and sucked her
under. Once she came to the surface, struggling feebly, and
then she went down and out of sight.

Silvestre looked at the spot where she had gone down and
said, "Well, let's tie the ropes together. We've got to pull them
across."

Three hours later the last of the men and horses were over,
with the dismal swamp behind them, at last under way, over a
plain trail, marked by hoof marks and droppings from the
Governor's horse. These signs gave odds that all was well. The
Governor was safe. Perhaps even now the spoils of Ocale lay to

his hands. In double file the thirty cantered through the open woods. At the end of two leagues mulberry and walnut showed through the pine, signs of a richer country. Silvestre rode at Tovar's side, their animals beating in rhythm, the mild warm air in their faces, and suddenly all the bad hard trails, the hunger and despair, his false exaltation, the confusion of lost unknown places, the sleeplessness and fatigue he had known seemed, all at once, never to have been.

"I feel drunk and yet not drunk," he said.

"That's the joyful stage of fasting," Tovar replied.

As the sun climbed between eleven and noon, the thirty rode out of the forest into a rolling valley and before their famished eyes maize fields appeared, dark green and dusty with ripeness. They gave a lusty shout and galloped down upon them. Shouts answered and coming through a lane dividing the fields they saw the Governor's Aceituno, the Governor astride and raising his hand in salute. In a few minutes he was up beside them.

"Welcome to Uqueten," he said. "There is plenty for all. I've had bread cooked and ears roasted, but first you must attend to your horses." He singled out Silvestre. "Well done."

"Gold?" one of the lancers asked.

"Ocale is further on. Be careful you don't founder your horses."

The lancers turned off into the fields and riding through them gathered the maize into their sacks. It was a good harvest, three and four ears to the stalk. They came into Uqueten loaded down. Great heaps of maize lay in the yard among piles of cobs and shucks, and all about the Governor's men sat shelling the grain. But they arose and met their comrades and helped them with their gear and showed them where to tie up for feeding. After this was done de Soto took the men before a house where two Indians were pounding out maize in log mortars. "Spies," he said. "I found them lurking in the fields and rode them down."

Silvestre felt the saliva rush into his mouth. In front of the house lay stacks of bread, piled high in earthen platters. "First to you, Silvestre," the Governor said and handed him three pones as large as plates. "Two for you, Tovar, and all the rest of you. In those pots are roasted ears. Take four apiece for the march. The devil is in his gut who asks for more."

Hands trembled as they reached for their portions and Silvestre felt the tears start to his eyes and then he sat on the ground, nor did he look up until he had filled his emptiness. Then, feeling an overwhelming thirst, he asked for water. The spring was in a clump of trees and he and Tovar went there to drink. For a while they lay on the ground full length, at rest. Perhaps they dozed, for when they returned to Uqueten the pack mules had been loaded with sacks of grain and fourteen riders mounted and in their harness. De Soto was giving final instructions. "Now when you reach the swamp, make the army cross over to you. The sight of food will give them speed and courage."

The succour came in good time, for those who went as guards found the army weak and scattered, eating herbs and roots and, what was worse, without any man knowing what he ate. Tuesday the last of the stragglers arrived at Uqueten. Some who had strayed were wounded and a crossbowman named Mendoza was slain, but the supplies sent by the Governor had revived their energy and at Uqueten each man and beast had his fill. The fields were stripped, the stalks cut for fodder and when the bread gave out, men ate the raw ear or hastily roasted it. After a short rest the Governor ordered the march to proceed towards Ocale, the land of hope and promise. The weak and unfit were left behind with ten horses too blown to travel, with orders to follow on the morrow.

Tovar and Silvestre rode with the wayward. This was de Soto's way of tacitly recognizing Tovar's quick and successful manner of crossing the swamp, but he made no direct reference to it, nor did Tovar go as a captain; yet the place of honour was at the front and Silvestre felt that perhaps his friend would soon again be in the Governor's favour. Refreshed by food and rest, the horses went at a good pace and the men, eager to reach their goal, pushed them along. On this same day, Tuesday, July 29, with the two Indians taken at Uqueten for guides, the army came to a town of some ten houses with one, obviously the cacique's dwelling, larger than the rest, set at the end of a square. The town was abandoned. Fields of maize grew about and there were several hanegas of last year's crop still in the barbacoas, jars of beans and two deerskins of bear oil. Fourteen small dogs ran about the yard and these the men quickly caught and killed, for they had had no meat since leaving the Port. The eastern face of the cacique's dwelling opened on a portico. The poles which held it up were round and highly polished. Some were painted red, some yellow, and some a blue Silvestre had never seen. He dismounted and walked inside. Benches ran along the walls and at the far end a platform extended into the open room. It was covered with moss and over this moss lay a hide, pricked and coloured and very soft to touch. The ashes of the fire in the middle of the floor were still warm.

Tovar was studying the markings on one of the poles in the portico. The Governor, Añasco, Ortiz, and the two Indians were grouped together in the town yard. The Indians were talking, Ortiz listening, and the Governor watched impatiently.

"Have you heard the name of this town?" Silvestre asked.

Tovar did not reply but ran his hand over the smooth coloured post.

"Suppose we'll make camp or go on to Ocale?" Silvestre continued.

Tovar turned and looked squarely at his friend.

"This is Ocale," he said.

5

APALACHE

Apalache

ORTIZ stood in the yard of Ocale and looked towards the forest. On one side it was open but towards Acuera the trees grew close and from the ground to the tops of the water oaks the long grey moss covered the branches, tangled in the undergrowth which crowded through the long wide arms of the oaks. Only in the very tops of the highest trees did it blow freely and there the dry grey streamers hung motionless or, moving slightly, shifted the still and heavy air. In that direction Espindola had gone four days ago to gather the crops of Acuera. He had had time to go and return. Perhaps there was no cause for worry, but Ortiz remembered with concern the speech and bearing of the cacique as he refused the Governor's offer of peace. Ortiz had gone out in the usual way, with a pine branch in his hands, to Ocale's temporary quarters in the forest. After he had delivered the presents and told who de Soto was, he made the demands of service. Ocale had listened to the end of his talk and then rose to reply. When the cacique stood and his people stood, Ortiz knew that the overtures of peace were about to be rejected. Ocale did not conceal his contempt. . . . "The Master of Breath has hung war on the sky. So be it. I will not stand about with shamed face, so be it, so be it, now that the Master of Breath puts the red sticks down. You tell me the cacique Pope has given my land and my people to a cacique you serve and who lives across a great pond. This Pope must be a fool to give what is not his and you must be fools to make war for another. I devote you all to death. You have no women, so you cannot breed. I will take your hair and you will be no more. So be it."

After Ortiz had returned and reported the failure of the negotiations, the Governor ordered the men not to wander from camp. He doubled the wood details and due to these precautions Ocale had taken no hair, but every movement of troops, every disposition in the camp was watched by day and night. The woods were covered with tracks of bear and panther. They turned and twisted in the right way, but Ortiz knew they had not been made by animals. The Indians were waiting for some careless slip. Perhaps Espindola had made this slip.

He looked once more at the surrounding forest and decided he might risk taking off his armour. He couldn't hear well for the smiths beating out shoes, but the woods felt all right. The birds showed no sign of alarm, the afternoon sun was hot, his plates heavy, and it was not the time of day for mischief.

He walked down the slope towards the spring in the bottom of the glade. It was a pleasant site. He could understand why the Indians were loath to give it up. He had tried to tell Ocale the Christians were only passing through, but he lacked the words to convince him. How could he explain to Ocale that his beloved town had sorely disappointed the army or that the Governor thought only of Apalache? Apalache, where Narváez had come to grief.

"A beautiful pool of water, Ortiz."

"It is indeed, Father."

He saluted the priest and looked down at the fountain. It boiled from its white sandy bottom, swelling and turning in all its clearness, throwing up sand and particles of shell with the water, casting them away from the jet in the centre, rolling them, making them sparkle until they sank gently, scattered through the pool, settling slowly about the bands of fish.

"One can see the bottom. How clear it is." Father Francisco spoke without lifting his head. "Almost one could reach and touch the eyes of that crockadile."

"He must be twenty feet below the surface, Father."

"Of course. And the varieties of fish. All swimming together in innocence as they did before the Fall."

[216]

"But they are not innocent. Fish are like Indians. They kill only when there is no danger to themselves. The pool is too clear for stratagem."

"Is the Governor worried about his halberdiers?" the priest asked suddenly and looked apprehensively towards the east. "Father Luis went with Espindola to Acuera."

"He thinks only of Apalache," Ortiz replied.

"Apalache," the priest said with annoyance. "I fear it will be like all these other provinces. Great toil ending in disappointment." He sighed. "God keep us."

Ortiz watched him walk up the slope to the town yard and then looked again into the pool. He counted the different bands of fish—gar, trout, flounder, catfish and skate, sheepshead, spotted bass and the ominous drum passing and repassing one another in the transparent fountain, as harmless as butterflies. He watched them float to the surface or sink to the bottom of the pool, growing smaller and smaller until they disappeared, to reappear on the other side no bigger than flies, gradually emerging as out of another world, growing before his eyes until on the instant they leapt to their proper size and shape. Others rose more gently, on their sides, upright, or at an angle, floating to the top to diverge and find their kind, and they swam together diving and rising in a perpetual pageantry.

"Looking for treasure, Señor?"

Ortiz raised his head. The sword-and-buckler had come up to his side, a small wiry man dressed in a habit of a sad colour. Ortiz regarded him a moment, then said, "I was looking at the fish."

"Why do you lower your head?"

"You are melancholy."

"Señor, to lose a fortune makes one melancholy."

"You are too easily discouraged."

The man shook his head. "Soon now I shall lose my life." He added quickly, "Not that I fear death. But to come so far to die and on so poor a venture. It is this thought which makes me melancholy."

"Who can number his days?" Ortiz asked.

"I have a premonition."

They stood in silence awhile. The man's words had struck Ortiz, had released a feeling of uneasiness lurking behind his own mind all day. To come so far to die. It was not death which troubled his head. With him it was another thing. He turned abruptly from the fountain and walked away. Under the arbour made for the beloved old men of Ocale the captains off duty had gathered. He joined them. As he came up, Moscoso was saying, "Throw the dice for it."

"There are no riches there," Lobillo said. "Narváez would have found them."

"There may not be but the Governor is going to Apalache and he wants a bridge built over the river."

Gaytán spoke up. "He'll have to come back. Don't you think he'll have to come back?"

"It doesn't matter what I think," Moscoso replied. "Throw for who builds the bridge and who goes with him."

"The land has proved barren," Maldonado said in his heavy voice, "but who can tell what lies to the north of us? I'll go with the advance and command the foot. You stay and build the bridge, Lobillo."

"No, I'll throw for it," Lobillo said haughtily.

"No offense, Captain. You didn't seem anxious."

"I can eat as little as any other man or stand as much. I was saying it's plain what this country is."

"What horse goes?" Vasconcelos asked.

"There's enough food here to take us back to Port," Gaytán said irrelevantly.

"Fifty horse and a hundred foot," Añasco said, coming up. "I have just come from the Governor's quarters."

"The army stays here where there is food. There's no recklessness in that." Biedma spoke for the first time.

"Who spoke of recklessness?" the Constable asked.

"I understood Moscoso . . ."

"I didn't say the advance to Apalache was reckless, Señor,"

[218]

Moscoso said quickly. "But I will be plain. I will tell you what I told the Governor. We march to Apalache. Well and good. The Indians say there is much maize there. They also say the Apalachians are great fighters and very jealous of their land. Very well. We go there and what do we find? Probably no more food than we found here. Barely enough to last the army a month, unless the halberdiers discover much at Acuera."

"And winter is before us," Gaytán added.

"What do you think we should do?" Tinoco asked sharply.

"I think what I think. It is the Governor's place to command and ours to obey. He orders me to Apalache. I go to Apalache."

"I think the Governor has sunk his fortune in this discovery. That's what I think," Gaytán said with a stiff smile.

"What do you mean, Señor?" Tinoco asked truculently.

"I mean nothing."

Tinoco stepped forward. "Do you impute ignoble motives to my cousin, your lord?"

"I am the King's officer."

"He is the Adelantado, both your civil and military lord."

Gaytán was standing, his hand on his sword. Moscoso stepped quickly forward. "This is unseemly," he said. "I order you both to your quarters." Slowly the two men dropped their hands to their sides. "Unless you can discuss these affairs with civil tongues."

Silence fell over the group and the captains refrained from looking at one another in fear of discovering the mark of shame on a companion's face. Maldonado reached into his purse and brought forth his dice. "Throw, Lobillo," he said with forced heartiness. Lobillo took the dice and shook them in his large hands, his hands opened and they scattered over the white sand floor. In relief the captains gathered around. Kneeling, Lobillo swept them up and gave them to Maldonado. Lobillo had made them rattle with his quick nervous shakes, Maldonado made one wide low shake and they fell in a heap at his feet. "You see, Lobillo, they obey me. It is an art to call your fortune."

[219]

"Which do you choose?" Lobillo asked, looking up from the ground.

Maldonado paused for an instant, looking at the younger man. "I go with the Governor," he said.

"Then it is arranged," Moscoso said. "You will build the bridge, Lobillo."

"Señors, look!"

Ortiz was pointing to the forest where it screened the trail to Acuera. Still but alert, the captains sent their eyes scurrying, darting, straining at the depths behind the trees. Moscoso looked stubbornly at Ortiz. "What is it?" he asked.

"Not on the ground. Higher."

"Where? Where?"

"There!" Ortiz pointed.

And then he could feel their eyes, blurred by surprise, grow sharp. By the quality of the silence he could tell they saw the halberdiers. Three of them swinging from the topmost branches of the water oaks. The bloody trunks hung like meat, the arms and legs dangling above and below, here an arm tied to a leg, there a fist thrust between the moss. The three heads swung alone on lower limbs and from under their chins the moss fell like beards. Two of the heads fell over as in sleep while one looked before in endless gaze and out of the hole between the lips blew the little black flies. It was here, where the stillness bred such a motion, that all eyes came to focus.

"Who's on watch in that quarter?" the Constable asked in fury.

Moscoso was hurrying away from the arbour, the captains scattering to their horses, some on the run, some half-walking, looking over their shoulders at Ocale's vengeance. Not until all had fled the arbour did they cry, To arms.

The woods were searched for Indians but none was found, nor did the camp settle down until dark when Espindola returned and reported the loss of the men, slain in the fields at Acuera. The small amount of maize found at Acuera forbade any further thoughts of wintering at Ocale and the Governor pushed the preparations for his advance and on the following morning set out with his horse and foot.

When Espindola reported no other losses, the death of the halberdiers was accepted apparently by the army as an unfortunate but unavoidable casualty, but the sight of the quartered bodies remained with Ortiz many days. He carried it with him as he went with the Governor. It returned in idle moments, although the march was so swift and bold there were few of these. It was not the simple violence of the image which made it cling to his mind. It was rather his own shifting attitude towards this violence. In the usual Indian wars when a party sets out to quench crying blood with blood, to take hair is enough, for then the beloved spirit of the dead may be allowed to rest. Often after such a foray the friend-knot is retied and the path made white. But when the danger is great or the insult insupportable, hair is not enough. Only the severed body or bodies divided up and brought into camp will requite the injured party. What other thing could show so full a vengeance or so great virtue in the war leader and his waiter, or the purity of the holy fire—unless it was to refuse to dance in triumph about the objects of triumph and hang them in broad light of day before the dull eyes of a contemptible enemy. This was the final, supreme and beautiful achievement of contempt.

So had he felt that afternoon in Ocale as he lifted his eyes to the trees. The captains dicing for their parts in the conquest had seemed ignoble and helpless before the daring and secrecy of their enemy. He could not then feel with them the shock of the act, their anger and hidden fear. But now, seven days out of Ocale, his sympathy and understanding had changed, with the Indians of the abandoned towns following, drawing closer in to the column and no sign of Apalache or of the Governor letting up in his search, with the main army far behind and the fifty horse and foot surrounded by people waiting to scalp and defile their bodies. He could read this thought in the eyes of all and he understood. Not that the men feared to die or lacked courage. What they lacked was belief in the conquest. It was

[221]

this which kept the outrage to the three halberdiers always before their minds, the grotesque exposure of severed arms and legs, an arm snatched from its socket and tied unnaturally to a leg, or another as unnaturally alone. There was the violence and the horror. But why? Was it because, stunned by the sight, the Christians could no longer evade the shame of their flesh which they hid so carefully, even from themselves?

Was it this or was it fear of a thing which they could not grip? They had been surprised and their power and pride openly mocked. And this at a time when they could show nothing for all their toil and danger. If treasure there was, it grew each day more elusive and each day the memory of Narváez more clear. The Indians never closed, yet they always threatened. Even the twenty men and women taken by Añasco at Bad Peace had eluded their captors by a stratagem, though the false chief fleeing had been thrown by a hound and held until he was taken again. Shorn of his ears and hands he had been set free, but this act did not restore the captives. The men were saying—he had heard them—Nothing in this land holds.

2

How deep in the land they were. Ortiz recalled the towns, Itaraholata, where an Indian crowded up to Maldonado to wound his horse and would have snatched the lance from his hands had not the Governor by chance come up, although Maldonado was a good knight and one of the best men in the army; Utinamocharra, Bad Peace, Cholupaha which they called the Town of Surfeit from the abundance of food, dried chestnuts and sweet wild ones, maize and beans and squash. And now this town they had left reluctantly, at a slow pace, the foot loaded with bags of maize strapped to their backs, the horse with a double share of grain behind the saddles.

The river they must cross was not far but it took too long to reach it. The officers spoke sharply but the men did not hurry. They kept their heads sullenly down, plodding along, and when they saw the river they stood about and stared at it.

It was out of its banks, the current swift and muddy. Some-where above there had been heavy rains. The Governor gave orders for pines to be felled and then took his engineer to find the best place to throw a bridge. The men went to work on the trees without spirit; the day was hot and sultry humours rose from the earth. When a tree fell close to a crew of cutters, barely missing them, they dropped their saws and drew their daggers. Maldonado had to ride between to prevent a fight. Not hearing the saws, the Governor came up to find what the delay was about. Harsh words were passing. "What is this, men?" he asked. One of the cutters spoke up, "It's not enough that we go through the same woods to nothing but they try to kill us."

"We cut the pine and it fell."

The Governor looked from man to man. "Get on with your work and watch what you are doing."

The men did not stir. Juan Gaytán had been leaning against a tree. He stepped forward and the twigs snapped sharply be-neath his boots. "Excellency?"

"Yes?"

"We are many days out of Ocale." He paused.

"Well?"

"There's no sign of Apalache."

"It's in front of us."

"Like the golden casques of Ocale?"

De Soto regarded the Treasurer with contempt. By now, sensing the emergency, almost the entire body of horse and foot had gathered in the woods. As the Governor turned away, he looked at first with surprise upon his men as they drew around him. Some dropped their eyes, others returned his gaze, but it was plain that all, or almost all, shared the Treasurer's views. The Governor showed no haste. He sat erect, isolated by the silence, his bridle hand jerking with the restless movement of the horse's head. And then when it seemed that he would never speak, he said evenly, "Surely, Señores, you are not asking to turn back your steps."

"Not I," Añasco blurted out, as though all that time he had

[223]

held in his breath; then he said more calmly, "But I think the men would feel better if you ordered the army to join us."

The Governor sat slightly back in his saddle. "Let that not disturb you," he said with a trace of impatience. "I'll order it forward when I find supplies enough to feed it. I have hopes of Aguacalaquen. The guide says it is a large town one day from here."

There came a pause.

"There's no gold in this country, Excellency."

The Governor leaned forward until he located the man who had spoken. It was a sergeant of foot. "You have lost too much salt, sir," he said briefly. And then he laid his lance across the saddle and folded his hands on the pommel. "I never promised you more than sweet liquors out of the hard flint. I can't even promise you that. The hard flint, yes—long toilsome days and watchful nights and a Lent sharper than ever His Holiness enjoined. But remember this. After every fast there comes a feasting." He took his lance deliberately and tightened his grip on the handle. "Captain Maldonado, you will hurry with the timber. We must lay the bridge today." With that he turned and rode away.

The River of Discords was crossed with as much labour as the stream before Ocale but by Monday, August 18, the Governor brought his men into Aguacalaquen. Like the other towns it was abandoned, but there was one important difference. Forewarned, the Indians had gathered their crops and hidden them. This discovery promised to postpone the bringing up of the army, another precarious movement forward, and with now two rivers between the advance and the main body. That night in the lodges of the town there was open discussion of the Governor's dilemma. Would he order the army to come up anyway, through a ravaged country, and take the risk of finding provisions further on, take the risk of choosing blindly the right trail to Apalache, or would the present circumstances force him to return while there was some food left? After his words at the river none looked for the prudent course.

What appeared to all as his stubborn and wanton recklessness seemed to be justified when on the following day Ranjel, his secretary, and Villalobos took a man and woman in the maize fields. The woman showed where the grain was hidden and the man disclosed the hiding place of seventeen people belonging to the town. When Gallegos brought these into camp it was found that he had taken the daughter of the cacique. The girl was used to force her father to come in. The cacique would have liked to free her without placing himself at the mercy of the Christians and, as at Bad Peace, sent in his stead a slave, but the woman exposed the ruse. Ortiz discovered that the woman and man were of the same fire and had polluted that fire by sleeping together. As this was a crime punishable by death, the two Indians were as anxious as the Governor to move on. With their help Aguacalaquen finally gave himself up but not until the fourth day of negotiations and then only when his daughter was brought into plain view of the woods, with the hounds straining at their leashes to rend her. An Indian with the rank of Little Trailer came first, blowing on his flute, and after him Aguacalaquen walked alone, his body smeared with white clay, swan's down on his head and in his hands green pine branches for a sign of peace. To the ball ground he came where the Governor waited and there Ortiz stepped forward and grasped his wrist, his elbow, and his arm near the heart. The Governor did the same and then Aguacalaquen spoke. "What do you want of me?"

They sat upon the ground under a great oak to confer, the Governor upon his chair facing the Indian, watching him carefully as Ortiz opened the conversation. The officers and men gathered around in a circle, listening as the cacique and Guatutima, a man of rank taken with the seventeen, told of the country beyond. The Christians showed little patience during the long hours of talk. They shifted from place to place or walked away during the long pauses the Indians kept to outface their captors. A man who had been leaning over the shoulders of his companions would turn after a break longer than usual and push

[225]

through the crowd, so that it stirred restlessly, or another would make his way to the rim of the circle and stare, turning and jerking his head. At such times a red film clouded for an instant the cacique's eyes, but only by this did Aguacalaquen show his contempt for his enemies.

The Governor's indifference matched that of the Indians. Often he would sit for half an hour between questions, never moving, staring before him, and when the name of a town such as Uriutina or Napituca would be mentioned, he would deliberately and with great skill shift the talk and not ask specific questions until the following day and then casually, as if the questions were of little importance. Not until the twenty-second of August did he broach the subject of Apalache directly.

By then even Ortiz, accustomed to such matters, felt weariness at the game and all showed alarm, for the woods round about, perhaps from some signal of Aguacalaquen's, thronged with Indians. Moscoso doubled the watch and took other precautions against surprise and on several occasions the captains pressed the Governor to send for the army. Each time he nodded abstractedly without giving satisfaction and returned his attention to the council, as though he meant to sit down in the town all fall. After the last appeal, made by Añasco, he said, "Soon now," and took his sword and made the sign of the Cross in the loose earth at his feet. He raised his eyes and asked negligently, "After Uriutina and Napituca how many towns to Apalache?"

The question was never answered. Guatutima and the cacique drew back as from a blow, spoke rapidly together, looking over their shoulders into the tree above them. They stood up and withdrew in haste ten paces from the council ground. Ortiz followed quietly. Not until he was free of the overhanging arms of the oak did he stop. He had heard the bird but not until the Indian's alarm did he take in what bird it was. Quickly he collected himself and faced the Governor. He had not moved and was looking towards Ortiz for an explanation.

"The bird, Excellency. It lighted in the tree."

De Soto made a movement of his head but he restrained

[226]

himself and did not look up. Not so the men. They were all straining to see and the word *bird, bird,* travelled to the back of the crowd.

"Bird?" the Governor asked incredulously. "Why did they flee a bird?"

"It is the Kind Ill Messenger."

"Well?" The Governor frowned.

"It warns of disaster. The Indians regard it with awe as you have seen. I've known war parties at its song to break up and return to their towns."

A light came into the Governor's eyes. "Good. Tell Aguacalaquen the bird threatens him because his words are crooked. Tell him quickly before it flies away and then ask him all I want to know about Apalache."

Ortiz spoke standing and when he was done Aguacalaquen replied that it was not to him but to his, Ortiz' cacique, the Kind Ill Messenger brought warning. He had not twisted his tongue but spoke straight. It was well known among all the tribes that Apalache had strong bold warriors and many towns and long fields of maize, for it was a rich land. And it was in Apalache that others like themselves had gone and found the truth of his words. The people of Apalache drove them away and on the shore of the big water these other strangers killed their deer and made large piraguas and sailed away.

Ortiz only half-listened to the Indian's words. He was thinking of that sword-and-buckler back in Ocale, the man's deep sense of depression, far out of proportion to the disappointment of the common hope in treasure. And now the Kind Ill Messenger had brought to a head his own feeling of futility and dread. It was only a bird, he knew the priests if he confessed his distress would say he was possessed and exorcise the evil spirit; and yet he could not dismiss it. He had been too long with the Indians, and it had not come to sing its warning until the mention of Apalache, that place of disaster to Christians which indirectly had cast him away for twelve years in this land. Would it again lose him? Had he come so close to escape not to escape? Would this Governor lead him to riches or to the deep places of Florida, where he must give up forever his Christian nature and make himself into an Indian? A young man can forget his birth and his name, take on strange habits and a strange way of living, but he was no longer a youth. This shifting of knowledge, this double nature, it was not a good thing to think about. Nor the restless moving, ever deeper into the interior, ever further away, and with each league's travel no closer to the end of travel . . . following at the behest of this Governor. What did he seek with his long-sighted eyes? Gold? He had found gold in Peru. Does a man risk a fortune gained through untold hardships and at the cost of his youth to find a greater? Perhaps. But so great a fortune?

But whatever the secret need which brought de Soto here there was no doubt about his men. They had come for gold. And he had never seen or heard of gold in all his twelve years in the land. Traders went great distances with their wares of shell, arrowheads, salt and pearls. If there was gold, they would have traded in it, for it had a lustre suitable for gorgets and bracelets, though not so beautiful as mother of pearl . . .

"Well, what did he say?" De Soto's voice was impatient.

Ortiz looked up. Aguacalaquen no longer spoke. He stood by Guatutima, silently regarding Ortiz, all his composure now restored. Ortiz turned away and in that moment he met the faces of the Christians. Suddenly he understood his power. He hesitated only a moment and then made his decision. His voice was calm, his gaze steady. "Excellency," he said, "the Indian replies that the Kind Ill Messenger comes with a warning, not for him, but for you. He says that others like us went to Apalache but did not stay because there was no road over which to go forward, nor any other towns beyond the dwellings of the Apalachians, for on all sides there is water."

The silence was oppressive as de Soto rose to his feet. Without looking at the Indians he said, "Take them away and see that they are guarded well. Añasco?"

"Yes, Excellency?"

"Choose eight men and take word to Moscoso to bring the army forward."

The Governor took a step to go to his quarters but the men surrounded him. They came close about, yet they kept a respectful distance and all showed how depressed their minds were at the information, and all, both officers and men, counselled the Governor to return to the Port that they might not be lost, and to leave this land of Florida.

De Soto let each man have his say and when they were done, he spoke.

"These things appear to me incredible," he said. "Nor will I return until I have seen with my own eyes what these Indians report." He raised his voice slightly. "In the meanwhile be in readiness for the saddle."

3

The Governor left the camp in charge of Maldonado as a rebuke to his men for their lack of faith and escorted Añasco and his eight guards as far as the River of Discords. As it was late in the day when he set out, he left word not to expect him back until the following day. The camp settled down in gloom and in fear, for its strength had been reduced by eighteen men and these among the best lancers in the army, the Governor taking ten with him to make sure of the crossing. When night fell, Maldonado set the watch doubly strong, both of horse and foot, and the men drew together about the fire in the town yard as though loath to separate and there they sat with little talk.

Ortiz withdrew to himself. He felt he must adjust himself to the failure of his ruse. It had not worked. He had seized the one moment when it had seemed possible for him to force events to do the bidding of his private will, but a stronger will had prevailed. Now for good or ill his fortunes were bound to the conquest. Indeed they were bound to one man. Hope of escape, even hope of riches, now drew all of his wit and skill to the furtherance of this man's purpose. Who was this man, what was he, blind chance had thrown in his way? Could de Soto compel all this emptiness to be filled with his desire? Ortiz raised his eyes with their dark speculations to the dark forest lying spread about, how far no man knew, beneath the stillness of the night, and as he looked he discovered that his gaze had stopped upon a figure half in shadow, half in the light of the fire. He knew the man slightly. He had been pointed out as a former friend of de Soto's, his second in command until broken in Cuba over a love affair. Tovar. Yes, Nuño de Tovar, that was the name.

Ortiz studied him a moment as Tovar faced the men in the silence his rise had caused. With his legs apart, his waist two hands might span, and the long body rising to the deep chest and shoulders, he had somewhat the frame of a giant hourglass. The head sat well above the shoulders, not too large or too small. The oval-shaped face had a bare look, as if the features did not quite fill it up. As he looked more closely, Ortiz saw that this very exposure concealed the man better than a mask, for by some trick of nature each feature was set apart, forcing a separate regard, so that one did not look at the face but at the broken nose, the high brows, the large eyes beneath, protruding under the lids in a kind of sensual arrogance.

Tovar took a step nearer the fire. In the very movement of his body there was irony. He said, "What did you expect when you signed on for this conquest?"

After a long pause a voice said from beyond the fire, "Another Peru, not these forest deserts."

"Peru," Tovar answered, mocking the word. "What do you know of Peru?" he asked and paused, looking in the direction from which the voice had come. Silence greeted his question. He continued, "The first province we found in that land was so poor the Inca levied upon it a tribute of lice. The inhabitants were little better than the beasts of their forests. They screamed like cats and were given over to the abominable crime. Nothing did we find there but misery. A new and strange disease consumed us like rotten sheep. It struck the lancer from his saddle, or it fell quietly in the night, so that by morning the sick were too weak to lift hand to mouth. It came as a swelling on the face and head, or like warts on the body, the colour of ripe figs, about the bigness of figs, hanging from a string and flowing with quantities of blood. For seven months the army lay stricken." He paused deliberately. "So did we enter on the trail which led to the Inca's gold."

"Do you expect, Señor," the voice said, slipping into the night, "so fortunate an end for us?"

Tovar seemed not to hear the voice. He stood with slightly lowered head, withdrawn, silent. "In Caxamalca we waited for the Inca to appear," he said, suddenly breaking his silence. "Pizarro had hidden his handful of men in the two large golpons which fronted on the square. The sun swung high over the mountains, and still we waited and watched. Then at last we heard the quickened throbbing of the drums. Out of the drums there came a thin high wailing of wind instruments and, thickening the beat, the chant of Indian voices. So it stood for a while, and then out of their camp, the Inca's soldiers began to pour into the fields on either side of the road. They rolled forward like masses of lava, so slowly it took them almost three hours to draw nigh the town. A haze of dust blowing before them overlay the square. Dancing and singing, bands of servants swept the road before the Inca's litter. On either side of it marched companies of warriors. The Canari guard walked next to their lord, some two thousand of them arrayed in cloth of azure, rich in ornament. They carried themselves like peacocks and the shout they gave on the downbeat of their tread was like the peacock's cry. Into the plaza they filed until they crowded every part of it, and the noise they made stifled the air. I looked up at the sun. It was far down the western slope.

"Then suddenly the plaza grew still. Into the silence walked a prince of the blood. He was attired like the Sun's messenger, with his garments girt about his loins, bearing a lance all studded over with golden nails. Out of the staff-head coloured plumes fell to the ground. But the herald faded from our eyes. Atahualpa had reached the gates. With even pace, over the tops of heads, the bearers whose life it was to stumble made the royal litter to glide like a lazy bird, but a giant and oriental bird, for the litter was lined with feathered robes and pillows of down, and out of the feathers jewels played with the failing light. Atahualpa's chair was of beaten gold, and the canopy raised over it, held in the hands of princes, was mounted with plates of silver overlapped with plates of gold. The Inca lord sat like an idol and about his feet his embroidered robes lay as stiff as death. At his neck hung a collar of emeralds—fifty-two stones and each one the size of a pigeon's egg, and from these stones hung topaz likened unto the sun and moon and the moon's fifty-two phases. Two fingers of hair fell at his ears and about his head circled the royal llautu. For sceptre he bore a golden axe. This he held rigidly in his hands. Thus did he enter with the lord of Chincha at his feet, and thus did he come to a halt in the centre of the plaza. Seconds passed. He moved slightly, turning his head. His voice at last broke the silence. 'Where, then, are the strangers?' he asked."

The fire had died down. Its glow reached to Tovar's lips, but his eyes were in shadow. Through the dark shadows his voice reached: "The priest slipped out of the doors of the golpon. He harangued the Inca as though he understood the Christian tongue, gave him his breviary. Atahualpa looked at the book and then angrily let it fall to the ground. 'Give him the sword for his sacrilege,' the priest cried out. At that moment Pizarro waved his scarf, the signal for our assault. From the fort sounded the heavy explosion of the falconet. With the cry of chivalry on our lips and the bells ringing on the horses' plates we charged into the plaza.

"The Indians never recovered in their first confusion from the pounding charge of the horses. We drove them against the walls and buildings, their dead piled up behind us. Once I saw the Inca's litter dip and roll like a boat in a storm. Then into the cries and tumult there came a terrific crash, a gasping silence, a long wail of despair. The wall for some thousand paces had given way and the Indians were spilling over into the plain. They began to run. The flight turned into a rout. The Christians remaining in the plaza surrounded the Inca. The pikemen, the lancers, the swordmen laid his guard down in ranks, but as one rank went down, another took its place. The Canari guard had made a wall of death about their lord. No word of encouragement did the Inca give to his men. Aloof, he watched the furious struggle for his person as if it were a show set forth for his pleasure.

"The shadows began to creep up the mountains. With one last effort we charged the litter, took hold of it and tumbled the Inca out of his chair. Atahualpa was in our hands. At the sight the Canari guard gave up in despair. Some few fled, but the most of them stood about like stricken cattle."

Tovar paused, stood for one long moment there in the yard at Aguacalaquen; then slowly, in a steady but subdued voice, he said, "We, the victors, drew together in this strange place, thousands of leagues from Christendom, on the backside of the world, and in awe viewed what our hands had done. The dead and the hurt lay heaped in the plaza. The mighty host of the heathen lord was broken and scattered. A kingdom of such riches as we had never imagined lay to our hands. And we, one hundred and seventy men, had done this thing, no more, no less, for of our number not a man that day had lost his life. Pizarro alone showed a wound, one in the hand, got in fending for his royal prisoner."

The bare line of Tovar's mouth closed. The silence rushed into the void left by his voice, swung over the heads of the soldiers huddled in the yard at Aguacalaquen. From out that crowd the same voice spoke, "That was Peru! Peru is not Florida."

Tovar turned his head until he had located the exact spot from which the words had been hurled, a challenge across the dark. "You are right, Señor," he replied. "Peru is not Florida, but it has bred Florida."

Suddenly Ortiz felt the chill before-morning air clamp his shoulders, thread his spine. He felt the eyes in the yard unfasten, heard the rustle and shifting of men drawing their cloaks about them. When he looked again, Tovar was gone.

4

After that night the soldiers ceased to complain and during the next ten days, the time it took Moscoso to bring up the main body of the army from Ocale, they kept watch, made forays, with such strictness and zeal that the Aguacalaquen Indians, in spite of many ruses, were unable to release the cacique or surprise the camp. The army had suffered on the way, for the land over which it had passed lay waste. In spite of his impatience the Governor delayed another three days to let the men rally their strength and then on the ninth of September he moved off, passing over the river of Aguacalaquen with Guatutima for guide. There were no Indians in sight, but on either side of the path, following the line of march, the call of quail came out of the woods. Towards the end of the day, in sight of a small abandoned village, a lone Indian stepped across the path and came towards the wayward, blowing his flute. The Governor halted to receive him. He had come, he said, from Uçachile, a cacique of many parts, which he described, who promised great services in return for the release of Aguacalaquen. De Soto replied that the cacique was not a prisoner but went along to guide him to Uçachile's town.

The next day, Wednesday, the army came to Uriutina, a town of pleasant aspect and abundant food. Here another messenger came with a red leather belt from Uçachile and bearing the same request. De Soto answered as before with courtesy and sent in return a velvet cap and a plume, giving the same specious excuse—it was Aguacalaquen's pleasure to accompany the Child of the Sun a way on the path. Then on Friday, September 12, several Indians came to visit their lord and when they left Ortiz understood that the white path would soon change its beloved colour. "My lord," he said to de Soto.

"Yes?"

"I've learned that our nation has been devoted to death."

"How?"

"These subjects of Aguacalaquen's who have just now left came to tell him so, to warn him his rescue was preparing."

"Devoted to death?" de Soto asked, his eyes shifting from the path to the woods around it.

"Among the Timucuans when they sanctify themselves for war, according to the old beloved speech they devote to death in advance the prisoners they will take. They may vow to kill all they meet on a certain trail, or all enemies during a certain number of moons, or only the great warriors of the enemy, or . . ." Ortiz paused, "they may devote to death an entire nation."

"And this death?"

Ortiz turned his back and pointed to the armour which hid his scars.

On Monday early the army moved out of Many Waters, a town where the march had been delayed three days by rain. Almost at once the wayward ran into a bad swamp. "Here is a place we may expect trouble," de Soto said and ordered Moscoso to place the men in three columns, the mules carrying the powder and artillery to march in the centre column. The hogs were driven up front, the captives sent to the rear, except for Guatutima and Aguacalaquen. Chained and under heavy guard, they went with the Governor's household. As the difficulties of the swamp grew every step more apparent, de Soto turned to Ortiz. "There must be another way around. It is too populous a country for one trail." His voice became casual. "I fear Señor Guatutima who has given such abundant information has a reason for bringing us this way."

[235]

"They draw an ambush like a bow," Ortiz replied. "Once the enemy walks in, the wings close about."

De Soto spoke to Romo. "Tell the captains in case of attack to bring the two outer columns together and form a square. The centre will make a smaller square within."

All day the army marched through the swamp, picking its way, through streams with currents running in opposite directions, over high promontories of spongy ground. Without warning a man would stumble into a pool over his head, a horse go down under a hidden snag. The swamp was full of down timber and treacherous pools, so that all the way it was toilsome and when the halts were called a man thought himself lucky to find a spot of ground dry enough to sit upon. And yet nowhere was there sign or sound of Indian. More and more it looked like ambush and then in the silence of the gloomy way—for no man spoke and only the sloshing of legs and chains made a noise, a dreary noise akin to silence—towards eventide the thought came to all that dark would find them in this watery waste with no dry bed to lie upon. Angrily de Soto turned his eyes upon Guatutima, but the Indian gave him no response, picking his way through the trees, dragging his chain with a shortened pace and only stopping, and that easily, when it snagged a root.

At vespers the scouts gave a lusty shout and rode back to tell of firmer ground with Napituca just ahead.

"What do you make of it?" the Governor asked.

Ortiz was slow to answer. "An ambuscade would have cost the life of Aguacalaquen. So the Indians must have reasoned. And so . . ."

"And so we must look for a stratagem bringing small risk to their lord."

Ortiz bowed his head. "Only if that fails will they give battle."

"It will fail but it must seem not to fail," de Soto said and then he rode into the empty town of Napituca, Ortiz following hard at his heels.

The houses were scattered through a magnolia grove. Be-

[236]

hind the town there were gardens and behind the gardens, over-grown in scrubby pine and a tall brown grass, the old fields ran up against the forest. Before it stretched a large green plain sur-rounded on its south side by a dense forest. Open avenues of pine ran down on the other two sides and there before the pine two lakes drew together against a narrow tongue of land. Leav-ing Moscoso to quarter the men, the Governor and Ortiz gal-loped over the plain to the nearest lake. It was the smaller of the two, measuring less than half a league in circumference. It was clear of growth and mud, but very deep. Eight feet from the bank the Governor's horse lost bottom. The second lake lay beyond, away from Napituca, much wider and so long that it disappeared towards the northeast like a river. On both waters lilies lay in great wide patches.

The Governor studied the plain, the lakes, the forest, the town. "It is too wet to fire the grass, it is too open to surprise the town." His gaze came to rest upon the forest across the plain. "There will come our trouble," he said, "if trouble comes."

"The plain is fine for cavalry," Ortiz said.

"A fine place . . . a very fine place for stratagem."

Dusk now lay over plain and town in a fine haze and across it, muted and lingering, the trumpet sounded calling all to chant the evening hymn to the Virgin. Ortiz and the Governor listened a moment and then, lifting their bridles, put the horses into a slow gallop towards Napituca.

Ortiz sat up, awake and alert. He had the feeling that he had been called from sleep. He breathed carefully and looked quickly around. On the floor of the lodge the men lay wrapped in their cloaks in the stillness of the last deep sleep of the night. The air thinned the stale warmth in which he had lain and he felt a clammy chill at his loins. Outside, near to the town, he heard the cheerful mock bird calling. He searched for his head-piece and the thought flashed through his mind that the bird was very low to the ground. He slung his dagger and sword and stepped over the sleeping bodies into the street outside. He

[237]

stopped and drew his cloak against the air. The close-at-hand bird no longer sang but at a distance another answered answering another and then all through the forest back and forth ran the song of approaching day. The bird in the tree began again. Ortiz sharpened his ears. The call was the mock bird's call but it was too low and too easily located. And there were too many. He had had his doubts. Now he was certain. The travelling signal of Indians, many Indians, had brought him from his sleep.

He slipped through the town and where the last lodge melted into the timber dropped to the ground. Under his cloak he wore only a breechclout and his belt. The cloak he unfastened and laid it aside with the headpiece. He hesitated and then undid his sword and slowly, like a cat, began to crawl towards the singing tree. He moved a hand, one foot at a time, as he had been taught to do. A branch of dry leaves caught on his rough body and shook. Suddenly the singing stopped. He softened his breath. He should not have tried this with the sticky night sweat still on him or he should have greased himself. He waited five, ten, fifteen minutes. The singing resumed but on a lower key, and he began to move again. When he reached the down log some ten paces from the tree his ears told him was the singing tree, his face and back were running with sweat. He picked up a piece of rotten bark, put it over his head and in a very slow movement looked around the edge of the log. There the Indian was where he had expected to find him, perfectly still behind the tree, a trailer on the lookout and—fortune smiled—with his back turned. Ortiz crossed himself. On beyond he thought he saw a slight movement in a thicket but it was still too dark to see. Very carefully he drew back behind the log and, with his face in the direction of the trailer, waited.

There was no further reason for him to wait. He had verified a certainty and, he would confess it, indulged a vanity. Stalking the stalker. He had not been able to resist that most difficult of the stratagems of war. It was a criminal act, he the tongue of

[238]

the army allowing himself to be so gravely exposed. Then why was he still here and why did his blood beat with such exultation? He gave himself no answer but reached forth his hand. It was trembling. He held it above the ground until it grew as still as a snake's head in a knothole and then put it down and felt the half damp leaves give under it. From the log to the thicket was an open space twice the length of his body. If he could pass that, the rest of his way would be masked. He slipped his knife in his teeth. His hands felt the air, felt the ground before they touched it, his bones began to twist and bend.

He moved when the Indian sang, kept still when he was silent. He did not forget after every forward movement to look behind. The fronds of fern brushed his back. He eased himself flat upon the ground: the open space was safely passed! It took several seconds for the muscles in his back and shoulders to untie, then more swiftly he advanced on the tree. He watched the Indian's legs through the ferns. If they moved, even slightly shifted weight, he stopped. Once the Indian turned and looked in his direction, sensing, Ortiz knew, that all was not right, and took a step towards the thicket. Ortiz sucked in his breath and reached for his knife. From the south came a call, very soft and low, of the morning bird. The trailer turned, listened, and from his throat came the low trilling answer. Ortiz rose to his knees. His heart fluttered, he stifled his breath. To wait, he *must* wait, for the song to end. To break it off would give the alarm. It died away and he sprang.

They were rolling on the ground, his knife driving under the heart, his arm clamping the throat. He waited for the spasm before he loosed his hold and then he stood up and put his foot on the dead man's neck and reached for his hair. His heart was galloping and the whoop of triumph trembled at his lips but he clamped together his teeth. He circled the skull with his knife. It began to slip and in two minutes he had the hair in his hand. Behind him he heard another call, very close by. He turned and gave the answer, then upright he slipped around the trees, passed the watch and at the edge of the town walked into a lance.

"Halt!"

"Ortiz!" He gasped his name.

Slowly the lance withdrew from his chest. "Where have you been?"

He stepped through the clearing and looked into Tovar's eyes. They travelled over his body and came to rest on the hair dangling in his hand. "Don't you think you'd better give me that?" Tovar asked easily. "The Governor might ask questions."

Ortiz looked at the scalp. Four crow feathers crushed and stained with blood still clung to the hair. "Hold this," he said and took his knife and split the scalp down its centre. One part he gave to Tovar and the other he kept. "This ties the knot of friendship," he said.

Tovar turned the hair over and looked at it from all sides; then he said, "You'd better wash that blood off your body."

Tovar followed him to the spring and stood by in silence as he bathed himself. As he stepped out of the chilly spring, he wondered what the day now creeping behind the last taut darkness of the night would bring. Did the Governor understand the danger? He was a wise lord and possessed of a strange self-confidence but he could not know what it was for a whole nation to be devoted to death. During his years of captivity and adoption he had never known it. Each spring, when the snakes crawl from their holes, when the war captain beats his drum three times around the house and with the calumet streaked black and red gives the signal of blood and death, he had taken his knife, his club, his hickory bow, his sack of parched maize and joined the warriors in the long house to sanctify himself for war. And three days and nights he had fasted from sunrise to sunset and drunk the black drink, watched closely by the Waiter lest he profane the fast and raise the burning wrath of the holy fire against the town. Not until the third year, after close tutoring, did they trust him to know and obey the rites of war on the path where, parched from thirst and hunger, he must not eat or drink but await the few crumbs and drops of water handed out by the Waiter. Nor dared he sit or lean against a tree, though spent from weariness, or sit in the daytime under shade, or on the ground during the whole journey, but upon such rocks as the ark of war rested upon, so that by such mortification the Master of Breath would give hair to the party and return them safe to their homes.

But that was Indian fighting Indian. These warriors now gathering in the forest by the hundreds, had they come to destroy or be destroyed? Did they sense what the Christians meant in their land? And would they change their beloved old ways of fighting, which change they must to conquer?

Tovar was handing him his cloak.

"Daybreak," he said. "You had better get into your harness."

When Ortiz stepped out of the lodge, girded and spurred, the echo of the morning trumpet calling the army to Mass whirled in his ears. Already a third of the men had gathered and sleepy voices were murmuring in undertone. Those late to the call were hurrying from their quarters, swinging their swords, some alert and with brisk step, others still drawn in sleep. Ortiz looked once at the sky. It was streaked and pocked. Momently the light grew. He made his way to the Governor's side at the right of the altar. De Soto was abstracted and did not notice him come up, and throughout the grove there was a feeling of haste and tension. The Mass would be rushed. This day it came the turn of the Governor's nephew to say it. Ortiz looked at the young priest's face and thought it was not a face to serve either God or man, and yet change the eyes and he must look as the Governor looked in his youth. The priest approached the altar. The army was kneeling.

He heard a slight movement and saw the officer of the day whispering into the Governor's ear and the Governor's voice, "Hold them." It was low and abrupt. The Governor returned his gaze to the altar and kept it there, as if there was only one sacrifice and one passion. But the moment the Mass was over he sprang from his knees and called Ortiz. "There are two messengers. We shall now learn their plan."

The two Indians were waiting on the edge of the town. The sun's rim was just rising over the tops of the pine. It flashed off the lakes and in this first morning light the tawny bodies glowed under their coating of grease. Blue paint circled their mouths, but their faces were vermilion. A single sheaf of feathers came out of the knot at the back of their hair. At their sides hung their clubs and quivers. They held their bows like staffs. All of this Ortiz noticed as the Governor went forward to greet them. Smiling, he invited them to his quarters. Moscoso, Gallegos, Lobillo, and Tinoco drew near but a little apart.

The Indians did not move but said they were only messengers unworthy to sit with the strange lord. They had come from seven caciques now gathered in the forest, subjects of Uçachile and friends of Aguacalaquen. It was their wish and the wish of Uçachile to be at peace with him and to help in his war against Apalache, a people hostile to Uçachile and to themselves. In return for this help they asked only for the release of Aguacalaquen and his people.

The Governor replied that he too wanted to tie the knot of friendship and that nothing could please him so much as their aid in his journey to Apalache. Let the seven come to him and he would receive them as their dignity and prowess deserved.

The mighty and powerful lord would understand that the seven were afraid to enter his camp before the knot was tied, lest they be detained; but let him come to the plain with Aguacalaquen and the seven would meet him there and, on neutral ground, negotiate the business. Afterwards as friends they could freely visit.

All of this Ortiz put into the Timucuan tongue. As he spoke, the envoys observed but seemed not to observe the Governor. When he was done, they said, "We go now."

Ortiz replied, "What? You are gone?"

De Soto waited until the messengers had turned their backs and were well started across the plain. Casually he turned and

[242]

walked towards his captains, but his voice was not casual. "Señores, from this moment until I appear on the plain, everything we do will be watched. In haste but without show of haste arm and mount the lancers. Those with the best armour hide in the lodges. The doors will have to be enlarged. Lobillo, go at once and have this done. Quietly, mind you. Mask the work by having men assemble, not too many, in front of the carpenters. The carpenters must make no noise."

Lobillo bowed and moved off in his great long strides. De Soto continued, "As soon as I leave with Aguacalaquen, I shall walk slowly. Mask as many other horses as you can behind the lodges, the rest saddled at their mangers, the riders near by. Captain Maldonado, with the foot it will be easier. Let them appear scattered and unarmed. A company of bowmen, a company of targeteers, near the forest. The moment the trumpet sounds, you will move off through the woods and take them in reverse. It is your duty to drive them onto the plain, if they have not already left the woods. In that case you will cut off their retreat. Have Lobillo take the same number of men and cut them off from the direction of the lakes. All other foot will form on either side of the halberds and follow the horse down the plain. Is this clear?"

The captains were silent, and then Moscoso spoke up. "You will leave with only six men?"

The Governor nodded.

"It will put you in great peril, Excellency."

Gallegos said, "I think it very unwise. This conquest hangs on your person. Any one of us"—Gallegos took in the group with his head—"will be honoured to take your place."

"Only I, Señores, can spring the trap."

Maldonado asked, "How far on the plain will you go?"

"As far as they expect me to go."

"That means at least two crossbow shots." Moscoso looked grave.

"It will give you a chance to test the mettle of your horses," the Governor said and smiled. The captains did not return his

[243]

smile. "No, Señores, I do not risk my person needlessly. To trap the trapper, one must walk into the trap. Remember this. It is sound strategy. And as for the risk . . . a risk is a risk."

From his place near the front of the lodge Tovar could see a short distance into the plain. Leaning forward in his saddle, he looked at the spot where de Soto, holding Aguacalaquen by the hand, had walked out of range. In his mind he tried to follow their progress. It seemed hours since they had set out, Ortiz just behind the Governor, the six guards in the rear, the Governor courteously attending Aguacalaquen as though no difference existed between them. But not so Ortiz. He would be scanning the forest. And the guards, they would be taking the measure of the seven caciques waiting in their paint and feathers, grown to the earth, waiting their moment of treachery. Around him in the lodge the lancers sat their mounts, the horses crowded head to tail, the lancers with their heads slightly turned, listening. There was no sound but the buzz of flies and the horses stamping the packed dirt floor. The fine thin dust rising from their feet blew slowly up and out into the open. A man sneezed. Cacho said suddenly, "Can you still see him?" And then as if he must apologize for breaking the silence, he said to the room, "You see, my orders are to dash forward with the Governor's horse the moment I hear the trumpet, the very moment. I'm to wait on no one. I'm to . . ."

"Yes, yes," Romo said. "We know that."

Moscoso was in the centre of the doorway, between Cacho and Tovar. Cautiously he leaned out over his horse's head and looked around the corner of the lodge. Slowly he recovered his seat. "There goes a man of wonderful great hope," he said.

After this there was a long silence and throughout the lodge came the sounds of steel striking metal, dully scraping as the lancers nervously felt for their weapons. In the yard the footmen no longer pretended to pursue the deception of going about their morning duties. They stood, a few sat, all of them very still and with their eyes fixed on the plain like runners who await their turn.

"Where is he now?" Moscoso asked. Tovar noticed the strain in his voice.

After a pause, without looking around, a man said, "He has stopped and is talking to the heathen chief."

"That is to give us time to put the army in position." Moscoso said this with an air of discovery, a thing all knew, and yet the men listened and their eyes responded as though it explained the unconscionable time it was taking de Soto to reach the council place. Through the grove Tovar could see Maldonado's men moving, half-bent to the ground, sliding to their positions in the forest. Behind him the men were breathing heavily. With surprise he noticed his own breath came quickly.

Suddenly a voice from the yard said, "He has come up to them."

A pause.

"They are talking."

"Now they sit."

From behind Tovar smelt the sour bitter odour of before-battle sweat.

"Ortiz has put the Governor's saddle on the ground. He is ..." The words died on the man's mouth.

Moscoso's horse leapt into the open. Men scattered before its hoofs. Tovar followed him. The two of them sat for a moment and watched the Indians streaming out of the forest. The six halberdiers were making a ring about the Governor, Ortiz was helping him to his feet. . . .

Moscoso stood up in his stirrups. "At them, knights! At them! Santiago, Santiago and at them!"

Their horses' hoofs pounded. The plain lengthened. The springy earth turned to mud under foot and yet the gelding was let all the way out and pushed Moscoso's bay to a nose. Were they already too late? The Governor and his guard were lost in the yelling, leaping mass of Indians. He glanced at Moscoso. His face was set but collected, all the pleasure lines gone from his mouth and eyes. Behind, the pounding of hoofs increased. Through the battle cries, the yelps, he heard the quick short blast of the trumpet. The trumpet? The signal. They had leapt the signal. He grew calmer. To his left Cacho passed on the Governor's horse. The dappled grey sped down the plain. Out of the corner of his eye Tovar was aware of the forest swelling and breaking with Indians. Overhead the air swished. Twice in front arrows flashed.

He began to distinguish the painted faces and then for an instant he saw the Governor. De Soto and his guard kept a broken circle and were fighting with their backs turned in. His throat tightened as he saw the familiar thrust and parry. And then he saw no more. In front the Indians were opening their lines, drawing their bows. . . . Beneath his armpit he felt a stinging. A giant of a warrior was raising his club to sling it. He levelled his eyes along the point of his lance. The point struck . . . he heard the grunt as he passed. The lance was bending, he rose in his stirrups and swung it around again in place; his eyes caught the page slipping down from Aceituno's back, the Governor mounting, and then nothing but chests, thighs, and backs where he jabbed. Very far away rolling along the forest came the sound of dry thunder. It repeated haltingly . . . the arquebusiers. This struck him in a delayed thought, just as the Indians surrounded him. The gelding leapt and pounded the air. He dropped the bridle and grasped the cutlass and laid about him. The gelding parried, turned, pawed, swerved to miss the blow of a club . . . a voice shouted, "The Governor is down." When he was free to look, he saw Viota helping the Governor up upon the back of a fresh mount.

Tovar found himself alone. Under the impact of the cavalry the Indians had fallen back from the forest towards the lakes. Their dead lay on the plain. A few wounded near the forest were dragging themselves towards its shelter. Everywhere they were fighting well and squads on the fringe of the battle were doing damage with their arrows, but the horse was pressing the main body too close for them to get the full use of their bows. Lobillo was working towards their flank and Maldonado's men waged a battle of their own on the edge of the plain. The foot had made few gains in that direction. Even as he watched, three Christians went down. In the lapses of the sound of the tumult he could hear the arrows' thud as they struck the bucklers. The crossbow was too slow. And then Sagredo's horse stumbled and fell. Sagredo got to his feet but the Indians were upon him. Tovar spoke to his gelding.

In a few thrusts he scattered the Indians. One of them lay at his feet, jerking and beating his head along the ground. "Relieve him," he said to Sagredo. "I must have struck the spine." Sagredo stooped and grasped the Indian's hair, drew his knife and calmly cut his throat. He said, "Look at his nails. Long as knife blades."

"Look sharp. Here come more."

Retiring slowly and giving Sagredo the cover of his lance, Tovar fell back among the halberdiers as they advanced and there left Sagredo. The battle had now swept across the plain towards the lakes. The wings of the Indians were wavering but the centre stood firm. De Soto had withdrawn and was collecting a squadron of horse, some forty or fifty in one long line. Towards this line Tovar made his way but before he could reach it the trumpets blew. The upright lances struck the air like rods; the men leaned forward in their saddles; in a wavering line they charged and struck the centre of the Indian mass. Through it they rode to the open plain on the other side. Without stopping to dress the line the squadron turned and again rode down the Indian centre, already staggering from the first blow.

Tovar reined in his mount. The battle was over. On all sides the Indians began to break and run, at first with some order under the whistles and signals of their caciques, but the horse closed in and drove them hard. For some minutes they still held their ground at eight or ten points but their clubs and bows were no match for the lances and the weight of the horses. They fell where they were or melted into the general rout. A small body made its way into the forest but Maldonado soon closed this, the natural line of retreat. Lobillo cut them off from Napituca. In their desperation they plunged into the lakes as the only relief from capture and death. By the time the arquebusiers and bowmen got up they had swum out of range. Bolts and shots were fired at random but no harm was done and de Soto ordered firing to cease.

The second lake was too large to guard and all who fled there swam away and escaped, but those in the smaller lake were quickly surrounded. Moving among the lilies, with only their feathers showing, they looked at a distance like a flock of birds just settled in their flight. Ortiz called on them to surrender. He told them their position was hopeless and that the Governor, admiring their valour, would treat them well. Not an Indian came out. They swam slowly about in the water, shouting insults. As he rode up, Tovar saw one climb onto the shoulders of swimmers and empty his quiver of arrows at the bank, then slip into the water and swim away.

The Governor re-ordered his line, six of foot and two of horse alternating in one long chain about the lake and then he took his stand near Ortiz. "They must see their plight is hopeless. Tell them to give up."

Again Ortiz repeated the same proffer of clemency and again they returned the same insulting replies. "What can they hope for?" the Governor asked.

"For night," Ortiz replied.

Tovar's wound, now that the fighting was over, began to pain him. The arrow had gone through his plate and coat of mail just below the arm guard and had come out through his back. There was no present need for him at the lake and he rode back across the plain toward Napituca to have it dressed. On his way he ran into Silvestre in charge of a squad counting and burying the Indian dead. He pulled up beside him. "How many?" he asked.

"Some forty dead or dying."

"Have you heard our losses?"

"Two dead and some eight or nine wounded. Look, you are hurt yourself."

"It's nothing. I'm going to have it dressed."

Silvestre called out. "Vásquez, take over."

"It's nothing."

"I'll dress it," Silvestre said. "The leech is not fit to bleed an Indian."

The shaft of the arrow had to be broken and even so it was a slow business working the plate loose and removing the shirt of mail, for the arrow was cane and the point had splintered at the steel links. As he bent over and gently worked it back out of the flesh, Silvestre said, "Now, hold yourself. I'm going to probe with a bodkin."

Tovar ground his teeth on the dagger, the back of his eyes drew against the sudden scald of pain. The pain ran down to the wound. "That's fine," Silvestre said. "I got the oil in boiling and it went all the way through."

Tovar distinctly had not slept, for he watched the change of light as the day waned and the flies, one a green-bottle fly, bumping against the rafters of the lodge, but dark had come and taken him by surprise. He sat up and listened. The town was still and the plain beyond. It could not be late and yet the very stillness told him the night was advanced. Suddenly he felt alone and abandoned. Clumsily he wrapped his cloak about him and walked into the dry chill of the September air. The gelding, hearing his step, gave a low whinny. Nobody had unsaddled him. With his left hand he untied the bridle and mounted and once on the edge of the town stopped and listened. It was all quiet in the direction of the lakes, but under the bright clear moon he could vaguely make out the forms of the long-drawn-out circle of men. It must be seven or eight hours after the battle. Could the Indians still be in the water? A familiar

[249]

voice called across the dark, waited and called again. Tovar turned his horse's head in the direction of the voice. It spoke in Indian and must be Ortiz.

At the lake he felt he was drawing within a circle of be-witched ground. Two or three heads jerked over their shoulders and without greeting turned back to their vigil. He recognized de Soto and Ortiz standing by the water, motionless and look-ing before them. There was nothing to see and yet they watched after the manner of men who expected to be surprised by what they saw. A little to their right were several horsemen. They were also stilled and sitting at attention. One of these was the Constable. "How many have surrendered?" Tovar asked as he rode up beside him.

"None," the Constable replied. After a pause he gave a start. "Oh, you," he said. "How is your hurt?"

"A flesh wound."

"Those damned heathen are still swimming around in that water. I don't see why they don't drown. It's cold." His voice was irascible and baffled. "They've been trying to slip out ever since dark." He turned back to the lake and to his watch. It might never have been interrupted, so quickly did the Con-stable become reabsorbed in what lay before him.

Tovar was puzzled. Why did all show such a strain of watching? The Indians had no chance to escape. The army was assembled and spread at such close intervals every foot of the shore was covered. They were bound to surrender or drown. Surrender they must, but what if they drowned? Surely there would be others to seize for bearers and servants. He did not understand. He did not understand until his eyes fell upon the wide light-splotched surface of the lake and saw—a great and silent vacancy. Dark banks of lilies in promontories and islands reached out from the shore. Here and there near their borders he thought he saw a head but the longer he looked the more unsure he was of what he saw. The bright sheen was playing tricks with his eyes, for distinctly that large flat mass of lilies had not been in that particular shaft of light when first he

[250]

looked. He had searched that spot for heads and had found it empty. Perhaps the lilies had broken from the parent body and floated into the light. He looked more closely. There was no current, the air was still, yet it seemed to be moving, drifting slowly towards the shore. No, it lay perfectly still on the water.

To the left he heard whispers and the soft push of hoofs. A body of lancers was quietly drawing down to the shore. Out of a deep shadow some ten feet from the bank a number of the flowering pads lay innocently upon the water. These pads the lancers watched. Slowly, so slowly that the eye was almost deceived, they began to move. Tovar looked quickly at the first mass he had seen. It had disappeared. Back to the others. They were drawing to land. Suddenly the horses splashed into the water, the lances speared downward, the Indians rose from beneath the lilies and dived. For a short distance he could follow the riffles they made. From different parts of the lake came the report of arquebuses and then stillness returned to the watch and out of this stillness de Soto said, clear and distinctly, "Call again, Ortiz. For the last time promise them amnesty. If they resist me further, when they do come out, I will put them to the sword. Tell them that I have eyes that can see in the dark. Tell them whether they come hidden by flowers or under the water they must at last stand forth and face the lances and the thunder I carry. No mercy unless they come now, in peace." And then under his breath, "They must not drown."

Ortiz' voice floated across the lake. Tovar could not follow the meaning but the tone of his words was low and caressing and it seemed to carry to every part of the water. And then he paused, waiting for some response, but none came, only the small waves lapping the shore. Tovar too waited and he heard his blood timing the hollow laps of the waves. He wet his finger and raised it. There was not a breath of wind. What then stirred the water so regularly? His eyes travelled from the shore to the centre of the lake and it seemed to him the darkness had thickened there and, did he see or feel it, flowed in a certain way, turning at a slow whirl like a dying wheel. And as he looked, it

[251]

came to him: there at the centre of the lake were the Indians caught in their dilemma, swimming against death, spending breath for breath in the late night chill. And from where they were to the shore where the Governor stood, directly, materially in the movement of the water which their defiance raised, momently at his feet they sent their answer.

Now all was clear, the extra strain of the watch, the Governor's stubborn persistence in his efforts to bring them to land. A second time, here as upon the plain of Caxamalca, the Indians had summoned death to stand between the Christians and their prize. Word would pass to other tribes how their brothers at Napituca had swum until they could swim no more rather than wear the strangers' chains. Everywhere this choice would raise an endless war, the one thing de Soto most feared, the thing he had tried to avoid by his friendly policy. Tovar watched him pace the shore in long slow strides, watched him pause and look out over the lake and then down at his feet. Suddenly he turned and mounted and rode off around the water.

Tovar waited until he had disappeared and then joined Ortiz. After a long, a very long while Ortiz said, "They no longer try to escape."

Tovar said aloud, "They steal away the victory."

The two men spoke no more but listened as the water in constant but fainter rhythm struck the earth. The Constable and Romo and Moscoso and Moscoso's two brothers drew near and Moscoso said, "What a dry, cold wake." The Constable drew in his breath, "It is indeed a cold one."

"What o'clock?" Romo asked. His companions looked hastily around as though time lurked somewhere in the night, to overtake and surprise them.

"In Andalucía the cocks would be crowing," the Constable said and again the men fell silent and again only the water was heard, lapping the shore. Time passed without change and with restless gaze all watched the lapping water as men wait upon the slowing breath of life and to Tovar it seemed the lake did gasp and labour like a human throat and, startled, Romo exclaimed,

[252]

"It breathes." As he spoke the sound ceased and each man sought his neighbour's face and, during the pause, the Constable cleared his throat. "It was I you heard," he said.

Slowly as a false dawn breaks, from behind on the plain, a red glow rose overspreading horse and man. Red quivering lines slipped out into the water. The men grasped their weapons and turned in alarm and saw a large fire starting on the plain. Tenders were busily feeding it, and riding before the glow, with the flames growing brighter at his back, the Governor made his way to the lake. "I thought he was on the other side," Moscoso said.

De Soto rode through the silence, drew up and looked into the inquiring faces. "Ortiz," he said, "Call to them again and tell them I've built a fire to warm them. Once again I offer them their lives." His face was hard and set and his words, offering cheer, cheerless.

Ortiz reflected a moment and then began to speak and while he spoke, the sky lit up with a leaping yellow light, the plain as far as Napituca, and falling across the water the reflection reached to the middle of the lake. Plainly now Tovar could make out heads and shoulders by the score, moving around some kind of a centre, slowly, moving just enough to keep afloat. Perhaps it was an illusion but he thought he saw groups clustered together and held up by their hair. His face grew warm to see men of courage exposed in their extremity. He did not dwell on this. The army was under a great necessity.

Ortiz' voice broke off.

"What did you say?" the Governor asked.

"I told them, Excellency, that never had you seen in the land of the Sun, your home, warriors of such valour and strength. I told them your heart was moved to pity and mercy, so that you relented of your last talk and gave them one other chance to come out of the water. As proof of your good faith you had caused the fire, which they saw, to be lit on the plain to warm and comfort them. Furthermore I told them they must not be disheartened by defeat, since you were a lord all the world feared and obeyed and that wherever you went you took much hair. These things I told them, Excellency, and . . ." Ortiz hesitated.

"Yes, yes."

Ortiz had spoken rapidly. Now his voice slowed. "And I asked them, 'Do you choose to go by the spirits' way like old women? Like men cast away without burial? Who is there to send you on the way? Who will lay your pipe at your side, or your club and arrows to guard you, or the pouch of maize to nourish you? And who will dress you in your fine brave clothes, or hang gorgets about your neck, feathers to your hair, or bracelets to tinkle as you walk?' And then I made this end: 'Will you never sit down in the beloved grounds of the Breath Master? Must you haunt forever the paths of this world?' "

All stepped back so that the Indians might see the fire better. They did not have long to wait. Three swimmers broke away from the main body and came slowly towards the shore. So slowly did they come the water barely broke around their shoulders. They came close enough to show the feathers lying over their ears, dragging the water. And then they hesitated, turned and swam away. Ortiz called softly to them. They turned and again drew close and again withdrew. Several times they neared the shore while Ortiz spoke and motioned to the fire until at last they rose dripping from the water and staggered towards the hands outstretched to help them. One stumbled to the ground and lay with his arms flung out before him. Blankets were brought to wrap them in and after a while they were led away to the fire. From this time on, others gave themselves up, by ones and twos but so reluctantly that at daybreak less than fifty had surrendered.

More fires were built closer to the lake and the Governor himself attended to the feeding and care of the prisoners. Those still in the water, seeing their companions walking about unharmed or resting before the fires, began to come in more rapidly and at ten o'clock two hundred, spent and hungry and bloated from spending twenty-four hours in water, gave themselves up

[254]

in a body. Half of these lay for hours motionless where they fell and the Christians to honour their courage did much for their comfort and saw that they had food to eat and water to drink. As their strength returned, they were put in chains and guards set over them.

Only seven now remained in the lake. Neither entreaty nor promises moved them to come out. It seemed that they had recovered the spirit the others lost and from the bank, as he watched, the Governor called out, "Who are they that strain God's courtesy?"

Ortiz made an answer. "Uriutina, Excellency, is the headman of the revolt. He is the Far-Away-Cacique of their army and with him now is the Little-Far-Away, the Far-Away-Warrior, the Little-Far-Away-Warrior and three other caciques, allies and kinsmen of Uriutina and Aguacalaquen."

The Governor listened in a brisk nervous way to these degrees of rank. It was plain that the Indians in the lake no longer interested him. They were merely the last irritating obstacle to be cleared up before he set out on his way. Tovar saw that he showed no wear from the battle or the long night watch and fortune looked out of his eyes. Twice he had triumphed, but better than triumph he had consolidated the army behind him. Until the battle of the lakes he had dragged his men by force of will through their difficulties, had dismissed their frailties and a growing distrust of the narrowing, unknown trails. But now he had shown he was equal to his purpose. He knew how to wait and how to act and he had exposed his person to a greater risk than any other under his command. Now his will was the army's will. No longer would he need to force it. He was free for his task. This he knew and it was this which fed his impatience and made his brief examining glance briefer than usual. As the Constable came up to ask what was to be done with the captives, he rode away with him, saying to Ortiz, "Be pleased to send the Urriparacoxit Indians in after them."

The Urriparacoxit took off their flaps and waded into the

lake. They swam to its very centre and there took the remaining seven by the hair and brought them out. There was little struggle except with Uriutina. He was the last to set foot on land, nor did his strength seem greatly impaired by the long hours in the water. The paint on his face was streaked and his feathers drawn and gapped, but when he gave himself up, it was done with indifference and a marked haughtiness. He refused to take any food and drink and asked instead that a messenger to his country be brought before him, and to this man he said,

"Look you, go to my people and tell them that they must take no thought of me. I have done as a chief what there was to do, in no way offending the holy fire, nor did I part from our beloved ways of fighting, but I struggled and fought until I was alone. And if I took refuge in this pond, it was not to flee death or to avoid dying, as befits me, but to encourage those who were there. And when they surrendered, I did not give myself up until the Urriparacoxit took me by the hair and brought me out. Say all this to my people and tell them further they must not, out of regard for me or anyone else, have any-thing to do with these strangers. They are a nation of witches and will prove mightier than we who speak the old beloved speech. And say this: If I must die, I will die. So be it."

Ortiz turned to Tovar. "I was right. It is a war to the death. Deliver these Indians to the guard. I'm going to report to the Governor."

The Governor forbade the messenger to leave the camp and on the following day, as the Indians were divided among the men, he went among them and released the caciques so that they might be better treated, using soft words to induce them to peace and harmony. And to show them greater honour, he sat them at his table among the captains, in order of their rank, and Uriutina he put at his right hand. Just as the arrangements were made and the heads bowed for grace, Uriutina gave a loud whoop and struck the Governor in the face. He fell backwards from his chair and the Indian jumped on him. For a moment the captains sat frozen to their seats and then all sprang up at once. From both sides they stabbed the rebel and he fell down in his blood. Moscoso and Romo helped the Governor to his feet. He stood dazed from the blow, blood flowing from his nose and mouth. He leaned over and spat two teeth to the ground. In the confusion the other Indians had escaped to the yard, and from there momently the whoops of defiance and confusion grew.

The Governor shook his head and called for his sword and casque, but several minutes passed before he could collect his wits and then he said, "Would to God that those Lords of the Council were here to see what it is to serve His Majesty in this country!"

Tovar was reclining in front of the pot of beans. Benito was sitting with his legs crossed, chattering to Silvestre of his feats in yesterday's battle. The slave who had fallen to Silvestre's lot was dipping up the beans and squash. Tovar had just held out his bowl to be helped when the whoop shattered the peace of the noonday meal. For an instant Tovar let his head turn in the direction of the sound, but it was an instant too long. Out of the corner of his eye he saw it coming and ducked. He missed the pot which the Indian threw at his head, but the scalding beans and liquor struck him. Before he could clear the stuff from his face, his sword was gone from his side. He opened his eyes and batted away the blur. Silvestre was rising with his lance, in disbelief, his face drawn tight. He leapt across the fire and lunged at his slave. Benito stepped out of their way, stumbled and Tovar caught him in his arms. In a frenzy the boy pushed away and stood clear. He said shrilly, his voice breaking, "He almost had you. I parried." His eyes were bright and wild. As he turned, Tovar saw the blood welling from his open neck, spattering his shoulder, the dark stain growing from under his shirt. The boy started to Silvestre's aid.

"Wait," Tovar said and caught his arm.

"Let me go," he said like a child in a fit of temper and jerked to free himself.

[257]

"Wait a minute, you are hurt. Here, lie down. I'll fix you up."

Benito struggled for a second and then he saw his shoulder. His face turned white, he felt behind him for the ground and sat docilely down. He did not move but looked up as though he were listening. Once he said, "Is it bad?"

The whoops and shouts of command and the stamp of feet seemed to Tovar to come from a distance. The fingers of his left hand were still numb and clumsy. They got in the way and the string he had torn from his shirt was sticky and slipped as he tried to tie the artery. He looked up for help and saw an Indian in the loft of a barbacoa defending himself with the up-roar of ten men. Before he could look away, the Indian hurled the lance, grabbed his chest and toppled from the loft to the ground.

A voice said, "Can I help?"

"Yes," Tovar said, "get the leech." His voice was not his voice. He pressed his hand against the neck and against his palm he felt the pounding artery. "Do I hurt, lad? No, don't shake your head."

The boy's lips had turned a dirty blue, the fuzz above the upper lip glistened with large drops of sweat. "Just a minute now," he said and then Silvestre came up and pulled out the lac-ing of his undershirt. Tovar stepped away and began drying his hands while Silvestre fumbled at the neck. Tovar looked at the boy as though his gaze might stay the spending life. He saw the lids flutter heavily over the glazing eyes. In panic he stooped down. The blood no longer spurted. "I believe it's stopping," he said.

Silvestre did not answer, but in a little while he sat back on his haunches, his useless hands hanging between his knees. "Yes, it's stopped," he said. Presently he stood up and took his lance and walked slowly towards the sound of tumult.

Tovar carried the limp body to their quarters. It was very light. He laid it upon a skin and covered it with his cloak. Later, when he came out, the fighting was over and men were passing with their slaves all going in the same direction. He spoke to Francisco de Saldaña who was leading a large surly man by a cord tied to his neck. "Where are you going?" he asked.

"The Governor has ordered us to put them to death, but I'm taking mine to the halberdiers for execution. It is not a worthy thing to kill a slave."

He passed by and Tovar noticed how small a man he was and how neat in his person. Upon the edge of the yard the Indian stopped and jerked back. In fury he seized his captor by the crotch and collar and raised him in the air like a doll. Tovar began to run. Saldaña struck the ground and the Indian was stamping him with his feet. Before he could come up, others closer at hand arrived and despatched the slave. They were bending over Saldaña's senseless form trying to revive him.

Tovar felt a sudden draw in his stomach and walked away, into the yard at the place where the Urriparacoxit stood in line with their bows in their hands. Opposite, at the other end of the yard, he saw a squad of Indians tied to a post and on either side of them, extending to the limits of the square ground, piles of coppery bodies. They lay in careless disarray, as if they had been dropped from a height. He heard a thick muffled voice say, "Again." Swiftly the Urriparacoxit raised their bows. The bows twanged, the Indians at the pole crumpled, two leapt high and another two stood rigidly facing their executioners until their knees buckled and they fell forward on their faces. He heard the thump and saw the dust rise, but before it could settle halberdiers were dragging them away and others walked between guards to take their places. "They wanted a war to the death," the same thick voice said. The voice worried him, he could not quite place it, but he could not take his eyes from the doomed and as each lot fell the sharp gnaw of vengeance dulled and the hollow place in his chest filled in.

"That's enough," the voice said at last. "Deliver the youngest to those who have good chains and are vigilant."

In a flash the voice's identity came to him. Distorted as it was, it could belong to no other. He turned and for one moment looked into the Governor's swollen and misshapen features,

[259]

grotesquely familiar, with the strutting lips fixed in a snarl. De Soto looked away. So close, so fatally close had the Indians come to success, outnumbered, in chains, with only pots and firebrands for weapons, and in the moment of the Governor's triumph when nothing existed to mar the perfection of victory. Now he understood Ortiz' anxiety, his neglected warnings.

Later Tovar and Silvestre buried the boy Benito. They sewed the body in skins, weighted it with sand and poled the raft to the centre of the lake and there dropped it in. It sank quickly. A few bubbles rose and broke, the raft shook slightly and then grew still. What remained of Benito was gone. The lake had swallowed him. One second he was there. One second more and there was nothing. Between the beat of two seconds pressed the last dark violence of life and not a riffle to mark its wake, here two thousand leagues from Christendom. Two thousand leagues . . .

Tovar looked away. On every side the forest drew down upon the lakes and the plain and from their broken depths he heard the silence beat like the beat of wings. Surrounded, abandoned. In sudden alarm he realized that already the boy was growing dim in his mind. In his need he returned his eyes to the water, with some half-formed thought to call up his image from the dark blue depths. He leaned over the raft, looking down. He drew back and grasped the pole which lay to his hand. An icy band circled his forehead. He steadied himself. He had seen not Benito but the swollen, unnaturally distorted face of de Soto. It lay for an instant on the glassy surface, wavered, then quickly vanished.

"He'll wait safely here until Judgment," Silvestre said and pushed down on his pole.

Noiselessly the raft moved towards the shore.

5

The army remained five days after the revolt of the captives, recovering from wounds, although it was much later before

[260]

de Soto could take anything but gruel in his mouth, and then on the twenty-third of September, 1539, it left Napituca and came to the River of the Deer, so named for a large buck sent as an offering of peace by Uçachile. It took over a day to bridge the river and on the twenty-fifth the army passed through two small villages and a town called Apalu and at night reached Uçachile. Here captains going in opposite directions to forage brought in a hundred Indians. News of the battle and deaths at Napituca had driven the Indians to cover. All along the route of march the towns were abandoned, nor did Uçachile remain to be thanked for his venison.

Impatiently the Governor pushed his march. Leaving Uçachile, he set out on Monday, the twenty-ninth, and passed all day through a thick wood, coming at nightfall into an open pine forest where he camped. From here a lad named Cadena went back for a sword and the Governor ordered him to be hanged for both offenses. Kind-hearted gentlemen intervened and Cadena was saved, but afterwards men straggled less. Two days out from Uçachile the army reached the town and river of Axille, upon the border of Apalache and on Wednesday, October 1, the Governor first set foot upon the eastern edge of the country he had so long sought. Moving swiftly, he came to the river and swamp of Ivitachuco, taking by surprise the inhabitants of a few scattered dwellings to the east of the river. All except a few women escaped and raised the alarm. On the other side, hiding in the tall swamp grass, the Apalachians made their first stand. For two days and part of another they held up the army, but the crossbowmen were brought up and under cover of their fire the bridge was laid and the army passed over with the loss of only three men. The Indians abandoned Ivitachuco, leaving it in flames, and darkness settled over the burning town as the Governor moved in.

The following day, Sunday, October the fifth, he reached Calahuchi and took two men, a woman, and a large amount of dried venison which the Christians who were always short of meat were glad to find. Here the guide ran away. Another was chosen, an old man who led the army at random until he was thrown to the dogs. On the sixth a woman brought the Christians into a pleasant country of open forest, maize fields and small scattered dwellings until at last, at day's end, she led them into Anhayca Apalache, the seat of the lord of the whole country. From here the Governor sent Arias Tinoco and the Portuguese captain, Vasconcelos, in opposite directions to explore the land. One at the end of eight days, the other nine, returned and reported many towns, large fields and quantities of provisions. Everywhere the Christians went they found maize, beans, pumpkins and the dried plums of the country, more than enough to sustain the army over the winter. On every hand men were saying how much more fortunate was this conquest in its captain than those who followed the luckless Narváez, and none seemed to remember the gloomy prophecies of disaster or the reluctance of all to follow him here.

He quickly set about putting the place in a state of defense, for by day and night the Apalachians made war in the fields and woods surrounding the town. But this war in no way prevented the supplies from coming in. The foraging details were strengthened and each night the storehouses grew heavier with grain.

Now that he had found a place where the army could safely go into winter quarters the Governor began to think of the garrison he had left at the Port. If he could bring the foot to Apalache by water, the horse might cross overland before the bad weather set in and thus re-united the army set forth in the spring. Hearing that the sea was only eight leagues away, the Governor sent Añasco with a mixed body of troops to find it. After being misled by a guide, Añasco passed through a town called Ochete and from there went to the coast, near the place where Narváez had made the vessels to sail away to his death. There was no doubt about the location. Crosses had been cut into the trees and near by upon the ground lay the skulls and headpieces of the horses, mortars for grinding flour, and a great tree whose trunk had been split into stakes and with the limbs

[262]

made into mangers. Añasco left a sign on the tallest tree, one that could be seen far out to sea, and then returned to Apalache to make preparations for his journey to the Port.

He set out on the seventeenth of October with thirty lancers and in eleven days passed over the one hundred and thirty leagues which it had taken the army two months to travel. At Uçachile and other towns he found the Indians already careless. He went through at a gallop and camped always in the open for three or four hours of rest, and in this way managed to avoid attack, and if any Indian was found by the trail he was lanced, lest he give the alarm. Arrived at the Port he despatched two caravels to Havana in which he sent to Doña Ysabel twenty women taken at Ytara and Potano, towns near Ocale. Calderón set out for Apalache by land with the cavalry and some crossbowmen of foot and a week later Añasco loaded the foot and supplies in two pinnaces. What he was unable to carry he gave to Mocoço or destroyed when he fired the Port.

Calderón arrived with the loss of two men and seven horses. For a while there were misgivings that Añasco's luck had forsaken him, and the Governor ordered planks and spikes to be taken to the coast for building a piragua, into which thirty men entered well armed from the bay, going to and from the sea, waiting the arrival of the pinnaces and fighting with the Indians who went up and down the estuary in their canoes. Finally on November 29 Añasco arrived at the port of Apalache. On the same day, in a high wind, an Indian passed through the sentries unobserved and set fire to Anhayca Apalache, two portions of which were instantly consumed.

Now that the army was safely together again, reunited under great danger and toil and quartered in a country of plenty, the Governor began to lay his plans against the coming of spring. He ordered Maldonado to take fifty men and run the coast westward in the brigantines, explore it and discover a harbour to which he could bring the army and re-establish connections with Havana after he had made a wide circuit through country never before seen by Christian eyes. For now he felt that he was

[263]

upon the outer edges of that rich land known to Cabeza de Vaca. Among the captives taken at Napituca the Royal Treasurer, Juan Gaytán, had a youth who stated that he did not belong to this country but to one afar in the direction of the sun's rising, from which he had been a long time absent visiting other lands, that its name was Yupaha and that it was governed by a woman. She lived in a town of astonishing size and had many neighbouring lords her tributaries, some of whom gave her clothing, others gold in quantity. The youth was questioned closely and he showed how the metal was taken from the earth and how it was melted and refined. Those who knew aught of such matters declared it impossible for him to give so specific an account unless he had been a witness of the operation. The army was confident and its hopes high. Spring seemed a thousand years away.

During the five long months of waiting the Indians gave them little rest. They laid ambuscades and surprised the wood details, freeing the slaves who were taken along to carry the loads, filing their chains with flint. The very day that Maldonado went away eight lancers rode out to scout and came upon two men and a woman picking beans. The men stood their ground and before they could be killed wounded the Christians and three horses, one of which died in a few days. Two Portuguese, Simon Rodriguez and Roque de Yelves, rode a short distance from town to gather fruit and were trapped in a tree. Roque jumped to the ground and was shot through the back as he ran for his horse. Rodriguez was shot in the tree. He was found at its foot filled with arrows and scalped. Near him lay Roque with an arrow sticking out of his chest. He told what had happened and, asking for confession, soon expired. One of the horses showed a spot of blood, which seemed a wound of no consequence, but in a few hours the animal was dead. Opening him up, the Christians found the arrow had passed through the stomach and intestines to the hollow of the chest, lacking four finger-breadths of coming out through the breast leather.

The Governor, hoping to put a stop to these assaults, led a

strong party against the hiding place of the cacique which he learned through spies was less than a day from the town. Laying his plans, he surrounded the place at night and struck at dawn. After a long hard fight through a trail blocked by palisades he reached the centre of the Indian retreat and there took the cacique who was too fat to flee. But the Apalachians in no way let up. For weeks, as regularly as the watches were set, the Governor sent parties against them, but nothing availed to bring them to peace. If their noses were cut off, or their hands, they made little of it. They were burned crying defiance from the stake. Not one out of fear of death denied that he belonged to Apalache and when they were asked whence they came, they proudly said, "From whence am I? I am from Apalache."

Out of patience, the Governor called the cacique into his presence, and he came crawling on all fours, for his legs would not support his weight. The Governor threatened him with death unless his people put an end to their attacks. The cacique replied that to his shame the messages he had sent were ignored, but if the Governor would let him meet with the head men of his nation and inform them of his danger, they would listen to his talk. Knowing this to be an old ruse, de Soto sent as guard a full company of horse and foot and cautioned the captains to keep a sharp watch. The following day the companies returned with the cacique missing. In the dark, between midnight and dawn, a spell was cast upon the eyes of the guard and Apalache had been spirited away through the air. It was plain, they said, there could be no other explanation for as the Governor knew one so burdened with flesh could never have escaped under his own power. De Soto kept his peace and pretended to believe what was said, for the captains were men of worth.

Because the Governor showed great skill in their method of war, the Apalachians were never able to do more than worry and harass the army, but the Christians were unable to relax their vigilance, so with the first signs of spring they looked more impatiently for Maldonado's return. Three days having elapsed

[265]

beyond his allotted time, the Governor let it be known that should he not appear at the end of eight days, he would go thence and wait no longer. Before this time Maldonado came in, bringing with him an Indian from the province of Ochus, sixty leagues from Apalache. He had found a sheltered port with a good depth of water, where boats could draw close in to shore. And he brought a blanket of sable fur better than any the Christians had so far seen in Florida. The Governor was highly pleased and he ordered Maldonado to Havana for fresh provisions which he was to bring to the port of his discovery later in the summer, where the Governor promised to have the army. If for any reason the army was delayed and they did not meet, he was to run the coast and then go back to Havana and return the next season.

Thus preparing against future want, the Governor gave the order to go forward, directing his men to carry enough maize for a march through sixty leagues of desert. The cavalry loaded the grain on their horses, the foot strapped theirs to their backs, for the slaves being naked and in chains had for the most part perished during the winter. On the third of March, 1540, the army in high spirits and with higher hopes cut all communications with their base and marched out of Anhayca Apalache into the wilderness.

Behind them, while the rearward was still in sight of the town, the Indians slipped out of the forest and silently drew towards their dwellings.

6

CUTIFICHIQUI

Cutifichiqui

Tovar could not sleep. He lay upon his back in the lodge where Patofa's Waiter had led him, with his eyes resting upon the patch of sky at the smoke vent. How many of these lodges had he slept in the last two months! Tired, often exhausted, each night he had not slept in the open, he had fallen upon the skins and at day had risen to be on his way. Even in the dead of night he had risen, passing half-awake through the ghostly towns, with no memory of places, for darkness is without location, with little memory even for names—only feeling, one long dry strain, although the saints bear witness the heavens and earth were not dry. Last year it had been the swamps and the gloomy tangled way. This season it was water. He had never seen a country with so many large and ugly rivers. And the rains. He had marched wet, slept wet, eaten cold damp maize.

How deep they had come into the land! And now they were come not only to the wilderness but to the edge of a wilderness deserted even by the Indians. And all upon the doubtful word of this boy Perico. No wonder he couldn't sleep. He must try to unravel the truth, the probable truth, for the absolute truth neither he nor any other man could hope to learn with the little they had to go on. Did Perico lie, or were the Indians trying to mislead them? The first month out of Apalache there were very.few, save the Governor, who still had faith in Perico. Nothing but rivers, and a few tribes, rich enough in food but in nothing else, none of whom had heard of Yupaha, until at last they had found the Altamaha peoples.

Their river, unlike all the others they had crossed, flowed eastward, presumably to the Ocean Sea. For the first time confidence returned in Perico's story, for had he not in Anhayca Apalache said that Yupaha lay towards the rising sun?

This was in the boy's favour. As they travelled up this river, thickly settled with generous and friendly peoples, they heard accidentally of the cacique Çamumo. At the time he, Tovar, did not see it, but now, looking back, he saw plainly that this was the next encouraging sign. The report of this cacique gave out that he never laid aside his arms because he lived on the borders of Cutifichiqui, his enemy. The Governor sent word that he might come as he pleased, thinking the Indian feared to present himself before strangers unarmed. He arrived with his bow and his knife in the midst of armed followers and for welcome the Governor gave him a plume mounted on silver. It pleased Çamumo very much, and he said to the Governor, "You who come from the sky, I shall eat in these feathers, make war in them; sleep with my wife in them?" And the Governor told him he might do all these things and then he questioned him about his enemy, Cutifichiqui.

It was only later that Perico made known that Yupaha and Cutifichiqui were different names for the same place. Now that Tovar reflected, this seemed strange and not in Perico's favour. Why was the boy so long in making the connection? Had he lost his way and used Cutifichiqui to save his neck? Obviously it was a name of power and prestige among the Indians along this river, for all the tribes mentioned it with great respect, and Patofa circumstantially. Could it be possible that Patofa had connived with Perico to rid his town of the Christians and send them to their ruin? This seemed unlikely, and yet all was not plain at the conference between the Governor and Patofa.

After the feasting and the dancing Patofa had led them into his council house, a large rotunda set upon the mound. He, Tovar, was among the last of the Christians to enter. As he stepped inside upon the hard-packed floor, he saw before him dimly the cane benches rising in three tiers against the wall.

Patofa sat down in front with his chief men around him, and behind on the different levels the warriors arranged themselves according to their honours. Between the first warrior and Patofa, on the other side of a partition, de Soto took his seat. By the time all were placed it had grown entirely dark. The silence increased with the darkness, and as they waited, upon what or for what he did not know, he felt as if he were in the hollow of a tremendous drum. Instinctively his hand crept to his sword. Around him he could hear others reaching for their weapons, when suddenly, near the centre of the rotunda, there came a crackling sound; then a small yellow flame leapt a few inches from the ground. No hand had set it nor had he smelled fire as he came in. But quickly bright clean flames stood straight into the air, rising out of a spiral of canes winding about the centre pole. Slowly the flames ate into the cane, following the course of the sun, casting a soft glow upon the dusky bodies and upon the Christians. Alone among the hundreds of faces Perico looked ill at ease.

Four Waiters, singing and bowing, passed the black drink in gourds. Afterwards the pipe with the long white stem went its rounds. When all had drunk and smoked, Patofa arose and spoke to the Governor:

"I have seen you only today, but it is a long time since I have received you in my heart. That was done the first time I heard of you. So be it. My desire to serve, please, and give you contentment is so great that these words which I speak are nothing to the feeling I bear you. Thus the tongue casts only the shadow of the thought. So be it. But of this you may be sure. To have the rule of all the towns on this river would give me less delight than this sight of you. Do not look for me to offer what is your own, this person, these lands, these vassals. All I possess you will use as with your own, and in so doing you will confer upon me an everlasting favour."

Patofa resumed his seat. The Governor kept a formal pause and then he stood up and, in courteous terms, thanked the Indian for the talk he had made and for the generous reception of him and his people. Then the Governor grew more particular. Was there not a large province four days' travel towards the east? Patofa conferred with his oldest councillors, which to Tovar seemed to take too long a time, except that by now he had grown accustomed to the deliberate formality of Indian ways. At last Patofa replied that towards the northwest there was the province of Coça, a country of great plenty and with very large towns, but to the east he knew of no such place. The Governor paused; then he asked if Cutifichiqui did not lie four days away.

Patofa knew very well of Cutifichiqui and if the strange lord was going to make war on the Lady of Cutifichiqui, he would give all he desired for the war, both in supplies and warriors, but the Governor must understand there was no path over which to go. The two towns had no communications because of an old and long-standing war, except at those times when they made raids on each other. These raids they carried out through obscure and intricate parts and it always took from twenty to twenty-two days to go and return. In this time they had very little to eat.

The Governor now turned to Perico and asked him to explain the discrepancy between his report of the distance and Patofa's. Perico could not answer the Governor's question, but he would stake his head that Cutifichiqui lay only four days' travel hence. By this time the fire had left behind it a long tail of white ashes. It had reached the pole and was flaring from the last bundle of cane. Patofa arose and pointed to the flames as a sign that the conference was over, and then he led the way, surrounded by his warriors, out of the rotunda into the night.

Now that Tovar reflected, there was little reason to believe that Patofa and Perico had connived together. There was too much proof that this Cutifichiqui existed and Patofa had every reason, besides that of friendship which had showed itself genuine enough, to aid the Governor in his search for Cutifichiqui. It must have seemed rare good fortune to the Indians to find, out of the sky, so powerful an ally against an enemy they feared and against whom they had made so little headway.

All the evidence pointed to some confusion in Perico's mind, either deliberate or——

Tovar sat up on his skins. Through the stillness of the night he had heard a cry, like that of a soul being torn from its body. He heard it again. He reached for his sword and ran out of the lodge. The noise was coming from Ortiz' quarters. Christians were running from all directions, half-dressed and with weapons in their hands. Tovar stooped at the entrance and looked up into the oily glare of a pine torch in Ortiz' hand. The occupants of the lodge were sitting or standing, half asleep, and looking at the floor, in the far corner of the room. There, pressed against the clay wall, lay the boy Perico, beating the air and muttering through his foamy lips.

"What's the matter with him?" Tovar asked.

Ortiz shook his head.

The lodge was rapidly filling up. Pressure from the rear jostled Tovar further into the room. Over his shoulder a voice called out, low and sibilant, "He's possessed!"

Perico opened his eyes and began crawling away from the wall; then he fell back upon the floor as if two hands had pushed him. He lay for a moment floundering and kicking. Tovar was pushed aside and he looked around to see Father John the Evangelist going towards the Indian, sprinkling holy water upon the floor, into the air, upon the boy's head. He kneeled and held his cross before him. The Indian cried out and began crawling away. He rolled under a bench and lay there, moaning like an animal.

"Bring him out!" the priest commanded.

Nobody seemed willing to do his bidding.

"Bring him out!" the priest repeated.

Tovar went forward and laid hold of Perico's feet. The boy kicked him. Angrily, he jerked him out from the hiding place and held his legs while Father John stooped and pressed the cross to his lips. At this the Indian caught the priest's sleeve between his teeth and tore it apart. "Hold him!" the priest called out.

[273]

Several men came to Tovar's aid and held the boy upon the ground. Father John laid his right hand on the black, tousled hair.

"I exorcise thee, thou unclean spirit, in the name of Jesus Christ. Tremble, O Satan, thou enemy of the faith, thou foe of mankind, who hast brought death into the world, who hast deprived men of life, who hast rebelled against Justice, thou seducer of mankind, thou root of evil, thou source of avarice, discord and envy!"

The priest spoke in a low rapid voice and when he was done, Perico gave a great cry of anguish and then lay upon the floor as limp as a broken weed.

"What's the disturbance?"

Father John turned, all who were in the lodge turned, and looked into the stern features of the Governor.

"I have just exorcised the boy Perico," the priest said.

"Possessed?"

"I have no doubts, Excellency."

De Soto hesitated. "It may be a ruse," he said; then he looked down at the figure outstretched upon the floor. "There is a great discrepancy between the distances he gives and those reported by Patofa."

"Baptize me, Father, or he will kill me."

Perico's voice carried faintly into the room. Low and halting he began to speak, half Spanish, half Timucuan, telling how the devil with many servants had aroused him with a command not to guide the Christians through the wilderness, on pain of death. And Satan appeared with the body of a snake and the head of a man, hissing and coiling before his very face. The servants whipped him with their tails and bruised him, as all could see by looking at his body, and would have killed him but for Father John who gave him the cross to kiss. At that moment Satan turned himself into a flame and vanished. He begged, therefore, to be made a Christian, for only by the cross would his life be spared.

The Governor looked hard at the boy. In his silence there

was doubt and in his voice. "You believe he was possessed, Father?"

"If you could have seen him, my lord."

Men crossed themselves hastily and looked behind them.

"It's possible the boy may know of a shorter way. And certainly," the Governor added reflectively, "it would be Satan's strategy to strike us in our weakest place." He walked over to the boy and examined him closely, Ortiz following with the torch. "He seems to be bruised," he said rising, "and there are signs of a lash, but it's your province, Father, to decide upon baptism."

Father John drew near to the Governor. The Governor continued, thoughtfully, "I only ask that you consult Father Francisco and the rest of the priests. I should not presume to advise you, but if the boy was possessed, then he should be given solace and protection. But you must decide tonight. We already strain Patofa's hospitality. Supplies for our journey will strain it further and that journey begins tomorrow. On no account will I delay." Then crossing himself and looking with a backward glance at Perico, he went out of the lodge.

Deprived of his bed by the priests, Ortiz followed Tovar to his quarters. Outside the two men paused by a jar and in silence dipped up a gourd of water. Ortiz drank and after him Tovar and then they stepped aside to ease themselves. After several moments Ortiz spoke.

"Do you know what I think?" he asked.

"What?"

"I think Señor Perico has lost his way."

Tovar considered a moment. "I suppose de Soto would have scruples about throwing a Christian to the dogs."

"Perico thinks so."

2

"Steady there!" Tovar jerked the bridle and the gelding righted himself. With the current as swift as it was, it was im-

[275]

possible to guard against the loose and slippery stones on the river's bed. He had seen two animals shoulder-slipped at the bank. It said much for the horses that more had not already been hurt. He looked from bank to bank. One solid line of cavalry.

They had stood in place now for hours so that the foot, crossing above, might not be washed away and drowned. It would have been much quicker if they could have crossed on the croup, but all had thought it too dangerous and he supposed it was. Even by tying the men together, thirty and forty at a time, many had fallen and come up half-drowned before a hand could be reached. But not so the Indian bearers. Eight hundred of them and not one had lost his footing, although at times in mid-stream the current had pulled them towards the horses. How carefully they had wrapped their bows in skins and slung them with the quivers to the packs. When the rains ceased, there would be more bows than crossbows dry and ready for action. For an instant he wondered if their friendliness was a piece of cunning, but there was no reason to doubt them. All the evidence pointed to their enmity with Cutifichiqui. Anyway, he had enough to worry about, guiding the last of the arquebusiers across. He cupped his hands and shouted above the water's roar, "Ready?" De Guzmán called back, and he saw the arquebusiers, all tied together, pick their way clumsily down the bank. He rode towards them and held out the butt end of his lance. The file leader reached for it like a blind man. He spoke to the gelding. Slowly the horse began to pick his way.

Would the rain never let up? As if in answer it came hurtling in sheets down the river, spattering the surface with gluey bubbles, pocking it. A pox on that scoundrel Perico. Four days now and no sign of Cutifichiqui.

At the bank Silvestre met him. He sat for a moment and then looked inquiringly at his friend. "Pass the word to husband the provisions. The Governor says we are likely to find ourselves in want."

"Husband them—we only brought enough for four days."

"It is not my order. I only pass it on."

The cavalry was climbing onto the bank and Tovar rode with Silvestre to join them. Silvestre went to the head of the column and he waited for the Portuguese. "Husband the maize," he said.

"You know what you can do," came the reply.

"On you," he said automatically. There was a short pause while they took their place behind the escort, and then the army moved forward. He saw the Governor disappear behind a giant pine. The trail was narrowing. Up to now it had been very straight and wide enough for three men to ride abreast. They had been moving less than a quarter of an hour when a halt was called. This was unusual and he rode forward to see what it was about. The Governor was surrounded by the Patofa guides and Perico. The Indians were pointing to the northeast.

"What's the trouble?" he asked.

Biedma said, "The trail has given out."

It had happened as Ortiz had foreseen. They had reached the borders of the unknown, untenanted wilderness, without a path, without a guide, with little food and no way of getting more. It had come, the thing that in Cuba Tovar had seen as clearly as a vision, when, walking after the priest down the aisle of the log church, he looked up and saw the wilderness growing out of God's altar. At last the Governor had met his adversary. Tovar waited for the conference with the guides to end—a formality and a waste of time—and the rain fell, making more desolate the solitude, and then the army moved forward. All morning it marched, and men said Perico had lost the way out of fear of the devil. At midday the rain let up and the sun came out. It broke through the tops of the pine, lightened for a moment the heavy mists hanging to the trees, and then went under a cloud. The light neither brightened nor lessened its steady grey flow. The laurel showed momentarily more colour, then faded. No other change was visible throughout the long smooth plain of unbroken pine. The marching was easy, too

[277]

easy. They had had to push against the rain. It had resisted like a wall which gives with each thrust but is never breached. But this was another thing. The flat needle-covered ground offered no resistance. Tovar could see the army's pace was half again as fast, the foot shambling along, the Indians keeping their effortless swing in a parallel column, bending slightly forward under their loads, except those who had carried the maize. They walked upright, their eyes now upon the ground, now upon the trees before them.

In the late afternoon they came to a creek and made camp along its banks. The cane was green and the horses had this to eat. The Indians wandered through the forest and returned with herbs and roots. These added to the slim stores, for there was no mess as yet entirely without grain. But there was little cheer at the fires. The Indians retired early to their camp, drawing together in sixteen bands of fifty each. Tovar saw their sentries go out and then at command each band sat down in a circle with the backs turned in, rings within rings. Twenty-five men made the outside ring, then fifteen, then ten. The band leader sat at the hub, facing the opening through which the Indians, with his permission, passed. They had taken no such precautions on the other nights.

Already the fires in the scattered Christian messes were dying away. Close about the men lay, drawn to the fading glow. Even as Tovar watched, the dim, red light sank into the earth. The reclining forms receded, disappeared. He looked again to where the Indians were. The darkness had swallowed them, swallowed the wilderness and the roof of the world. Far above, among the tops of the pine, beyond them, the outer darkness soughed and the night beat softly down the air, over the path their tread had that day made where no path was, over the plain, its smooth-needled floor, the smoother grass that on the morrow their feet would bruise. To its very margins, unseen, unknown, it ran and the empty waste it filled with its own emptiness, a boundlessness binding and as it bound darkening all that was to come. The black void pressed against his eyes. Plainly from

[278]

its depths Tovar heard a voice say, "When?" and afterwards "Where?" The words did not die but travelled as from some point far out in space and they came towards him, wavering, fusing, and passed as the wind passes, so that for a long time he heard them behind him in no way diminishing or increasing their sound. Suddenly he understood that he was standing, straining at the dark, with his ears roaring as if they were under water.

When he awoke, he was lying on his back looking up the long straight pines. The tops were patched with light. Half awake, he heard a quick gobbling rush of sound running from tree to tree. In the first instant of recognition it seemed to him to be the noise that day makes, and he lay in a haze of wondering awe.

"Thousands of them."

He sat up. "Thousands of what?"

"Turkeys," Silvestre said.

All through the camp men were jumping to their feet, arquebusiers loading their pieces, squads of Indians slipping in and out among the trunks, bending over with their bows in their hands. "God, there's enough meat to feed this army for a month," he said and then he felt his mouth grow moist and the hollow pull at his stomach.

"The roost must go for leagues," Silvestre said in a whisper.

"God, God, God," Fernández said over and over under his breath.

And then the trumpet sounded. Voices cried "No," and cheerful, vibrant, explosive, the gobblers mocked the call, drowning the horn, until there was such a din that it did not grow quiet until Moscoso rode through the camp saying the Indians had been sent to hunt, it was too shy a bird for Christians, and there was no time.

As he rode along, here and there through the trees Tovar saw the birds fly from their high perch, slanting towards the ground, and for the first hour of the march the forest continued to ring with their calls. At sunrise they gradually ceased, and the wilderness returned to its solitude. Hour followed hour, with the path always behind, never before, and the silence increased with the gloom. Each halt looked like the last, the same stand of pine down which the eye seemed to seek a way, only to find the same terrain, a creek banked with laurel and cane, a dark-surfaced pond, here and there groves of oak, and then pine. With each league the horses moved more slowly. The green cane and short measure of grass they had eaten ran at their tails. The men scarcely spoke, lest they speak the one thought growing in their minds. More and more the Governor glanced at the guides. Perico averted his eyes. At the noonday rest the Indians who had been sent to hunt came in with six turkeys.

In the early afternoon the army was stopped by its fourth great river. The banks were miry and overgrown with brambles and briers, and the water flowed deep and hard, dividing around a small island thick with brush and trees. De Soto called for swimmers to find its depth, and they stripped them of their clothes and waded into the water, sinking deep in mud, cutting their way with axes until they reached the stream's bed. Swimming and walking, they came to the island and from there passed over to the other side. One recrossed, reporting that with the help of the cavalry the foot could make it, although for a hundred paces at the coming out the horses must swim. Moscoso and several of the captains advised the Governor to wait for the morrow, reminding him that the men and animals were tired from marching and weak from the little they had eaten, but he replied that the river might rise and since there was no food to restore their strength, it would be best to cross at once. Other axemen went in to clear the way and cut a path at the end of the island, where the supplies were piled to be loaded on the horses' backs. Then the foot and the cavalry passed over together. Each lance gave a stirrup or the tail of his horse to the men struggling with the current, and in this way the army reached the opposite bank without loss. The day was fast spending, but the Governor pushed on for half a league to a pine grove. Here the cooks who had been sent ahead gave out a soup made from the turkeys, but so far did it have to stretch that it was little more than flavoured water and when it was drunk made the hunger sharper.

The following day broke grey and cloudy. After Mass the men stood about waiting or they wandered restlessly from mess to mess, asking for food. Tovar felt the sense of waiting. He thought at first that it was because he lacked his puchero. This was the first morning he had not had a few grains of maize to eat. Without food the beginning of the day delayed; there was a hiatus more empty than his stomach. Indeed the pulling and gnawing filled it with a violence to its very top. It was not his stomach but his spirit that felt empty. He sat down and mended his harness, patched his boots, and then took his kit and shod his horse. Still he felt a loose and driving energy. He wandered through the camp, came to a group of men talking in high meaningless tones. He asked them the trouble and the only reply he could get was that they had sent for Ortiz.

"But why Ortiz?"

"To find whether Saint Jorje is dying."

"But Saint Jorje looks well."

"But he has been passing blue water."

Saint Jorje turned his wide dark eyes upon Tovar: "Blue, all blue, like the sky it was blue. My water has been bewitched and I must die."

Ortiz arrived and heard the story. "It was as blue as the hem on Her Ladyship's gown in the chapel of the Mater Dolorosa in Badajoz."

"What have you eaten?"

"What have I eaten? God save me I've eaten nought but a tough root with a little white flower."

"Eat no more such roots," Ortiz commanded. "You will not die but your blood will thin."

"What a land is this to turn a man's water the colour of the sky!" Saint Jorje said.

[281]

Tovar followed Ortiz to his mess. They passed the priest of the Holy Trinity. He stopped them and asked Ortiz when the march would begin. His eyes were bright and his words rushed forth with warmth. "Our Lord's blood is too strong for his belly," Ortiz said as they passed on. They approached the Governor's quarters, placed between two large oaks, and saw Perico and several of the Patofa guides surrounding the Governor whose glance turned upon Ortiz. "I want your help," the Governor said, and Ortiz replied, "Your service, Excellency."

And then it came to Tovar. For the first time since leaving Patofa the morning trumpet had not sounded assembly, and in that moment he understood that the army was lost . . . the Governor's voice rose in harsh, insistent tones. How was it that among eight hundred Indians there was not one who knew the way? Ortiz' voice, liquid, meaningless, the Indian's, a long speech, soft and guttural, rising and falling, and then Ortiz' again. "The war leader says that they have never seen the towns of the Lady Cutifichiqui, they have never come so far as this, for always they have fought at the rivers and hunting grounds, lying in ambush and taking or losing hair. The Governor must remember that all of this was told him before the setting out."

"They have served us well. I do not blame them," de Soto said flatly, and then he turned on the boy Perico and his eyes flashed. "You shall be flung to the dogs for lying and bringing the army into this empty waste."

Perico begged the Governor to believe that he had not lied. He was lost, it was plain that he was lost, but he had not wickedly led the army astray. Five years had passed since he had been in Cutifichiqui and in that time the trails had dimmed.

The Governor pointed to the dogs. "They at least will eat," he said.

Ortiz interposed. "Perico alone understands the Patofa people, Excellency." De Soto looked hard at the boy, then strode angrily away.

Thirty minutes later, with a squadron of horse and foot,

he set out to find a path. Later in the morning Tovar took an Indian and went into the woods hunting what roots and blites they might find. All afternoon he wandered where the Indian led until towards the end of the day he made signs that it was late and time to return. The Indian grunted and pointed to a clump of weeds. Tovar kneeled and began digging and as the roots came out of the ground and he held them in his hand, the Indian brought other plants which looked so like truffles that he had to look away to hide his trembling mouth. Tears, sudden and uncontrollable, blurred his eyes. And then through his hazy sight he saw a body of strange men and horses coming through an avenue of trees. He stood up, his knees weak and shaking. They were Christians! As they drew closer, he saw that they were dismounted and leading their horses by the bridle or driving them before them with sticks. They came in no order but they came silently, and it was clear that they, too, were lost and in worse plight than his own companions. Their weapons were slung to the saddles, footmen dragged themselves along, holding to the stirrups. Others wandered aimlessly in and out of the trees. Their eyes lay back in their heads, glazed and hollow. Their feet moved without guidance. Never had he seen horses so thin, or men. As he looked from face to face, they seemed all alike, with the same cast of the bone which kinsmen show. One walked before leading his horse, more splendidly attired, but his face lay back in his casque. He walked slowly but firmly. His sword swung gently at his side, the hilt thrust forward. The hilt was familiar. He knew one like it . . . the Governor's. Of course, the Governor's. They must have had the same. . . . He looked up and saw de Soto's eyes, dark and burning, turned upon him.

Tovar did not move. He waited until de Soto, coming towards him, stopped. De Soto paused a moment and then he asked, "How far is it to camp?"

The voice was infinitely weary but it spoke with the old intimacy of Golden Castile, Peru, and Spain, but not until that moment had it spoken so in Florida. Tovar forgot his hunger, where he was, and he said, "It's not far. I'll take you there." He did not need to ask if they had found a trail.

3

The following day de Soto called the officers together. They sat around him upon their saddles, all except Añasco. He leaned against a tree, bracing himself by his lance which he thrust before him. A shaft of light, glancing across his chin, flecked the red curls of his beard. It was the first bright morning in days. De Soto looked slowly from hollow face to hollow face. His eyes came to rest upon Tinoco. "You found nothing?"

"Nothing, my lord."

"And you, Vasconcelos?"

"We rode until the horses gave out."

Overhead the yellow butterflies swarmed, dived, hung to the air like a flowering bush and then blew away.

Juan Gaytán followed their flight. "We ought to turn back while we can," he spoke without emphasis.

"There's no maize behind us," Lobillo said. "We have eaten it."

"We might make it," Moscoso began in argument, broke off.

"Those rivers," Romo said.

"It's a bitter thing," Añasco said from his tree, "to turn back, to sweat again the old bitter sweat."

"It's a bitter thing to die," Gaytán replied.

There came a pause and then de Guzmán interposed evenly, "Let us be perfectly frank with ourselves. We are thoroughly lost. We are thin and weak. We are going to get weaker. Even if by the grace of God we find some way out of this waste and discover habitations, will we be strong enough to defend ourselves? I doubt whether my horse will go out of a walk."

For a moment there was silence and then Añasco lunged from his tree and hurled his lance at the ground. It swung to and fro, quivered to a stand. "If there was only something solid, something to strike," he said.

[284]

Moscoso regarded him diffidently. "You'd better save your strength," he said.

But Añasco did not hear. He strode to his weapon and jerked it from the ground. "Something this could strike, some . . . some . . ." defiantly he swept his head towards the forest, "some demon of the woods."

He had said it. Panting heavily, he sat with a backward lurch to the ground. Romo and Gallegos shifted to make place for him. For an instant de Soto's eyes met Tovar's gaze; then he straightened himself on his saddle. "Señor Constable," he asked quietly of Gallegos, "you alone of my captains have not spoken. Perhaps you will tell us what you think?"

Gallegos raised his head, looking into space. "I was thinking, my lord, of my wife, how in Cuba at our setting out she asked to come with me. I was thinking how well I did to deny her."

Gallegos broke his own silence. "But I wander from the purpose at hand. Naturally we must go on, find some way out of this . . ." he waved his hand.

"How?" Gaytán asked.

"Go on," he said.

"From nowhere to nowhere? From the middle of nowhere? Who will guide us?"

"We shall go on," the Governor said quietly. "Our situation is by no means hopeless. Even the horses know it's bad, but there's a little grain left, enough to feed a few men ten days. I'm going to ask Señor Añasco and the Constable to pick eight men, men that can swim, and the fattest horses, one to go up the river, the other down it, and allow themselves five days to go and five to return. The army will move back to the river and wait for them there, for they must take no risk of useless wandering as they return. Besides the men can fish." De Soto rose and the captains rose.

"And what, my lord, shall we eat over these ten days?" De Guzmán asked.

De Soto frowned. "There are the hogs, Captain. I brought

[285]

them for just such an emergency. A pound of flesh to the man each day. This cooked with herbs will keep life in us."

"The Indians do not find enough for themselves."

"You can look for no help from the Indians. There is nothing to feed them and I shall dismiss them to their homes. Well, gentlemen, let us be off."

"What if we fail?" Añasco asked.

"You must not fail."

No sooner had Añasco and the Constable set out than the Governor called Romo and Lobillo to him. They must take the same number of men and their rations of pork and the last of the grain, go into the country away from the river, keeping always a northerly direction. Romo set out with a full detail but Lobillo could find only four horses fit for travel. As soon as they were gone, the Governor called the Indians before him and released them from their service. They appeared loath to leave the Christians in their extremity. Their speeches of farewell lasted far into the day, and with each speech de Soto grew more restless and when it began to rain, he took it as an excuse to send them off without more ado.

The army gathered at the river bank and watched them swim away. The water was filled with feathered heads, and then it was empty.

"They are gone," Tovar said.

"Yes, they are gone," Silvestre replied.

The two friends stood for a while longer on the bank without speaking, when from behind they heard the screams of the hogs. "There's our pound of meat. Let's go get it," Tovar said.

De Soto and the officers were standing in line, waiting for their portions to be weighed. The Governor went unarmed, save for a dagger at his side. Almost it seemed deliberate, this neglect of his arms, as if he understood he must now choose other weapons for a more private strategy. For the next three days he went among the men, jesting since he could bring no

[286]

present comfort, and all strove to hide their sorrows in his presence. At Mass the army prayed devoutly for deliverance and Father Francisco spoke of our Lord's long vigil in the wilderness, and when it came the moment to raise the Chalice, he found a poisonous worm crawling up the side of the cup. Taking the sacred vessel he held it high before the altar and, kneeling, prayed that God might strike dead the worm. In the eyes of all there was fear as the worm followed its slimy way to the rim of the cup, slothfully drawing its back and swinging its head over the Sacred Blood. "Die, venomous worm, thou cousin of Satan," prayed Father Francisco in loud and sonorous tones, and his voice rang through the spaces of the forest. And as his voice grew more fervent, asking our Father not to abandon his own, suddenly the worm shrivelled and fell to the ground. "It is a sign," the priest's voice rang out. "He dies that we might live." Singing out loud and clear above the priest's words, the Governor's voice rose in a *Te Deum* and the united voices of the army, in relief and jubilation, swelled with the praise of the only salvation.

And that very afternoon, at the end of three days from the time of his setting out, Añasco rode into camp with two men, and the coats of their mounts shone darkly from their toil. Twelve leagues away they had found a town, a small town, with one barbacoa of maize and thirty bushels of parched maize. "Listen," de Soto cried in the midst of the army, "for he brings you life." Leaving directions for those captains still out, he buried a letter inside a gourd at the foot of a pine, and in the bark of the tree he cut these words: "Dig here." And the following morning before light the army had set out for the town of Aymay, called by the Christians Succour. And there was no road save the one Juan de Añasco had made moving along through the woods.

That same day, Monday, April the twenty-sixth, all riding and walking the hardest possible, the men drew near to the town, some sleeping two leagues off, others three and four, each as he was able to travel and his strength held out. The Governor wore out two horses and mounted the third, his last spare, and at sunset reached the town. Behind him, walking and leading their mounts, came Añasco, Biedma, Gaytán, Diego Tinoco, pushing himself along with the banner of Castile, and behind them Tovar, and each man entered the town ten and fifteen minutes behind the other, and Tovar behind the mare and the gelding, prodding them with his lance. The guards whom Añasco had put over the maize brought hominy they had prepared and they took each horse from its master and gave it a cup of maize. The Governor said harshly, for his voice was spent, "Take care. Don't founder the animals. I'll throw in stocks the man who founders his animal." No man looked at the Governor. With trembling hands they reached for the bowls of moist brown grain. Añasco took off his gloves to eat. Biedma and Tinoco with their gloved fingers shovelled the food into their mouths. Gaytán turned his back while he ate, but Tovar sank his face into the bowl and ate like a dog.

"Now, Señores," said Pedro Morón, the sergeant left in command by Añasco, "I have prepared a delicacy. Pray follow me."

In single file, like children at school, the men marched behind Morón into a lodge. Standing back like a server, Morón waved his hand. "Your dessert, Señores."

There upon a stool lay a large bowl heaped with strawberries. The men looked down in disbelief, then all at once broke into tears.

4

How fragrant was the land! With roses blooming sweeter than those in Spain and endless groves of mulberry trees in season, strawberries running wild over the ground. What a godsend was this fruit! Tovar breathed deep drawing the fair land in and slowly let his breath expire. Before him hundreds of men crawled along, picking the berries. Their voices called cheerfully across the savanna, or they shouted from the trees.

But there were those still too famished for cheer. Eight men sat in a mulberry straddling the limbs, picking the fruit silently, in rapid methodical movements. Viota sat split by a branch, his arms hanging at rest, his legs loose and relaxed, gazing into space. For the first time in months, indeed for the first time in Florida, had Tovar seen a man eating his fill.

How the fruit helped out with the grain! There was less than eighty bushels. Even with the greatest economy this could not last very long. And how much longer must they wait in Aymay? Most of the army had come in on Tuesday in varying degrees of exhaustion and Romo with the four Indians he had taken, but Gallegos and Lobillo were still out. They might not arrive for days. They might even miss the directions left at the foot of the tree and the fact, the stubborn fact, remained that as yet Cutifichiqui was as remote as the day the army set out from Apalache. But Perico understood Romo's Indians. There was hope in this, despite the Indians' silence. All morning the Governor had tried to make them talk, but neither bribes nor threats could make them show the way to their towns. Finally the Governer had leaped to his feet and shouted, "They lie or you lie, Perico! By my dead friend Compañón they shall take me to Cutifichiqui or burn. Tie the largest one to the stake. Let him burn slowly, like his wits. And you, Perico, if you live, it will be in Cutifichiqui."

Captain Espindola chained the Indian to a tree and the servants piled logs and brush about his feet. The Indian showed no fear or interest in his coming ordeal. He listened with indifference as the priest offered baptism and salvation. When pressed to answer, he said he did not understand the strangers' gods. There were three and then one which made four and yet there was only one. He shook his head, nor would he speak again as Perico repeated the Governor's offer of reprieve. He had only to put the Christians on their way. By dying he could not keep them from his town, he could only delay them. Was death worth this delay? But the Indian would not answer and Espindola turned to the Governor. Was His Excellency ready

[289]

for the business to proceed? De Soto rose and inspected the placing of the wood. "It is too high," he said. "The flames won't reach the body. Take it down to the hips."

"He will be longer dying as it is, my lord."

"Take it down," the Governor ordered peremptorily. "I use him for an example to make the others talk."

The torch was set, the dry brush flared, the flames settled, crackling at the bottom of the pile. And then Tovar had gone to feed the broken-down horses their warm meal gruel. He fed them with his hands, rubbing their coats to raise their spirits, and as he worked listened for cries or sounds from the stake. But there was nothing. Nor would he hear anything. He had known from the start that it was a waste of time to burn the Indian.

Always the thing the Governor pursued withdrew as he advanced, and the deeper in the wilderness he went the more confusing grew the way. Even when the Indians spoke true, by the time their words came through several mouths the sense was twisted so that never could he be certain of where he was or where to go, and yet always he went on. If the Indians resisted as they were resisting now, as they had resisted in Apalache ... surely this Florida was no Peru. But did the Governor recognize the difference? Would he allow himself to recognize it? That loss of patience, the sudden condemning of the Indian to the stake when he must have known full well he would be none the wiser for the fire. Could it be that he knew, at last, what Florida was? And feared it? And set his will, hardened it against all those who would steal away his desire? If only he had understanding behind his fear! Perhaps he understood. Had he not taken him, Tovar, again into his household and set him those tasks he was best fitted to do? Would de Soto forgive without understanding? He thought not. In this there was hope.

Through the trees Tovar saw Silvestre approaching. He was walking rapidly, with a light spring to his step. He hailed him and then went forward to greet him.

"Great news," Silvestre said. "At least it may be great news."

[290]

"What?"

"The Constable has come in with an Indian woman. Cutifichiqui is only two days away and she will guide us there."

"At last . . ."

"The Governor orders you to give out a double ration of maize for all. He has chosen an escort of the strongest horses. Tomorrow he means to go ahead and let the army follow as the men and animals are able."

Before the sun came up, the Governor was stirring. He ate a handful of fruit, three cakes of maize and then called to him Moscoso and set him over the army. He made one last inspection of his escort and threw out eight horses; then he mounted and turned to Moscoso: "We will meet in Cutifichiqui," he said and his eyes were bright.

He was about to give the command to go forward when three men walked into Aymay leading their mounts. The first of these was Lobillo. He came wearily forward. Even at a distance Tovar could see the hollows and the eyes set far back in their sockets. He came up and bowed without speaking.

"What news?" de Soto asked.

"We found trails."

"Where?"

"Two days out we found them. Running north-north-east."

"Did you follow them?"

Lobillo shook his head. "The horses . . ."

Suddenly the Governor looked at the two men just come up. He snapped his eyes upon Lobillo. "You had four men, Captain. Where are the others?"

"Their horses gave out."

"I asked you a question, Señor."

Lobillo put out his hand and rested it on his mount's neck. With his other hand he motioned to the rear. "Somewhere back there."

The army had gathered to witness de Soto's departure. It now grew very still, waiting for his face to compose itself. At last he began: "I send out four captains in this army's great

[291]

distress. One of them returns, bearing news of a town and food. Another comes in with four Indians, and another telling of populated lands, but with the greatest gift of all—a guide to Cutifichiqui. But you . . ." Lobillo's eyes were now on the ground before him. He was breathing deeply. "Mount your horse and go find the rest of your command."

"Yes, my lord." Lobillo's lips barely moved.

"Well, be on your way."

"A little food, Excellency, first."

"The men you abandoned do not eat."

Lobillo reached for the pommel of his saddle and pulled himself into his seat.

"You will find those men and bring them safely into this town, on pain of death," the Governor said.

Lobillo could still be seen through the trees as de Soto and his escort disappeared, travelling west by north, with the Indian woman seated upon a mule, riding at the Governor's side.

The Governor and his men travelled until they came to a river and there made camp for the night. Juan de Añasco he had sent on ahead to arrange for interpreters and canoes, for the woman guide said the town lay on the other bank. Eagerly the Governor pushed on and the horses, half-spent as they were, caught the spirit of their masters. On the way a messenger came from Añasco saying he had taken three Indians who reported that the Señora was making preparations to receive them in her town. One of these he had sent on to announce the Governor's near approach.

The trail began to widen, running now by the river, now out of sight of but always within reach of its sound. And where they went the air was sweet and smelled of a rich land. The same roses as at Aymay bloomed wild along the way, growing in the shade of the forest, bare of leaves, blossoms hanging to the thorny wood. They rode through oaks, live-oaks, groves of cedar and liquid amber. They rode past thickets of yellow plums, the fruitful mulberry, and everywhere the mast lay deep upon the ground. And then the path turned, through the trees the sun flashed from the water, and they came out of the long shade to the river. So sudden was the change Tovar had to turn his eyes away from the brilliant light.

Standing among the canoes drawn up along the far bank, men, women, and children looked silently across at the Christians. Upstream in the trees he could see the outlying lodges of the town.

Añasco rode up to the Governor. "Welcome to Cutifichiqui, my lord."

The Governor dismounted and walked with Añasco to the edge of the river. "You have spoken with the Indians?"

"I have, my lord. It is an amiable and gentle people. Six of their principal men came over to ask if we came in peace or war. I gave the usual reply and begged food and portage. They retired to consult the cacica."

As Añasco was speaking, Indian flutes sounded in the forest and all eyes turned in the direction of the town. Dancing, raising and lowering their bodies as a bull swings its neck, the flute players came out of the trees. The light ran from the bright tassels of the wooden flutes. Turning and bowing, blowing into the ground or straight overhead, casting their rude music where it would fall, the pipers led the way to the canoes, following close to the shore. Behind them walked six men of authority, and then warriors with bows as long as their bodies. They did not dance but bore themselves with a grave and stately mien. The six wore crowns of feathers and they were clothed down to their feet. "The head men," Añasco said.

By now the escort had dismounted, drawing behind the Governor's chair which had been set upon level ground some twenty paces from the river. Down stream the pages had taken the horses to water. Perico pointed and cried, "The Señora!" The Governor leaned forward in his seat, around him his men caught their breath. The Lady of Cutifichiqui was drawing into view.

[293]

She sat high upon the shoulders of her servants. The litter that bore her was covered in a soft white linen and she was all in white. Her hair flowed loose about her shoulders and she sat with an easy grace, looking before her. The bearers walked with slow and careful steps, so that her chair seemed to drift like a boat upon the air. Over her head two youths held fans of herons' wings and from the long staffs in their hands they shielded her face from the sun. Trailing behind, walking lightly upon the smooth red bank, came her women with baskets of fruit and behind them, at the last, were other servants bearing fardels of skins and cloth upon their heads. So clear was the air and so unhurried her progress that, by the time her train reached the place where the canoes were moored, she seemed no longer distant and strange but familiar and like one who is close at hand.

She alighted and entered a canoe that had been prepared and sat in the stern upon two cushions, under an awning. Six of her women sat at her feet but no paddlers or any man whatsoever entered the boat. At a signal the canoe into which the head men had embarked shot into the water, tied to her bow and began to tow her where the Governor waited. On all sides canoes skimmed over the surface of the river, the paddles dipped and flashed, the arms of the paddlers reached to the water and rose in unison. As she drew near, the Governor rose from his chair and went down to meet her.

"She's a girl," Biedma said.

"And beautiful," the Constable said.

She sprang lightly to the bank and stood for a moment scanning the faces of the Christians. Her feet were as small as a child's, enclosed in buskins embroidered in seed pearls. Her skirt was white and of the softest doe and over her shoulders she wore a shawl of mulberry cloth. Her eyes were black, her skin the colour of almonds. And then Tovar's gaze came to rest on the pearls, four strands of them, as large as hazel nuts, falling to her waist.

She was moving. Surrounded by her women but walking

a little before them, she approached the Governor without fear or curiosity. He was smiling and bowing. She inclined her head and then began to speak in low courteous tones.

"Excellent Lord, be this coming to these your shores most happy. My power can in no way equal my wishes to serve and please you, but with the purest good will I tender you my person, my towns, my people and these small gifts."

Her retainers dropped skins and fardels of cloth at the Governor's feet and then she took from her neck the necklace of pearls and with perfect ease dropped them over his head. As she was small, he bowed to receive them and then he took from his finger a band of gold set with a ruby and placed it upon her thumb. After the courtesies of greeting he led her to a stool her people brought and he sat facing her in his chair.

The conversation was long, broken by Perico translating to Ortiz and Ortiz to the Governor, but the bearing of the Señora and the tone of her voice gave emphasis to the words which, so indirectly, promised relief. Half of her town she would turn over for the army's quarters; if necessary she would move her people into another close at hand, although this she preferred not to do because the town, with many others, had been cursed. She would share her grain, but he must understand that she had only two barbacoas to last until the new year's crop was gathered and that was many moons away. But she would send her hunters to hunt and at Ilapi there was stored seven barbacoas of maize. If his people were many, he could send part of them there. All that she had she would freely share. Pointing to the horses, she asked if they ate meat or grazed like deer. The Governor replied that they partly grazed and partly ate maize like a man. She looked at them apprehensively and said they must eat a lot, for their bellies were big. The Governor assured her that his men and beasts would be frugal in their appetites, so that she and her people would not come to want, an unworthy return for her generous and hospitable reception. . . .

Tovar's attention wandered. From long practice his eyes

ran swiftly over the assembled Indians, measuring, examining. They were different from all the others he had seen in Florida, more like Christians, he thought. It was not only that they were clothed. He examined their garments—well-tanned buskins on their feet, shirts made from the finest skins, black leggings with colored fringes as they are made in Spain. And there were white strips of leather for ties. But he did not find what he unconsciously sought. Something was lacking. And then it came to him: they had no gold. Gifts of mulberries and plums, sable fur and the strong-smelling skins of cat. Rich and welcome gifts, but not what the Governor expected of Cutifichiqui. Perhaps there would be pearls enough to please him; those he had received were worth their weight in gold. There must be great numbers in the town. All the women had necklaces and armbands, those upon the girl at the Señora's right seemed particularly fine . . . the girl was looking at him. He had the feeling that she had been looking for some time.

And then the Señora rose, her attendants shifted, the girl stooped to pick up her mistress' stool . . . the Governor was taking her by the hand . . . the procession moved off to the river.

The canoes shoved off, the paddlers bent forward in unison. In a ragged line the boats shot athwart the current, bobbing, diving through the light brown stream. The eyes of the Christians fastened upon the boats, as if their looks propelled and guarded them. They watched them ride onto the other bank, saw them turn again, empty, into the stream.

The Governor now released his eyes. "Strike off Perico's chains," he said. "We pass over to Cutifichiqui."

As he spoke, he looked like a younger man.

5

Lying upon the piazza of his lodge, in the midst of the companions of his mess, Tovar felt the soft cane mat give beneath the weight of his body. He felt the stain and sorrows of the march fall away and, letting down his guard, knew what it was to be at peace again. He tried to remember when last he had known such utter comfort and peace. The effort was too great and he gave it up. All around him, in the eastern quarter of the town, Christians were taking their ease, lying upon the skin-covered beds or sitting in the porticos, idle, breathing the soft mild air, the Indian women passing with baskets of fruit and wafers, dried strips of venison, great bowls of beans, and salt.

Salt!

What a feast day!—the people serving without fear or servility, as they might welcome kin come out of a far country. He asked himself why these Cutifichiqui, saving of course the Patofa, were the first to come in peace, openly and without guile, civil in their manners, kind and generous in their acts. Out of the corner of his eye he saw Silvestre sit up and look around. "Even if there's no gold, I'd be willing to settle," he said.

About him the men sighed.

"There are pearls. I should judge a great many," Tovar said.

"There may be gold," Chaves added.

"There may be," Tovar said. Absently he studied the design of Cutifichiqui. Like Patofa and Ocute it was laid out about the chunghe yard. He stepped the yard with his eyes, some three hundred paces long and about fifty wide. At the river end was the square ground, enclosed by four long houses, where at the moment most of the Indian men had gathered; at the other end stood the temple and rotunda. The private dwellings, two, three, and sometimes four houses to a group, lay back from the long sides of the yard. Into the buildings on the western face the Indians had withdrawn. At the middle of the yard stood the chunghe pole, the four square pillars declining to an obtuse point, some thirty feet in the air. From its top hung a cedar branch, brushing the pole when the wind blew. He wondered what it meant, hanging there at the very centre of the town. And then his eyes came to rest upon one of two poles near each corner at the temple end. It was not high, some twelve feet he judged, but it was not the height which caught his attention. Dangling from the pole fell a number of scalps, with the hair on and strained to hoops five or six inches wide. There were two he looked at a long time. The hair on these had all worn away, and they were as dry and white as parchment.

A shadow fell across the portico. He looked down, into Ortiz' eyes. They were smiling in the brown mask of his face. "We've happened here at the end of the Mulberry moon," he said.

Chaves swung around. "Don't come walking like an Indian. Make a noise when you come up."

"Mulberry moon?" Silvestre asked. "What's that?"

"It's a time when people eat, dance, and walk as twined together."

"I'd like to twine," Chaves said.

"We've been invited to the dance," Ortiz said.

As they were speaking, the Señora's litter passed out of the square ground and the Indians in procession moved down towards the river. Tovar and his companions followed and stood at a distance watching. The Señora stepped from the litter and dived four times into the water, and all her people dived after her, and then the procession made its way back to the town.

"Where are the women?" Chaves asked.

"They aren't allowed in the square at feast times," Ortiz said. "They might pollute it."

"How can you feast without women?"

Ortiz did not answer.

"I always wash before I feast," Tovar said and began taking off his clothes.

He and his companions jumped into the river and others from the town, seeing them, came down and with them the Governor until all who could swim spent the afternoon in the water. By the time they had dressed and fed their horses the sun had gone down. In twos and threes they gathered before

[298]

the Governor's quarters, waiting for the messenger to conduct them to the square. They did not have long to wait. Coming across one end of the yard, the messenger took his way. He neither hurried nor delayed but came at an even pace. The Christians knew at once that it was he and waited silently. Suddenly the silence was broken.

"Are you going to assist at these heathen rites?" Father Francisco asked with a harsh voice.

Tovar looked around in surprise. He had thought the priest was at his prayers.

"The Señora has asked it, Father," the Governor replied.

"It is a feast of death," the priest continued. "I forbid it."

It was now dusk but Tovar thought he could see the colour go a shade lighter in the Governor's face.

"It is unseemly and dangerous. Do you know to whom these rites are made?" Father Francisco did not wait for an answer. "To the moon. To the pagan goddess of the woods and fields and streams. To her these lost and deluded souls make sacrifice. I call on you, Hernando de Soto, to take no part in it. Furthermore I enjoin upon you to fulfill His Majesty's will and forbid the savages their evil and ungodly practices. Nigh onto a year have we been in this land and to none of these savages have we brought the Word or taken them from death to life."

The Governor faced the priest. He spoke coldly after a moment in which he delayed to collect his thoughts. "I have dedicated this conquest to God," de Soto said, "but there is no time now to save their souls. First the conquest must be made and the land pacified. When all of Florida I have added to the Crown then, Father, we shall bring them to grace."

The priest had scarcely restrained himself. He blurted out, "It is of Christian souls, your soul, I now think."

All colour had fled the Governor's face, but his eyes remained even. At the centre of the dark pupils there were two dead flecks of light. His lips parted. "We do not go to assist at these rites. We go to pay our respects to the Señora. And I go on business." His voice grew smoother. "You may, but I cannot forget the courtesy I owe this Lady for saving our lives. Heathen bread you have eaten, Father. Did it grate upon your bowels?"

The two men faced each other in the haze of the spending day, and then slowly the priest raised his hand and thrust his finger at the Governor's face. "The Bread of Life is not served at the devil's board."

The Governor lifted his shoulders as though shaking off a weight and faced the Indian messenger. None had seen him come up. He was waiting silently, with a wand in his hand. The Governor nodded and the Indian turned, and the Governor, the officials of the Royal Hacienda, all those who had come together, followed behind his soft footfalls. As they neared the grounds, coming to one of the openings between the houses, the pace increased, insensibly keeping time to the hollow beat of the drum. When it came his turn to enter, Tovar looked back. Kneeling in the dirt, Father Francisco had bowed his head in prayer, his face turned away from the town.

The dancing had already begun. Around a great fire in the centre of the grounds the Indians moved in a circle, a circle within a circle, with turkey wings in their hands to shield them from the flames. They did not look up or in any way notice the arrival of their guests. To one side the musicians sat with their legs crossed beneath them. One was beating a loose wet skin tied about a pot, the other shook a rattle as if he knew the night was long and feared to grow weary. They were singing in time to their music, and at certain places in the song the dancers turned.

Tovar waited for the Christians to climb out of his way to their beds in the northern end of the house. The Señora was alone in the middle bed. He looked for her women, but she was the only woman in this gathering of men. Behind her the beds were crowded with warriors, up to the roof of the house. Their dark faces looked dimly out, and he thought of the choir of angels in the picture hanging at the altar in the parish church at Badajoz—until he saw their eyes, glowing steadily like hundreds of cinders. The Governor stepped before him, bowing to the Señora. She pointed to a pile of skins, and there beside her he took his seat.

Tovar could see nothing but the bounding flames and the flickering bodies of the dancers, moving always in rhythm, the same stamping of the feet, the same turning before the fire; and as they turned, its light ran streaming down their greased and coppery bodies until their flesh seemed all aflame. He knew this was witchery for his own blood began to exult and he grew restless and secretly crossed himself, thinking of Father Francisco's warning. From time to time dancers dropped out and others took their places; then suddenly all of them stopped, without signal, and walked away. After a while the Señora spoke to an old man, and he rose and began to speak. He spoke for a long time, and the people listened quietly. After he was done, the dancing began again.

So the night wasted.

During one of the pauses the Governor said, "Your ladyship, as you see, we travel alone, without women. My men are young . . ." He did not take his eyes from her face as she listened to his words through Perico's mouth. Once the pauses were established, the interpreter's part made the speeches grow at once more formal and free.

"There are women in the town who have been put away for adultery," she said. "These you may have. And the girls if you please them."

"Will your ladyship deliver these to me?" he asked.

The Señora shook her head. "Their bodies are their own to do with as they please."

"My men must woo?"

"They must buy. A girl often, before she becomes a bread-maker, sells herself for a day or a season to a youth who has won a name or comes laden from the hunt. Except at those times when it is forbidden. Until the dances are put away it is forbidden. Tomorrow your men may choose girls they are able to please."

"If it will offend your warriors?" he said.

"She who has had the most lovers is desired by all. To be loved by your warriors will make all more desirable."

The Governor bowed his head. The ostrich plumes in his beaver bent in slow grace over the Señora's head.

"But the bread-makers," she continued, "these you must pass by."

"And how will my men know the maidens?"

"By their flowing hair."

The Governor leaned forward. "Is your ladyship betrothed?" he asked.

It seemed to Tovar that their bodies touched. It was an illusion of the shadows cast by the fire, for the Governor was meticulous in his deportment and whatever the intention of his question, nothing could make him violate by a direct, familiar manner the formality of the occasion or the nobility of their persons. Tovar was as certain of this as he was certain that Lord Christ was born of the Virgin. And yet the image of their bodies joined remained as sharp in his mind as if the thing had been done.

Later, weary of the dancing and the talks, he left the square. From time to time in the last dark hours of the night he had seen many of the Christians slip away. Nor did the Governor notice or call them back, perhaps because it was near day and the time for the taboo to lift. As he passed out of the square and went where the women were gathered with the children, on the benches outside the grounds, he knew it was not weariness which had sent him wandering at so strange an hour. The old women sat with veiled eyes but the younger ones smiled at him, or they laughed frankly together. In the growing light he looked from face to face, but she was not among them. He crossed the chunghe yard to the Indian side of the town. The town was empty. He went from lodge to lodge, more rapidly as he drew to the far end. He looked once toward the rotunda and temple, growing solid now in the grey air. No use to look there. Or was there? He took a step in that direction, halted. Surely she would not go into the temple with her lover. . . .

It was out. He was jealous of this savage girl and angry—angry that he could be so disturbed over any woman again, angry at his foolish behaviour. He had seen her only once. He had happened to be in her way and she had stared from curiosity as she had stared at the horse, the, to her, strangely bedecked warriors. And yet ... no, it was a vanity to think the girl would remember or had chosen him from among so many. She had taken a lover to pleasure her and when the pleasure was past, her love would pass. So it was with these people. On this continent, this land, unknown to Christian geography, love was still innocent.

Beyond the town stood a knoll overgrown with walnut and cedar. On the near side it was open and the trees spaced as if they had been planted. He began to climb. He liked this innocency in love. To love without thought of sin. It was good. And yet they were a moral people. Once given in marriage the woman was bound. The Señora had been careful to stress this.

In the east the sky was beginning to streak. To his left he could hear the river. Beyond him along its misty banks lay the narrow fields, now dark green with the young maize, the tender shoots bending low with dew. There was no fatter land in heathendom, or one more pleasing to the eye. Wide, open forests free of thickets, hummocks of mulberry and oak lying close about the town, and everywhere a great plenty of game, if he was to judge by the gifts of skins and fur, enough to reshoe the army and with plenty left over for jerkins and hose. What a land for ease and riches and pleasure. Never had he felt so gay, not since Cuba, when, in his despair, seeking the thing which without reason or cause had undone him, he had walked into God's house and found the wilderness sprouting from the altar. He had fled the sight but could not flee the dread or, fleeing, ever escape it, or know what it was except that it was evil and an evil unnamed in the Christian calendar. Now it no longer haunted him. The dread had fallen away, like harness from his back, and he walked free again. What had happened to release him? Was it a thing of the moment, a mere reprieve?

[303]

Beyond the forest the sun was rising. Before it the sky opened out like a shell. Cutifichiqui! To lost and starving men it gave meat and bread. Could it be the promise of life, its restoration, the life that was death to cherish, which brought him such comfort? Surely it was more than fear of death which that day in Havana, under the full fury of the noonday sun, had left so cold a chill at his heart.

He threw up his head, grew still. Somewhere to the front he had heard a noise. He looked around, moving only his eyes. They stopped upon the side of the hill where it fell away in a dip. Distinctly now he heard a flapping and once, he was not sure but he thought he heard a sharp moan of pain. He slipped through the brush, the dew spattered his sleeves, but he made no sound. Cautiously he parted the two cedar shrubs and saw it: upon the ground a hawk was in distress. A long thin snake had several times wrapped about its wing and body. The free wing beat the ground and the air, its beak struck at the weaving head, black and no larger than a thumb, but the head bent and swayed, always out of danger, circling and diving to entangle the bird further in its coils. He watched the fight a moment and then stepped through the cedars. With a bound the hawk spread its wings and flew silently up the air. Silently the snake sped away and turned a corner of the dip.

He ran after it, angry that a creature so loathsome should have the bird of princes in its grip, saying as he ran, I will bruise its head. He came to the turn and drew up short. The snake had veered and was disappearing behind a drift of dirt and leaves. Out of his eye he saw the black whip-like tail, the chocolate body. The tail jerked out of sight; not a leaf stirred or so much as trembled. In the full clarity of the moment it seemed to him a symbol of the whole mystery of the coming day, for he saw the end in the beginning, how the power of that twisting flight could pass over so frail a thing and leave no sign. This was an instant reflection, for his full gaze was stopped by what he saw in front of him.

He felt no surprise at the sight of the youth and woman, but a feeling that they had been waiting for him to come. All was logical, as in a dream. The youth lay stretched upon the ground, supporting himself on an arm, his neck drawn back, his eyes pulling him towards the woman. His face was grey and stained by pain. Sweat pocked his forehead and cheeks and his breath came in short harsh gasps. The woman was very still, squatting between his outflung legs. She was entirely absorbed in what she did, but her back was turned and Tovar could not see and yet he knew at once what it was. If they had heard him approach, neither gave any sign. Each watched the other out of the silence they made.

He drew closer and saw her hand. The youth's hose was open and in disarray and there at his middle she held him, worn out and at her mercy.

Tovar may have spoken, perhaps his boot fell heavily to break the spell. The woman stood up without haste or alarm and stepped away. As she rose, the youth dropped upon the ground. From the entire length of his body he drew a sigh and then grew very still. When Tovar reached him, his eyes were closed, his face pale but no longer drawn. It was young Herrera. After a while Herrera fluttered his eyes and looked up at Tovar. "You came in time," he said weakly. "A moment more and she would have gelded me."

"Are you able to walk?"

"In a minute." And after a pause, "You won't say anything about this?"

Tovar helped him to his feet. He said, "Even with an Indian it is best to be formal."

Herrera averted his face and began to arrange his clothes. "I meant nothing carnal," he said. And when Tovar did not reply, half-turning but still averting his eyes, he added, "I'll go back now."

He limped off down the hill, breaking through the underbrush, and for some minutes after he could no longer be seen Tovar could hear the noise he made.

The girl had not moved. She was waiting as he knew she

would wait, as he had known from the instant he came upon them it was she for whom he searched. She was smiling, and her smile told him all he had need for knowing, if need there was. Words would have burdened the theme and he thought, as he went towards her, how little use they had for speech, how it confused the act, went beyond it. He stood for a moment and as openly returned her smile. Then he took his silver chain from around his neck and dropped it over her head.

Laughing, she ran deeper into the grove, and he followed her.

6

He should have foreseen what would happen, but the first few days at Cutifichiqui passed in one long idyl; and yet in all that time he had the feeling of a man acting in a dream, when those desires impossible to the awakened senses are gratified, but gratified in that timeless haste which ever flees but ever finds the day. Even after the rest of the army came up and he looked across the river and saw the gaunt men and wasted horses, saw their hunger and their need, even then he did not admit to himself how their arrival must, of necessity, put an end to the false relations existing between the Indians and the Christians. As long as there was only the Governor's escort in the town, both peoples could disguise the true meaning of the occupation. The very numbers of the army must hasten the crisis and the decision, for in spite of the Señora's hospitality the hour would come when either the Christians or the Indians must be deprived of food. And the women? Would the Indians continued to submit in this?

There was only one course to take. The power of the Indians must be summarily broken; they must be divided up, baptized and brought into the knowledge of the Christian faith. But this policy, the inevitable end of the conquest, the Governor was slow to put into effect. He delayed, neither conquering nor moving on but ravaging the land, taking away the liberty of the Indians without converting them.

The reason for this, Tovar thought, was plain. De Soto delayed for the Señora's sake, allowing her a specious sovereignty which maintained her dignity but in no way interfered with the army's well-being. Gift maize ate as well as tribute maize. Here Tovar let the matter rest, not doubting because he would not let himself doubt that the Governor would act when the time came, or when the Lady pleased him less. If he preferred to dally and play the game of visiting prince at a foreign court, let him play, so long as he could be brought to settle and go no further into the wilderness. Yet Tovar did not completely delude himself. As great as were the Señora's charms they could not for long supplant that image of a richer Peru which had fixed itself in the Governor's mind. This consideration alone disturbed the perfection of his days. He consoled himself with the thought that pearls were staple treasure, and Cutifichiqui had pearls. If not gold, they could be traded for gold.

He repeated this to himself, coming from the woods into the town, with his leman, Tsianina, beside him. Absorbed by his thoughts, he did not see Silvestre until he had laid a hand upon his arm.

"It's well," Silvestre said, "we are still at peace."

"How so?" Tovar asked.

"Love has left you little strength for war."

"I've enough to put you on your back."

"I have another kind of back," Silvestre said and, laughing, the two friends cast aside their swords and stripped them to the waist. Soon they had fallen and were tumbling over the ground. The idlers gathered to witness the sport. The betting ran high and the shouts of encouragement when, suddenly, there came the cry to arms and a commotion from the Indian part of the town. Tovar reached his feet in time to see a Christian holding to the loft of a barbacoa, kicking at Indians trying to pull him down.

The Governor arrived and quelled the disturbance and threw the Christian into irons. As the man was led away, the Indians, pacified, scattered to their dwellings. But the damage was done. No longer would it be the same at Cutifichiqui. This Tovar understood as he watched the Governor's face grow dark with anger and heard his sharp rebuke to the man. "Disobey again and I shall hang you," he said, and the man replied, "It has not been your custom, my lord, to deal so strictly with us when there was food and we hungered." To this the Governor gave no reply, but later in the day he ordered the Constable to take a large part of the army away to Ilapi where the food was more plentiful.

Afterwards he entered the temple and opened the places of the dead. Thus suddenly was de Soto brought to a decision. Tovar knew what a grievous thing it was in the Indians' eyes to rob the dead and he wondered if the thing was done with the permission of, or despite, the Señora's wishes. As the Governor took no measures to seize the Indians which he must have done if he no longer expected to rule them through her power, it appeared as if she had connived at the sacrilege.

She stood apart and watched the small dark opening through which the Governor had passed. Her women were very still and her councillors and they averted their eyes as the pearls were brought out into the yard. But the Señora watched closely the door and her eyes grew puzzled as she saw the delight upon the Christian faces as basket after basket of pearls was brought and set by Añasco to be counted and weighed, and the King's fifth set apart from those to be divided according to each man's station and worth. There were chains and bracelets, gorgets for the neck, and some wrought cunningly in the shape of figured birds and babies. At last Añasco called out: "Two hundred pounds." Here was a fortune indeed!

At last the Governor came through the temple door, holding three Biscayan axes in his hand. As he approached the Señora with a question in his eyes, Tovar glanced towards the Indian side of the town. Not a man, woman, or child was on the streets. The lodges were still, the mats had been dropped over the doors; no sound of life stirred behind their darkened mouths. Even the dogs had slunk out of sight.

"Where got you these?" the Governor was asking.

Tovar returned his attention to the Señora and listened as she told how many years ago other strangers with beards had landed on the coast. Before they sailed away, the axes had been got in trade for food and other things. This she had heard from her aunts and uncles, for she was too small a child to remember.

"That must have been the Licentiate Ayllón," Biedma said.

"And this river the Saint Elena," Moscoso added with excitement.

The Governor interrupted. "How far is the sea?" he asked.

The Señora twice swept her hands in the air. "Two days' journey away."

"Now is good fortune with us," Moscoso said, turning to all of those standing about. Tovar noticed that the Governor disliked his enthusiasm and the fashion in which he addressed the captains and the men.

The Señora walked to the baskets of pearls. Her people did not follow her. Pointing to them, she said, "Do you hold these of much account? Then go to my town, Talimeco, and you will find so many your horses cannot haul them away."

"Let them stay there," the Governor said quickly. "To whom God makes a gift, may Saint Peter bless it."

It was clear what the men thought: the Governor wanted Talimeco for his own domain. Only in the light of their own greed could they interpret his words, but Tovar knew better how to understand them. Only his foolish wish had seen a drifting in the Governor's policy. What else could have made him think de Soto had looked upon Cutifichiqui other than as a place of rest and food, once it was discovered the tales of gold were false? Enough riches had been found, with the promise of more, to make the men want to settle and take the known goods for the unknown promise of the wilderness. This explained the Governor's manner when he heard of the sea, and his sudden blessing of the pearls at Talimeco. Blessed or unblessed, if there was such treasure there as the Señora said, the army would know of it. He, Tovar, would see to that. Then surely the Governor would think hard and long before he went against all his men and the officers of the King's Hacienda.

7

Tovar rode by the last house of Cutifichiqui into the forest, Tsianina walking at the side of the horse. He had tried to get her to mount his mare, but she was afraid. By signs and by saying Talimeco over and over he had made her understand where she must take him. Once he had thought to bring Perico in and make it plain, but he did not trust the boy. Already the woman seemed able to foretell his will and, strangely, he felt that he had dwelled with her all his days. He watched her as she went over the path, the soundless fall of her feet, the slightly rounded hips, the easy carriage of body and head, and the way her movements seemed to melt into the forest growth, never violating or disturbing brush or leaf, or the stillness through which she passed. Her face was turned away, so he could not see her eyes, and yet he knew she saw and heard everything stirring in the woods that might do harm to him and her. He spoke to her, dismounted, and put himself at her side.

Half a league from Cutifichiqui they came to the first deserted town. The grass grew high in the streets, and where the houses touched the forest, saplings and bushes grew all about, some in the very doors of the rotting lodges. Here and there the wind had torn away the roofs, but the walls stood firm, except those made of mats and these hung in strips or lay dragging the ground, leaving gaping holes. He walked up to one of these open gaps and looked inside. The ashes of a fire lay white and dry near the centre pole. All the pots and bowls lay about as if the owners had been called suddenly away. Upon the benches the bedding skins were covered with dust. In some he could see where the moths had eaten. He understood why Tsianina would not enter with him but waited outside. Surely a curse hung over the town. Was it a curse that he could ever under-

[310]

stand? he asked himself, when towards late afternoon they came upon Talimeco.

It was only a good league from Cutifichiqui, up the river, but they walked slowly. Tsianina, sensing his errand, was not her usual wanton self when they were alone together. And for the first time he felt the need of speech with her, understanding how persistent was the memory of disaster, so great that even now the Indians did not like to go near the old towns, fearing that there was still evil enough lurking there to do them harm. They had fled, leaving everything behind. He had opened the barbarcoas and found them piled with garments of cloth and feathers, grey and vermilion feathered cloaks, white ones, and cloaks made of different colors, closely fashioned and warm for winter wear. They had left their food, too, but the rats and weevils had wrought havoc of this.

That such disaster would come about for the going out of a fire. He remembered the Señora's face as she had told of the sacrilege. She had mentioned it when first they met her, when she had stood so slight and comely, facing at her ease the strangers. Little then did he know what were her secret thoughts and fears. And then later, as all alike, the first among the Christians and the first among her men, sat around the cane spiral fire in her house, she had brought it up again, how once Cutifichiqui had been a great people with many towns and many caciques owning her aunt's rule. And she seemed not to make a tale of it, or to boast of her once fair towns and the people in them. Rather she told it to herself as if to mind her what a wasting wrath was sacrilege. The people dying by the hundreds, the stench of the ghost breaths falling from the rafters until the fires in the lodges burned blue. Witches had been stabbed and burned; warriors who had sinned against the holy rites confessed and were driven to shift for themselves in the wilderness; adulterers were caught and publicly shorn of their hair, and the old custom of shooting to death by arrows was tried—and still the people died. And then one of the

[311]

tenders of the holy fire fell sick, so sorely sick he must crawl to feed the flames.

When it was plain he was dying, he sent to the cacica, the Señora's aunt, and said that she must come at once, that he had a thing of such importance to tell her if he died without revealing it all the people would perish. As soon as the sick man saw his mistress, heavily wrinkled with age and sorrow, he trembled so it appeared he would be unable to speak. But at last his mouth began to work brokenly. I am going to die, he said, so it makes no difference whether I die of sickness or by man. I know that I am evil for having concealed so long what I am going to say. I am the cause of the death of my nation; therefore I merit death, but let me not be eaten by the dogs.

The cacica reassured him to draw forth his secret. Then he told how when his companion was away he fell asleep and let the fire go out. Fright seized him. As he was still alone, he called the first passer-by and begged of him fire to light his pipe, which the man brought knowing it was forbidden to touch the holy fire except to tend it. Thus the fire was relit with profane fire. Soon after the sickness came.

The cacica assembled all the old men in council and by their advice it was decided that very day to go and wrest fire from a town as yet untouched by the evil, and to abandon Talimeco and all the dwellings of sorrow. The messengers needs must travel two whole days, since on the way they found no tree burning from the lightning's stroke. Fire come directly from the sun they might have taken. About the wrested fire, purified by blood spilled in its taking, the new town of Cutifichiqui was built. Here the sickness fell away and the people grew as joyful as after the green maize dances, when all things are renewed and freed from pollution. Yet they were few and their greatness broken.

Looking upon Talimeco, Tovar grew still before the full measure of the calamity. Never had he seen so fair an Indian town nor one so large. It made five of Cutifichiqui. And as he looked, things seemed now not so simple as when he first set out to find treasure enough to force de Soto to bide in this land. He walked through the long empty streets, and the grass which grew where the feet of dwellers should be passing swished and struck his boots gently and with the noise of rough silk. He could break it with his little fingers; yet slowly and secretly, beyond the eye to measure, it was overthrowing all that man in his power and pride had built. Each lodge stood greater or as great as the Señora's house at Cutifichiqui, and above and below all were covered with cunningly wrought mats and roofs of cane that looked like amber tile. He came to the end of a street where four long houses were set somewhat apart. The first of these he entered. From the floor to the roof tree it was lined with shelves, and the shelves were piled with the dry white bones of the dead, not in order but as if they had been hastily laid away. From the long bony toes, mingling with ribs and thighs, the spider had cast its web, and the webs drooped with dust. Slowly he walked through the room. He paused by a skull larger than the rest and took it in his hands. The holes of its eyes gaped with emptiness, on the mound of the skull he saw the marks of an old wound, where a club had struck; the mouth hung open thirstily, drinking the silent and invisible air. So would it hang. . . . Carefully Tovar laid it down.

The other houses were like the first, crowded with the bones of hundreds of dead. He looked in, but he did not enter. At last he climbed the great mound where the temple stood. He had seen it rising through the lower branches of the trees before he saw the town. When first he set out from Cutifichiqui, he had thought he could not wait to see what the temple held, but now he delayed and went first to the chieftain's hall. It was like all others he had seen in this part of Florida, except larger. The posts of the buildings were painted in reds and blues and carved in figures of the panther. Inside carven heads of men looked fiercely at him from the foundation pillars and from the walls hung bunches of herbs, now as dry as tinder, swan's down, eagle feathers. Weapons lay or stood against the walls. The bed skins were of bear and fallow deer. There were storehouses piled with dyed and figured skins, a summer dwelling house and a hall for receiving visitors. Tovar turned away and, at last, let his eyes rest upon the temple.

Its roof was high and steeply pitched and made of slender stalks of cane, split in half. It was adorned with rows of sea shell and periwinkles, and in between fell skeins of pearls and seed pearls half a fathom long. Now in the late afternoon sun the whole roof glowed with many fires, strong or delicate as the rays struck the upturned shells. As he watched he understood the influence of this heathen god and why the Indians feared and loved him. More magnificent were the Sun's places of worship in Peru, but here too he ruled the seasons and struck down those who grew careless in his service. Tovar was troubled and fearful, for certainly only God the Father held sway over life and death. He crossed himself and entered the wide doors, between figures of warriors holding weapons in their hands, as though to guard what lay inside.

An odour like stale cold incense struck his nostrils as he stood for a moment in the dimmer light. And then he looked upwards. The upper part of the temple above the walls was adorned like the roof outside with rows of shell and pearls. From the beams hung many-coloured plumes and feathers and, in between, strings of pearls of so thin a thread that the pearls seemed to be falling out of the roof. As he looked, the room grew less dark and the pearls shone with a dull grey lustre, and from the walls high up, near the ceiling beams, figures of warriors leaned forward, out over the wooden chests which lay beneath. So still were they and so still the ropes of pearls which hung from their necks they seemed incorruptible in this house of corruption. He looked hastily at the breastplates of hide, the round and oblong shields, the sheaves of arrows, the bows which hung to the walls, and then his eyes came to rest upon the chests piled high upon the narrow shelves.

Warily he went forward and knocked off the lid of the first one which came to hand. He looked in and stepped back with a kind of horror. The skin hung like smoked leather tight to the bones, and on the breast, neck, arms and thighs he saw dull, grey maggots crawling as big as tumble bugs. Then he looked again and thrust his hand among them. He laughed loud and harshly. His voice came back to him from the high rafters, strange and sepulchral, as he dropped the pearls back into the chest. They fell through his fingers, rattling like peas upon the skeins of pearls which adorned the dead.

Hastily he went from chest to chest, prized off the tops and looked inside. He found evidence enough that the Señora spoke true. Although the pearls were darkened by the heat which the Indians use to open the oyster, yet were there enough to repay each and every man for the risks of the conquest. But best of all he felt well assured that there were oyster beds to be worked, if only the Indians were put to this service, and then the pearls must come to their hands as rich and with as good a hue as those come out of the East.

He was on the point of leaving when he saw a chest larger than the others. A giant of a man it must have held, he thought, as he lifted the top and looked inside. The bones were as the others, bedecked with trinkets and pearls, with pipe and club and the great hickory bow laid close to the hand. He was lowering the lid when he saw a dull yellow gleam near the knuckle bone. He reached down and untangled a chain of jet beads. He brought them slowly into the light. At the end of the chain hung a small gilt cross.

Tovar stood perfectly still outside the temple door. Unnoticed, the beads slipped through his fingers, swinging from the cross which lay in his open palm. Here his eyes were fixed, on the spots of moulding flesh which tarnished the slender bars. And here his thoughts were fixed by one thought. It was not the Sun god's wrath alone which brought troubles dire and a curse upon this land. Not his own will but another's had set him on this track, to find in the adipose substance of the dead the sign of salvation. And to bring it forth tarnished. Other things now grew sharp and clear. That look and bearing of the Señora's which he had so simply mistaken. It was not from love she had

[315]

spoken of her town of Talimeco. Not willingly had she let her sacred places be ravished, her hospitality outraged, and her people brought to shame. Strange it must have seemed to her, this Christian lust for trinkets; and yet she was quick to use it for her vengeance. Upon Christian heads would she bring down the wrath of the Sun. So had she directed the Governor towards Talimeco.

The afterglow left in the train of the dying god flared angrily in the sky, the stains on the bars of the crucifix quickened in his trembling hand. He closed it and held tight his fist and then with effort dropped the frail jet chain about his neck. Beneath his shirt he felt the cross slip down his burning flesh until it came to rest against his chest, as cold and hard as splintered crystal.

8

"You cannot do it," Silvestre said. "It's unseemly. It's dangerous, and you don't have to do it. Who's to keep you from taking her with you?"

"None."

"Then why in Jesu name——" Silvestre broke off and looked at his friend, baffled and angry.

"I'm not marrying her in Jesu name," Tovar replied. A faint smile twisted his mouth. "I'm marrying her Indian fashion."

"I saw you," Silvestre said scornfully, "putting a stick down in front of her lodge and Tsianina sticking another beside it. It's like enough some witchcraft she's brought you to."

"No witchraft—our betrothal rites," Tovar said half in banter. "You might say we are already married. Her uncle showed me the couch I shall mount tonight—it was bravely decked with herbs and skins—'There's your bed,' the old man said."

Silvestre laid a hand on Tovar's shoulder. "I'm your friend. You've got to tell me the truth. Why are you doing this?"

Tovar met his eyes with a direct gaze. "I don't want to lose the girl," he said. "And I don't want to force her to go with us in chains."

"Then why don't you have a priest baptize her? You can't marry her. You are already married. But at least she'll be a Christian."

"She would not feel bound by that."

Silvestre dropped his hand. "You know what it looks like," he said in a low voice. "Almost as if you were turning heathen."

"Nonsense. What hurt is there in two sticks?"

"I only hope you find no hurt."

"If it will please you, I'll bring her later before a priest."

"No priest," Silvestre said impatiently, "will assist you unless you disavow this thing you are doing."

Tovar paused. "That I will not do," he said at last.

Even as he spoke, he wondered at his stubbornness, almost wished his hasty act undone, for surely he could have kept Tsianina with him, he flattered himself she would have followed him willingly, without this putting of stick by stick and of what he must do this night, slip into the Indian lodge when the ashes had been drawn over the fire, slip out again before day's dawning. . . . And yet he could not be sure. She was the Señora's waiting woman. It was as if he had thrown down his glove at the Governor's feet. Impulsively he had done it without knowing the meaning of his act. As a challenge the Governor took it, since he had not forbidden the marriage, which he might have done. . . .

"Tovar?"

"Yes."

Silvestre stood within the door. "I have this to say and then I am done. No good has ever come to you through women."

His fair face was uplifted gravely, half lost in shadows from the lodge; and then he was gone. Tovar followed him as far as the piazza, hoping that once more Silvestre would turn and ask for friendship's sake to stay his wayward purpose, but he kept on his way, never looking back. Soon he was lost to sight behind the dwellings.

[317]

It was true what Silvestre had said. No good had ever come to him through women, at least no immediate good, but the tale was not yet told to its end. A woman had sent him to the Indies. But had not she brought him fortune until another woman broke it? Now perhaps this Indian girl would mend it. But there was little comfort in such thoughts. He knew too well what little bearing any woman had upon the present act. He shook his head and raised his eyes. His gaze fell upon the fragile leaves, the innumerably complicated patterns of greenery between earth and sky, and he looked at the clear colourless light of the expiring day. Each leaf, each twig and branch, hung sharply defined. There was no movement, not even one late bird settling in the boughs, to mar the stillness. No spot, not one thin line quickened the spent sky. Everywhere there was peace and quiet. And yet the peace was no peace but the rushing silence which outrides the night. Even now, with the world at balance between time and space, the dark drew nigh and shook that balance. Well, let the night come, let it come and bring the binding act, for the hour of decision was past.

Only three days had passed since, returning from Talimeco, he had related what he had found. Three days ... He could not speak for the value of the treasure, he had said as he sat in council; he knew little of the worth of pearls, but the boxes of the dead held twenty fold more than the temple at Cutifichiqui, not to count the baskets of seed pearls and those unspoiled by fire. He spoke as one might number fardels of cloth both coarse and fine. From time to time he noticed the captains, especially Moscoso and Añasco, looking curiously at him. They wondered, he knew, at his lack of zeal, for his wish to settle was known to all. When he was through, the Governor nodded and waited, as was his custom, for an expression of opinion. Several minutes passed before Añasco craved his lord's attention. He begged the Governor to consider the advantages which a town at Cutifichiqui would bring to the conquest. A good base from which to explore the land at leisure and with fewer hazards. With the sea

[318]

only two days away, ships plying between Spain and Mexico and from the islands could stop to trade and unload supplies. They could establish a port in all conveniency upon the sea. It seemed to Añasco the better judgment to settle. After Añasco Moscoso spoke, adding that the men and horses were still sadly worn. No doubt they could find towns lying about which would feed the army, and certainly the treasure was no small thing. The Tinocos, Vasconcelos, Lobillo, all the captains gave counsel that it would be well to settle.

Tovar waited impatiently, listening to the idle words. With impatience he waited for the Governor to give the answer he knew he would give. Twice de Soto ran his hand through his beard; a film dropped over his black brown eyes, set so hard and round in his head, and then they looked clearly forth upon his captains. In all the country thereabouts, he had said, there were not enough supplies to support his troops for a single month. It were best, therefore, to make their way to Ochuse, where Maldonado was to wait. Should a richer country not be found between here and there, those of his men who would could always return to Cutifichiqui. He doubted not that it would still be here for the taking, unless the town was bewitched as he sometimes thought, for certainly it seemed to have bewitched his men. He looked about him and smiled. And by that time the Indians would have gathered and stored their crops.

It seemed so plausible, the Governor's reasoning, his voice pleasant and reasonable, laying forth not his own judgment but the logic of their situation. But in spite of his logic Tovar saw that many of the captains still thought it an error to move on. Yet there was none who would say a thing after de Soto had shown his mind. They listened to the Indians tell of Chiaha, a province twelve days' travel hence. The Señora was asked for bearers and then the council came to an end as in the past, with each captain receiving his orders for the march.

The next morning the Señora was put under guard. Perico reported that she had planned to flee to the forest with all her people. Why it was Tovar did not rightly know, but the Señora's arrest brought him to his decision. He acted not without reason, or reasons, mixed and confused though they were. Even now he did not fully understand why or what he had done. Almost he could believe that the curse of Talimeco had fallen upon him, that snare the Señora had tried to set for all the Christians and which instinctively, like the good soldier he was, the Governor had stepped around. That the curse had not worked him harm he had Tsianina to thank. She had given him herbs to chew and made him dive four times in the river. That night she scattered other herbs about their bed. So he kept free, at least, from the ghostly snare. But of one thing he was sure. The evil at Talimeco was not dead. He had seen its long reach and the damage it had done. *And he had felt it.*

Standing without the temple door at Talimeco, holding the rosary in his hands, his gaze held fast by the marks of corruption left by the unshriven dead, he had foreseen all that must happen at Cutifichiqui: the dropping of the false mask of courtesy, the stolen wives, the looted temple, all the indignities and loss the Indians had suffered and would continue to suffer at Christian hands, even the Señora's arrest. Then why had he delayed, waiting for the deed's violence? He was sitting cross-legged on the ground, mending a stirrup strap; Ortiz came up and said, "Guards have been set over the Señora."

Without pause, without looking up from his work, Tovar said, "I shall marry Tsianina Indian fashion."

There were half a dozen men around him; he could feel them stiffen. Ortiz made no reply but he saw the look of understanding in his eyes. "Ortiz, you must interpret my proffer of marriage," he said. Ortiz did not answer but dropped his head in assent. Tovar knew it would take little time for his words to reach the Governor's ears. I am marrying her to show honour where you have dishonoured. This is what he had meant and so it was understood. But was it all he meant? He had followed de Soto out of Cuba to aid, not do him hurt. Certainly it

[320]

was a gratuitous hurt, and foolish, and unjust to hold the Governor to account for all that he, Tovar, had hoped for from Cutifichiqui.

With a start he saw night had settled over town and forest. It came upon him that he had little heart to go through with the thing he had started, but turn back he could not. He had gone too far for that. He waited, his mind empty and unseeing, for the last restless sounds in the yards and lodges to withdraw and leave the town at rest; and then he looked towards the blots of darkness which were the houses of her kinswomen. He felt a cold twisting down his spine. At dawn he would owe to those who dwelt within a kinsman's dues.

Erect, with head borne high but stiffly, he walked across the chunghe yard, past the scalp poles, to the east of the chunghe pole. . . . The winter house loomed like a great misshapen tree. He hesitated a moment and then lifted the door flap. Inside a red, bright eye looked up from the floor, gleaming steadily. His hand trembled as he clutched the skin. The draft he made blew a dark film over the coal; he cursed softly and vehemently and, stooping, stepped inside.

He stood for a moment to get his bearings. The smoke had not settled and his eyes smarted. The odour of smoke and grease and skins, the faint strange odour of alien flesh, which he noticed now for the first time in the warm close room, rose from the floor; it drew heavily through his nostrils, stuck at his throat. With his hands before him he crept towards the middle bench staked against the right-hand wall. From the opposite wall he heard a body turn over. With their sharper eyes did they all watch his furtive progress? What were their thoughts? Had he allowed himself to be tricked? A sacrifice for the many Christian injuries? He put his hand upon his long keen knife . . . then from the wall blew the fresh smell of cedar, sweet spices . . . dimly he saw her naked form, her open eyes he could not see. What did she see and think?

Silently he stripped him of his clothes, his dagger belt he

laid under the bed. His hand touched her hair as he crawled in. He felt her turn. Their bodies touched in the enveloping dark.

His body lay still and heavy, stretched upon the bench. Her head lay in the hollow of his arm. By her breathing he could tell she was asleep, but he could not sleep. This had not been like the other times, for then he had been free, free in the image of the life he had foreseen for them here in Cutifichiqui. Now he knew that Cutifichiqui could be no different from the rest of Florida. Nor could he ever be free from the thing he had done. It had seemed to him, when first he entered on it, a kind of game, a game with a purpose but without rules to bind him in any way. Now he knew better. How far, even in what way, these heathen rites had bound him he did not know, but bound he was. Tsianina was of the Wind family. By marriage he was kin to the wind ...

In the darkness of the lodge he tried to smile, but it was no true smile which passed his mouth. Nor was the lodge so dark as he thought. A faint glow from the half-covered coals showed from wall to wall, showed plainer the forms of his inlaws encircling the room. In sudden shame he understood there had been witnesses to the act. Covertly he turned his head. All was withdrawn and still. Slowly he settled back upon the skins, his eyes fixed upon the rooftree.

Was it, after all, that he had been guilty only of adultery? It had seemed so simple and innocent, their joy together. He had not missed the protection and fellowship of a common faith. Indeed they had had a fellowship. They could not speak together but they had communicated by signs. A gesture, a look of the eye, oftentimes says more than words. But tonight there had been only feeling and darkness, feeling in darkness, pure and sharp, disembodied as a flame, drawing and consuming the flesh like dry dead wood until of itself it went out, spent by its own fury. He looked down at the vague shape of her head lying so close in to his arms. Tomorrow.... The innocence between them was gone now for good, ay, or for ill; but good or ill, they would never be parted.

Outside the wind pressed against the walls, the lodge trembled slightly. Cool, thin spears of air blew through the seams in the matting. The wind . . . did it speak to her? What did it say, her kinsman? Carefully he freed his arm and laid her head upon the skins. He sat upright in bed, listening; and then swung quietly over the side and began putting on his clothes. He passed quickly through the close, evil-smelling room. How soon, he thought, had he found his way about this dwelling. Outside he leaned against the flap, breathing deep of the clean May air. The wind blew gustily, dying and surging through the long avenues of the forest. It blew the late night chill through his clothes, took the skirts of his surcoat and flapped them against his thighs . . . his new kinsman was overfamiliar.

He had stopped by the scalp poles. The scalps were blowing out into the sky, the long hair streaming visibly in the light of the waning moon. They struck and wound themselves about the poles, tossed and uplifted by the fitful wind. The wind died and they fell, stilled, against the wood. Below he stood, quietly. What were these people who reckoned their descent from the wind and animals, whose gain in war was the skin of the head, who had never established their rule in the land they occupied but wandered like the beasts in a common brotherhood? Their towns were little better than lairs which, once abandoned, fell again into the wilderness; in their fields the weeds grew as high as the maize they had planted. These people he this night had pledged himself to honour, somewhat under their laws he had fallen, a thing no Christian, even a bad Christian such as he, should ever have done. And yet done it he had. What was it he had done?

Over the sky he felt the dark shifting. It was nothing he could see but he knew it was the sign that the night was fast spending. The forest grew black and solid, the lodges of the town more insubstantial under the paling moon, the chunghe yard one long shadow. As he looked upon this black wilderness, reaching God alone knew how far or how deep, he felt that he was shut in by a narrow room, but a room existing nowhere in space. And then it came to him that the high and tangled forests were but a succession of such rooms, each with its corridor, indefinitely multiplied, beyond the power of man to count. And the air of each was held in place by the air of all, constant in density. And then it came to him. Vaguely in Cuba he had felt it, then more clearly at Talimeco as a sign. Now it showed heavy but clear in his mind. All he had done took on its rightful meaning. Following de Soto, the Christians had stumbled upon the world and before any knew it, all were drawn fast by its coils. The world that was flesh was everywhere, its power each man knew in himself, its temptations and its triumphs. But this land was the very body of the world. Not through any agent but through its proper self it worked its evil. Where but in one place could this happen? Where but ...

He put out his hand and grasped the pole to steady himself. Had they perchance stumbled upon Eden, abandoned of God, running its unpruned seasons, ignorant of the generations of men, yet throughout all those generations growing heavier with the bloom that cannot die, the decay that cannot live, for the dry rot and the odour of that fruit which blooms and falls, falls and blooms, at the garden's pole?

The wind had fallen. His face was drenched with dew. His head awhirl, he crossed the yard to the Christian side of the town, opened the flap to his own lodge. His messmates were still asleep. He did not go in but reached for his cloak. Already the eastern sky had taken on more colour and depth. From the forest came an expectant hush. . . . He wandered without purpose, drew sharply up before two yellow spots of flame. In between upon a log stood the cross and before the altar, in the woodland choir, the priest. Two men knelt in the sod. It was de Soto and his clerk, Ranjel. Tovar knelt to one side of them.

Well might this Governor pray for guidance, for it was not gold he would be seeking when, a few hours hence, he set out again on his way. Daylight would find him entered in the lists of a grimmer tourney. His good fortune so far had brought him out of the very hands of the wilderness, but the bout was not ended. How would he deliver himself from his peril, how deliver him, Tovar, who saw and was bound, and how bring his army safely through? The cross was de Soto's weapon, but he bore it with pride. In avarice and pride the bands of horse and foot had entered into his train, of all the sins the most mortal save that one sin for which there is no atonement.

All was clear at last. The gage which lay between them, invisible as it was, was clear. All, all was clear.

The three men rose in silence. The Mass was finished. De Soto stood for a moment uncertainly and then half turned and looked toward the west. His legs sank down in shadow. A bluish-yellow light fell upon his breastplate and upon his face, so that his cheeks lay in shadow below the bone. It was still too dark to see his eyes well, but they looked out with a brooding forward stare. Behind, the trees parted and showed the sky. Riding high, the slim new moon was withdrawing before the approach of day.

"Shall I arouse the trumpeter?" Ranjel asked.

De Soto straightened his shoulders. His armour made a faint dull clank. "Do so," he said briskly. Then his eyes met Tovar's. The two men looked across the vague light at each other. Not until Ranjel had withdrawn did de Soto speak. "What," he asked with irony, "has the bridegroom left the bride so soon?"

In irony Tovar replied, "It is customary among the Cutifichiquians."

"A strange custom."

"There be many strange things in this land, my lord."

"The strangest of all is your behaviour. Just when I think I can use you again . . ." he paused.

"You will use me again, my lord," Tovar said evenly.

"Not a moon-struck man."

"Mayhap we are all moon-struck."

"What mean you?"

"*I* mean nothing, my lord."

De Soto waited, as though uncertain whether to stay or go; then he said distinctly, "You are right. I will use you. We leave

[325]

within the hour by this trail. It is the trading path to the west. The Señora and her waiting maids go a part of the way with us. You seem to have a way with women. I shall put them in your charge."

Tovar bowed slightly. "My lord, I shall be as wary as the guardian into whose care you have put us all."

The two men looked at each other across the gloomy light, and then they parted.

7

MAUVILLA

Mauvilla

THE leaves, falling, fluttered before Tovar's face. No wind was stirring, but they fell, bright yellow and vermilion, the colours flickering as they scattered, lost in the undergrowth or the forest beyond the trail. Overhead among the high branches the sunshine lay in patches along the bark, spotted the turning leaves. Where it fell, it lay thin and with a failing strength. Tovar lowered his head. He said to Silvestre, "What day is it?"

Silvestre thought for a while, "It's October, I know."

"What day is it, Ranjel?"

Ranjel called back over his shoulder, "Sunday, October the tenth, the year . . ."

"I know the year," Tovar answered. Around him the men laughed. The laugh ran a way over the marching column, broke and died.

Stealthily, as the leaves falling, the year was slipping away. Suddenly Tovar remembered that last day in Cutifichiqui. It had been spring then. . . .

What months and how many hundreds of leagues lay between! But in spite of his foreboding the army was still together, even larger in numbers, although smaller in fighting strength. There were numerous carriers and women slaves to fill out the bands. So jealous were the Christians they kept their women away from Mass. They kept them always by them, walking by the horses or among the foot, with their pots and bowls hanging from their backs. Several had babies slung in between the pots. Their clothes were worn and dirty. A few

[329]

went naked or were dressed in the faded shirts of their masters. For the first time the army looked less like an army than a people migrating.

But it was not unwieldy. The horses were in fair condition. The men were hard and lean. The ones who had lost their flesh looked like younger men, but young men grown old before their time. All now were veterans in Indian ways. They could forage or fight with equal ease. The weak who had broken down through the long march over the mountains recovered at Chiaha, or at Coça, or had been buried at one of these places. How many times Tovar had heard, "If only I had a little salt or some meat, I would not be dying thus. . . ." It looked now as if the greatest of the trials were behind them. Ochuse could not be many days hence. The Ochuse Indian taken by Maldonado and brought to Apalache was beginning to recognize tribal names. He had heard of the greatness of Coça, and now Coça was far to the rear.

Perhaps Maldonado had come from Cuba and was waiting at the trysting port? Tovar felt his heart beat a little faster.

The Governor had done it, or almost done it. No great kingdom had he found or any riches, but their lives and their weal he had guarded as best he could. Perfect in strategy, perfect in diplomacy, perfect in patience. Reckless at times but always he came out unscathed, as at Coste when he put himself and a few Christians in the midst of the hostile town. When the Christians, as was their custom, began climbing the barbacoas, the Indians took up clubs and fell to beating them. On the instant the Governor seized a cudgel and joined the Indians, calling to his men in feigned anger to bear with him. Later he made the cacique pay for this insolence.

But the greatest feat was getting the army safely across the mountains to Chiaha. By holding the Señora in hostage he had made all the tribes through which he passed give of what they had, but that was little enough and but for the generosity of the Chiaha they all would have starved to death. It took the horses alone a month to recover. It was on this march that the men began to desert, and at Xuala the Señora retired into the woods to make water and was nevermore seen, neither she nor her women. She took with her a small trunk of unbored pearls which the Governor had allowed her to carry, thinking to beg them of her when they parted.

Peacefully or by force the Governor took the supplies and what service he needed, just as with his own men when they held back, he went on ahead, drawing them after him. It would be the same with this Tascaluça whose town they were now approaching. Moscoso had gone before the army to prepare the way with presents. From what he, Tovar, had learned, Tascaluça was the suzerain of many provinces and of a numerous people, being equally feared by his vassals and the neighbouring nations. In the early days of the conquest, at the rumour of some great lord, the lancers would sit a little forward in the saddle and the foot would quicken its pace, hoping to find the treasure that always eluded them. They no longer showed such interest. It had been a long time since the word gold had been mentioned. Maize and women. This was all the Christians talked of these days.

Far to the front Tovar heard the blast of trumpets. His mare threw up her head. "The Governor is entering Athahatchi," he said to Silvestre. Silvestre met his glance, and together they spurred their horses.

They overtook de Soto as he was alighting in the yard of the town and joined him as he climbed the mound to greet the Indian lord. Tascaluça was a giant of a man. He did not rise when the Governor approached but remained passive, with perfect composure, as if he had been a king. Without invitation the Governor took off his helmet and sat beside him.

Tovar stopped a little way off. He had never seen an Indian of such size and authority. Around his head he wore a coif like the almaizal which the Moors wear and a pelote of feathers which fell to his feet. He sat high upon cushions and over his head an Indian held an umbrella, the size of a target, quartered in red and white, with a white cross in the middle of a black field, similar to that of the knights of the Order of St. John of Rhodes.

[331]

After a weighty pause, Tascaluça turned to the Governor. "Powerful Chief," he said, "Your Lordship is very welcome. With the sight of you I receive as great pleasure and comfort as though you were an own brother whom I dearly loved. It is idle to use many words here, as it is not well to speak at length where a few may suffice. The greater the will the more estimable the deed, and acts are the living witnesses of truth. You shall learn how strong and positive is my will, and how disinterested my inclination to serve you. The gifts you did me the favour to send I esteem in all their value, but most because they are yours. See in what you will command me."

Tovar looked quickly at the Governor so soon as Ortiz had finished translating the words, for Tascaluça's welcome was the perfection of irony and courtesy. The Governor showed nothing in his face, but he seemed for the moment lost for a reply. He looked covertly down into the yard; the wayward was entering. He took a deep breath and said that the cacique must dine with him. After only the necessary pause the Governor grasped Tascaluça's hand and stood up. The cacique showed nothing in his face, but he hesitated a moment and then slowly and with dignity arose. A servant reached for his cushions, the attendant with the umbrella followed. As they went towards the steps of the mound, the Governor, fitted out in his best clothes and armour, looked like a little boy holding the hand of a foreign tutor. Silvestre whispered: "He's as tall as that Tony of the Emperor's guard."

They seated themselves in a pavilion off the yard, and the Indians danced well before them. Afterwards Moscoso advanced with his company, the steeds leaping from side to side and at times towards Tascaluça, when he, with great gravity and seemingly with indifference, now and then would raise his eyes and look on as in contempt. Nor did he show any greater interest when the lancers rode at rings or jousted with reeds. As the day waned, he rose to go, but the Governor told him he must sleep where he was.

The muscles in the Indian's body tightened. He grew still

[332]

as a deer. Without moving his head, he let his eyes run over the town. Quietly, during the games, a company of lancers had spread about the mound. Upon its top the bowmen and arquebusiers had arranged themselves. Ten of the Governor's halberdiers stood at rest at the sides of the pavilion and all about were well-armed gentlemen and the Captain of the Guards. A red film passed over the Indian's eyes and then he spoke to his principal men, each separately as they withdrew.

"He means mischief," the Constable said.

The Governor shrugged his shoulders.

The next morning the Governor demanded bearers and a hundred women. Tascaluça spoke to certain Indians who remained about his person and four hundred bearers were gathered to carry the loads.

"Now," the Governor asked, "where are the women?"

"The women I will give you at Mauvilla," Tascaluça replied.

"You understand that we will pay you for these women," de Soto said. "In the meanwhile accept this as earnest of my good intentions." He took from his steward a scarlet cape and threw it over the Indian's shoulders; then he had his pages put some buskins on his feet and afterwards he ordered a horse to be got ready to bear him on the journey.

"Of course, you know he does not mean to give up any women," Ortiz said.

"I think he will change his mind," the Governor replied lightly. "He has seen that we always release the bearers when we come to a place where we may impress others. He has also seen that rebellion reduces them to slavery. You may be sure he has inquired into the difference in status between those we free and those we keep by us."

"I like not at all his putting off the payment until we reach this Mauvilla of his," the Constable said.

"What can he do?" de Soto asked. "His life is in pawn. If he plans mischief, it will turn out as at Ulibahali. Did not Coça himself ask his vassals to lay aside their arms? And were they not glad enough to do it when they saw our horses, besides fulfilling all our requests, even to women? No, gentlemen, Tascaluça is a giant in his person, but he blundered when he received us peacefully. But so you may not think me careless, I will tell you that earlier this morning I sent Xaramillo and Diego Vásquez to discover the temper of the Indians at Mauvilla. Let us march with our usual precautions, and you will find that all things will go well with us."

There was some difficulty in finding a horse able to bear Tascaluça. Finally the largest pack animal in the army was brought and this he mounted, attended by a large retinue of Indians, and always the attendant with the sunshade and another with his cushions kept at his side. That night the army lay in the open and the following day came to a river, a copious flood, which all considered to be that which empties into the bay of Ochuse. The town on this river was called Piachi. Here they got news of the manner in which the boats of Narváez had arrived in want of water and of a Christian named Don Teodoro, who had stopped among these Indians with a negro, and the dagger he had worn was shown.

It took the army two days to cross the river. Diego Vásquez rode into the wayward just as it was coming down out of the rough, hilly country which bordered the stream. He reported that a great many armed warriors had gathered at Mauvilla bent, it seemed to him, on trouble.

The next day at a fenced village messengers arrived with a great deal of chestnut bread. They talked with Tascaluça and straightway left him.

From here on the army travelled continually through inhabited country and, as the men scattered to forage, delaying the march, de Soto took fifteen lancers and thirty foot and pushed on ahead. He arrived before Mauvilla at nine o'clock in the morning, halting on the plain which surrounded it.

Xaramillo appeared suddenly out of the woods. The Governor looked sharply at his spy. "Well?" he asked.

Xaramillo raised his good eye to the Governor. He carried

so many scars his face looked like a hard piece of wood which somebody had tried to carve into features. His tongue had been split, so that he spoke slowly and with a lisp. "My lord," he said, "I pretended to leave with Vásquez, but at night I slipped back to a place where I could observe."

"Yes," de Soto said in haste, for he saw a group of caciques well attended by flute players and warriors coming through the gate of the town.

Xaramillo would not be hurried. "You see there across the plain. There were a good many huts built around the stockade. Yesterday they tore them all away, and day and night they have spent strengthening the wall. At night I've heard a great many going in. When the fires were high, I could see others with bundles of arrows on their backs. They've been dancing and whooping."

Tovar looked at the stockade. The timbers of the fence were sunk firmly into the ground. To the height of a lance the entire wall was plastered with mud. All along it there were embrasures, loopholes for archery, and towers overhanging the main gate. It took him only a glance to see how strong it was. On this day of all days the Governor should not have allowed the men to scatter. He looked at Tascaluça. His eyes were lowered but through the drooping lids the cacique watched closely the approaching Indians.

The flute players spread out and the spokesman presented the Governor with three cloaks of marten skins and then asked if it was his pleasure to come into the town or camp upon the plain.

"Where are the bearers and women you promised?" de Soto asked.

"I will give you these tonight," the Indian replied.

The Indians had gathered in a half-moon before the escort. They stood back from the horses but, although none among them had ever seen so strange and fierce an animal before, their eyes were fixed not upon the horses but upon de Soto. He returned their gaze easily and showed nothing but confidence in their good will, as the interpreters gave back the words. And then there came a short pause.

"Their intention is evil, my lord," Moscoso said. "Tell them we will sleep out in the woods." Moscoso hesitated. "Tell them you fear their town is peopled overmuch already."

"We cannot show fear," the Governor replied.

"But the army is strung out. It will be hours before it is all up."

The Governor drew back his head. "I'm impatient of sleeping out. Let us dismount and draw inside. Captain Espindola, keep sharp watch on Tascaluça."

Espindola felt the laces of his quilted coat, adjusted it over his plates. "The bearers, Excellency? Where shall I have them set their burdens down?"

De Soto glanced down the long line of Indians. They had dropped the supplies at their sides. They stood with the chains hanging from their collars, since one could not sit without all. Over every fifteen a halberdier had been placed. The guards leaned upon their weapons, at ease. "The weather is fair," de Soto said. "Bring them just without the walls. Reduce the guard by half and have them follow me inside. Ranjel, take three or four men and look after the horses."

Lightly the Governor jumped from his saddle. His men dismounted more slowly and, surrounding Tascaluça, followed the Indians towards the gates of the town.

2

Tovar wondered where the women were. There were some three or four hundred men in the town but no women. This looked a little suspicious, but the men wore no paint. That was encouraging. Still he did not quite like the looks of things. And then, just at the time the Governor had seated himself in one of the bed arbours, with Tascaluça at his side, nineteen girls walked in single file to the centre of the yard and began to dance. He had never seen a woman's dance before and watched

[336]

it closely. Perhaps this was a special act to show their parts, since Tascaluça's freedom rested upon the gift of women. But where were the others? Perhaps they waited in the lodges, to dance in relays. He let his eyes run idly over the town, counting the dwellings. Suddenly he became alert.

The Constable was a little way removed from the Governor who was chatting in low tones with Moscoso and Biedma. He hurried to the Constable's side, noticing as he went that Tascaluça had withdrawn to sit with the principal Indians at the farthest edge of the bed. His great head almost touched the roof. He was looking at the dancing girls. His eyes had become very small. The pupils were whirling in the red, mottled balls.

"Do you notice anything out of the way?" Tovar asked as he paused at the Constable's side.

The Constable followed Tovar's gaze. "The Indians," he said, "look somewhat ugly, but so have all of them when we first enter their towns. They seem to be making an effort to receive us well." He nodded towards the dancers.

"Look at the houses," Tovar said.

The corners of the Constable's eyes wrinkled in a puzzled way. "They don't seem to be occupied," he said.

"That's it," Tovar snapped, speaking louder than he meant, to be heard above the songs of the women. "Over each entrance the lattice door has been dropped. Look at the lofts. All closed by mats. They are usually open at this season of the year."

The Constable laid his hand upon his sword. "I think we had better take a look," he said.

Gradually moving on the rim of the crowd, Tovar came to a lodge smaller than most. The logs were too close together to see between. He leaned against the wall, listening. Not a sound. He moved in front of the door. A hot stench of bear grease and sweat blew past his nose. Without seeming to, he looked through the slats. The place was packed with Indians.

He was careful to show no haste as he presented himself before the Governor.

"Excellency," he said, "we have been led into a trap."

[337]

Without raising his voice, de Soto said, "Be brief."

"The lodges are filled with Indians."

Still without raising his voice or looking in the direction of the Captain of the Guards, de Soto said, "Captain Espindola, tell your men to withdraw quietly and without arousing suspicion. Tell those lancers without to mount their horses and approach the main gate. Send word to all detachments to hasten to the field. Yes, Señor Constable?"

The Constable had come up to the arbour with the shuffling gait peculiar to a heavy man in a hurry. "The houses are packed . . ."

"Yes, I know. Calm yourself. The Indians will sense that we know. Yes, Diego?" He barely turned his head as one of the guard came rapidly forward.

"My Lord, Indians are slipping sheaves of arrows beneath the palmettos."

"Where?"

"By the north gate."

"Thank you. And stand by."

Casually, almost absentmindedly de Soto took his helmet which rested at his side and put it on. It was his headpiece for dress occasions. Tovar noticed that the plumes had grown brown and somewhat limp. De Soto ran his hand under his beard and pushed it forward. For the first time in Florida had he used this gesture and only twice in Peru. It meant only one thing: he thought the situation grave.

De Soto raised his head, caught Tovar's glance for an instant and then looked up and beyond him. At the same instant Tovar felt a shadow behind him, a shadow with substance. He swung around and met, level with his sight, the tremendous chest of Tascaluça. Above and below the left teat were two ragged scars. Suddenly he thought of a buckler he had seen in Valladolid, torn on either side of the spike. He drew back half a dozen steps and still he had to raise his head to look into the Indian's face. The Indian was speaking.

"What does he say, Ortiz?" the Governor asked.

[338]

"He is angry, Excellency."

"What does he say?" There was the faintest edge of haste in the Governor's voice.

"He says that he is weary of following you about and asks leave to remain in this town."

"When he furnishes the women he promised, and bearers to the confines of his domain." The Governor's words were soft and gentle. "Tell him that his society gives me great honour, an honour I should be sorry to lose."

Tascaluça showed impatience.

"Tascaluça says that if you wish to leave in peace, you must quit Mauvilla at once and persist no longer in carrying him away by force. Neither bearers nor women will he give. . . ."

Tascaluça, even as Ortiz reported his words, turned and walked away. The gentlemen about de Soto and several of the guard stepped forward to interpose, but the Governor raised his hand. "No, gentlemen. We are few. We have not yet exhausted diplomacy."

An Indian dressed in a marten-skin coat passed at this moment across the yard. The dancers had disappeared; the spectators had withdrawn; the yard was empty save for this lone Indian. The Governor called to him. He ignored the summons. The Governor called again. The Indian turned and spat on the ground, moved on insolently. The Constable strode after him, caught him by the arm and turned him around and shouted angrily. The Indian jerked away his arm and the Constable pulled the coat over his head and left it in his hand.

It happened all at once. Tovar saw the stroke of the Constable's cutlass and the Indian's arm, the hand still holding to the marten skins, fall to the ground. It fell like the arm of a jester's doll tied to a cord of incarnation velvet, with an outward swing; then the blood spurted in all directions. From out the houses the arrows sped. They struck the ground, the poles of the arbour; they passed with a swish, volley out-racing volley. From the houses the Indians were leaping into the streets. As by magic the town yard was filled. They rose from the ground

[339]

with a whoop. Feathers lay close to their heads. Black and red were their bodies.

Tovar was engaged with seven at once. At a great distance he heard the Governor's voice. "To the gates. Don't stand to fight."

As he freed himself, Tovar saw the Governor fleeing in the midst of his guards. Twice he slipped and fell. Arrows hung from his quilted coat like ornaments.

The Indians were so numerous they were getting in one another's way. This, Tovar saw, worked in his favour. It was too late to follow the Governor. He plunged into the throng and slowly began to thrust and cut his way through to the north gate. Soon he discovered that he must only slash and cut. If he stopped to thrust, he would be quickly surrounded and taken. With his dagger he struck out at those who rushed him. There was no din of battle, the thundering crash of pikes, and the cries of chivalry such as is heard on European fields, but the cries were terrifying, short, galloping whoo-whoo-whoops, sharp and shrill, almost feminine in their tones. Behind him Tovar heard Moscoso's voice call through the noise, "Gallegos, Gallegos, come out or I will leave you."

Tovar was shoved between two centres of fight, saw out of his eye a halberdier at bay. The halberd was no weapon for this kind of fighting. He shouted, "Draw your sword." The man did not hear him. He heard nothing. His face was set and doom looked out of his eyes. When Tovar looked again, the Christian had disappeared. The halberd was thrust high in a brown hand. The whoops of triumph volleyed like sounds in a small room. Fury gave strength to Tovar's arm and he charged twenty paces in as many seconds; he saw the gates within reach. Caution slowed him down.

He felt something under his feet. He tried to step over it and his foot slipped away from him and he sat upon the ground. In one motion he rose up again, but at the instant of his fall he had looked into the face of Francisco de Soto, the Governor's nephew. He tried to speak to the youth; rough, dry, indistinguishable sounds came from his throat. He ran his dry tongue over the roof of his mouth, swallowed. "Follow at my back," he said.

Francisco did not move. Swinging to right and left Tovar despatched two Indians. For a moment he was free. "Get up," he ordered. Then he saw the arrows sticking through both of the lad's boots, up near the groin. Upon the bald place where his hair should be growing a red ooze glistened like a bloody cap. He looked like and yet unlike his priestly brother. "Can you crawl?" Tovar called out.

Wearily Francisco lifted the lids of his eyes, the lids drooped and the eyes swam in their sockets.

"I must go," Tovar repeated. "Can you crawl?"

Francisco's under jaw fell and he shook his head impatiently like a fretful child.

"God rest with you," Tovar said.

Above the wooden jaw the tongue replied imperfectly, "God go with you."

Tovar lifted his cutlass to parry the fall of a club. He was surrounded and now he thought only of himself.

He cleared a space to a house and put his back to the wall. It did little good to disable his assailants, so hard was he beset. He said a prayer and prepared to keep them at a distance as long as he could. He saw no hope of escape. Then he heard the Constable's loud shout. He cut his eye around. The Constable was coming methodically towards him, laying about with his heavy sword as a peasant cuts grain. With him were Moscoso and two halberdiers. Tovar dropped his dagger and put both hands to the cutlass. With this fresh force he kept his ground until the Christians drew nigh. "On to the gate," the Constable shouted as he passed.

The gate was closed, and it was a matter of a few minutes to open it, but then they were free. "Stay close in to the wall," Moscoso called back over his shoulder, "and below the loop holes." Half-walking, half-running, the small party reached the

[341]

central gates just as the Governor was clearing them. The Indians poured out, spreading around him and the two halberdiers who were with him. Within the threshold of the gate backed against the portal, stood Captain Espindola and one guard. The Constable struck the flank of the Indians. Across the plains, their lances levelled at the charge, rode Ranjel and Solís. They struck the Indians together. Two fell before the lances and the crowd gave back. At this the Indians began to grow unsettled. Solís rode into them, but Ranjel veered his horse and charged down the line. The Indians gave rapidly now, some of them fleeing into the town. But Solís had gone too deeply in. He toppled, fighting, and fell beneath his mount. Arrows grew out of the back and flanks of his mount. The horse kneeled and rolled over. With a sudden shock the Governor's voice rose above the whoops of battle. "Ranjel," he shouted, "go to the aid of Espindola. He is quite used up." Then the Governor turned his back upon the town. "Pedro, my horse," he shouted. At the sound of his voice Tovar saw the Indians pause and look his way.

Already the negro was bringing the stallion at a gallop across the plain. The Constable and Moscoso were running towards their horses staked in the woods. Espindola and the halberdier withdrew under cover of Ranjel's lance. Ranjel rode up to the Governor, his quilted coat of armour loaded with arrows. Deftly, giving a twist of the wrist at each pull, the Governor began taking them out; then his negro arrived. Leaping into the saddle, he said to Ranjel, "See to Solís, that they don't carry him within the walls." His last words he shouted over his shoulder, on his way to the rear to organize what horsemen had come up.

The Indians were picking up the sacks and bundles which the bearers had set down and were carrying them with shouts of triumph inside the walls. Tovar watched for a moment all the army's possessions fall into their hands; the pearls, the skins, the extra clothing, even some weapons, all the powder which the arquebusiers did not carry on their persons, the Sacred

Vessels, the moulds for making the body of Our Lord . . .

Espindola came up to Tovar, breathing hard. "Father Francisco, the Christian women belonging to the Governor and his page are still inside."

Tovar crossed himself. "God rest their souls."

"I saw them go into a house."

"Had they weapons?"

"The page wore a short sword."

"Let us to horse," Tovar said.

Espindola motioned him on. "I can't run," he said.

Tovar's legs struck the ground unsurely, and he saw how nearly he had come to being used up.

The Christians showed themselves greedy for every moment of time. Even the horses seemed to understand the desperate emergency. Tovar's mare, when she saw her master running in her direction, broke the bridle and ran onto the plain to meet him. The twenty or so lancers who were at hand acted as though they had rehearsed the movement. Swinging into a line of charge, the animals neighing shrilly, the squadron trotted after the Governor as far as the gates. The Indians rushed out to meet them but they did not venture far from the stockade. They stood uncertainly about, shooting arrows in swift succession and making obscene and threatening gestures. From the stockade volley followed volley, singeing the air. The horses leapt and plunged as the shafts went by. "Turn and ride for the woods," the Governor called out. "Perhaps they will follow us."

Behind him Tovar heard the wild yells as the Indians were drawn after their false retreat. They are hungry to use their arrows, he thought, and then he heard the Governor's voice, "Wheel!"

The lancers turned as a man. The horses reached forward their necks, their legs shot from under them. The charge struck the Indians midway of the plain and rode them down before they could recover themselves. Tovar felt his lance sink into flesh, saw the brown bodies fall beneath the mare's hoofs.

[343]

On all sides the Indians fell down, lanced and dying. As soon as the Christians got within range of the walls, the Governor gave the command to encircle the stockade. "We can do no more until the army comes up," he said.

But Don Carlos did not hear. He rode to the very gates, lancing as he went. He would thrust, the horse would pause, the Indian stumble and fall; then the horse would jump forward and Don Carlos would thrust again. Before the gates his horse seemed to balk. Its master tried to turn him, but the animal bent its head to the bridle and would not budge. Don Carlos dismounted and took hold of the horse at the bit.

"To his rescue," a voice shouted.

Don Carlos was standing with his hand on the arrow in the horse's breast. It had driven through the armour almost up to the feathers. The other arrow had passed through the Christian's neck, just above the shoulder. "She couldn't turn," he kept repeating. "When I stooped to pull it out . . ."

"We must get you to the rear," Tovar said.

"You must get me a priest," he replied.

The Constable and Silvestre rode up together. Each took an arm of the wounded man and, bringing their mounts close together, rode with him to the rear. Tovar closed in behind. His body shook and he lurched in the saddle, as the arrows struck the back of his quilted coat. Don Carlos' legs swung and danced beyond any control. From the heel of the right boot a stream of blood scattered behind him. There was no priest to hear his confession; so the Governor lifted him and spoke such words as might comfort a dying man. Soon after, Don Carlos' head rolled forward on his breast. The Governor looked at him a moment and laid him gently down. He motioned to two men to take him to the rear; then he stood up and asked suddenly, "Where is my nephew, Francisco?"

"My Lord, he is in Purgatory," Tovar said.

There were less than twenty lancers investing the town, but in such terror did the Indians now hold the horses, they no longer dared to come without the walls. They appeared above them, waving long feathered flags, beating their drums in a mounting frenzy, and emptying the knapsacks and bundles which they had taken, waving the garments and whatever their hand had seized before the Christians below. And they had the bearers stand high and show their broken chains and the bows in their hands. Tovar looked at the cloaks, shirts, odd pieces of armour, and weapons as they appeared above the parapet. He saw none of his own gear, but from time to time he would see a Christian lean forward and grasp tightly his lance, and lips spit out an oath. And then he saw Tascaluça's son, a man as great as his father but slimmer, leap up with his arms outspread. In each hand he held a silver chalice used to bear Our Lord's blood in daily sacrifice for the sins of man. . . .

By eleven o'clock all the army had arrived. First, Vasconcelos came up at a trot, his company of Portuguese strung out loosely behind him, their saddle bags loaded down with maize and beans. He had heard the sound of battle and had ridden towards it. De Soto ordered the saddles lightened and the men thrown forward to strengthen the line of pickets. At the back of the town Indians had already slipped away. The report came back that Tascaluça had been among them, wearing the scarlet cloak which the Governor had given him and many necklaces of pearls.

A hasty conference of the captains was called just beyond the woods. All sat their horses, facing the Governor. His Aceituno pawed the ground restlessly. "Gentlemen, we must storm it," de Soto said. "Surely the pioneer detail did not pack their axes in the baggage?" He looked towards Lobillo.

"No, my lord. They brought their tools with them," Lobillo replied.

"Good."

"It's going to be costly," Añasco said, looking towards the town. "It's strong and well manned. Why not invest it and starve them out?"

[345]

"Impossible," the Governor said impatiently. "There are Christians inside the walls."

"Think you they are still alive?" Moscoso asked.

"I have hope, Señor. I have hopes."

"They are alive," the Constable said firmly. "Else we had seen their scalps."

Juan Gaytán craved the Governor's attention. "It seems to me, my lord, that we must count the cost in lives it will take to rescue those within. And surely you can threaten the Indians with reprisals enough to insure their safety. Besides there are priests a-plenty still in the army."

The Governor's face grew dark with shame and anger. "Surely, Señores, you do not hold with Señor Gaytán?" His voice rose, quavering slightly in his effort of restraint.

"You must decide, Excellency," the Constable said briefly. "We can ill afford to waste any more time."

"Then," said the Governor, "we must storm from all four sides at once. Let an arquebus shot be the signal. Dismount sixty of the best armoured men. To these I will add twenty of my halberdiers, five to each party. Distribute the axes equally. Moscoso, you take the east side; Señor Constable, you the west. The south to Vasconcelos, and I will take the north. Añasco, mount some of the lighter-armed men on the horses and encircle the entire place. Captain Lobillo and Captain Calderón, you will cover our advance with the bowmen and arquebusiers. Once we have made a breach, you will follow the storming parties inside." The Governor paused and looked around at his captains. "Does every man understand clearly what he is to do?" Each captain nodded. "Are there any questions?"

"I have a suggestion," Moscoso said.

"Yes?"

"There are at least three or four thousand Indians crowded within a narrow space. I suggest we try to fire the town."

The Governor regarded his Camp Master for a few moments. "Very well," he said. "It will hazard our possessions, but we cannot set the lives of men over against our goods. Let

[346]

two men in each storming party carry fire brands. Now, gentlemen, be quick and may God go with you."

The captains sat for a moment their horses. De Soto repeated, "God go with you." In unison they replied, "God keep you," then quickly dismounted.

Tovar lay flat upon the ground, with his buckler before him. He looked to the left. The bands of bowmen and arquebusiers were in place, lying behind the brush they had cut and brought up to shield them. He could see the small streams of smoke from the brands which the arquebusiers had lighted. Before and behind, small puffs of dust rose where the arrows struck. From time to time he could hear the smack and thump as an arrow hit a buckler. The archery of the Indians was powerful and accurate. The crossbowmen would have to move forward another twenty-five yards before they would be close enough to make their bolts tell.

"What's happened to the Governor?" Men Rodríguez said. "We'll all be pinned to the ground, if he doesn't hurry."

"He's got to see that all are in place," Silvestre said.

Tovar could tell by Silvestre's voice that he was feeling the strain. The oily smoke from the burning brand blew by Tovar's nose. He coughed to ease the tension.

"They aren't making as much noise," a voice said at the other end of the line.

"They must have plenty of arrows. I've counted thirty in front of us."

"The more they put in the ground ..."

"There he comes," Silvestre said.

The Governor rode in view behind his lines at a slow canter. He seemed in no particular hurry. The plumes of his casque bent and fluttered as though he were on parade. The silver trappings of his horse glinted in the sun. In spite of the toils and sorrows of the marches, in spite of the early dews and the gradual wear of the weather, he managed to look as freshly groomed as on the first day he had landed in Florida. Or almost. The coarse quilted coat, which all the lancers had been forced to wear as the best protection against the Indian archery, now hid his gold-embossed plates, fashioned by the Emperor's armourer. And his mounts were no longer so brave and slick in appearance. The stallion he rode showed his bones; his tail was matted by burrs; there were galled places visible even at a distance. De Soto rode unhurried to the rear of the party he would lead and dismounted, giving the bridle to a page. He stepped over the prone forms of his men, swinging the heavy axe in his hand. He looked deliberately at the town, as though he had just come upon it; then he said without looking around, "Sagredo, fire your piece."

Sagredo aimed his arquebus at the walls; there came a sputtering of the match, the explosion, the yells rising from the ground.

The man at Tovar's left stumbled and fell, but he did not look around. He felt that he was holding his breath, but it was Time he held in his teeth; and then he was beneath the walls hacking away at the clay plaster. The yells and the whoops had reached a constant swelling. In spite of the volume there still seemed something feminine about it, something animal-like. The clay fell away and he came to crossbars as large as his forearm. These quickly dropped to his feet; the axe began to sink into the logs proper. The chips leapt into the air, spinning. His strokes seemed to smite the swelling noise and rebound. One log was through. He moved on to the next. Once he looked up and saw the men crowding close into the wall with their bucklers held over their heads. The Governor stepped back, gave his axe to the man behind him. He drew his sword and leaned into the wall. "Now remember," he said through his shortened breath, "we must try to reach the gate and open it."

Tovar withdrew to let in the men with pikes. Six logs had been cut through at the bottom, but they remained in place. "All together," the sergeant said. The logs groaned and then fell inside with a crash. Five arquebusiers stepped forward and put

[348]

matches to their pieces. The men recoiled and Tovar heard the explosions. Two dropped where they were; one had his piece knocked from his hand; all were wounded. He saw one reach under his arm and tug at an arrow as the Governor jumped through the smoke to disappear within the walls. A dozen of his men followed. Tovar stepped forward. The breach became blocked and no more could enter. Three men were fighting just within the breach, separated and surrounded. He saw the Governor lay about with his axe, and then a club fell upon the casque of the Christian in front of him. He fell backwards at Tovar's feet. Tovar raised his cutlass and parried the blow, stepping over the body of his companion. The reddish-brown bodies, streaks of black and vermilion, swarmed before his eyes.

The Indians lay at his feet as high as his knees and still they came on. He had fought until his arms burned and his blows fell light and he had not moved a foot from the stand he had first taken. And then one by one, as they were used up, the Christians were driven back against the wall, working their way out of the town. He stepped aside and let the Governor out. On either side of him thrust the bludgeon-like barrels of the arquebusiers. Tovar's ears split with the roar, he felt a scattered burning on his cheeks, heard loud voices crying, "Let us through." He stumbled around the edge of the breach and sat down outside the walls as the fresh detail moved in.

The Governor was leaning on his axe. His quilted coat hung in threads. He stood in that position for some moments, then he raised his head and listened to the turmoil within. He dropped the axe and drew his sword. Up to his armpits his sleeves were soaked with blood. "Once again," he said and stepping over the fallen bodies, fought his way into the town.

Two other times the storming party entered and was driven out. Fresh troops were brought up, but the Christians were unable to drive a wedge deep enough into the town to fire the dwellings. Noise from the other quarters told the same tale: the Christians were everywhere confined close to the breaches they had made. At each entry more and more men leaned or sat against the outside wall, resting and bleeding from their wounds. The footing had become more and more precarious. The ground was slippery from blood and the bodies of the wounded and the dead. Once in the surge of battle Tovar and the Governor were fighting shoulder to shoulder. Together they had struck down their men, and for a moment they were free. They turned and looked at each other. The Governor was breathing hard. His beard was flecked with gore. "The time has come to risk the horses," he said. "Hold this place until I return." Tovar nodded. "Will you hold it?"

"I'll try," Tovar said.

"Will you hold it?"

"I'll hold it."

At that moment a fresh group of sword-and-bucklers came up. Tovar threw them in a half-moon before him. Those still fresh enough to do service with their cutlasses he placed in a second line with orders to move forward where they were most needed. He placed himself in the centre and took a brand and hurled it at the nearest roof. He saw the dry palmettos grow black about the pine knot, saw it sink in, saw the black spread slowly and the flames shoot up. "It's caught," he shouted. But at once the Indians began to climb to the roof and tear away the fire. With nothing but their hands they tore at the burning fragments and hurled them towards the Christians. Suddenly the Indians fell back and three ranks of their feathered bowmen stepped forward, one behind the other, and released their arrows. Eight sword-and-bucklers fell and had to be taken to the rear. Tovar shortened his line. He was now no more than ten paces from the breach when the assault was renewed. Step by step he was being driven back, when from behind he heard: "The horses!" He dared not look over his shoulder. He felt himself being jerked aside; the lance missed his head by an inch as the Governor's stallion dashed into the yard, and behind the Governor the horse of his cousin, Tinoco, then a bay, then a sorrel, then the snow-white animal of Hernandarias, grandson to the Marshal of Seville.

The cutlass fell from Tovar's hand and he did not know it had fallen. Slowly he went out through the breach, and slowly crossed the plain towards the rear. His breath and his strength would return by the time he reached his horse. . . .

Suddenly he felt an overwhelming thirst and remembered the pond to the north of the town. He hesitated, saw the lancers in single file moving towards the town in hard short gallops. From the south rode another troop, also in single file, their shadows curving behind and to the left. He looked back over the town. The sun burned in a vermilion haze, beyond the western wall.

He stood by the pool. Around him men were drinking or staring at the water, or sitting in lassitude from the satiation of their thirst. He looked down. The sun's bloody reflection lay upon the surface and then as he kneeled he saw the black thickening pools overflowing the cavities and uneven places at the edge of the pond, the lazy bright pink streams, darkening upon their outer edges, browning the earth as they ran into the water. He stood up hastily. His vision was not distorted. From under the fence of the stockade welled this spring of blood. He felt a black swell of nausea, then his mouth began to burn and draw with thirst. He fell down and drank deep of the pond. When he raised his head, he saw bubbles rising slowly to the surface in front of a man's face. They did not rise in groups but singly, turning for a moment beneath a pink, iridescent glaze, to break. The man had certainly a great thirst; then Tovar noticed that his hands had slipped into the water in the position of rising. But he did not rise. Then it came to him: the mouth, the nose and eyes were plunged too far below the water. He seized the man by the shoulder and turned him over. An arrow stood out of the centre of his breast. About the broken links of his mail the blood no longer flowed. A pallor crept beneath the brown of his skin, the water rolled quickly off; a few drops remained, glistening coldly. From under the half-closed lids the eyes peeped furtively at Tovar. The lids drew back and the eyes set with a remote, an upward stare.

Tsianina saw Tovar before he reached the woods. She came out with a bowl of maize gruel, leading the mare in her other hand. She handed him the bowl silently and he drank it down in one deep gulp. Although she said nothing, when he handed her the bowl empty, he knew she had watched the opening into which he had gone, had managed to see each time he had gone out or in, had quietly and quickly with her small deft hands mixed the parched meal the moment he had emerged upon the plain. Suddenly he felt a great pity and tenderness and a new strength. His weariness fell away as she wiped the sweat and blood from his face, poured soothing juices into his cuts and bruises, searched him for graver wounds. He longed to reach out and touch her, but this he knew she would not like. Lifting his light, supple lance, he swung into the saddle. As he turned towards Mauvilla, he saw smoke rising up in three places and a squad of horse charging through the open gates. He touched the mare's flanks with his spur.

In spite of their quality, in spite of the horses, in spite of the firing of the town, the Indians did not yield at any point to the Christian bands. Lancers charged down the crowded streets, piercing and trampling underfoot those in the way; but as soon as they had reached the end of a street, turned and looked back, the Indian ranks had closed and it was all to do over again. Tovar arrived in the midst of this second stage of the battle in time to help free the priests and members of the Governor's household who had been trapped in the lodge. The enemy had unroofed their prison and were trying to enter from above after numerous failures to break through the latticed door. Steadily both foot and horse fought a way to the lodge, and in time. The priests, the pages, and the two Christian women ran out through the lane which the soldiers made, Father Francisco and Father Luis laying about with their clubs as they fled. But the Christians paid dearly for the rescue: two knights and their horses were struck down. There was time to remove the bodies beyond the reach of the Indians, and no more.

After six hours of fighting the Christians could show only this rescue as tangible evidence of their progress. Three houses had been burned, but the fire did not spread. The Christians held all the gates and from these points of vantage they sallied forth, always to be driven back. If they cleared a way, the Indians would give in one direction to flow in upon them from another. It was like fighting in a fluid mass, and a position gained could never be held because of the Indians' indifference to their lives—and the archery from the houses. Each was loopholed and at such close range the bowmen rarely missed their marks. More and more the most honoured and skilful men in the army left the attack, either killed or wounded or used up. Hundreds of the enemy had been slain, but this lessened no whit the fury of their defense or their love of death. "It is a dreadful thing, so rare is it," Ortiz said to Tovar, "a dreadful thing to see those whose honour in war is to kill without hurt to themselves dying like any Christian."

After three o'clock all understood that the crisis had been reached. If the Christians could not force a decision by nightfall, all was lost; and it was clear to all that by the present methods it was physically impossible to kill enough Indians between afternoon and dark to force this decision. In spite of the dead and dying the streets still held many more than all the bands of the Christians. In the houses were unknown and uncounted numbers. Soon now, after a few more rounds, on account of the loss of the powder fifty arquebusiers would be put out of the fight. Over twenty horses had been killed or wounded. This loss spread rapidly from mouth to mouth, while the casualties among the men were as yet unknown, but sufficient to cause alarm.

In a lull in the fighting the Governor looked up at the declining sun; then ordered all the horse to reform without the gates. He galloped from point to point, using the cover of the stockade, to organize the new assault. The same orders he gave to all. At the sound of six trumpets each party, mixed of horse and foot and carrying five brand-holders, would attack at once, surrounding and firing the houses. Nor would a party leave any

[353]

particular house until the flames were beyond the control of the Indians. Then, and only then, must they push on to the next. Valour had failed, skill had failed, the horses had failed. Humiliating to consider, only fire, the very violence of nature's element, gave the Christians any hope.

The towers above the gates had been cut down and with brush and dirt and the dead bodies of Indians a parapet of a sort had been made around the quarter of the town which Tovar's company held. Just without the gates he sat his horse, waiting. The Indians, sensing a graver threat, had quieted somewhat, shooting regularly but without the usual violence at those lying behind the parapet. Occasionally an arquebus went off. Bolts from the crossbows whanged intermittently. Tovar's mare stood docilely, but from time to time she quivered as though shaking off flies. And then the Governor rode up and took his place on the other side of Tovar. The six trumpeters filed in, turning quickly against the fence. Studiously they avoided looking towards the Indians. Tovar heard the drum-major's voice and then the shrill, surging blast of the instruments.

Together he and de Soto jumped over the parapet and struck the waiting throng. The arquebuses went off and the bows. With "Santiago!" on their lips the Christians charged and surrounded the first house. Tovar saw nothing but brown, painted bodies leaping towards his lance and the mare's legs pawing the air and wheeling. Black smoke blew between him and the foe like a curtain. The Governor's voice cried, "Santiago and the next!"

Between the second and third houses, as the blood leapt after his withdrawing lance and the tall, slim, muscular form swayed above the level of the mare's head, the eyes looking out defiantly through the crazy mask of streaked and smudged colour, Tovar recognized Tascaluça's son. As the hands, falling before the falling body, reaching to drag him from his seat, suddenly clenched the insubstantial air, he understood that his own sight had blurred for minutes or in one long breathlessness,

[354]

divided by the lunging of his arm in formal fury, striking out against a mass of gleaming bodies, without breath or blood, glistening red streaks, horrid smears of black, moving and whirling and striking in response to his own uncontrollable thrusts. Suddenly he understood that behind the painted masks and streaming feathers there were men fighting for their lives. For an instant he looked down upon the young cacique. In that instant the blow struck him. He lunged to one side, his fingers tingled, the lance was almost wrenched from his hand. He thought, I paused a second too long. He righted himself in the saddle and felt the waves of heat from the burning houses. He touched himself, shook his head. What had happened? A cold shiver drew his body together, his head cleared, he lowered his lance to meet the onrushing foe but it was a cross which pierced the soft-giving flesh. The shaft of an arrow, without splitting or marring the wood, had passed through the centre of his weapon, where the two pieces of ash were joined. So this had been the blow which almost knocked him from his seat. With this cross . . . , he said, and the words dried up in his head. The haze which had lifted for a moment drew again before his sight.

He found himself between the burning houses, driving slowly one lone Indian before him. Whirlwinds of smoke rose in the air and broke, scattering like the aftermath of an explosion. From the ground whirlwinds of dust made funnels before his eyes. The air, sharp and scorching, he drew in through his teeth stingingly. His armour tightened about his body, hot and suffocating. He fought like a man who has been drugged, in great and timeless leisure, out of any harm to himself, easily parrying the desperate blows of the Indian's club. The Indian's chest rose and fell, rapidly, spasmodically. Out of the grease of his body, great round balls of sweat gathered white and pure, breaking into little glistening streams down the black and vermilion flesh. Slowly, towards the burning house, step by step the Indian drew before the long staff of the lance which was a cross in Tovar's hands. Freed from the confusion and the frenzy of the melee, the threat of arrows hissing from unknown and unseen directions, alone with his enemy, surrounded by fire, alone and triumphant . . . so did Tovar prolong his sense of power, godlike in its aloofness, all danger to his person remote, playing with his enemy as upon a hunt, pricking him never deeper than half an inch to increase his fury, delaying the inevitable stroke of death.

And then from the earth, unforeseen, the whirling dust swept before his eyes, a puff of the red-glinting particles swept in under his helmet. Blinded he was sinking to the ground, and as he sank a hoarse and broken scream lifted in triumph. Still blind he managed to reach his feet from under the falling horse and through a blur to point his lance towards the Indian's chest. So they stood, facing each other. His mare he could vaguely see kicking in her death throes. In a moment his sight returned. The Indian was weaponless. He was looking at the mare and in that moment he, Tovar, understood whom the Indian felt to be his enemy. He drew back the lance, the Indian raised his head in such arrogance and dignity that he withheld a breath too long the forward thrust. Lightly, turning and leaping in one movement, the Indian hurled himself into the flaming house. The lance left Tovar's hand, but it was the cross he saw, by the Indian's side leaning out into the flames, browning in the windy heat.

He turned and fled through the flaming street. In the houses as he passed he could see glimpses of black moving forms, but from none were there cries. No cry had his enemy, in his final triumph, uttered. Drawing his hands before his flap, the feathers in his head black twisting quills, the Indian stood quietly looking out upon the enemy he had killed and the enemy he had humbled by his superior act of manhood. Nor did he ever move or cry out, even when his body and his face began to swell and break into boiling blisters. Then, remembering himself, Tovar had turned and fled but the sight of the red and whirling eyes he could not flee. They burned into his head until all was flaming red. Through billowing waves of red he fled. His head grew light, his legs moved but his body did not follow. Then one of

[356]

the waves grew into a great and angry blister, a swelling red-
ness. It broke with a hiss. . . .

He was leaning against the outside logs of the stockade. The
air was hot and charred. Behind him he could hear a crackling
roar. Hot cinders were falling, some still burning, at his feet.
Before him, on the plain, the Indians were fleeing and being pursued in all directions. Then he began to feel his hot and stinging face. He looked at his hands. His gloves were charred, his
jacket of armour black and rotten. As he stood up and began
walking away from the burning town, his boots fell from his
legs, flopping against the ground as he moved, and he felt like
some lumbering, heavy-footed creature, at times as if the earth
of this land were reaching out to take and bind him.

When he reached the woods, without seeing her come up,
Tsianina appeared and as before without greeting began taking
off the charred remnants of his harness. Deftly she cut the strap
which held on his casque and poured a cooling liquid over his
hot and throbbing head. She treated his hands and the burns
on his legs and gave him something to drink, a slimy cooling
draught, wonderfully healing but bad to smell. Binding up his
most grievous hurts, she gathered moss and leaves in a heap
before a tree and there she took him, propping him against the
trunk.

The noise and shouts of battle were fast spending. Troops of
horse were returning at a walk or galloping slowly into the
plain. The foot wandered aimlessly about. All along the edge
of the woods the wounded had gathered and their companions
were bending over them clumsily and solicitously. The women,
he heard, had been divided among the most gravely hurt. To
the left of the main gate small bodies of Christians and Indians
were still fighting. In front of the town the sky was grey with
ashes and cinders, some falling in jagged arcs like stars thrown
off their courses. But in this sky he saw the greyness that was
death, for although the Christians had, at great cost, destroyed

[357]

their foes, yet he knew without being able to tell why that in their triumph was the beginning of defeat. In his exhaustion and through the stings and aches of his wounds this thought overlay his heavy spirits, as fear and depression descend in the first awakening from a bad dream.

His eyes returned again and again to the burning town. In all of its many noises there was one noise, growing out of and yet apart from the flames, private, unique, and yet in some way as everlasting as truth. It sounded upon his ear and not even his own breath was more real, but he knew that the moment it passed, it had passed forever. Nothing in man or beast, on the earth or in the air above it, held comparisons or symbols by which it could be fixed and described. It was like pain, which though sharper than sensibility lacks memory: death without resurrection. He listened as to the unfathomable mystery of doom, told with accents clear and grammatical but told in a foreign tongue. In sorrow and foreboding he listened and watched, saw tails of whitish smoke creep up the spaces between the log fence, saw the red and wavering sheet of flame behind the open gate, and then . . .

He sat forward unbelieving. He was about to call out and ask if he was graced with a vision. But it was no vision, or a vision given to all, for he could tell by the movements and sudden awakening of interest of those Christians facing the town that they too saw. From out the gates, out of the very flames themselves, walked the nineteen girls who early that morning had beguiled the Governor into thinking the Mauvillians received him on a footing of peace. They came forward across the plain in one line, nineteen of them, and halted out of reach of the heat. Altogether they folded their hands before them in submission and one beckoned and made motions of surrender.

Three lancers rode uncertainly forward; among them he recognized Vélez by his barrel trunk. They rode until they came near, how near he could not say and yet every step the horses took he watched like a man stricken by a spell. Suddenly the maidens parted at their middle and three warriors stepped

[358]

forth and drew their long bows back to their ears. The bows grew straight but so quickly was another shaft fitted to the gut, and the gut drawn back in its arc that the eye might have been deceived into thinking they took only an overlong aim, had not two of the lancers charged forward, and had not Vélez leaned forward on his horse and the horse grown still, to fall, minutes later, in a forward lurch and throw its master to the ground.

The maidens parted in two groups as the lancers rode down their men. The third Indian outran them to the walls. There he climbed the gate post, stooped for a moment and did something to one of the logs and then dropped from the wall, jerked violently up, to hang between ground and sky at the end of his bowstring.

3

There was no way to disguise it: the victory, overwhelming as it was, carried for the Christians all the gloom and uncertainties of defeat. Bands of horse were sent out to lay waste the land and spread terror within the confines of Tascaluça's domains near enough to the camp at Mauvilla to threaten reprisals for the fall of that place. A number of Indians were captured for bearers, but not enough to replace those that had been freed. Of maize and other foods enough was brought in to sustain the army and the animals for a month, but this could not lighten the effects of the disaster. The lowest reckoning of the Indians killed was twenty-five hundred, not counting those burned to death in the houses or those others who had fled to near-by towns where, overcome by their wounds, they died in the fields and houses. The army had been handled too severely to be comforted by these facts. Twenty-two Christians had been killed outright, a third of these the most honourable and valiant men in the army. Two hundred and fifty showed upon their bodies seven hundred and sixty injuries left by the arrows and clubs of the foe. At night these wounds were dressed from

[359]

the fat of the dead Indians, as there was no medicine left, all of it having been consumed by the flames. Twelve horses were killed or died and seventy hurt, and all the supplies, the clothing the Christians carried with them, the sacred vessels for saying Mass, the wheat for making the Host, the wine, many weapons, and all the pearls were burned. There was nothing now to show for all their toil and trouble, except their wounds and their sorrows.

But the worst blow of all was the loss of the pearls. This Tovar sensed in the changed attitude of the Governor. He became gloomy and withdrawn and when one of his officers said that, as bad as was the loss of the supplies, they would be replenished by Maldonado's caravels, he changed the subject. Again, when an Indian reported that the gulf was only forty leagues away, he showed no interest. As his interest in the coast waned, that of his men increased. It was more eagerly discussed and the tenor of the discussion, though never openly voiced, exposed the wish of many to quit the land. The Governor was aware of this but he made no comment, either public or private. Between the times when he visited the wounded, with whom he was tender and solicitous, doing many things with his own hands to ease their hurts and bringing a frank, bluff cheer to support their spirits, he kept apart with his thoughts. But his aloofness, and what appeared at first as gloom, was not despair. On no occasion did he say or do anything that might lead one to think he despaired. It was something very personal to himself. Almost it seemed he carried on a private court of inquiry into the disaster, with himself as accused, as prosecutor, and as judge. When he was interrupted by pressing business, he always responded quickly, intelligently, and briefly. His self-confidence was unshaken; he never showed that his belief in the final success of the conquest had been shaken. It was rather that he felt the obstacles had become more difficult and that his own point of view must be changed, and radically, to meet the changed circumstances. Or so it seemed to Tovar, as he watched him during the slow weeks of convalescence.

[360]

In the first week of November a cold wind blew out of the north and lasted for three days. It went away and fine clear fall weather returned, but everybody grew restless. They had recognized the breath of winter. And then one day a strange Indian came into camp. Only the Governor and Ortiz, using the Ochuse Indian for interpreter, saw him. The next day the Indian had disappeared and with him the Ochuse cacique. The camp was filled with rumours: Maldonado had arrived; the Indian came as messenger; the Governor had secretly, without consulting any of his officers or the Royal Hacienda, decided to lead his army farther into the wilderness, to drive them to their ruin, out of pride and vanity and because he would not return to Cuba with fortunes wasted and hopes blasted. Many stout hearts argued the probable chances of success still remaining, but they were troubled and for the first time the Governor's interests were spoken of as personal and separate from those of his men.

One night shortly after, as Tovar was returning to his fire, he passed by a mess where a dozen men were gathered. It was late, he had just fed his horse after coming off sentry duty, and it seemed to him strange that any would be up at such an hour. But he thought little of it. In the loneliness of the watch he had been thinking of his escape from Mauvilla. It had worried him during his convalescence. He had three bad arrow wounds, which had healed under Tsianina's ministrations wonderfully well, but they had not hurt him so much as his burns for these burns had scorched to his soul, bringing always to mind the image of his foe leaping into the flames as to a sanctuary. His pride had never recovered from that act of defiance, which had snatched away his victory. The advantages of horse and weapon, his superior skill, his very manhood had been brought to seem mean and ignoble in his own eyes, for he knew that he, under the same circumstances, would not have had the fortitude to accept death by fire. Nor could he have gone through the ordeal without crying out. Could a mere heathen so mortify his flesh, lacking the example of Lord Christ to sustain him,

[361]

while he, a Christian, must have showed his feather? At times he thought that he could have matched the Indian in courage, in his conquest of pain; but always doubts would return. This debate with himself he went over again and again during those weeks after Mauvilla, coming never to any resolution. They kept him from following closely that other conflict which was brewing between the Governor and his army. At times he would try to understand the outcome, assess the temper of the army, the Governor's purpose; but always his own private obsession came back and he would forget the Governor and his army. Nor did he connect the whole train of events with his fears and the gage which he had thrown down at Cutifichiqui. On top of this, to confuse him further, he remembered how his lance had made a cross and that cross left burning by the Indian's side. To him it had been given as a sign, just as the rosary taken from the skeleton's hand at Talimeco had been given as a sign. But how to read this sign? This question he was asking again for the hundredth time as he passed near enough to the mess to hear without being seen. He would have gone by with no more than a curious interest, save that a certain tone in the men's voices made him halt. It was subdued, yet violent, like the voices of conspirators.

"Now that the pearls are gone, what is there to send to Cuba and keep alive any interest in this land?" a familiar voice was saying.

"To delude others . . ." The voice trailed off.

". . . false land."

"Peru . . ."

"In Peru the gold has just been touched."

At this place the shadows from the forest fell far out over the plain. Cautiously he drew nearer and heard the voices plot to go away on Maldonado's caravels and join the civil wars in Peru. He gathered that the numbers of the disaffected were considerable and that he had stumbled upon the leaders. This was very close to treason. He was certain that he knew to whom at least three of the voices belonged: at the King's Treasurer,

[362]

Gaytán, he was not surprised; Lobillo, he could understand; but Añasco . . . that gave him pause. Two of the men were half turned in his direction. They were Moscoso's brothers!

He was undecided whether to hear more or go on when he saw a figure withdraw furtively from the shadows at the back of the mess and slip silently into the night. For a short space the glow from the dying fire showed it plainly. It wore the robes of a priest, but no priestly garments could disguise that carriage, the clumsy furtiveness and purposeful stride, or the flat chin and pointing beard thrust insolently out of the cowl.

Had it come to this? Such distrust and fear, such isolation? Was there none upon whom the Governor could rely? Need he skulk in the dark, the open and forthright gentleman? Tovar felt a great sadness and pity and before he thought, he had turned his steps to follow. But his wits returned in time to prevent his folly. He made his way to his own quarters, now thoroughly apprehensive.

There had been no doubt in his mind that the man hidden behind the priestly garments was de Soto. Thinking wishfully, he had tried to reconstruct a doubt, but this vanished when the word went around that the army would not seek Maldonado at Ochuse but go forward into the country. The Governor had avoided an open test of strength. With his perfect tactical instinct he had called his officers together and told them that now that winter was near, he feared to risk a march to the coast. The army must settle down as quickly as possible and where grain was known to be plentiful. He had word of a province to the north of Mauvilla, a week's journey away . . .

None had protested. For once he had failed to ask for advice. His manner did not warrant gratuitous opinion. His officers received their orders and were dismissed. They retired without discussion and reported to their commands the information that as soon as the most severely wounded were able to travel, the army would push off again into the wilderness.

Later the captains bethought themselves and returned singly or in groups to petition the Governor to reconsider his decision.

[363]

What was said, the arguments given and the arguments replied, Tovar was not present to hear; but certainly they expressed the general disbelief in the land's treasure. To this he knew what must be the Governor's answer: Peru, Pizarro's many expeditions, his numerous disappointments and trials. It was made to hand and came, Tovar knew, readily to the Governor's lips. To those who would plead the need of replenishing their supplies the Governor could advance the doubts of finding Maldonado and the urgent necessity of seeking quarters before winter settled down. The signs promised early and severe weather. The one argument the Governor could not have answered no captain of honour would permit himself to make: the situation openly referred to by the conspirators—to go out of the land now would mean the Governor's ruin. Had any one of the captains been bold or base enough to say, "My lord, the question is this—whether you are willing to risk further the life of this army to forestall the publication of your ruin and the disgrace of failure." To this he could have made no answer. He must have accepted the risk of holding a weary and disheartened army with the same old promise in the presence of the release which Maldonado's ships would have offered. But since the arguments and counter-arguments avoided mention of the one thing which could have brought the issue out into the open, it worked underground in a rapidly spreading discontent, obscuring and weakening the belief of those, a considerable body, who still had hopes of Florida and were willing to follow the Governor to the end.

The discontent did not remain long below the surface. It happened to come Juan Gaytán's turn to stand guard the day after it was known that the army would not seek Ochuse. When the guard formed, he was missing. The officer of the day found him gambling with his companions and reprimanded him sharply for his delay. Gaytán looked up, the dice in his hand, and said insolently, "It's not fitting for a man of my station to stand guard." He returned to the game as though he did not mean to be interrupted. This was open mutiny and all knew it. Whether he came to this decision on his own, or whether it was a signal for the disaffected to rise never developed. The officer of the day did not reason with him. He turned on his heels and marched the guard to their posts; then he went straight to the Governor's quarters and reported.

It was the hour of the first night watch. Every eye in camp watched the officer of the day as he crossed the open square to the Governor's quarters. The silence was sullen and grim. There was no movement or talk, save at the dice game. Gaytán bent over the circle as though his only interest was in the cast and roll of the dice, but the attention of his companions was not so perfect. They followed out of their eyes the officer's progress. Tovar had armed himself and saddled his horse. Anything, he felt, might happen. The officer paused before the Governor's door, stooped and entered.

It could not have been more than a minute or two, but the strain grew unbearable. Then the Governor's equerry came out and disappeared in the darkness. A few moments later the Governor was standing in his door, with his casque on his head. His voice lashed out across the dark and empty spaces, "I am inspecting the sentries. Any man not at his post, no matter what his station, shall hang five minutes thereafter."

The silence boomed. The gamblers looked up from the game, frozen by the voice. None looked at Gaytán. He stooped, unmoving, with his hand thrust out over his knee. The light from the fire flickering over his long and swarthy features, over the Hapsburg nose—it was said he was grandson on the left hand to Maximilian—but his eyes were in shadow. No others were in view. It seemed to Tovar that the entire army was holding its breath. And then the Governor's stallion was brought up. He swung lightly into the saddle, the horse curvetted, a page handed him his lance. Slowly he rode towards the first post.

Tovar felt the sweat pricking his face as he forced himself to glance towards the ring of gamblers. It had scattered. A lone figure was running in the direction of the horses. A few moments later the sounds of a horse galloping came out of the woods where the fourth guard was accustomed to be posted.

There had not been time to saddle the animal. Suddenly through the camp ran a low and brutal snicker.

The Governor gave no other reprimand, nor did he show any less courtesy in his dealings with Gaytán, but that night His Majesty's Treasurer lost the esteem of the army and by his cowardice and the Governor's prompt challenge the army was spared internecine strife, which in its state of morale must have wrecked it. If Gaytán had held his ground, his faction must have gone to his succour. A faction there was, for in view of Gaytán's behaviour there was little reason to think that singly and alone he had taken upon himself the risk of defying the Governor's rule. So more and more, as the days passed, did the Christians feel the effects of the Mauvilla disaster. Of all the crises which de Soto had faced, this had been the most dangerous. When a governor is forced to maintain good rule by his own right arm, things have indeed reached a dangerous state.

During the following days the army responded better to its plight. Good order was restored; although the men accepted their destiny with grumbling, they accepted it. But after that night Tovar felt that tacitly, at least, two factions remained in the camp and there was never again quite the same unity of feeling and purpose.

By the tenth of November there was no further reason to hold on at Mauvilla. The wounded had all healed, except for two or three who could be moved on litters, and healed without the loss of a single life. Men took comfort from this, as a sign of God's care and benevolence. A Mass of Thanksgiving was called for the morrow, at an early hour so that the men could spend the rest of the day preparing to set out, at the latest, by the twelfth.

4

They gathered in the open, under a sky that was neither night nor day. Not a man in the army was absent, except those on guard duty, for this was the last Mass at which the priest would hold the Host up to the altar. Father Francisco had carried on his person a few wafers made before the moulds and

[366]

the wheat had been burned at Mauvilla. Sparingly they had been used and now there was one left. The priests and friars had met and discussed whether or not to substitute maize for wheat. It was decided that such a practice would be highly dangerous and without precedent. In the future all Masses must be dry Masses, as are sometimes held at sea. This was in no way so comforting as seeing God's actual body consumed for the sins of man; so on that morning, while the stars were still out and the half-moon still rode the sky, all had foregathered in great humility of spirit, in thanksgiving, and with melancholy and some fear.

Each Christian followed the service as though he understood for the first time the holy mystery. Many wept silently with the feeling and expression of true love for God and God's Mother and out of pity for their own sinful natures. In every heart there was forgiveness and longing. From station to station they followed Lord Christ towards the cross, shining upon the altar, under the open sky as was that first cross upon the hill of Golgotha. All drew together in compassion for the coming sacrifice. The fire of their tenderness ignited not only the straw but also the wood which the devil had cut from the mountain of mercy.

And then it happened. When Father Francisco had reached the place in the service where he was about to eat God's body, when the attention was most perfect and every heart had quickened in anticipation of the moment of truth, he turned toward the people with the holy Host in his hand, holding it upright above the paten. At this innovation there ran through the congregation a sound like a shudder; then a sudden descending quiet, but it was no longer the quiet of peace but a stilled waiting.

The blessed father paused a little while, gazing devoutly upon his God, while tears streamed copiously from his eyes. In the midst of his tears he lifted up his voice with the authority which God knows how to grant to those who serve Him, saying, "Hernando de Soto, come before me."

The Governor had been kneeling in the place to which his

rank entitled him. Without a word he stood up and walked over to the priest and knelt down at the foot of the choir. Again Father Francisco paused, as if to receive from God the words he would speak. Breaking the pause, he said with a celestial grace, "Do you believe that this which I hold in my unworthy hands is the body of our Lord, Jesus Christ, Son of the Living God, who came from heaven to earth to redeem us all?"

"Yes, Father, I believe it," de Soto said.

Again the priest said, "Do you believe that this same Lord is to come to judge the quick and the dead, and that upon the good he will bestow glory and upon the wicked eternal suffering in hell?"

"That, too, I believe."

"If then you believe this, which every faithful Christian must believe, how is it you are the cause of the many evils and sins we have suffered?" The priest gave him no pause in which to answer but continued: "How is it you do not take the advice of your captains and go out of this land, where for your sake this people have perished and are perishing? Or hearken unto me who have often warned and implored you?

"If until now you have not hearkened unto men, listen to the Son of the Virgin, who speaks to you. And fear that same Son of God, who shall judge you. By this God, whom I hold here in my hands, I warn, I beseech, I command that you now do that which you have not wished to do, which in your stubborn avarice and pride you have refused—Go out of this land! Follow the command of this Lord and I promise you escape for all. Disobey His command and receive chastisement by His hand."

He held the Host over de Soto's head for a second and then turned to the altar. De Soto remained kneeling, but his back was stiff and his head upraised. The priest moved rapidly through the rest of the service; but his motions, the sound of the trumpet, the shifting acolytes, the sacrifice itself went unseen. No eye sought the altar but the man kneeling at its foot. The elation of pity and worship was gone. Impatience, wonder, the gnawing of a fearful curiosity bound together the communi-

[368]

cants in a gross and worldly anticipation; and, when the trumpet sounded to announce the moment of contrition and joy, it told instead the near end of the service.

Ite missa est. . . . For an instant the silence slipped like a spring; then it tightened. The priest withdrew to the small brush arbour at the side of the choir and began taking off his vestments; the acolyte was putting out the candles; and still de Soto continued to kneel before the altar. The Constable's breath rose and fell like a torn bellows.

Not until Father Francisco had folded and put away the last of his robes did the Governor rise. He stood slowly up upon the swell of ground where the choir had been marked off and the altar set. Up to that moment most of the men had kept their knees from suspense and uncertainty. Now there came a great shuffling and clank of harness. Tovar felt his legs tremble and pushed himself up with his hands for balance. . . . The Governor had turned and was confronting his army. All the blood had withdrawn from his face. It was a pale and lifeless brown, but his eyes were black with anguish. So he stood, waiting for the quiet to return. As he waited, a cold light swept down, slanting across the heads of the men. Tovar raised his eyes. Up from the darkened earth, clear and flawless, the first light of morning streamed across the sky. In one corner Tovar saw the moon, as thin as a wafer.

"Fetch me the priest."

At last de Soto spoke, in great gentleness but firmly. So soft were his words that none moved to do his bidding; and then as he stood there waiting, Tovar came to himself and hastened towards the arbour. "Father, His Excellency . . ." he began.

"I have said all I have to say to Hernando de Soto. Through me God has spoken. Let him hearken."

Father Francisco was standing in all the arrogance of spiritual pride, his face flushed and his voice loud and slightly quavering. Tovar felt a flash of anger. He swallowed to collect himself. "You do not understand, Father," he said, as calmly as he could. "It is the Governor who wants to speak to you."

"He can want nothing of me."

"You scurvy priest!" Tovar laid his hand upon the other's arm.

Father Francisco drew back. He was a strong man but he could not free himself from Tovar's tightening grip. "You impious son——"

"Must I drag you there?"

"Loose me. I see the devil is not so easily routed."

Tovar relaxed his grip, Father Francisco jerked his arm free and strode out of the arbour towards the assembled army. Tovar followed close upon his heels and stopped several paces behind him.

In the presence of the Governor and the army Father Francisco recovered his poise. He said, "You would speak with me, my lord?"

The Governor inclined his head slightly but he did not look around. His gaze travelled over the uplifted faces before him, came to rest midway of the crowd. "Señores," he said in sadness, "you have seen what Father Francisco has done. You have heard the strange words he spoke to me." He paused, raised his hand and rested it upon the hilt of his sword. "I have called him before you to hear my reply." He raised his head slightly and continued, "I do not doubt that Father Francisco thinks God has spoken through him to me. To think otherwise would do him injustice, and that I would not do wittingly to him or to any man, as all of you know; but especially to him, for he has ever been God's faithful and earnest servant. But—" he drew in his breath—"it is passing strange that God chose the time of our greatest trial, when courage has been struggling with doubt, to call upon me, the Adelantado, to abandon the conquest I have dedicated to Him. To flee the land! To flee it empty-handed and with our work undone. To abandon Florida yet unpacified, abandon the thousands of souls now living in darkness; leave them without the knowledge of the only faith and the only salvation."

Gradually his voice had begun to rise until it rang out in full and resonant tones, flowing without hesitation and under perfect government. As he listened, Tovar thought it was too well checked. If once it should break.... Slowly de Soto drew in his breath; slowly, word by word, he released it.... "I cannot think that Father Francisco, impelled by what influence I do not know nor dare even to think on, understood what he, and mind you I say he, not God's priest, would have me do."

The priest stepped forward. "What mean you, Hernando de Soto?" The cold fury of his voice, the fury of righteousness outraged, struck in its suddenness like a challenge. As at drill the heads in the crowd turned from priest to Governor. In the pause which followed, a low excited murmur rose and died.

De Soto turned in his tracks. The crowd could scarcely contain itself. They recognized in his movement the familiar sight of his battle carriage: head drawn back, eyes alert but composed, the swift flowing of his body, as though it were all of a piece, without joint or tendon. Always at such times he gave the impression of immobility, but it was the immobility of a bow cranked and bolted. His beard moved slightly, the lips barely opened.

"I mean this, priest. In that moment when you held God's body in your hands, ready for the sacrifice, the sacrifice I and the army had gathered to witness, in adoration, in all humility of spirit, in thanksgiving and the need of our sinful natures, in that moment when we were upon our knees waiting for the consummation, what did you do? Did you complete the sacrifice? No. You turned away from the altar, you violently and without precedent delayed the blessed immolation. And why? I cannot tell you why. It is not given me to read men's hearts. But I can tell you what you did. When I was upon my knees, helpless before the divine Presence, that blessed body, my God"—here his voice slipped and quavered—"my God that I would not see again, for a long time, perhaps never again in this life, you in the power of your office, calling in His name, commanded me to reverse a decision of policy. Was it a spiritual thing you asked me to do? No. You commanded me in the name of Him who teaches us to deny the flesh to save the flesh its sorrows and trials. In God's name you attempted to usurp my authority. But I will tell you, Father Francisco of the Rock, that I, not you, am Adelantado, both civil and military Governor in this land, by grace of your spiritual superiors and His Sacred Majesty, the Emperor. In all matters pertaining to this army I shall decide. In all things pertaining to the welfare of our souls, you and your brothers may guide us. But to meddle in my domain . . . it was not well done of you, priest. It was not well done of you."

It was apparent that the Governor had the sympathy of the army, but they waited to hear Father Francisco. He was so long replying that the men began to move restlessly about. De Soto had relaxed, now that he had relieved his mind. He showed that he felt the growing sympathy, but his hand, resting upon his sword, trembled. At last the priest began to speak:

"I have long known," he said with feigned humility, "that I count for nothing in the affairs of this army. At last you have openly confirmed my belief of the opinion you hold of the good I might do it. So be it. On this count I have nothing more to say, except to add that when the prince mocks his spiritual adviser, he pares the devil's claws."

De Soto made a movement as if to speak. Father Francisco raised his hand.

"But there is one question I will put you, and in the sight of this army, whose fate rests upon your word. I shall ask you to answer me with a plain yea or nay." He paused and then continued with a reasonable tone, "Is it not true, my lord, that you, a layman, inevitably embroiled in the world's Corruption, are less fit to interpret God's will than I, God's annointed priest?"

Father Francisco opened his hands as does a humble petitioner, but one finger of each hand was out-thrust, as though prodding de Soto with the dilemma he had proposed. Softly, with a sharp edge of irony, he added, "No equivocation, Señor Adelantado. A plain yea or nay."

It took a little while for the crowd to understand the cunning of the question. When it saw, it began to stir and draw together as it does in the arena when the moment of truth has arrived. Every eye was fastened upon the Governor with delight, some few with pity, but all in a fearful fascination. It was now broad light and he stood upon the rise of ground, in sight of all, no longer able to disguise the workings of his face. Under his armour one could almost see him writhe.

"What, have you lost the tongue that spoke so glibly a few moments ago?" So gently spoke the priest his words were barely heard. The crowd leaned forward as if to see the blood they drew. "A simple yea or nay."

"In spiritual matters . . ." de Soto burst out. His voice was hoarse, ungoverned. Tovar saw large beads of sweat break upon his brow, and looked away.

"Yea or nay." The goading voice was grown suddenly peremptory.

To answer Yea meant that he must follow the command of the priest and go out of Florida. He could not, no Christian, could answer Nay. The dilemma was such as only a priest could put. There came a click. De Soto had dropped his hand from the sword hilt.

"Heed me, priest," he said. "I believe it is God's will that this land be pacified. Pacified it shall be. There is your answer."

Now it came Father Francisco's turn to pause. The pause lengthened into silence. The silence rose above the crowd in swelling waves, wave melting into wave until all the world whirled in a great and billowing swoon. There in the centre, upon the rise of ground, stood the Governor, pale of face but resolute in the knowledge of what he had done. He had given his answer. There was no more to be said; but he held on, waiting to hear the pronouncement of heresy, to receive the complete and formal statement of his peril.

But Father Francisco could not end his pause. Now that it was too late he showed himself to be thoroughly aware of the grave consequences of the situation he had forced upon them all. "Ay, then, it is nay," he said at last, in a voice so low that only those near the choir could hear him. With difficulty he raised his shoulders and looked towards the Governor.

"The devil knows how to wear the raiment of Paradise.

With it shining and dazzling the eye, who will look for the cloven hoof?"

The words fell at his feet. He turned like an old man and began walking away. His steps did not falter, but they moved wearily and without direction.

Tovar was the last to leave the ground. The Governor, like a mechanical man, walked down the rise, his men breaking and withdrawing to let him pass. By the time he had reached his quarters, the gathering had broken up, the men singly or in groups drifting across the plain. And then came the ring of the smith, beating out iron into shoes. Soon the usual noises preparing for the march filled the camp. Almost one could believe that nothing had happened, almost but not quite. There was the spot where de Soto had kneeled before the choir; there the altar had stood. Now neither choir nor altar, nor God, only a rise in the ground upon the plain of Mauvilla, somewhere in Florida. There upon this piece of ground, indistinguishable from any other, it had happened. There, there, there....

The Governor could not bring himself to say the word, and yet say it he had. Father Francisco was right: Nay it was. He had set his private will outside the guidance and discipline of the Church, the will which, unrestrained, serves only the senses, as the senses only the flesh. He, a layman, had undertaken to interpret God's mind. This is what his decision meant, no matter if he denied or disguised it. From here it is only one step further to supplant God's will by man's and call it divine—man made God, man with all his frailties and pride setting up the goods of the world over the good of heavenly grace. Where would this bring him? Where would it lead them all?

Gradually Tovar pulled himself together. His legs he set firmly under his body, his arms he placed at his sides, and then he turned his back upon the altar. He turned and faced the wilderness. Out of the north a cold wind had risen, sweeping sharply down the plain.

He said aloud, "This is the twelfth of November, 1540," and then: "I must hurry."

[374]

8
THE CONQUEST

The Conquest

I

TOVAR let his eyes travel over the gaps in the wall. He thought: They ought to be filled. But the Governor had given orders to leave them down and the gates open at night, to show the Indians how little he thought of them. It had come to this: The Christians must practice guile, now that they were come to the most populous territory they had found in all of Florida. No longer could they stand upon the strength of their arms alone. But it was a wearisome business making the rounds each night, by the gaps, the gates, and down to the river where the crossbowmen guarded the dugouts. It made the watches come too often, with only forty horses left fit for service.

He shifted his eyes over the town. The army had grown. Not a man lacked a slave. There must be seven or eight hundred of all ages and sexes to serve the Christians. Service they did render, but for every hanega of maize the Christians ate it took two for the slaves. He looked from house to house, at the people sitting or lying around the yard. All looked dully before them, their hands lying motionless in their laps. A few pretended to mend their harness. He turned abruptly to the five Indians sitting on the ground before the Governor's couch. The boy from Cutifichiqui was straining to understand their different talks. Five separate tongues and the boy with only a smattering of Spanish.

"Ortiz was the greatest loss we've had," Silvestre said in a dull, resentful tone. "In four words he could have understood what it has taken this boy all day to make out."

"We've come this far anyway," Tovar replied.

"This far? How far is this?"

Tovar lifted his hand, let it fall. "Guachoya."

"Guachoya? And where is Guachoya?"

He did not answer. A whole year's wandering since crossing the great river and now they were back on that river, but where they were neither he nor any man knew. Perhaps the interpreter might yet find out, might catch the word Sea, out of all these different tongues. The Indians of Nilco had said that their river would lead to the great river and that to an arm of the sea. There the Governor could build his pinnaces and send to a Christian land for the help he needed, horses and supplies of all kinds to continue the conquest. Even now, with two years gone by since Mauvilla, after all the things they had suffered, he still thought of conquest.

De Soto sat among the skins, leaning slightly forward, his breath quick with fever, his glazed eyes fastened upon the Indians. Mechanically he shifted his gaze from face to face, as though he understood the words, as if he would look beneath their brown masks and see the truth. No matter how often the boy stumbled or misinterpreted he never lost patience. His patience was terrifying, and his will . . . how much longer would it last? Already it had worn him to the bone. The skin of his face was drawn like a mummy's. His lips had an upward curl.

The interpreter seemed to be making no headway. Tovar got up from the bench and walked slowly to the gates of the town. Beyond them, a crossbow shot away, lay the great river. It swept by, half a league wide, endlessly, like a great yellow sloughing of earth that had liquefied. Tremendous trees passed bobbing upon its surface. Suddenly one would stand upright in a whirling pool, as slim as a sapling, then plunge, trembling, out of sight. On the far shore he saw several toy canoes laboriously working upstream. He wondered what tribe they belonged to. Somewhere this body of water was bound to reach the sea and the sea, habitations of Christians. But where? If only Ortiz were still with the army, there would be certainty again.

[378]

"If it would only make a noise," a voice beside him said petulantly. "It didn't make a sound that time." And then mysteriously, "I think of him whenever I see it go by."

The man was standing out from the gateposts. He had spoken without taking his eyes from the river. "That's strange," Tovar answered. "I was thinking of him, too."

"We were in the first barge," the man continued and Tovar wondered if the soldier had heard him speak. "It had taken us two hours to drag it upstream, and then we gave it to the current. We had six horses and forty men on board. All the way across he was gay. We were the first load, you see, and didn't know what was ahead of us. His voice somehow set us at ease. He seemed so free from danger."

Tovar remembered the concern of the army when that barge had been launched. It had taken a month to build the barges and while they were building every afternoon at exactly three o'clock two hundred long dugouts came down the river, drew nigh the banks where the Christians were and loosed their arrows. It was a brave sight, the paddlers standing in the boats, protected by the bucklers of the warriors, the caciques sitting in the stern under an awning, shouting orders . . . the boats moving like a great armada in action.

"You know," the soldier continued, "I can hear his words now, as plain as if he were by my side. 'A soothsayer once told me,' he said, 'that water would be the death of me. Now I know what he meant. Ever since we've been in this land I've done nothing but walk through water, sleep in it, float on it, drink it. And what have I got for my pains? A few feathers and a skin or two. What a fool I was to leave Italy where the sack of a town brought real gold, at least a bed to sleep in and a Christian woman. . . . In this land a man has got to be half fish.' We all laughed at him, he told it in such a wry way, and he laughed back. We felt good, for the barge, we could see, would land in the right place." The soldier paused, then said slowly and wonderingly, "He was the first to jump ashore. It was not a big jump, a few feet maybe. He stood there for a moment, poised,

[379]

with his sword in his hand; then he jumped. His foot slipped on the bank. He went down without a sound." The man looked hard at the river, his voice continued mysteriously, "We prodded with our lances, but he never came up. He went down without a sound and never came up."

"You are mistaken," Tovar said. "He died at Autiamque." The man looked up, startled, his face grown suddenly blank. "Francisco Sebastián?" his voice said, retreating.

"No, Juan Ortiz."

"Oh, Ortiz," he said with returning confidence. "Yes, he died in Autiamque."

A slight flicker of annoyance passed over the soldier's features, and he turned again to the river. Between that yellow torrent and the man's thoughts existed some close and secret communion. Nothing, Tovar saw, might intrude. The man was as completely withdrawn as though he had entered a room and closed the door.

Dispirited, Tovar turned away, wandering aimlessly. Were there many, he asked himself, who saw only one other casualty in this greatest of all casualties? There had been a time when each name struck from the roster had been felt as a common loss. Had death become so common a thing, except where it touched each man's private sorrow, that it seemed only the natural end to hardship and toil and trials beyond the tongue of man to utter? Or were men now grown too fearful or too spent to look into the common plight? He, at least, would face it. They were lost and without a guide. He repeated aloud, "Lost and without a guide."

He came to a platform the Indians had built in a maize field, where the women go to sing to the growing maize and watch for crows. He climbed up and sat down in the shade, but the shade of April is cold and he moved over to where the sun fell upon the rough-hewn planks. It was not strong enough to burn or make him uncomfortable. Its light warmth sank through his clothes, bringing him cheer. The little heat in the boards his body took quickly up, and the cool air blew up through the cracks. But he had underestimated, he found, the strength of the sun. It struck his face, his chest, his thighs with a growing strength. He reached out with his hands to turn over. . . . He looked at himself, leaning on his hands. In this exact position had he awakened in the lodge at Chickasaw and seen the roof in flames. He had been dreaming that he lay out on the plains at home, at Vista Hermosa while the cattle grazed. There was no other sound than the crackling roof. Quickly he prodded his companions awake. He remembered again the light from the fire falling across their naked bodies and their dazed looks. It was March, it was cold and they still slept in the winter houses. There would have been time to snatch clothes and weapons, but before they could recover their senses the Indian whoops leaped up from the ground. His companions grew still in their tracks and then broke out of the door. He followed hastily wrapping his cloak about his body.

Never had he seen such confusion. Naked men fleeing in all directions, blinded by the smoke and the flames, horses neighing and galloping over foe and friend alike, shaking their broken halters. Animal screams from the burning stalls, the utterly abandoned cries of hogs trapped in their sties. Shouts of Christians mingled with the cries of triumph from their foes. As he fled to the woods, he saw the Governor, armed and mounted, lance an Indian, then go over the head of his horse with his saddle. As he sought the darkness of the thicket, he said, "This is the end." But it was not yet the end. God who chastises His own as He pleases shut the eyes of the Indians and made them think that the horses stampeding were cavalry gathering for the charge. And so the army was saved.

But the town was in cinders. Lances, armour, weapons, clothes all were burned. If by good luck any one had been able to save a garment from the burning of Mauvilla, it was here destroyed. Half of the army remained naked and only kept from freezing by drawing close to the burning houses. The next morning, under the grey sky, the Christians took account of their losses. Fifty-nine horses burned to death and twelve

Christians lost, either by fire or at the hands of the Indians. Bautista's wife, heavy with child, had rushed back into her dwelling for her pearls and was burned. Her husband went to her aid, but the flames leapt between them. Someone who saw him said that each time she screamed he would beat his bare breast, giving way a few feet as the flames rose higher. All thought it God's blessing when he was found later, lying in a heap, black from the fire, with an arrow through his neck.

Now that he looked back on it, this sad ending to the first winter they had spent after Mauvilla was decisive, for it was more than the hardest blow ever to be received by the army. It had been a hard winter, not so cold nor so long as at Autiamque, for there the quarters were strong, well-fenced, and the army never lacked for food. The winter at Chickasaw had been hard in another way. It was due to the changed relations between the Governor and his men. Nothing on the surface showed this change, except that the Governor no longer confessed to Father Francisco but went instead to his nephew priest, and one felt that this was merely a formality. It was rather that the men performed their duties in a too perfunctory manner. They seemed to feel, even those of the Governor's mind who preferred every risk to the certainty of poverty, that his decision there at Mauvilla had in some way relieved them of all responsibility. Fewer and fewer went to confession; and at Mass, when there was no blood or body to lift to the altar, the congregation sullenly and unreasonably connected the absence of God's body with the Governor's defiance. It was almost as if they had shifted all responsibility for their lives and perhaps their souls, even, onto his shoulders. He, in turn, withdrew from the companionship and society of his captains. There was nothing overt in this. It happened that his discipline grew more harsh and he more incommunicable.

All were glad to see the winter at Chickasaw come to an end. The day before the night of the fire, preparations for the march were completed, and the Governor and Moscoso had gone to the Chickasaw cacique to beg of him two hundred bearers.

These bearers were promised for the morrow; but, returning to camp, the Governor said to Moscoso, "This has all the signs of an Indian night. Set a strong watch and pass the word out for all to sleep in their armour, with horses saddled." It was never explained, but Moscoso put three of the most worthless men and the poorest horses on duty. He either failed to see that the precautionary measures were taken or the men still refused their natural share of responsibility. It never came out in Moscoso's trial, for the trial was held between two people, Moscoso and the Governor, and the judgment handed down was unequivocal: Moscoso was found guilty and broken to the ranks. No other Camp Master was set in his place, but it came about that the Constable assumed his duties.

The following three days was a time of complete bewilderment. Some effort was made to salvage weapons and armour, but with half of the men absolutely naked in the severe March weather, the Christians could do little but keep fires going and stand between them. And then on the night of the third day the Indians returned again, and again the army was saved. A heavy shower fell, loosening their bow strings, and they retired to their towns. When this became known, the situation resolved itself at once. The Governor marched to a village on the slope of a hill about a league away. Near by was a grove of fine ash for lances and saddles. Only then did the army's torpor fall away. Two bear skins were made into bellows and with gun barrels a forge was rigged up, and here all the weapons were retempered, saddles made and bucklers, and lances as good as those of Biscay. Some contrived mats of dried grass sewed together, one as a top piece, the other for a gown. Many who laughed at this expedient were compelled afterwards to practice it.

At the end of eight days the companies were re-armed and the squadrons resaddled and mounted, and no horseman lacked a good lance. As it turned out, this refitting came not an hour too soon. The Indians came against them one morning at four o'clock, formed in three squadrons, each from a different direction. In all haste the Governor drew up his army into three bodies. Leaving one detachment to guard the camp, he threw the other two into battle formations, just as day was breaking. The ground was open and advantageous for cavalry, his charge well timed. Many Christians displayed great valour that day and no one failed to do his duty. Unfortunate was he who did not defend well his life or who failed to prove to the Chickasaw the quality and arms of the Christians, for the Chickasaws were bold and cunning fighters. As the battle was going in favour of the Christians, a friar cried out without reason, "To camp! To camp!" causing the Governor to go to its succour. But for this the Indians would have paid more dearly for their insolence. As it was, they retired for good, and with little loss on either side.

So it came about, now that he could look back, that the disaster at Chickasaw made for the quick and resolute recovery of morale and fighting prowess. Faced with annihilation, the men freed themselves of the winter's sloth and made the Governor's will their own. Whatever fate he led them to, they followed willingly. But was the will enough?

So long as the Governor's will maintained its pure, direct drive, so long as it followed avidly the promise of the world, followed it without weakening or allowing the golden image which drew it on to tarnish, that long and no longer would the expedition hold together and thrive. But . . . but in these last two years' journeying, in the fights, the idle days in conquered towns, Tovar had forgotten the Wilderness, that old adversary whose dangers and powers appeared so clear to him at Cutifichiqui, in Cuba as a vague but terrifying threat, and now as a grim and foreboding reality. Against this had de Soto's will and, after Chickasaw, the will of the army, been matched and matched with no other aid.

So far the army, in spite of its greatest disasters, in spite of the gradual attrition in men and horses, had kept intact. The horses were few, but still over half of the men were alive. Ortiz was dead and the Governor ill, but he had lost none of his cunning or his skill in ruling. He might yet be restored to strength, get contact with a Christian settlement. He might even stumble upon the golden city. . . .

A noise in the maize brought Tovar out of his thoughts. He stood up and saw eight horsemen riding slowly in his direction. Añasco was in the lead, his eyes straining with the air of a man looking into the wind. As he drew near, Tovar hailed him.

"Where are you going?" he asked.

Añasco drew in the bridle. "The Indians tell the Governor that they have never heard of the sea or of any towns to the south of us, except on the east bank. Quigaltam, I believe they call it, the greatest lord in this part of the country. They say he lives about three leagues down. The Governor doesn't know whether to believe them or not. You know the situation. He has sent one of the Guachoya Indians with a message to this Quigaltam . . . the usual thing, he is the child of the Sun and where he goes all obey him. He will be rejoiced to have Quigaltam's friendship. He must come to see him and bring something that is held in most esteem in his land. Me he is sending to prove or disprove what the Indians say of the lack of towns on this side. I don't particularly like it. It's bound to be swampy and hard going all the way."

"You have always brought us luck," Tovar said.

Añasco nodded vaguely and lifted his bridle.

"God go with you."

Añasco did not reply. He was looking before him, at the tangled mass of trees and looping thickets through which he must pass. Tovar watched him take the short path down to the river. In a few minutes he had disappeared.

2

It came to Tovar, on his way to the Governor's quarters, that he had not seen him since Añasco's return. That would be almost a week now. What could the Governor want with him? He had not called him into his presence since Cutifichiqui. To send him scouting? Añasco had found no signs of towns, only

[385]

canebrakes, thick scrubby depths and bogs coming out of the river. So impassable was the country that he had made only some fourteen or fifteen leagues in eight days. Perhaps the Governor felt their situation desperate enough to try again. But if Añasco had failed . . . And anyway why would he call on him, when there was Vasconcelos, the Tinocos? . . .

The lone halberdier standing outside the door said, "He is expecting you. Just go in and, Señor, if he does not recognize you, shake him a little. He dozes a great deal from the fever."

Tovar lifted the skin, turned inquiringly towards the guard. "I hear a voice," he said.

The guard came up and listened. "It is nothing, Señor. Only a page. Enter."

The skin fell behind Tovar softly. He stood, waiting to be noticed. The page was the rascal, Cacho. He stood screening the bed where the Governor lay.

". . . and Mosquera has lost his skill at throwing."

"How so?" came the voice from the bed.

"Last night at dice he lost a principality," the page continued archly.

"Principality?"

Only now Tovar recognized de Soto's voice, so dry and cracked it was.

"Yes, Excellency. They stripped him down to his buskins. His horse, his weapons, his jerkin and coat. The coat had a population as large as Seville's."

A dry chuckle rose from the bed.

"His brother, the ex-Camp Master, went his bond for horse and weapons. The leanest of his women he gave in pawn."

"And the Constable? How fares he?"

"In melancholy and with his honour. Juan Gaytán, in melancholy, but without his honour. Wednesday last, while on his knees at prayers—he prays much these days for a salty breeze—his serving boy was on his knees between his mistress' . . ."

"Enough. Enough."

"On Thursday, His Majesty's accountant, Señor Añasco,

after his failure to discover escape for us by land, delivered a lecture on military art and science."

The boy stepped back, swelled his chest and threw up his head and said in a sharp and rasping tone: " 'Concerning Homer's military discipline, the works of Stratocles and Frontinus, a man of consular dignity, are still to be read with profit. Æneas perfected the theory at large, publishing many volumes of warfare which were abridged by Cyneas the Thessalian. Likewise Pyrrhus the Epirote gave us tactics, and his son Alexander, and Clearchus, and Pausanias, likewise Polybius, and Eupolenas, and Iphicrates; Possidonius, also, the stoic. . . . All of these have I seen and read and yet think it not much to purpose to mention particularly, well aware that it hath been the manner of those writers to apply their style, for the most part, not to the ignorant but to such as are already acquainted with the matters they treat of. . . .'

"At which Captain Vasconcelos, in his Portuguese manner: 'Read you no book telling how to find a road out of the wilderness?' "

"Stop, you scoundrel," the Governor said.

Cacho paused; continued:

"On Thursday Father Dionisio of Paris forgot himself and rubbed the air where his belly was wont to be, sighing, 'In this land every day is Friday.' And, for truth, Your Excellency, the whole town is covered over with fish, so faithful are the Guachoya Indians. . . ."

"That reminds me," the Governor said. His voice was no longer mirthful. "Go find what's happened to Tovar."

Tovar stepped forward, "Here am I, my lord."

Cacho turned, the Governor leaned forward. In the silence his hand played with the covers. His eyes were wide and dark, looking out through a glazed film. They were straining as eyes strain at an object in the distance. Tovar moved a little forward. The Governor said, "How long have you been here?"

"Only now, Excellency."

"Oh," de Soto said wearily and lay back on his bed. From

[387]

across the room his breath came quickly. An embarrassed smile came on his face. "The lad here has been amusing me." And then, "Cacho, fetch me water."

As Cacho passed, he came close to Tovar, "None comes to visit him," he said in a whisper.

"Come closer," the Governor said softly. "I find it difficult to speak."

Tovar moved swiftly to the side of the bed. "My lord, I had no idea you were so sick."

De Soto waved his hand, then it sought his throat and moved his garment. "I know that each one has much need of sympathy for himself, now that the danger confronts us all of never being heard from . . . but the boy has a good heart."

"Your Excellency, I'm sure none knows of your condition. I shall . . ."

De Soto raised his hand in deprecation.

"It is not for that I've called you here."

Cacho entered with a gourd of water, went forward and put his hand behind the Governor's back and lifted him up. De Soto drank thirstily. "Prop me up a little higher," he said. "Thank you. Now tell Juan de Guzmán to come here."

The boy went out. "I shall send Tsianina to you, my lord," Tovar said. "She has an art of making cooling drinks."

"You are kind. Father Luis has let me wear a splinter from the Holy Cross. It has a great reputation for curing fever. I have hopes of it. But now . . ." His mind seemed to wander for a moment, then: "Things look bad for us. You have heard the reply the cacique of Quigaltam sent me."

"Some insolence, I've heard."

"I shall quote it: As to what you say of you being the son of the Sun, if you will dry up the great river, I will believe you. As to the rest, it is not my custom to visit any one, but rather all to visit me. If you desire to see me, come where I am. If for peace, I will receive you with special good will; if for war, I will await you in my town. But neither for you, nor for any man, will I set back one foot." The Governor paused for breath,

[388]

then he said: "It grieves me I am unable to cross the river and abate that gentleman's pride, but that must wait. But apart from Quigaltam I am uneasy. So many Indians come and go. I feel that we must strike such terror in their hearts that they will leave us in peace until I recover. The cacique of Guachoya tells me that the Nilco people have returned to their town. Guachoya and Nilco are enemies, but they might, particularly if we stay on here any length of time, forget their differences and fall upon us. I want you to take fifteen horse, Guzmán his company of foot—he will go up the river in canoes in company with a detachment of the Guachoya: I insisted that Guachoya accompany you; it will make such a blood feud between them as to prevent their uniting against us—together, with you in command, you must fall upon the Nilco and do such damage that our names will strike terror for a hundred leagues around. Spare the women and children, if possible. It might be best to leave many badly wounded. But you will know what to do."

De Soto closed his eyes. His lips drew back from his teeth. From where he was Tovar could smell his hot foul breath. The eyes fluttered open. "I will tell you something. It came to me through the Bishop of Burgos. De Vaca told the Emperor that, following the coast on his way to the South Sea, he came first to a land where cotton is grown, and then to a land of turquoise, and then—" his voice was low and vibrant—"and then beyond, to a land where all was golden. You see the importance of your mission. You must not fail. Nothing must keep us from reaching the sea. From Cuba we shall get all we need, men, horses, cattle on the hoof, powder, new weapons."

His voice gave out.

"I will not fail you, my lord."

De Soto raised his hand in dismissal. Tovar looked hard at the sunken features. The lids were so thin he could see beneath the dark stain of his eyes. He looked for a moment longer and then turned and walked softly towards the door.

"Nuño."

He stopped and faced the bed.

[389]

"In my will I left a thousand ducats, five hundred to you and five hundred to Doña Leonora, to avoid delicacy or doubts."

"My lord."

"Tell them without to send in Captain de Guzmán the moment he arrives."

3

It would not be long now. Tovar judged he had come steadily for ten hours since leaving the others. If only the gelding held out, he should be back in camp before day. Never had the gelding shown his stamina so well. He had given him his head, so there was little danger of going astray. Between Nilco and Guachoya the path was well beaten, but on a night such as this there were many false shadows and numerous paths which fed into the main trace. Yes, he had done well to give him his head. He had done well, too well, at Nilco.

Two leagues out of Nilco he had waited for the foot. It was only an hour behind him. Everything moved smoothly, as smoothly as the plan laid down in council. While it was still dark they crossed the river together, horse, foot, and Indians. So well had they planned, they came within sight of the town just at dawn. A scout discovered them and raised an alarm, but his warning came too late. The lancers rode hard at his heels and struck, as the people were running from their lodges. A perfect surprise, perfectly carried out. The ground was open fields with the houses scattered for half a league. Not an obstruction in the way, nor a warrior among them in readiness to draw a bow.

The cries of the women and children still rang in his ears. Whenever the lancers seized them, they turned them over to the foot; but as the day advanced the bloodthirsty spared neither young nor old, neither women nor children. The crossbowmen shot the old men in the place which told their sex and once he had seen a baby thrown into the air as target. It was all too easy. None resisted little or much. In those few places where the warriors gathered the most valorous broke through, lancing, bearing down scores with their stirrups and the breasts of their horses, giving some a thrust and letting them go—this had been his order, for the greater number of wounded the greater the terror and the farther it would spread.

This time, at least, he had not failed the Governor. There could be no doubt about the success of the expedition. Almost a hundred dead had been counted. That would mean some three hundred wounded. In a population of five thousand, the numbers he judged to be living at Nilco, there would be eight or nine hundred warriors. Over half struck down or disabled! Not to count the eighty women and children taken prisoner. And the effect on the Guachoya had been as telling, perhaps more telling than even the Governor expected. At first they hung without the town, watching. Later they had plundered the houses and gone off with their plunder, fearing, no doubt, that he or Guzmán would take it away. By now they would be, fearfully and circumstantially, reporting to their cacique what they had seen.

What the Governor expected of him had been in every way satisfied, and here he was hurrying back to camp, with no feeling of triumph or elation, but a stubborn and growing shame . . . and fear: fear that the success had come too late; shame at the brutal and bloodthirsty action of the foot. During the last three years cruel decisions had been made, but they were single acts, for specific and pressing reasons. This occasion, he supposed, was specific enough; but at least in the past hostility and immediate danger had forced the particular act of cruelty to save a greater violence. The Governor had prided himself on the economy of his violence. After strategy and diplomacy had failed, then the lance. And then, too, the men had got out of hand. Like dogs they had sensed the situation. Their fears had closed their eyes and armed their hands. Into this orgy of blood they had plunged that they might forget the pit upon whose edge they balanced so precariously.

There was hope, if only he could arrive in time, that the

[391]

news might relieve somewhat the Governor of his growing worries. Their parting had shown he knew how sick he was. He must ride harder. His news might be the means . . .

"Steady, Grey."

The gelding had planted its feet in the path, its head an arched shadow in the vague but solid arms of darkness. Gently he plied the spur and spoke to him. Delicately the gelding set down his feet, shying as he advanced; then he stopped and whinnied. There came a low answering whinny. Three shapes rode out of the forest and surrounded him.

"Tovar?"

"Silvestre!"

"The gelding gave you away."

"Am I so near to camp?"

"Two and a half leagues. We are an advanced scouting party, to learn the results of your foray."

"Complete success in every way. The Governor?"

The pause hung between them, growing like a bubble.

"Well?"

"He is dying."

"Dying?" Tovar's voice sounded flat and remote.

"When we left. He sent us here to rush the first news . . ."

"Dying?"

A voice spoke through the dark. "We were supposed to be relieved day before yesterday." The voice added wisely, "Nobody has relieved us."

"I don't think there is any doubt of it," Silvestre continued. "He commanded that all the King's officers should be called before him, the captains and the principal personages." Silvestre's words came through the darkness as out of a void, formal, disembodied. "When they were gathered, he said he was about to go into the presence of God, to give an account of his life. Since God had been pleased to take him away when he could recognize the moment of death, he, His most unworthy servant, rendered Him hearty thanks. He confessed his deep obligations to us all, whether present or absent . . . for our great qualities, our love and loyalty to his person, so well tried in the sufferance of hardship—qualities, he said, which he ever wished to honour and had designed to reward when the Lord should be pleased to give him repose from toil and greater prosperity to his fortunes. He begged us to pray for him, that through mercy he might be pardoned his sins and his soul be received into glory."

Silvestre paused.

"Yes?" Tovar said.

"Even as he spoke, one could see him balance eternity somewhere before his eyes. And then he asked that we relieve him of the charge he held over us, as well as the indebtedness he was under to us all. Especially he asked to be forgiven any wrongs we might have received at his hands. Finally he directed us to elect a principal and able person to be Governor, one with whom we should all be satisfied. This, he said, would abate somewhat the pains he suffered and moderate the anxiety he felt at leaving the army in a country, he knew not where."

"The Governor said these things?"

"With such quiet dignity and so much reason that, but for his quick short breaths, one could not believe him so near to death. Baltazar de Gallegos responded in behalf of all, consoling him with remarks on the shortness of the life of this world, attended as it was by so many toils and afflictions, reminding him that to him whom God earliest called away, He showed particular favour. With many other things appropriate to such an occasion. And finally, since it pleased the Almighty to take him to Himself, amid the deep sorrow we not unreasonably felt, it was necessary and becoming in him, as in us, to conform to the Divine Will. And then, as to the election of the Governor he ordered—whomsoever his Excellency should name, him would we obey."

Out of a thin pool of nausea Tovar felt his fatigue rise in his throat. He swallowed once. "And whom did he name?"

It seemed to him that Silvestre waited an interminable time to answer, but at last he lifted his head. The outlines of his face, square and firm, protruded through the dark. "Moscoso," he hissed.

Tovar was dismounting. "I must have a horse," he said, "the freshest you have."

"There may be time," Silvestre said, standing by his side, holding the head of his own mare.

"I must be off."

"There may be time. He has taken extreme unction and now lies next to the earth, the cross of ashes at his head." As Tovar felt the strange saddle beneath him, he heard again, "There may be time."

The horse moved surely through the night as though she understood the urgency of his errand. He tightened his hand about the lance and gave himself to the rhythm of her forward steps. Branches slapped his face and body, tendrils snatched at the lance. From above the moon fell in narrow beams, across the animal's neck, spotting the ground, breaking but never illuminating the darkness. Moscoso . . . how bitter must that decision have been. In public, before the captains and the most esteemed of his army to admit defeat. His last command a confession of failure, for he knew well enough Moscoso had only one policy: to leave the land, if leave it he might. He had chosen Moscoso, accepted the full measure of humiliation rather than risk divisions and conflict over the command. The Constable would have tried to do what the Governor would have done; but the Constable's hand was not strong enough, and he would bow to the new Governor's policy. Bitter, bitter must have been de Soto's decision.

If only he were not too late to pay one last act of homage. Perhaps the Governor had mended somewhat. Perhaps his despair misled him, misled them all into thinking . . . he had heard of men's spirits, loosed by fever, wandering near without crossing the dark border. He sank his spur into the horse. In a moment they were rushing down the long, narrow corridor. The air pressed against his mouth, against his eyes, like a cool, damp cloth. The black walls opened and closed around him.

4

The corridor declined, the walls spread suddenly out, the horse gave a lurch. . . . He was riding through opaque light, visible yet blinding, streaming out of the dome-like roof. I have strayed, he thought, into a cavern. He drew on the bridle, but the horse went on. He pulled harder, the horse still rode on. His arm was like water, his eyes began to blur . . . a black fluid curtain rose up before him. "Beyond," he heard the voice, clear and sepulchral, "beyond lies the abyss." With one last desperate effort he jerked at the bridle, the reins tightened, the animal slowed. Within his head hammers pounded. The walls of his skull felt as thin as paper.

Acrid steam rose from the horse and stung his nostrils. He shook his head and slowly he opened his eyes. There before him, in the full wash of the moon, stood the wall of Guachoya. The cool, uncertain light fell over the town, upon the runway and the fields surrounding it, but dark and ponderable stood the wall, rising out of its shadow. He had arrived! At last, at last . . . He turned the horse's head towards a gap in the western face. It was closer and would save delay at the front gate.

He jumped down and his numb legs gave beneath him, but in a moment he was on his feet, whispering his name at the gap, lest the sentry take him for an Indian and cut him down. But no sentry challenged and he hurried through. It was only some thirty paces to the Governor's quarters. He crossed them in as many seconds. No guard's voice, no hound, no troubled dreamer called out to mar the deep silence of the night; yet he had scarcely stepped inside the walls when he felt a strange disturbance in the town. All was quiet, but there was no repose. Once behind him he felt a stealthy presence, furtive steps such as some shade might make, escaped from Purgatory. Hastily he looked over his shoulder. No one, nothing, stirred in the yard, the streets, the empty spaces between the houses. But there was little comfort in this. In all he saw he felt the kind of emptiness around which an ambush is drawn and from the houses watchful eyes crowding every inch of the vacant town. He remembered the open gap: always a guard had been posted there; Silvestre's scouting party, its relief overdue. He hastened his steps, stopped short before the Governor's quarters. The guard there, too, was missing. Fear and shame filled his heart. Did Moscoso think there was no longer any need, or had his carelessness again, as at Chickasaw ... ? No, a repetition of that disaster was unlikely. But what was it? His gaze came to rest upon the entrance. Even that seemed unfamiliar, bare and too open. Then it came to him. The skin which served for door was gone!

The moon streamed through the opening, falling aslant the hard dirt floor. He put his hand on his sword and entered. His shadow fell before him, outstretched upon the floor, and he saw that he was alone in the empty lodge. He stepped aside, out of the light, and his shadow followed, sliding into the dark, uncovering the armoured figure in all its length touching the earth which had claimed it. Grey and insubstantial lay the cross of ashes, drawn at its head. Upon the breast glowed the cross of Santiago. The plates were highly furbished and, strange to behold, so bright did the moon shine upon them, upon the harness from casque to spur, it seemed to his dazzled eyes that the source of the light came not from the moon but the body itself. He found it easier to look a little to one side of the figure.

He was come too late. At the first glance he saw that all his haste had been to no avail. The Governor was dead. He waited for the surge of grief, but nothing moved in his heart. It lay within him like rotten cork, his body like stone. And yet, drawn by the thing he saw, he could not leave. *Too late, too late, forever too late,* galloped in his head with the strain, the sharp edge of his ride.

"It was not like you, Nuño, to tarry."

Had he heard aright? He looked towards the casque. It was

closed but shining like a thing alive. Fearfully, lest he mock himself, he whispered, "My lord?"

"Yes, Nuño?"

The words were clear, spreading in his ears like reverberations of sound, everywhere yet nowhere. He collected himself. "Then I have come in time," he said.

"There's only one time at the Moon's Inn."

He must be out of his head, he thought. He said aloud, "My lord, what mean you? You do not lie at the Moon's Inn. You are in Guachoya, with a roof over your head. Some one has taken the skin flap from your door. It is that which makes you think you lie in the open." He paused, said firmly, "I shall see that this is remedied."

There was barely a pause and then he heard through the casque: "There is no remedy. For you or me, or for any who come to this land. It is the Moon's Inn for all, heathen and Christian alike. It can never be more than a temporary abode, a stopping place of the variable seasons, where the moon is host and the reckoning counted up in sweat, in hunger, and in blood. Ayllón, died of a fever; de Narváez, a marker of tides; the great Admiral who first ventured beyond the Christian chart, returned in chains; where now is Compañón, my brother and friend, or my other brother, de León, who would cheat me of my dues; the Marqués of Peru who learned in pig sties how to give out the yellow gold and rule lands and men, or his brother Almagro, and all those who returned with pelf and profit? Where lie they now? Where Hernando de Soto, Governor of Cuba, Adelantado of Florida . . . ?"

"My lord, you lie before me."

There was a moment of silence. Tovar ventured further.

"This time, at least," he said, "I did not fail you. Do not despair. All may yet go well. The will remains. . . ."

"The will is not enough. It is not enough for one bent on his own destruction. Did I lead the chivalry of Spain to the sacred groves, the blessed land of Jerusalem? No, I am the alchemical captain, the adventurer in gold. Gold the wanderer. Pursuing,

[397]

I found the world's secret, the alkahest and the panacea. They are one and the same. The universal menstruum is this . . ." Slowly from the ground the arm raised up, the bony hand reached forth, white and shining, and the voice, thin and distant, "Only the dead can prophesy."

Tovar dropped to his knees. "My lord, say you have forgiven me that one time, in Cuba . . ."

The hand moved towards his lips. He bent forward, his lips kissed the air. Where the figure lay a shadow fell, blocking the light. He felt a presence in the door behind, leapt to his feet. But there was no one there. He stepped back, and the moon, unobstructed, streamed in through the opening. Particles of dust whirled in the milky light to settle slowly upon the cross of ashes, and upon the empty floor where the armoured body had lain.

He stared for a moment and then, with sword in hand, fled into the open. He ran into the first lodge he came to and shouted, "Where is the Governor?" The sleeping men sat up in their sleep and stared. He lingered a moment, then ran again into the streets towards the gates of the town. The guards there, at least, would know. As he drew near, he saw a shadowy group of figures standing at the side of a pit, others moving inside it. His voice rang through the stillness, "Where is the Governor?"

The men swung around like thieves surprised at their trade. A hand grasped his arm. "Be quiet, fool," the voice said. "I am the Governor."

Tovar turned and looked into Moscoso's startled and angry eyes.

"Oh, it's you," Moscoso said and released his grip.

"What have you done with the Governor?"

Moscoso drew him to the edge of the pit and pointed to a bundle of skins into which men were shovelling sand.

"That?" Tovar asked. "That, the Governor?"

"All that's left of him." Moscoso looked curiously at Tovar. "We are weighting it with sand to make sure it will sink."

"Sink?"

"Yes, in the river."

"But at night, like conspirators?"

"It's the best way. He had given the Indians to understand he was immortal. First I put him secretly into a house, but he began to stink. There's no smell so mortal as death. So, again, at night, I had him buried here within the gates and rode horses over the place to disguise it. But the Indians saw the loose ground and began pointing to it. They had seen him ill. Guachoya came to me and asked what I had done with his brother and lord. I told him de Soto had ascended the sky, as was his custom; that, as he would be detained there, he had left me in his place; whereupon Guachoya brought in two youths and told me to strike off their heads so that the Governor would not go unattended. I told him he had gone well attended." Moscoso did not disguise his irony.

"All ready, Your Excellency," a voice said from the grave.

"Good. To the river with him. Secretly now. No noise." Moscoso turned hastily to Tovar. "It's the only safe burial. When we leave, they would steal his body."

The men lifted the shapeless mass of skins and passed with it out of the gates. They walked out of step; then in step with the deliberate caution of bearers straining under a heavy load. At the bank the body was lifted silently into the canoe, when those appointed to do the last service for their lord stepped in and, arranging themselves, shoved off. The river was high, pouring by the landing like some molten flood of metal, rushing to fill its mould. To the far shore the moon lighted its sleek and boiling surface. The dark high forest shut it in. Tovar could see the paddlers struggling to give the boat direction, and then the current took it, drawing it out and down, swiftly down until, black and shapeless, it bobbed like a piece of flotsam, at a far uncertain distance.

The boat floated aimlessly, then it took shape again, appearing in splotches of light, disappearing. He saw the rowers bending to their task and the boat moving slowly towards shoal water. It passed around a bend. After a long while the dark prow emerged noiselessly from under the foliage near the landing. A man jumped out. The boat jarred as it struck the bank. One after the other the burial party stepped upon land. No one spoke. Moscoso's head turned questioningly towards Tinoco. Tinoco nodded and then he crossed himself. All, hastily as men who have overlooked some courtesy, crossed themselves in turn.

They stood upon the edge of the stream, will-less to move, while the flood of water passed by, hurrying to the sea. Tovar felt a shudder run from man to man.

At his shoulder a voice said, "It is the turning of the tide."

"To your quarters, Señores," Moscoso said in a loud voice; then he whispered, "Go quietly all."

Tovar heard their steps withdraw, heard the silence overtake them. He turned at last. They were crossing the patch of light which reached but did not go beyond the walls. Their tarnished mail glowed fitfully as they walked, and then, as the gates opened to receive them, grew suddenly dull. At the threshold they hesitated and looked into the darkness beyond. One by one, as though taking leave of his companions, each man crossed alone, shades in a deeper shade.

Tovar moved forward into the light.

THE END